EMPYRION II:
THE SIEGE OF DOME

Other Books by Stephen R. Lawhead

Fiction

Dream Thief

Empyrion I: The Search for Fierra

In the Hall of the Dragon King

Warlords of Nin

The Sword and the Flame

Non-Fiction

After You Graduate

The Phoenix Factor: Surviving and
Growing Through Personal Crisis,
with Dr. Karl Slaikeu

Rock Reconsidered

Turn Back the Night: A Christian
Response to Popular Culture

The Ultimate Student Handbook,
with Alice Slaikeu Lawhead

EMPYRION II:
THE SIEGE OF DOME

STEPHEN R. LAWHEAD

Crossway Books • Westchester, Illinois
A Division of Good News Publishers

Empyrion II: The Siege of Dome. Copyright © 1986 by Stephen R. Lawhead. Published by Crossway Books, a division of Good News Publishers, Westchester, Illinois 60153.

Book design by K. L. Mulder.
Illustration by Kernie Erickson.

Second printing, 1986.

Printed in the United States of America.

Library of Congress Catalog Card Number 85-72913

ISBN 0-89107-381-7

And though the last lights off the black West went
Oh, morning, at the brown brink Eastward,
Springs—
Because the Holy Ghost over the bent
World broods with warm breast and ah! bright
Wings.

G. M. Hopkins, God's Grandeur

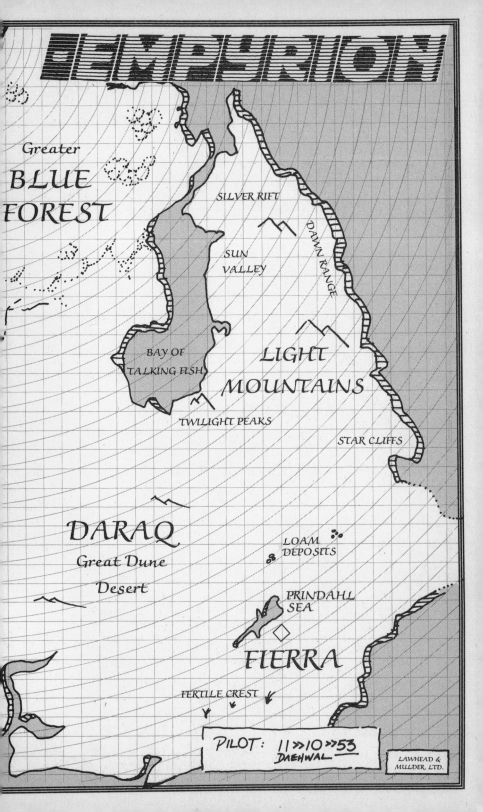

PROLOGUE

In the year 98 A.A. Colony suffered a killing contagion that severely decimated the population. This was the time of the Red Death, and many whom Cynetics had raised up were alive then. These were the Original Ancestors, of whom little is now known, except that they were wise in the ways of Expertise and Machine Lore.

The disease spread despite heroic efforts of the Medico Expertise to contain it. Quarantine measures proved ineffective, and it soon became apparent to the Ancestors that most of Colony would succumb to the Red Death—so termed because of the blood welts that formed on the skin of the victims at the slightest pressure.

I have seen old records which indicate that the Red Death struck with frightening suddeness, producing chills, vomiting, loss of muscular control, slurred speech, lethargy. The eyeballs of the afflicted were said to become red from burst blood vessels in the eyes. Mucus ran freely from nose and mouth, making breathing difficult, and later impossible as the lungs filled with fluid. Victims of the Red Death drowned in their own mucus, choking, gagging, whimpering in agony as each touch brought a new and painful blood welt to swell the skin. Where these welts burst, a vile, suppurating crust formed. But at this stage, the victim was normally comatose and beyond care. Death followed within thirty-six to forty-eight hours of the disease's onset.

In those terrible days one Ancestor in three was taken by the Red Death. The Ancestors knew that for Colony to survive, healthy breeding stock from each Expertise had to be preserved. Those selected for survival were sent out from Colony to live apart in the Hill Country. Others, fearing the disease, attempted to escape by exiling themselves to the wilderness also; but lacking tools and provisions, many of these died from hunger.

In time, the exiles who had managed to live by eating fish and small mammals returned to find less than a fourth of Colony left alive. The surviving population numbered four thousand. Not one of the Original Ancestors survived.

The Ancestors attempted to replace every Expertise, organizing survivors to form the HSCs—Human Survival Cells. Each HSC was dedicated to preserving its own Machine Lore, and in this way each Expertise was preserved—all except one called Biogenics, which many survivors believed had created the Red Death.

It has been said that from this time Cynetics turned its face away from its people, abandoning its children because they fell away from the worship of true spirits. The Cult of Cynetics grew up among the survivors who believed renewed contact with the Divine Spirit would aid them.

The Four Thousand became the Progenitors of old, who reformed Colony after their own desires, vowing that nothing like the Red Death would ever happen again. Thus began the First Age of Empyrion.

Feodr Rumon
Interpretive Chronicles, Volume 1
After Arrival 2230

ONE

Orion Tiberias Treet lifted his face from the page swimming before his eyes, sat up, and glared around, red-eyed, at the untidy stack of blue plastic notebooks he had been reading nonstop for the last few days. He rubbed his whiskered jaw and stood creakily, began swinging his arms, pacing and stretching to get his blood circulating.

Five days—maybe more, he couldn't tell for sure—in the subterranean Archives of Dome, reading Feodr Rumon's *Interpretive Chronicles,* had given him an ache in his head to match the one in his stomach. He had not eaten since returning to Dome, even though, upon entering the Archives, he had found the provisions he and Calin had left behind on their first visit—a time that now seemed impossibly remote.

The food had long since spoiled, but the water in the sealed jar was good; so he drank sparingly from it and settled down to discover all he could of Empyrion's lost past. He knew he might never have another chance to read the notebooks, and knew, too, that once he left the safety of the Archives, he might never return. Several days of hunger were worth the price.

Upon leaving the Archives he would be a hunted man; so Treet was in no hurry to leave his work. He would have to leave soon, though. Already hunger was making him light-headed and weak. If he waited too long, he might not have strength or wit enough to successfully elude capture and provide some help to Tvrdy and his allies.

Of course, not knowing what had happened since his escape from Dome, he was at a distinct disadvantage in the strategy department. He assumed the worst. That way he would not be unduly disappointed.

He wondered what he would find when he decided to leave his hidden enclave, wondered whether there had been a Purge, and whether Tvrdy and Cejka had survived or been brought down. Assuming that they had survived, he wondered how to make contact with them, or with anyone else in a position to help him.

These matters he pushed from his mind whenever they intruded, and he forced his attention back to his reading. Old Rumon's *Chronicles* offered a wealth of information to be mined. He had only to pick up one of the ancient notebooks to be transported to some long-forgotten age of Empyrion's past. A past which Treet sincerely hoped would offer a clue as to how he might begin averting the catastrophe he had so clearly seen looming over the future of the planet.

This once-strong hope had turned into a wormy anxiety. For now, having returned, he was far less certain that he'd read the signs of disaster aright. I was so sure of myself before, he argued. Nothing has changed—so why do I doubt myself?

Doubt was a mild word for it. Whenever he thought about what he had committed himself to, snakes began writhing in his bowels.

Treet had lived his life trusting his instincts, never looking back. Life was too short, he often told himself, to spend even a second in regret. Now, it appeared that his ever-trustworthy instincts had betrayed him and backward glancing would become a way of life.

On the strength of his gut feeling he had left the Fieri and their magnificent civilization to return to Dome on the narrowest of chances that he might somehow forestall the doom that only he seemed to see.

On the strength of his gut feeling he had sacrificed his own best chance for future happiness by alienating the only woman he'd ever really loved, the only woman who, quite possibly, had ever loved him.

On the strength of his gut feeling he had set in motion a series of events which had caused the messy death of a beautiful friend. He missed Calin—would have ached for the loss of her had not grief numbed him. Still, the thought of her death and the sting of his own guilt for the part he played in it were never far away. And the gruesome battle between him and the demented Crocker, which had claimed the gentle magician's life, was replayed nightly in his dreams in brutal, bloody detail.

All this—the torment of those memories, of second-guessing himself, dark bouts of self-accusation—he struggled to hold aside long enough to learn as much as possible about Empyrion Colony's past in the short time he had to give to the task. And, despite his growing uncertainty about his mission, he still felt this to be crucially important.

So, ignoring all else as he ignored the vacuum in his stomach gnawing at his concentration, he returned to the nest he'd made for himself on the floor and opened the notebook he'd been reading for the last few hours. The binding, brittle with age and cracked in a dozen places, bore the handwritten tag *Volume 19*, signifying he was one-quarter of the way through Empyrion's Third Age, as classified by Rumon.

He took out his bookmark—a folded sheet of paper bearing the notes he had scratched with an old polymer stylus found in a nearby bin—and read what he'd written:

Colony Foundation	=	1 AA
Red Death	=	98 AA
Plebiscite Rejected	=	309 AA
Colony Splits	=	311 AA
Second Split	=	543 AA
First Purge	=	586 AA
Directorate Installed	=	638 AA
Flight of the Fieri	=	833 AA
Fieri Settlement Est.	=	1157 AA
Cluster Closed	=	1270 AA
Fieri Scattered	=	1318 AA
Directorate Overthrown	=	1473 AA
Second Purge	=	1474 AA
Threl Established	=	1485 AA

It was the record of civilization born to turmoil, much the same as any civilization. But what made Empyrion's record so sad—and this was the part that really got to Treet—was that the colony had advantages never possessed by any other civilization he'd ever encountered: they had started out with all the tools for creating Utopia right from the very beginning; they had all of history to teach them how to organize and govern themselves. They might have chosen to recreate Eden.

Instead, they chose Hell.

Treet's list of major historical events was the record of a society descending inexorably into tyranny. From the rejection of the first citizens' plebiscite to the establishment of the Threl, Dome had consistently chosen the downward course, evading at every turn the opportunity to rise; choosing—not once only, but time and time again—the collective will over individual rights, manipulation over liberty, expedience over benevolence, repression over freedom.

Through years of upheaval, through painful splits and bloody purges, the leaders of Dome relentlessly pursued the downward track. It was all right there in the notebooks—the damning evidence of a society throwing away human rights and freedoms with both hands, shedding all the higher and ennobling qualities that enlightened governments had fought so hard for since the dawn of time.

Yes, Treet thought gloomily, it was all there, faithfully recorded in the notebooks.

He still had nine fat notebooks to go, but was beginning to doubt whether he could finish before hunger made it impossible. Already the hand-lettered printout pages swam before his eyes, and his concentration was so fragile he was forced to read a single paragraph several times to get anything out of it. But at least he had discovered that catastrophe had taken place in Empyrion's past to shape its future—a future he was living now: the Red Death.

Based on Rumon's scant reference, Treet strongly suspected a genetic experiment gone haywire. Perhaps they had been attempting to adapt an indigenous lifeform or create a new bacteria strain for some purpose past remembering. However it was, once the contagion was loosed upon the colony, nothing could stop it. The disease had killed, by Treet's calculation, close to twelve thousand people, three-quarters of Empyrion's total population; by comparison, not even the plagues of the Old Middle Ages were so devastating.

When the Red Death had finally run its course, Empyrion was changed forever.

Treet found his place in the book and began reading. In just a few minutes he was exhausted, but struggled to keep at it for a few hours more. In the end, he had no choice but to admit defeat and lay the notebook down carefully. He had to have something to eat. Now. But before he could eat, he'd have to find a way past the guard station outside the Archives and then a place to hide until Tvrdy could be contacted.

He took out the map he had found on his first day back in the Archives. There was no telling how old the map was, or how accurate. Though it only showed two lower levels, one of which was mislabeled Archives Level, he supposed it could be trusted to point the way to the Old Section where he hoped to find refuge.

Treet stood and steadied himself as spots like tiny black fireflies swarmed before his eyes. He left the hidden room, taking a last look behind him as he entered the dry pipeline and made his way back to the Archives floor. As he walked along, one arm outstretched, touching the side of the pipe, he thought again about how he might elude the guards. Surprise would be on his side, he figured, for whatever that was worth. And he supposed that he might find some sturdy hunk of something to use as a weapon. Beyond that, he had no notion of how he might proceed.

He retraced his steps to the junction box and continued along the second pipe until he reached the metal ladder leading to the Archive floor, placed his foot on the first rung, and hauled himself up. It was then that he heard the clang and groan and felt the tremor of a heavy machine rumbling across the floor above.

anais Director Tvrdy crept along the darkened tunnel, pausing every few meters to listen again. He heard only the tick of his own footsteps echoing off the endless tile. He hunched his coat over his shoulders and wished for the millionth time that Pradim had not been killed. He would have trouble finding another guide—*if* he were ever to find one—who could be trusted so completely in so many delicate areas. Over the years, Pradim had become less a tool than a confidant and friend, and not incidentally a strategist of impressive powers.

If he missed the blind guide, the Cabal would miss him more. Reeling from the defeat Jamrog had forced upon them—for that's what Sirin Rohee's sudden and as yet unexplained death was: a crippling, paralyzing defeat—Tvrdy fought now just to maintain his position within the Threl. One way or another, Jamrog meant to have his head.

And one way or another, Tvrdy meant to keep it. If staying alive meant abandoning his Directorship, so be it. Only a fool like Hladik would insist on clinging to his dwindling power to the death. If Tvrdy allowed Jamrog to kill him in his bed, the Cabal was finished. And if the Cabal, small though it was and ill-equipped, passed from Empyrion, all resistance to Jamrog's rule would effectively vanish.

That was why he was making this journey now, alone, in the stark, predawn hours of a bleak and hopeless day, to make contact with Giloon Bogney, legendary leader of the faceless nonbeings, the Dhogs.

A message had been sent through the Rumon messenger network—Tvrdy didn't know how Cejka managed, but was thankful for such a clever and resourceful ally—and, what was most miraculous, an answer in the form of detailed directions had been received. Giloon agreed to a meeting in the Isedon Zone, that empty ring of ruined Hageblocks that formed the no-man's-land between the Hages and the Old Section. The condition was that Tvrdy come alone and bring some proof that he was in fact a Threl Director.

Tvrdy hated the thought of meeting the repulsive nonbeing alone in unfamiliar territory, but he was desperate. He would see Giloon, find out what his help would cost, and, with luck, estimate what that aid would be worth. The fact that Giloon had replied at all was a good sign; the crude map he'd sent was a better one. The Dhog wanted something, or he would not have responded at all.

Tvrdy came to a place where the tunnel ended, opening onto a deserted plaza lined with the charred stumps of once graceful feng trees. He consulted the Dhog's drawing and confirmed what he already guessed, that this was the entrance to Isedon, center of one of the original cluster of long ago; the only one still remaining. The dwelling-blocks on either side of the square—those still somewhat intact, at any rate—were smaller than in Hage, and were built in the ancient style: straight lines and flat surfaces. Tvrdy much admired the style and had copied it in his own kraam. The decrepit structures were dark and empty now. At least he supposed they were empty. The feeling of invisible eyes observing him intensified as he moved hesitantly to stand in the center of the plaza, overgrown with wireweeds and squatty lofo bushes that had insinuated themselves into crevices between the broken paving stones.

Tvrdy stopped when he reached the center and drew a shaky breath to calm himself. The air smelled foul and old, rank with decay. He shivered involuntarily; the place was a pest hole. He looked furtively around, imagining all sorts of crawling vermin creeping in the rubble of the tumbled buildings, and pulled his coat more tightly around him. The stiffness in his left arm reminded him of why he had come.

He and Cejka had had Cynetics' own luck that day when the Invisibles found them in the Archives. In the confusion of the Travelers' escape, he and Cejka had—he still didn't know precisely how—convinced the savage Mrukk, Commander of the Mors Ultima Invisibles and Jamrog's personal lackey, that killing two Directors outright and without proof of treason would be a mistake that would be paid in blood.

Mrukk, his face rigid with hot frustration at seeing his quarry racing away on Fieri skimmers, had made the decision to try to stop them, leaving Tvrdy and Cejka behind as he turned his attention to the fleeing spies. Cejka's men had attacked the small security force as soon as the shooting started on the landing platform.

Cejka lost several good men that day—Tvrdy himself had been wounded—but the Directors had escaped.

Then followed one demoralizing setback after another as all their careful plans failed or were neutralized by some evasive tactic of Jamrog's. The Saecaraz Subdirector seemed always to be one step ahead of them as the rebel Cabal scrambled for leverage to force events their way. So far, success had proven as elusive as a Hage priest's blessing, and as costly. They had lost many followers, and their network of agents and informants lay in ashes.

Tvrdy was startled out of his morose inventory by the appearance of a short, thick-limbed figure scuttling toward him over the slanting stones of the deserted plaza. The man wore a long cloak that dragged at his heels and held a short bhuj in his right hand; the wide, flat blade glimmered dully in the murky light as its owner scrambled forward on stump legs.

The Dhog leader came to stand before Tvrdy, his face begrimed, the hair of his beard virulent, matted, and greasy. A vicious purple scar divided his low forehead like a jagged lightning bolt, parting his hair and plunging diagonally down to the left cheek, warping the left eye so that it looked upward askance, as if Giloon were continually watching the sky-shell of Dome for a sign.

"So, Tanais!" he said, his round face splitting like an overripe fruit. Ocher teeth shone through the mat of hair, and his pudgy nose wrinkled in wry good humor. His voice was coarse gravel grating on glass, a sound to inspire abhorrence. An odor like that of rotting meat came off the Dhog's filth-encrusted clothes—actually, rags patched with rags—offending the nostrils as much as their appearance assaulted the eyes. On his chest he wore the medallion of a Jamuna Hage priest: a double-ended arrow bent into a circle.

Tvrdy took this in with a grimace of disgust, almost gagging, but forcing a sickly smile of greeting. Why had he come? There was no point. The odious creature could do nothing for him. His heart shrank in despair, but he reached into an inner fold of his yos and brought out a packet which he offered.

The Dhog spat and looked at the packet. "Giloon don't needs it. Giloon be knowing you, Tanais, withouts it."

Tvrdy replaced the packet, actually relieved not to have the Dhog paw through his personal documents. "Thank you for agreeing to meet me. You took a chance, giving me directions."

Giloon tilted his face up and laughed. The sun had risen, but the weak light filtering in through the stained crystal panels overhead remained dusky. Very likely Old Section residents knew only two variations: twilight and deep night; their days were spent in the dim half-light of eternal gloom.

Giloon's laugh died. "What Tanais wants of Giloon Bogney?"

"Is that who you are?"

The Dhog raised the bhuj and laid the flat of the blade against his cheek and rubbed. "Who else? Anyway, as Giloon a nonbeing it matters no big much, seh?"

"I want your help," Tvrdy said simply. He had been prepared to use elaborate persuasion and rhetoric to state his case, but decided to cut the interview as short as possible so that he could get away. There was no point in drawing out the hopeless affair.

"Help!" Giloon spat, dribbling spittle over his chin. "Help he wants!" He spun the bhuj in his hands and leaned on the haft, looking at Tvrdy with wild amusement on his dirty face.

He's insane, thought Tvrdy. I never should have come. "Help, yes."

"And what you be giving in return? You slicing Giloon's throat, seh?" He drew the blade tip of the bhuj across his neck.

Tvrdy took a deep breath and said, "If you help us remove Jamrog from power, we will grant the Old Section stent—you will become a Hage."

"And Giloon being a Director?"

Tvrdy grimaced, swallowed his revulsion, and said, "Yes, you would become a Director."

The Dhog squirmed—whether with delight or torment Tvrdy couldn't tell—raised his face once more, and laughed deep in his warty throat. "Giloon liking a man who lies big and fearless! You eating the night soil with both hands, Tanais, but Giloon liking you. That is why he not killing you now. Directors must be talking, seh? We talking."

● ● ● ● ● ●

The two women walked along the shore of the glimmering quicksilver sea, Prindahl. Chattering rakkes strafed the shallows for the quick yellow fish, scattering diamonds among the waves with every plunge. It was still early morning, but the day was warm and fair; a seaward breeze flipped the wavetops and swept the hair from their foreheads as the two ambled along, steeped in the comfort of each other's company.

Presently Ianni stopped, finding a place to spread her fishing net. Already barefoot, she lightly doffed the saffron knee-length trousers she wore beneath the belted tunic and waded out into the water.

Yarden Talazac watched for a moment and then sat down on a large flat rock nearby and let Prindahl's cool waters lap over her feet. Face turned toward the small white disk of Empyrion's sun, she let the rays warm her skin and allowed her mind to drift as she listened to the shimmering beauty of Ianni's song.

Ianni, like most Fieri, had the gift of song in her soul. She could spin a melody as easily as she cast the light net in her hands while wading the crystalline shoals. Ianni's songs were webs of fragile, sparkling beauty: fine and delicate and intricate, possessed of a poignance that made Yarden yearn for places she'd never been, for things she'd never seen and did not know.

Fierra itself, the shining city of the Fieri, came very close to fulfilling Yarden's nameless longing. It was all she could have dreamed of and more: a spacious, gracious city filled with gentle, loving people; an entire civilization whose highest aim was the pursuit of truth and the nurture of beauty in all its varied forms.

In Fierra there was no want, no trouble, no pain, no violence of any kind. In fact, none of the noxious weeds that had poisoned other societies had taken root in Fierra. It was a charmed, enchanted place. Charmed and enchanted by the Presence, the all-infusing Spirit of the Infinite Father, whom the Fieri worshipped in nearly every word and deed. Here in Fierra, among these inspired people, it was easy to believe in their God, easy to feel His relentless, questing spirit drawing the faith of all men and women to Himself.

Yarden wanted to believe. In the last weeks she had felt the prickly, fidgety squirm that signaled an inner awakening. This stirring in her soul she knew to be, in part, a deepening desire of hers to actually become a Fieri. In believing in the Fieri's God, she would be like them in a most fundamental way. There was more to it than that, but the rest remained inarticulate and unformed. Her heart had its reasons that her head could never know. She was content to let the matter rest there for the moment, to let belief come to her in its own time and in its own way—if it would.

As for the rest—a whole realm of thought and feeling she was ignoring, holding back, and denying, most of it having to do with the disturbing person of Orion Treet—she simply refused to entertain even the smallest fragment of a thought or emotion. She had shut him out of her life the moment she turned her back on him at the airfield and had maintained her stoic decision ever since.

Ianni's song stopped and Yarden shifted her thoughts, focusing her sympathic awareness on her friend. The two women had grown so close in their months together that it was easy for Yarden to receive Ianni's thought impressions—they came through clear and strong. In fact, Ianni had developed a habit of mindspeaking whenever she thought Yarden might be listening to her.

Bohm returns this morning. The balon will arrive soon. We could go to the field if you wished.

Yarden opened her eyes and looked at Ianni, who was still standing with her net in her hands, gazing into the water. No, she thought, and wondered if Ianni would receive her answer. I don't want to speak to Bohm about . . . the trip.

You cannot forget him, Yarden. He will need our prayers.

I mean to forget him, thought Yarden. That's exactly what I intend doing—as quickly as possible. He made his choice, and I have made mine. I will have nothing more to do with him.

She closed her eyes once more and lay back on the rock, feeling its sun-soaked warmth seep into her. She *would* forget him.

THREE

Asquith Pizzle let the rudder line go slack in his hand as the sleek sailboat turned itself into the wind, scarlet sail flapping. He gazed at the Fieri woman sitting across from him, now regarding him with a quizzical expression.

"I feel like letting it drift for a while," he explained.

"Are you hungry?" asked Jaire, reaching for the bundle riding in the sling between them, her henna hair flaring red-gold in the bright sunlight.

"Starved."

"You're always starved." She laughed lightly. "What an odd word."

"I'm still a growing boy." It was true—spending every waking moment with Jaire made him feel like a youngster whose fondest birthday wish had come true. "I could look at you forever," he said, speaking his thoughts aloud. Never in his life had a woman as beautiful as Jaire allowed him within fifty meters; most hung out "Forget it, Buster!" signs the second they saw him coming. Jaire was different. And despite the fact that she was, technically, an alien—or maybe because of it—he was ankles over elbows in love with her.

Jaire favored him with one of the dazzling smiles she gave so effortlessly, bent her head, the lights off the water filling her eyes, and with deft fingers tugged open the bundle in her lap, bringing out the sweet fruitbread she had prepared. "I am going to the hospital tonight," she said, passing him a thick slice, over which was spread a soft nut-flavored cheese.

"Is someone sick?" He took a bite and savored it.

"No . . ." Jaire shook her head. "It is my—what is your word for it?"

"Shift. Your work time is called a shift." He had been teaching her Earth English, as she had been teaching him Fieri.

"It is my shift." Jaire worked at the Fieri's single central medical facility—a hospital devoted mostly to the care of expectant mothers and the delivery of babies. There was little disease among the Fieri; so being a physician meant obstetrics and pediatrics almost exclusively.

Also, since disease had long been in decline, the medical profession among the Fieri ranked about the same as the position of computer operator back on Earth, as far as Pizzle could tell. Not that the Fieri worked all that hard at any particular occupation. Theirs was a culture wholly given to job-sharing. No one, apparently, held down a single career. Each of those tasks necessary to the maintenance and functioning of society was divided among any number of people.

And since there was no such thing as wages—they simply had no concept of money—it didn't really matter who did what. People tended to do what they liked to do, receiving training in several different occupations and then pursuing them most casually. This had the effect of removing such societal ills as avarice, ambition, and stress from the work environment. The Fieri ascribed no status to what a person did; they were more concerned with the quality of the life being led.

"How long?" Fieri work schedules bewildered Pizzle; he didn't see how they kept all their various tasks and commitments straight.

"Ten days."

"Every night?"

She laughed, "Yes, every night. You will have to ask Preben to take you to the concerts instead of me."

"But I don't want to go with Preben—I want to go with you. I'll miss you."

Jaire passed him another slice of fruitbread and looked at him in that mysterious, enigmatic way Pizzle regarded as her Mona Lisa look—a look she had begun giving him a great deal in the last few days. It hinted at both humor and high seriousness, combined with several other elements he couldn't decipher. Something completely female, and therefore foreign to him. He had no idea what it meant.

Pizzle continued, changing the subject. "I've decided what I want to do with my life here. I want to learn all I can about your people—every single thing."

"That will not take long." Jaire lifted the sweet bread to her mouth and chewed thoughtfully. "There is not much to learn."

"I disagree! There's everything to learn." He held up the half-eaten slice of bread. "For example, I don't have the slightest idea how or where you grow your food, or where you go to get it, or how you divide it up. Or how you get along without money, or anything like that. Where I come from, *everything's* money! Without money you can't live."

"You have told me about money before. Forgive me, but I still don't understand it."

"Never mind. But you see what I mean? There's a whole world to learn." He waved his bread in an arc that took in the whole of the Empyrion horizon, glittering with the sun off the distant pavilions.

"And what will you do when you learn everything?"

"I don't know. Write it down, maybe. It doesn't matter. I want to know all about you." Pizzle tucked the last morsel of bread into his mouth, lay back, and closed his eyes, letting his mind drift in the glory of the day. He felt positively reborn. Nothing else mattered but that he was here and that he would always stay here, just like this, now and forever. He felt his shriveled soul expand, shaking out folds and wrinkles he'd thought were permanently impressed.

He breathed a long sigh of profound contentment and let the gentle waves rock him to sleep as Jaire composed a nursery song she would sing to her infant charges later that night. Yes, thought Pizzle dreamily, this was the life. Heaven itself could not be sweeter. A man would be a fool to leave—for *any* reason.

• • • • • •

Treet hung on the metal ladder in an agony of indecision. Should he go back and wait until whatever was happening up there in the Archives was over, or should he risk discovery to find out what was going on? This debate raged for several minutes, and would have gone on longer, but his fingers grew tired. Rather than drop back down, it was easier to go up—which he did with utmost caution, inching up the ladder, watching the hole overhead for any sign of discovery, ready to let go and fall the instant he saw anything suspicious.

He saw no reason for retreat, however, though the clangor and rumble grew perceptibly louder the higher up the ladder he went. At last, clinging to the top rung, he pushed his head up just above floor level to see that nothing had been touched near his secluded hole. The sounds he had heard came from a point midway between him and the inner doors of the enormous circular room. A quick check confirmed what he already guessed—that the outer doors were now sealed tight once more. Whoever was running the machine stood between Treet and his only exit.

Wasting no time, Treet pulled himself the rest of the way out of the manhole and darted to a nearby stack of electrostatic filter frames, crouched, and peered cautiously around. He saw no one nearby, so began threading his way through the mazework of discarded machines and obsolete junk, creeping with all the stealth he could muster.

The din grew as the incessant clang began to include other sounds as well: the screech of rending metal, the groan and pop of fibersteel breaking, the crash and clatter of objects being thrown and smashed against one another. Treet worked his way toward the activity, pausing frequently to look over his shoulder. If he were caught now, it would be over before it began. Fortunately, the noise of the wreckage covered any inadvertent sounds he made, allowing him to get closer than he might have otherwise.

What he saw when, crouching behind a plastic water tank, he peeped out across a cleared expanse of Archive floor was a huge orange machine lumbering across the floor and stirring up the fine gray powder into a thick haze. The thing was little more than an engine on treads, with a flat metal plate hung on the front for banging a pathway through the accumulated jumble. A half-dozen Saecaraz stood watching the mayhem as the improvised bulldozer rammed the circle larger, punching the perimeter outward from the center. The heavy metal plate smacking against the treads created the deafening clang that he'd first heard.

The Saecaraz seemed intent on what they were doing—creating more room, Treet guessed, though why they should care about that now puzzled him. After all, the Archives had been ignored and unvisited for generations. Perhaps it had something to do with the events which had taken place here recently. Treet did not especially want to see those events replayed; so he ducked down and looked across to the doors. He saw that one was open and, wonder of wonders, was unguarded.

He backed away quietly and, keeping a safe distance from the Saecaraz, moved around the cleared circle to the doors. He had reached the halfway point when the machine stopped. The wash of noise evaporated into silence. Treet froze. He could hear the voices of the Saecaraz. Apparently they had finished their work and were leaving. They were coming toward him!

Treet continued on, hurrying to stay ahead of them, but taking pains to remain silent and unseen. The voices were closer behind him when he reached a place where two pathways crossed among the towers of cast-off equipment. He hesitated. One path appeared to lead directly to the door, while the other bent around and wound back into the welter. With the Saecaraz closing on him from behind, he chose to make a stab for the door rather than muddle through the maze.

He dashed for the door, thinking that if only he could reach it before the others reached the ring of steps he would have a chance of slipping through unseen. The Saecaraz were coming perpendicular to him now, making for the same path he had chosen. From the sound of their voices, Treet guessed that some were approaching from behind him, and others were just ahead, having chosen different paths to the single exit.

Treet put his head down and ran for it, but had not gone more than three paces when one of the Saecaraz stepped onto the path ahead of him, his back to Treet. Treet skidded to a stop.

The man turned toward the door and moved off. Treet remained unnoticed, but knew now that he had to get off the path. He glanced around and saw a stack of vent covers and stepped onto it. The stack shifted under his weight, and Treet was pitched backward into the path, while the vent covers cascaded around him in a clattering avalanche. The insidious gray film that lay thick over everything in the Archives powdered up in dusty clouds. Heart beating wildly in his throat, he looked up to see that the Saecaraz ahead of him had not turned around. Was the man deaf?

Furiously scrambling for his feet and scattering more of the infernal vents, Treet picked himself up. The startled shout from behind him caught him with his rear end poised in the air in the act of standing up. He glanced behind him—two Saecaraz Hagemen stood together, both wearing expressions of amazement. The foremost of the two shouted again, this time for the help of his comrades. The Saecaraz ahead of Treet turned around and started running toward him.

Treet stood for an instant, poised for flight but with no-where to go. Then, without thinking what he would do, he threw himself forward, crashing through the stack of vent covers and into a glassy wall of electrical insulators. He tore down the wall, and stumbled through the breach—heaving ceramic insula-tors big as a man's head behind him as he went—and fell into a tightly packed corridor on the other side, the sounds of the chase close behind.

He flew down the corridor, formed by banks of heat de-flector shields, and ran headlong into a dead end. Panting, Treet halted and turned to meet his pursuers.

FOUR

Horatio Crocker plowed through the heavy underbrush, searching for the trail he hoped he would find somewhere just ahead. The robot carrier tagged faithfully along behind, riding its treads over the foliage Crocker tramped down.

For six days Crocker had stalked the lonely hills. Dazed, senses numb, whimpering pitifully to himself, he pursued a meandering path that roughly paralleled the river. On the seventh day he had come to the edge of the Blue Forest—a tractless expanse terminating the desolate hill country like an enormous curtain of deep blue-green vegetation.

He had no thought but to lose himself in the darkness of that many-shadowed land—and even this was not a conscious desire. He simply moved because he could not stop moving. At first there had been some urgency in his flight, but as time and again he glanced fearfully over his shoulder and saw nothing to cause him alarm, he gradually relaxed and pushed a less hurried, though still wary, pace.

He did not know why he ran, or where. All consciousness—that part of himself that knew himself, spoke to and governed himself—had been obliterated. He had a ghostly recollection of a shattering event back there in the hills: of blood and death, and an agony like a firebrand cleaving his skull and burning into his soft brain tissue. His mind had become an inflamed and tortured thing, and he bellowed out his pain to the empty sky.

As day gave way to day, Crocker retreated deeper and deeper into the core of his being in an effort to escape the drumming pain. He moved with the same cunning and stealth as a wild animal, and with as much self-regard. He ate when he was hungry and slept when he grew tired. He drank from the river, never far away, though he had water in three canteens in the carrier. He considered the robot a companion, accepting it as being alive in the same way that he was alive. In the space of a few days, he came to derive comfort from the machine's presence. It followed him—moving when he moved, stopping when he stopped, purring idly while it waited—giving Crocker a sense of kinship.

When, on the sixth day, he had stood atop a high promontory and saw the hillscape descending in rippled steps to meet the forest, he knew that he would go there and seek solace beneath the dense dark mass of its interwoven canopy. No one would find him in there; nothing would hurt him anymore.

Without so much as a backward glance, he had pushed his way into the thicket fringe that rimmed the forest, protecting it like a daunting barrier reef around a vast, serene, imperturbable lagoon.

Now he labored, pulling himself through brush grown so lush and tangled that it was a solid wall. Above the wall he could see the tops of nearer trees; he watched these to mark his progress, lifting his head now and again as he thrust arms and legs and torso into whatever openings he could force through the growth. His clothes snagged and tore. His hands bled. But he did not heed the little pain, for it was drowned inside the greater, all-pervasive pain that he had become used to.

As he pushed past a broad-leafed shrub, thick-bodied and twice as tall as a man, he stuck his hand into a hole in the dense covering of leaves. An instant later the bush erupted in a flurry of flashing wings and screams. He threw his hands before his face as the shrieking birds took flight, and then, with instinctual quickness, reached into the feathery melee and closed his fist on the warm body of a bird as its head appeared in the hole, its wings half-unfolded for flight.

In the same motion, he brought the creature to his lips, put its head in his mouth, and bit down hard, feeling the crunch of delicate bone and hot blood spurting over his tongue. He drank the thick, bittersweetness and then spit the head out, tossing the carcass away. He smiled and wiped his mouth. "Meat," he muttered to himself.

• • • • • •

"How Giloon knowing Tanais be doing as he says when big noise finished?" The Dhog leader put his loathsome face close to Tvrdy and smiled maliciously. "Tanais Supreme Director be forgetting his Dhogs, seh?"

Tvrdy stared at Giloon, trying not to show his disgust. They were sitting in one of the dwellings across the plaza from where they had met. The kraam had been hastily appointed for the meeting: two filthy cushions had been put down on the grimy floor and a much abused table between them. Beside the low table stood an improvised brazier made of cast-off pieces of fibersteel riveted and bound together with wire. Foul-smelling chips—dried dung, Tvrdy suspected—burned in the brazier, giving off a thick, noxious smoke. There were two skewers with chunks of ratty-looking meat and a few sorry vegetables sputtering on the odorous coals.

Giloon reached over and turned the skewers expertly, casting a sidelong glance at Tvrdy and grunting with satisfaction. Tvrdy wanted to be away from this stinking place, but his opinion of his squat companion was changing. Giloon Bogney might well be crazy—probably was—but his madness bore a wide streak of stubborn self-interest that, under the proper circumstances, Tvrdy recognized as extremely useful. So, the Director sat in the ruined hovel, permitting himself to be alternately offended and insulted by the Dhog's presence and broad insinuations.

"You don't know me," replied Tvrdy, "if you think I would turn my back on any who gave aid when I asked. Saecaraz and Nilokerus may forget any service when it suits them—"

"But they be remembering any crime!"

"Yes, that's true. But the Tanais are not like that. We live by our word."

"When you getting fat on it."

"Watch your tongue! We make sure the terms are right before we make a deal. We never have to go back on our word—unless, of course, the other party attempts treachery."

Giloon chuckled, an ugly sound, full of malicious glee. "Giloon being a Director then, because Dhogs doing what Giloon says." He snatched up a skewer and thrust it at Tvrdy, who took the unwholesome thing and looked for a place to throw it. "Dhogs helping you, Tanais. Giloon giving his word, seh?" He tore off a scrap of meat, raised it in salute, and flipped it into his mouth.

Tvrdy followed his host's example and swallowed the meat without chewing. "I will send men to you—Rumon and Tanais, perhaps Hyrgo too. They will train those among you who are fit enough to fight."

"Dhogs not needing your training."

"We will face Invisibles armed with thermal weapons. You *will* be trained."

Giloon begrudged him the point with a grunt. Tvrdy continued, "You will give these men any aid, supplies, or information they require. Hold nothing back. If we fail, Old Section will not become a Hage and you will not become a Director."

"What we having, you having." Giloon spat on the table.

"My men will bring supplies with them which they will share with you—as they see fit. You must keep your people organized. There is to be no trouble between us. This is of the highest importance."

"You think Dhogs needing your aid, your training, your supplies? You throw us out of Hage, our names being erased; you taking away our life and thinking to starve us. If you be finding us in Hage, you kill us. Ah, but Dhogs live! We go down into the pits, we taking what you throwing away, use it. We living a long time this way, and we being still alive to roll your bones, Tanais."

Tvrdy put the skewer down on the table and leaned forward, his face hard, his tone steel. "Listen to me! You call yourself a leader—act like one. If you do not control your people, you will be of no use to us. If we do not have help, we will fail. And then how long do you think you will be allowed to live?"

Before Giloon could answer, Tvrdy went on, "When Jamrog is finished with us, he will turn on you. Rohee tolerated the Dhogs because you were useful to him: those who displeased him, he made nonbeings and sent to you. He used you as a threat to enforce his will. Jamrog is not like Rohee. Jamrog lives only to destroy. He will see the Old Section razed and the Dhogs slaughtered. I know him; that is his plan. Your head is full of night soil if you think to survive the Purge."

Giloon had sunk into a sulky silence. He fixed Tvrdy with a murderous glare and said nothing.

"You don't like what I've said, but you know the truth when you hear it, seh?" Tvrdy sat back, folded his arms across his chest, and returned Giloon's stare boldly.

The silence spread between them, but Tvrdy let his words sink in. Giloon frowned and fingered the bhuj's blade in his lap. When at last he spoke, his voice was a hissing whisper. "Giloon maybe kill you, Tanais."

"You'd kill your only friend for speaking the truth? Then you have much to learn before you ever become a Director."

Giloon sniffed, picked up the bhuj, and slammed the blade into the table. "Giloon being a leader greater as you. I control my people."

Tvrdy rose. "See that you do—your life and the lives of all your people depend on your cooperation."

"There being no noisy guts between us, Tanais." Giloon climbed to his feet and led Tvrdy out of the kraam and back across the square. Tvrdy saw the ghostly shapes of Dhogs watching from behind piles of rubble. As he moved away, the nonbeings came out of hiding to watch him leave, so that when he turned to give some last words to Giloon he saw a whole throng, gray as the shadows they inhabited, gathered at the far end of the plaza, watching silently.

"My men will begin arriving tomorrow. They will come one by one, or in twos. Receive them and make them welcome. We will soon have rumor messengers so that we can talk, but it is best if we do not see each other again until the plans are set. Do you understand?"

Giloon nodded, eyes squinted up at the Director. Tvrdy guessed some sign of official recognition of the Dhog leader before his people would go a long way toward smoothing future relations between them; so he took off his cloak and placed it on Giloon's shoulders. "There," he said, "now my men will know that I recognize you as a Director."

The Dhog's face squirmed into a great grin. He raised the bhuj and touched Tvrdy on either side of the throat with it, then turned abruptly and, hitching the cloak around himself, swaggered off across the ruined plaza to join his people.

Tvrdy watched him go, then turned and fled the Old Section as fast as decorum allowed.

Treet gulped air and watched the Saecaraz come toward him. There were four of them. The two others had presumably gone for help. They slowed as they came nearer, and Treet sized them up: two were taller, heavier-looking, their bodies bulky beneath their black-and-silver yoses; the other two were slighter of build and not as tall, but looked more fit. Clearly, he would have trouble taking on all four, but it looked like he would have no choice.

So, figuring his best advantage lay in initiating the fight, he lowered his head and charged into them, bellowing as he ran. He plunged his shoulder into the first Saecaraz and sent him sprawling into the deflectors, spun off the block, and caught the second man as he attempted to dodge away. Treet gave him an elbow shot in the small of the back and shoved with all his might. There was a crash and a groan behind him as Treet dove for the onrushing feet of the third, who gave a yelp of surprise as his legs were cut from under him. The man landed on his face and skidded into his crumpled partner.

Treet came up running. The fourth Saecaraz stopped in midstride when he saw Treet gathering himself for another charge. For an instant the two stood looking at one another; then Treet yelled and lunged forward. The Saecaraz backpedaled and spun, tangled his legs and went down. Treet dashed for him, placed one foot square on his breastbone, and ran right over him and back into the main pathway, reaching the door seconds later.

He paused only long enough to pull the door shut and seal it, then ran for the first of a succession of doors leading to the guard station and the lower levels of Hage Nilokerus beyond. Once beyond the second set of doors, with those doors sealed behind him, he paused to listen and heard someone coming toward him from the opposite way.

The two Saecaraz who had gone for help were returning with the Nilokerus from the guard station. He could hear their feet pounding down the corridor—one, maybe two doors beyond. There was only one thing to do. Turning to the door he'd just sealed, he tapped the entry code into the lock and opened it again, then dashed the fifty meters to the next door, went through it, and pressed himself flat against the opposite wall and waited.

A moment later the Saecaraz appeared, followed by three Nilokerus with weapons drawn. They slipped through the huge doors and raced toward the next one ahead. Treet waited, holding his breath and praying none of them would glance back and see him standing there playing chameleon. None did; all five, hurrying to get to the Archives, pounded straight ahead.

Treet inched his way to the door and slipped through. He waited until the corridor was empty and then sealed the door he'd just exited. Then, listening carefully, he made his way to the next set of doors, which he also sealed behind him. No one seemed to be following him. They would not know he had evaded them until they conferred with the others inside the Archives; that would give him a minute or two before they came racing back after him. The doors would stop them only momentarily as they reentered the code at the lock, but every second counted.

He was thinking about how best to lose himself in Hage as he burst through the last set of doors—which is why he failed to see the Nilokerus guard waiting for him on the other side.

• • • • • •

Nilokerus Director Hladik was reclining in his suspension bed, stroking the soft flank of his hagemate as she fed him cherimoyas from a silver bowl, when a chime sounded in the next room. A moment later his guide came silently into the sleep chamber.

"I told you I was not to be disturbed," Hladik said.

"Forgive my intrusion, Hage Leader," said the guide tentatively, his fingers sifting the air, eye sockets staring emptily into space. "It is from Supreme Director Jamrog."

Hladik sighed and lifted his deeply creased face. "Since Jamrog has become Supreme Director, I have not had one moment to myself. Well, what is it, Bremot?"

"The messenger did not say. You are to go to Threl High Chambers at once. Jamrog is waiting for you there."

Eyeing his bedmate hungrily, he said, "I must go, Moira, but wait for me and I will return soon." She yawned as he kissed her neck, then pulled a sheet over her body and went to sleep.

Hladik pulled off his hagerobe, donned a yos, and strode into the next room where Bremot stood waiting. "I hope Jamrog is brief this morning. I wish to return as soon as possible."

The blind guide led his master through Nilokerus Hage to a lift. They rode the tube down to Greengrass level and entered a guarded corridor where an em stood waiting. At the sight of their Director, the two Nilokerus snapped to attention. Hladik frowned, but passed by without a word, too much in a hurry and too preoccupied to offer the obligatory reprimand.

Under Bremot's precise control, the em sped along the empty corridor as it bent around and down, dipping below Kyan and coming up on the other side in Saecaraz Hage. The corridor had been constructed well before Sirin Rohee's time, and had served many Nilokerus Directors, providing a well-used shortcut to Threl High Chambers.

At one time Hladik had dreamed of becoming Supreme Director. But he feared Jamrog, and in that he showed wisdom. Jamrog's ambition was fiercer than his own; he knew Jamrog would ruthlessly remove any rivals to his claim. So, in those early years of Rohee's reign when the Directors were still vying for position and favor in his regime, Hladik had tipped his hand—a risk, certainly, but a very small risk—and let it be known that he considered himself successor material. Jamrog, still assembling his power base then, had been in no position to challenge him since Jamrog himself was a Subdirector and, technically, wielded an authority inferior to Hladik's.

This had forced Jamrog into the position of having to win Hladik over through gifts and favors. And Hladik allowed himself to be won, selling his ambition for the Supreme Director's kraam, but at a very fine price. He had never regretted his choice—except now, when Jamrog interrupted his intimate affairs for trifles.

Eventually Bremot brought the em to a stop and led them to another lift. They rode to the upper levels of Threl High Chambers. "Wait here," said Hladik as he stepped from the compartment. "This will not take long." Bremot nodded and remained in the lift.

"I suppose you don't know anything about this," Jamrog cried as he entered the Threl meeting room. No one else was in attendance, save Opinski, Jamrog's guide, standing quietly in a far corner of the room.

Hladik glanced at the flimsy yellow communique fluttering in Jamrog's hand and said, "Of course not, Supreme Director—seeing as how you have not yet shown it to me."

"Read!" Jamrog threw the sheet in Hladik's face.

Hladik took the transcript and read it. "Yes, I see."

"That's all you have to say? *I see?*" Jamrog fumed.

"I see, yes. I see no reason for you to be upset by this—" He snapped the sheet with a finger. "—this routine report."

"Your own guards caught someone in the Archives, and you call it routine."

"A Dhog, Supreme Director. What else?"

"A Dhog in the Archives. On the day before Rohee's funeral?"

"Coincidence. What else could it be?"

Hladik shrugged, outwardly trying to remain unconcerned. Inwardly he seethed. Why had those idiots allowed the Saecaraz to be contacted first? The communication should have been sent directly to him if Nilokerus guards were involved. Or perhaps Jamrog had intercepted it? "What do you suggest, Supreme Director? I fail to see—"

"You fail to see a great many things these days, Hageman," Jamrog barked, then dismissed Hladik's hurt expression with an impatient flick of his hand. "All right, I may be oversensitive just now, but it's only because I am concerned that nothing interfere with Rohee's funeral. Everything must take place precisely as I have planned. The people must witness a glorious spectacle. There must be no distraction."

"What could go wrong?"

Jamrog dropped into the Supreme Director's thronelike chair and passed a hand over his eyes. "I have not slept for two days, Hladik. I'm tired."

Hladik approached and sat down next to him. He waved Jamrog's guide away. Opinski withdrew discreetly. "Now, suppose you tell me what's really troubling you, Jamrog. I know there is some other reason you sent for me."

Jamrog stared upward and then closed his eyes. "I'm so tired."

"Rest then. Rest now so that you can enjoy your triumph tomorrow all the more."

"How can I rest when Tvrdy plots against me? He is out there even now, scheming with that Cabal of his to steal the bhuj from me—and I have not even been installed yet."

"That is but a tiresome formality—it gives the priests something to do. No one, not even the ridiculous Tvrdy, doubts that you are Supreme Director now. Besides, you have worn Tvrdy down. His power is gone; the Cabal you speak of is smashed. There is nothing left. He has no choice but to accept defeat gracefully if he would save his skin."

"You do not know Tvrdy at all if you believe I have won so easily. He will resist me to his last breath."

"Forget him. He's nothing."

"What if he is behind this incident in the Archives?"

"Well, what if he is? He will have discovered nothing. His agent was caught before he could make a report. There is nothing to worry about. If you wish, I will have the man brought to the tank and questioned and—" He hesitated.

"Yes? I'm listening. Go on."

"I was about to suggest having him conditioned after questioning and returned to his master. That way, if he is one of Tvrdy's men, we will have eyes and ears inside Tvrdy's network."

Jamrog's eyes narrowed with cunning. "Sometimes I underestimate your resourcefulness, Hladik. Yes, have the man conditioned and then allow him to escape."

Hladik forced a laugh. "Think of it! We will have an agent inside Tvrdy's network."

"Not an agent, Hladik," Jamrog said, his eyes narrowing to slits. "I want a weapon."

"It will be all right, Asquith, you'll see. You wanted to go to the concert and since I cannot go with you, I asked my friend to take you." Jaire was pulling a reluctant Pizzle along the upper gallery of Liamoge to the receiving hall. "She'll be here any moment."

"It won't be the same," complained Pizzle in his nasal whine. "I'd rather not go if I can't be with you."

"You'd miss a good concert—they're doing the *Naravell* tonight. You said you wanted to learn all about our ways, and I promised to introduce you to people who could teach you. My friend is much more knowledgeable about music than I am, and she'd be disappointed if she couldn't meet you."

"She would?" Pizzle asked suspiciously, not at all certain he wanted to meet anyone who wanted to meet him. That, in his experience, always betokened disaster at the hands of someone even less socially acceptable than he was.

They came to the wide, curving stairway and descended. "She's here!" said Jaire, giving Pizzle's arm a squeeze. They were only halfway down the stairs, and Pizzle didn't see anyone in the hall. Jaire propelled him down the stairs and out the doors to the curving drive outside. A sleek blue two-passenger evee was just pulling up to the entrance.

Pizzle saw only the single occupant sitting in the center of the passenger seat and purposefully turned his head away so that he didn't see her clearly. He heard the evee door open and, eyes on the ground now, saw two buff-booted feet come to stand in front of him. Jaire embraced her friend and they exchanged greetings, which Pizzle ignored.

Jaire said, "Asquith, I want you to meet my friend Starla."

Pizzle sighed and looked up. He'd heard of people claiming they'd been shot by Cupid's arrow. For him, it was as if he'd been impaled on the pudgy little love cherub's spear. He stared, transfixed by the vision before him: a young woman clothed all in white with buff-colored accents, her fine, platinum hair swept back by the light evening breeze, looking at him with pleasure and excitement mingled in her large, dark, oak-brown eyes. She was half-a-head shorter than he was and wore a silver bracelet on each wrist; her arms, bare in a sleeveless jacket, were tanned and smooth, as was her elegant, graceful neck.

An impartial observer might have said that her eyes were too big and perhaps too wide set, her chin too small and her nose a little thin. Certainly, her lower lip protruded when she was not smiling. But in Pizzle's eyes, she was, if possible, even more beautiful than Jaire—his fantasies made flesh.

"Starla," he said, repeating her name. And again, "Starla."

"I'm pleased to meet you—" She hesitated.

"Pizzy," he said, and embarrassed himself when he realized he'd just given her the least favorite of his many objectionable diminutives. "Just call me . . . Pizzy. Everyone does."

Starla laughed lightly. Pizzle reconciled himself to the name in that instant; it was worth all the years of misery and embarrassment if that name could evoke such a sound from one so lovely. "I'm pleased to meet you, Pizzy. Jaire told me you liked music . . ." She paused again because Pizzle was staring at her. Glancing at Jaire, who nodded toward the vehicle, she said, "Mmm, shall we go?"

Jaire took Pizzle by the arm and pushed him forward, saying, "Yes, you'd better hurry or you'll miss the best seats. I'm sure you'll both have a wonderful time." She took Starla's hand, placed it in Pizzle's, and bundled them both into the evee. Starla leaned forward and pressed their destination into the console; the car rolled silently away. Pizzle did not look back to see Jaire smiling in smug satisfaction.

• • • • • •

Stepping into the forest was like stepping into a cathedral. Enormous trees with smooth trunks stood like huge pillars, holding up a dense, blue-green layer of leaves, a vaulted roof a hundred meters above the forest floor. In fact, there were, Crocker noticed at once, two forests: the older, taller forest formed a towering leaf roof over a younger forest of slender trees and squat, fleshy shrubs all sewn together with innumerable vines and creepers. Around the massive smooth columns of the supporting trees, braided pathways wound and converged and split, only to join and rejoin again.

The light filtering down from the leaf ceiling was bronze-green and soft, melting into the humid, water-drenched air. Vaporous wisps snaked along the forest byways, curling upward like tendrils of a growing plant to evaporate on unseen currents. And everywhere beneath the forest roof there was the rich, heady smell of damp, fecund soil and vegetation run riot—odors as palpable as the chitterings, clicks, and chirrups of the host of insects hidden in the foliage.

Higher in the leaf canopy, the shrill, chattering calls of birds and jarring whoops of mammalian tree dwellers—along with all sorts of murmurings, cooings, blarings, gruntings, yawpings, toatings, and gugglings—let Crocker know that the forest brimmed with unseen life, even as the heavy air reverberated with its raucous music.

The Blue Forest was a world unto itself, and Crocker felt secure here. As he walked further into its majestic fastness, the oppression of the open spaces fell away. He took the thick closeness of the forest and wrapped it around himself like a robe. He would be safe here among the creatures of the forest; he would become like them, and like them he would survive.

He struck along a path wide enough for the robot to follow and began moving deeper into the interior, the last glimpses of blue sky and green hills disappearing as the forest closed behind him. He walked along silently, moving with caution and stealth, adapting himself to the ways of the forest.

Like an animal, Crocker wandered the soft pathways, pausing now and again to sift the air for scent and sound of water. It had been exhausting work burrowing through the brushline to the forest, and he was thirsty. Eventually he came to a place where a small brook lapped around the gigantic roots of one of the forest pillars. He knelt down, cupped his hands, and drank.

The water was warm and had a distinctly earthy taste. He sipped and swallowed and spat the rest out. To get clean water he'd have to find a deeper source. Without thinking about it he moved off along the little brook, following it as it made its way over and around the roots of the giant trees and through stands of rushes with large lacy fan-shaped leaves. The brook took him deeper into the forest, deeper into the living green solitude.

At one point he pushed through a bristle-bladed hedge and found himself in a walled clearing. He looked up and saw the walls of the hedge rising above him for many meters. The clearing was carpeted with thick, bluish moss made up of tiny coiled filaments like wire springs. The sunlight striking through a thin place in the leaf canopy fell to the forest floor like heavy gold. In the center of the clearing lay a pool of deep blue-black water, filled from a spring which welled up from the center of the pool, splashing and sending ripples to the pool's outer rim.

The forest's discordant music, muted by the hedge walls, sounded far away. In the clearing, only the gentle plipping of the spring as it ruffled the water could be heard. Crocker stared at the water for a long moment and then began mechanically stripping off his clothes.

He lowered himself into the pool, feeling its chill refresh and revive him. He sank down into the ooze of the cool mud bottom and let the water close over his head, then kicked off and swam the length of the pool underwater, coming up for air when his head touched the far bank. It felt good to swim, to feel tight muscles relax as the knots loosened.

After a few minutes of swimming, Crocker felt wholly restored. He climbed out on the spongy bank and lay down in a patch of sunlight to dry off. The sun filtering down from the upper boughs warmed his skin, and he closed his eyes and went to sleep, his mind blank, unthinking, undreaming. He was part of the forest now—as much as any of her natural creatures. And, in his own way, just as wild.

SEVEN

Yarden watched as the dancers whirled and spun on the grassy field before her, their shimmering clothing reflecting the sun's last rays. Three men and three women, each tracing a complex interaction of movements with each of the others, danced for an audience of a hundred or more rapt spectators. Several musicians sitting around the ring of observers accompanied the dance on their instruments: long, hollow tubes, curved into polished semicircles. The flutelike instruments emitted low, rich, mellow tones, and though the musicians were scattered throughout the crowd, their music formed a single, seamless stage upon which the dancers performed.

Never had Yarden seen such exquisite movement, so lithe and free and—there was no other word for it—holy. The music and the dance were one and the same expression, so beautifully did they complement one another: sound giving impulse to movement, dance giving visual emphasis to the music, and each doing what the other could not do, thereby creating a total experience greater than the sum of the parts.

Yarden stood entranced. She'd seen dancers perform before, of course—some of the best in the world—but never with such abandon—almost as if they were creating their intricate movements spontaneously, yet in complete harmony with the others, for each dancer moved as an individual and as a member of a larger body at the same time. She knew they must have performed together for years to be able to create such intricate and harmonious movement.

This appreciation made the dance all the more wondrous to Yarden. She knew the cost of such perfection and loved the dancers for their extravagance. She watched with total concentration, savoring every fleeting, endless moment as the dancers spun and leapt and turned, coming together, forming patterns, breaking apart to create new patterns, until all the field and music and spectators coalesced into a single, creative awareness, joined by the movements of the dance.

When the dance finally ended—the dancers breathless and

exhausted, the music trailing off in whispers—the audience all exhaled as one, and Yarden realized that she, like all the others, had been holding her breath. She sighed, closed her eyes, and savored the moment, knowing that she had experienced true beauty and had been touched by it in a most intimate way.

She felt a nudge and opened her eyes. Ianni smiled at her and indicated the crowd, typical of Fieri gatherings, moving away silently. Yarden saw that the dancers, having gathered themselves together, were smiling at each other and talking together in low tones, their faces flushed with satisfaction and exhilaration. It seemed somehow wrong to Yarden that this performance should go unrewarded by the audience; there should be some recognition paid the dancers—applause, at least.

"I'll be right with you," she told Ianni. Turning to the dancers, she approached hesitantly. One of the women in the ensemble glanced up as Yarden came near. She smiled and held out her hands in the Fieri greeting, but Yarden stepped close and put her arms around the woman. They embraced and Yarden said, "Thank you for sharing your dance with me."

The woman pressed Yarden's hands and said, "It is our joy to dance. If you find pleasure in it, praise the Giver. He gives the dance."

"Your dance is praise itself," replied Yarden. "I will never forget what I've seen here today. Thank you." She then rejoined Ianni, who was waiting for her a little way off.

"Why did no one acknowledge the dancers?" asked Yarden as they walked back across the meadow toward the Arts Center, a palatial edifice made of rust-colored sunstone, with numerous wings and pavilions radiating from a common hub. "Or praise them for their artistry?"

"Praise belongs only to the Infinite," Ianni explained gently, as she had explained so often to Yarden since becoming her mentor. "Would you have us praise the vessel for its contents?"

"I don't know. It just seems that one ought to show some appreciation for the dancers, for their art, for the joy they bring in the dance."

"The joy of the dance was theirs."

"They shared it with us, then."

"And we paid them the highest tribute—we honored the beauty of the moment, and respected the serenity of the performance."

Yarden thought about this. "By leaving like that? Without a word, without a sound—just leaving? That was your tribute?"

Ianni, a tall, dark-haired woman, slender with long graceful limbs, folded her hands in front of her and stopped walking, turned to Yarden, and said, "We shared the moment together, and we took it to ourselves. We have hidden it in our hearts to treasure it always. What more can one do who has not created? It was not our place to judge, only to accept."

They walked again, feeling the warmth of the day and the pure rays of the sun on their faces. After a time Yarden nodded, saying, "I think I understand what you are saying: the artist practices her art for herself alone, but she performs as an expression of praise to the Infinite Father for the gift of her art—a gift she shares with her audience."

"Or with no audience at all."

"Yes, I see. The audience does not matter."

"Not to the performance, no. But if the audience is moved to praise the Infinite too, so much the better. Let praise increase! Of course, an artist is pleased when the audience is pleased. That is only natural. But, since she performs her art for herself and for the pleasure of the Infinite, the audience's response or lack of it is of no concern."

"The only concern is how well she has performed."

"Yes, whether she has used her gift to her best abilities. If she has, what does it matter whether she had an audience or not, or what the audience thought about the performance?"

Yarden understood, though she still thought anyone who could create such beauty as she had just witnessed ought to have more for their trouble than mute enjoyment, no matter how appreciative the crowd.

They continued on in silence until they reached the nearest of the outflung wings of the Arts Center. "Do you wish to return to the paintings?" asked Ianni. They had been viewing Fieri commemorative artwork in the gallery before their stroll of the grounds and their encounter with the dancers. Yarden looked up at the imposing entrance to the gallery and hesitated. "Or we could come back another time."

"You wouldn't mind?"

"Not at all." Ianni smiled. "One can only absorb so much."

"And I've absorbed all I can. Now I need time to think

about what I've seen." She took Ianni's hand and squeezed it. "Wasn't it beautiful though? I never imagined anything could be so perfect, so right, so expressive."

Ianni eyed her thoughtfully. "Perhaps you have an artist's heart, Yarden. Would you like to learn?"

Yarden shook her head sadly. "I could never dance like that."

"How do you know? Have you ever tried?"

"No, but—" Yarden's eyes grew wide with the possibility. "Do you think I should try?"

"Only if it appeals to you."

"Oh, it does. You have no idea how much!"

. . . . . .

The place where they brought Treet was an underground complex carved into Empyrion's bedrock, a cave with square-cut walls and passageways—the Cavern-level bastion of the Nilo-kerus. It was here that Hladik maintained the infamous reorientation cells: row upon row of stone cubicles, barely big enough for a person to stand upright or stretch out full length. Each cell had independent heat and light controls so that one cell could be floodlit and heated to a swelter, while the one next to it was plunged into total darkness and bone-chilling cold, depending on the whim of the reorientation engineer.

Treet was dragged roughly from the Archives vestibule, through an endless succession of corridors and galleries until he was handed over to the keepers of Cavern level. He had kept his mouth shut and answered none of his captors' questions, since it was clear from the beginning that they had already decided what to do with him and anything he said would make no difference.

From the conversation of the guards, he gathered they thought him a runaway—someone who had left his Hage to lose himself in Dome's underground mazeworks, hoping perhaps to make contact with the Dhogs. They presumed he had sneaked into the Archives when they themselves had entered. It did not occur to them that he had been in the Archives all along. Neither did it occur to them that he might be a Fieri spy.

For that he was grateful. At least they considered him no

more important than the typical runaway, which meant that he might be released sooner or later if he kept up his part of the charade.

"Your name?" asked the bored Nilokerus officer, glancing up from a green screen. He sat behind a large console and gazed at his prisoner with weary, watery eyes. The air in the caves was warm enough, but humid, and the stone was chill, making the atmosphere clammy and hard on the sinuses. "What is your name?"

Treet thought fast and said the first thing that popped into his head, "Stone." He tried to make his tone properly contrite, still hoping he could yet convince them it was some sort of mistake.

"What were you doing in the Archives?" the officer asked, punching keys into the terminal before him.

"I—ah . . ." Treet tried to come up with a plausible explanation. "I saw the doors open and I went in. I didn't know it was—what did you call it?—the Archives."

The intake officer looked up. "Were there no guards to stop you?"

"I suppose they didn't see me."

The guard gave a snort of contempt—whether for Treet's answer, or for the slackness of the guards on duty, Treet couldn't tell. "Hage?"

Treet said nothing. He was desperately thinking.

"Your Hage? Answer quickly."

"Bolbe." Treet blurted the name, and then gritted his teeth, hoping that he'd chosen a good cover.

The officer punched a few more keys. "No Stohn in Bolbe," he announced. "What is your Hagename?"

Mind whirling frantically, Treet searched his memory for a name that might serve him now—a name he had heard in passing that could be documented. "Bela," he said finally, with what he hoped was the right amount of resignation. Wasn't Bela the name Yarden had told him was the name of her Chryse keeper?

The officer shifted in his seat, tugging on his red-and-white yos as he punched in the name. "Yes," he murmured at length. "Here it is. Bela. You are a second-order ipumn grader."

Treet nodded and lowered his eyes.

"You will be returned to your Hage, Bolbe—"

Treet started to breathe a sigh of relief. His dodge had worked. Evidently, Bela was a common enough name.

The Nilokerus officer continued, "—after reorientation."

"No!" shouted Treet. The Nilokerus loafing in another corner of the room looked up sharply. "Please, I've never done anything like this before. I'll go back gladly. I'm sorry."

The officer gazed at Treet, hesitated. Would he let Treet go? With a shrug he said, "Standard directive punishment. No exceptions." He motioned to a nearby guard. "Take him to J-5V. Begin reorientation at once."

"No!" Treet screamed again. "Please! No!"

Two guards grabbed his arms and pulled him away; he was marched down one of the branching corridors and shoved into a cell. He heard the fizzling crackle of the barrier field as it snapped on, and he was left alone in the darkness of his cell.

EIGHT

Crocker came instantly awake, fully alert. His sleep had been deep and long, but a part of his awareness remained sharp, even in sleep, so that he awoke when he heard the faint rustling in the dry vegetation on the side of the pool opposite where he slept. He did not move, but merely opened his eyes to see a fat, furry creature the size of a small but well-fed pig ambling out of the brush.

The sounds of the forest were hushed now as the denizens of the day settled to their nests; the forest's nocturnal population had not yet begun to stir. Night came quickly to the world beneath the leaf-roof of the forest, and Crocker gazed out across the evening-dimmed circle of his bower at the intruder, his pilot's eyes keen in the failing light. He watched the animal pause in its slow shamble to the water, raise up on short hind legs to sniff the air, and peer into the murk with tiny round eyes. The thing had stubby legs that curved under its bulk and a long, fleshy tail that it carried straight up in the air. Its face was long and pointed, like a rat's elongated snout, but its eyes faced forward and its ears were the velvet exclamation points of a rabbit.

The animal appeared happy with its survey of the glade and continued down to the water's edge. Crocker eased himself up on palms and toes and made his way around the pool, maintaining careful silence on the cushiony moss. He came up behind the creature as it poked its long muzzle into the water and slurped noisily. Crocker eyed his prey for a moment—the creature was totally oblivious to any danger—and then, gathering himself for the spring, pounced on the animal, his hands quickly finding its short neck.

A terrified squawk bubbled from the creature's throat as it wriggled furiously. Crocker picked the animal up and shook it, squeezing the soft neck until the feeble fight went out of its body. The animal gave a convulsive quiver and died with a gasp.

He was standing by the water's edge, examining his catch,

when out of the brush behind him came a ball of bundled fury, charging right for him. He spun around, flinging the dead animal aside, just as his feet were swept from under him. He went down on his hip and squirmed to his knees as the burly ball of lightning attacked, long ears flattened to its back, sharp incisors bared.

Crocker saw enough in that second before the animal sprang to know that he was being challenged by the mother of the creature he had just killed—it was an exact replica of the first animal, but easily twice its size. He put his hands up and rolled backward as the animal leaped for him, catching it under the chin and pulling it over the top of him, his legs lifting its body up and over with the aid of its own momentum. The animal raked at him with its short, clawed feet and snapped at him with its long jaws as it went over, and then it was sailing through the air to land with a heavy thump on its back a few meters away.

The animal grunted and came up snapping, gathering itself for a second charge. Crocker did not wait, but leaped headlong at the animal. It twisted away, but Crocker landed on its back and his fingers found its neck and dug in. The creature yelped—a confused, mewing sound—and tried to roll over. But Crocker, adrenalin pounding through him, clamped his knees against its fat sides and kept his place on its back. The fleshy tail lashed his back ineffectually and the animal stumbled, grunting and squirming, digging its short claws into the moss and flinging patches skyward.

Sitting atop the thrashing beast, Crocker was overcome by a sudden rush of pure ecstasy and, with his hands buried in the creature's neck, choking the life from its body, he threw back his head and laughed. The sound rang in the glade, shivering the leafy hedge round about—a strange, strangled sound of tormented delight.

He laughed until his sides ached and then, as the unearthly echo died away, looked down to see that the animal beneath him struggled no more. Gradually he released his hold and got up. The creature lay still, unmoving. He looked at it for a long time and then knelt down beside it and put his hands on its body.

The fur was luxurious, thick and fine; the flesh beneath well-muscled, but soft. He stood abruptly and walked around the pool to the place where he'd entered, then stepped back through the hedgewall. There, patiently waiting for him on the other side, stood the robo-carrier. Since it could not force its way through the thick hedge, it had simply stopped on the trail to wait for its human controller to return.

Crocker retrieved the camp pack from its rack and then went back into the glade, opened the pack, and dumped out its contents. There was a utility knife among the articles in the pack, small and of no use as a real weapon, but Crocker took it up and went to the larger of the two animals he had killed.

Within a few minutes he had the rear haunch of the animal skinned and had cut away a large section of its liver; his hands were steeped in gore to the elbows. He sat back on his heels to look at his handiwork, the smell of blood heavy in the air. He raised the piece of liver to his mouth and licked it, tasting the thick sweetness, then hungrily devoured the still-warm portion. When he had finished this delicacy, he wiped his mouth with a blood-streaked arm and, taking up the knife again, began hacking at the meaty loin of the hapless creature.

When he had freed a good-sized piece of the haunch from the rest of the carcass, he sat back and, nostrils flaring with delight, began tearing off still-warm strands of meat and devouring them, smacking his lips and grunting his pleasure at this fine feast.

• • • • • •

The concert had been over for hours, but Pizzle still sat with Starla in the soft night, gazing at the sky and talking in the empty amphidrome. The *Naravell,* a moving retelling of the long years of the Wandering and a monumental piece of music by any standard, went by Pizzle as if it had been a jingle for foot powder. He could concentrate on nothing but the entrancing creature beside him.

Starla had shown herself to be charming, fascinating, captivating, engaging, bewitching—all this, and she had not spoken more than a half-dozen complete sentences throughout the course of the evening. Mostly, she had listened raptly as Pizzle discoursed on whatever subject happened to pop into his head—everything from *Arabian Nights* to Zen. Her presence, like a heady wine imbibed too quickly, had not only loosened his tongue, but made everything he said seem to him wise and wonderful and sparkling with wit.

He spoke like one drunk on the sound of his own voice, but it wasn't his words that fascinated him—it was that *she* was there listening to him. He would talk just to have her listen, just so he could watch her listen—for he'd never experienced anything so marvelous in all his drab life. For indeed, his whole life did seem lackluster and inconsequential up to the moment of meeting Starla.

Pizzle paused for breath—his voice was going hoarse—and Starla laid a hand on his forearm and said, "Let's walk for a while."

They'd been sitting for hours, but Pizzle hadn't noticed. To him, the evening had been but a moment as it sped by. "Sure, sounds good," he said, getting to his feet. He looked around and saw that the amphidrome was dark and empty. "Cleared out fast, huh?"

Starla led him up the aisle and out of the amphidrome and along the broad boulevard planted with feathertrees—slender trees whose long, supple branches grew delicate blossoms like goose down. They walked along for a while in silence. Pizzle, having interrupted his monologue, could not now think of a single word to say. He was absolutely tongue-tied.

"Smell the air," sighed Starla. The feathertree blossoms sweetened the warm night air with their light fragrance.

"Mmm, nice," said Pizzle. He looked at his ravishing companion. If Starla by daylight was a vision, Starla by starlight was a dream. Her platinum hair shone like silver, and her eyes were liquid pools of darkness fringed by long, sweeping lashes. "You're nice, too," he said, and blanched. Without premeditation he'd just given her his first compliment. What a night!

"I must go soon," she said. They walked on a little further in silence. "We could go to another concert sometime . . . if you like—"

"Oh, I would," agreed Pizzle heartily. "Tomorrow night. Okay?"

Starla laughed. "I don't know if there is a concert tomorrow night."

"Then we'll go sailing. Anything. Please? Say yes. I'll come pick you up. Where do you live?"

"Very well," Starla agreed. "We will meet again tomorrow evening."

"What about tomorrow morning? As a matter of fact, I'm free all day tomorrow."

"But I work tomorrow."

"Where? What do you do? Tell me about it. I want to know about everything you do. I want to know all about you."

"Most often I serve the Clerk at the College of Mentors. There are twenty-four of us, and we help Mathiax administrate the Mentors' resolutions." She stopped and smiled at Pizzle. "But the day after tomorrow I am free."

"You are? Good! Let's spend the whole day together. Okay? Say yes."

"Yes." Starla laughed, a warm, throaty sound, full of good humor. "I'd like that very much." She paused, glanced down at her feet and then up into Pizzle's eyes. Growing serious, she said, "I know you are a Traveler, and that you come from another world. Jaire has told me much about you. I must seem very plain to you after all you've seen." Pizzle opened his mouth to tell her just how wrong she was, but she silenced him with a gesture and went on. "Forgive my presumption, but it's hard for me to think of you as someone so different. I think we are more alike than different. And though I don't know you very well, I like you very much, Asquith Pizzle. I would like to be your friend while you are here."

He looked at her, standing against the heaven-scented background of the feathertrees, and swallowed a lump in his throat the size of a melon. "No one has ever said anything like that to me," he said. "I'm going to stay here forever."

NINE

Cejka, Director of Rumon Hage, took up his ceremonial bhuj, turned the flat blade so that its polished surface faced the correct quadrant, thrust out his chin, and squared his shoulders. Though his days as a member of the Threl elite might well be numbered, he would appear among his own people as their worthy leader: imperious, unafraid, powerful. Opposites, to be sure, of how he really felt. Covol, his Subdirector, arranged the hood of his black-and-red striped yos, nodded once, and stepped away. Cejka began walking slowly, a phalanx of Hage officers and functionaries behind him, leading his delegation through Rumon to the docks where they would board one of the official funeral boats that would take them to Saecaraz, where Sirin Rohee's funeral was to be held.

As they moved through Hage, he thought again about his message from Tvrdy. Though the Cabal had suffered crushing defeats of late, it was no small tribute to his own skill and cunning that his network of rumor messengers was still virtually intact. For this he was thankful.

The meeting with the Dhog, Giloon Bogney, had been, in Tvrdy's estimation, a success. They had gained the nonbeing's promises of support—though at a very high price, it seemed to Cejka. Hage stent for the Old Section? Such a thing was inconceivable even bare weeks ago. No doubt Tvrdy had only done what he'd been forced to do.

Ah, Tvrdy, my friend, thought Cejka gloomily. What is to become of us? Jamrog will not let us live, I think. Already I feel his hands on my throat. I hope you know what you are doing. An alliance with Dhogs! Unthinkable!

Be that as it may, Cejka now had to select the men who would go to the Old Section to begin training the Dhogs in the ways of covert combat. That, too, rubbed Cejka the wrong way—teaching Rumon secrets to nonbeings. But Tvrdy had insisted. There could be no holding back now. Jamrog had gained the Supreme Directorship, and the only way to survive a Purge was with an army at your back—even if it had to be an army of Dhogs. It was to Tvrdy's credit, Cejka reminded himself, that he'd not only considered turning to the Dhogs; the ever-resourceful Tanais leader had actually joined forces with them. This was something Jamrog could never have foreseen.

The Rumon entourage, purposefully a large one so Jamrog would have no cause to accuse Cejka of being unsympathetic, passed slowly through the streets and byways of the Hage, followed by other Rumon Hagemen making their own way to Saecaraz to see the funeral spectacle. A delegation of Rumon priests, chanting loudly and raising a din with their cymbals and horns, took up a position in front of the official party and led the way to the dockyard.

The entire waterfront area was crammed with boats and people waiting to jam into boats. There was an air of festivity and high spirits among the populace. After all, it was a special day—no work in the Hages and free food for all in attendance at the funeral. It promised to be a tremendous spectacle, and no one wanted to be left out; all who could were making their way to Saecaraz.

"There is the funeral boat," said Covol, pointing out the red-draped decks and gangway of the large tridecker. Cejka led his entourage to the gangway and boarded the boat, which was to pull away from the dock as soon as the last official squeezed aboard.

Cejka made his way to the topmost deck and took his place at the forward end, his guide on one hand and his Subdirector on the other. There arose a commotion from below, and when he asked what was taking place Cejka was told, "Some Hagemen have attempted to board, but they are not of the official party. There will be a slight delay while they are put off."

"Oh, let them come along," replied Cejka impatiently. "If there is room, let them all aboard. It will only make our number appear larger, which cannot hurt. No delays! We must arrive at the scheduled time."

The Hagemen were allowed aboard, the gangway was pulled in, and the boat drew slowly away from the wharf, backing carefully through the small, congested harborage of Rumon, the scene ringing with voices of pilots and passengers as all made for the river beyond.

Kyan's gray and turgid waters were choked with watercraft of every size and description. Anyone in charge of a vessel of any size was ferrying Hagemen to the funeral. There were tiny two-seat paddleboats, large triple-deckers, Hage pleasure barges, and a host of the solid, double-decked cargo boats, all crowded with people making their way to Saecaraz for the big day—and every last one flying a red funeral banner.

The festival atmosphere was inescapable. A Supreme Director's funeral was a rare event in the first place, and Jamrog had appropriated huge sums to be spent in making Rohee's funeral the most lavish of any in living memory. Cejka distrusted this, though Jamrog's motive escaped him.

"I would have thought Jamrog content with a private cremation," Cejka whispered to Covol as he scanned the enormous flotilla stretching out both ways along the river. "Why, a man could walk across Kyan without getting his feet wet! Look at them out there. We'll be lucky if half the population of Empyrion isn't drowned today."

"Perhaps Jamrog seeks to gain more than the approval of the populace with this tactic," replied Covol, a small man powerfully built and possessing a quick mind. He would one day make a good Director.

"Say what you think, Covol," directed Cejka. "There are none among us in Jamrog's keep." It was true. Cejka had rigorously maintained the purity of his own ranks for years; he knew there were no traitors in his top echelon.

"By making much of Rohee's death, he will gain favor with those whose loyalty is easily won."

"Of course."

"But he will also create the illusion of being greater than Sirin Rohee himself. Only a divine can pay homage to another divine, so the priests say."

"I see," said Cejka thoughtfully. "He will be seen not only as Rohee's successor, but as greater and more powerful than Rohee ever was—and all because he makes a greater show of Rohee's death than Rohee himself would have. Yes, I see."

"For the price of a day's food and drink, the populace will see him as Cynetics incarnate."

Cejka sighed heavily. "I am afraid you are right. And we—we support the illusion by seeing to it that our whole Hage turns out to glorify dead Rohee—a man who was barely worth his night soil all his life long."

"It is strange."

"More than strange, Covol. We will see a frightening thing today. We will see a man make himself a god. There will be no stopping him now."

"Yet, he must be stopped," said Covol, wanting to believe that it was possible. "We will find a way."

Cejka looked at him sadly and then turned his eyes back to the river, saying, "Kyan will run red with the blood of our Hagemen before Jamrog will be stopped. Enjoy the funeral today, Covol. It is our own."

· · · · · ·

"An artist must be pure of heart," said Gerdes, "for true art is the expression of the artist's innermost being. To create beauty, one must *be* beautiful"—she pressed her hands to her bosom—"in here, in your heart of hearts."

Yarden listened intently. They were meeting in Gerdes' home which was, like most Fieri homes, an exercise in studied simplicity: spacious and comfortable, open to the sun and air. The room in which they sat facing one another across a low table of polished wood opened onto a meticulously tended garden. Fine paintings hung on the walls, delicate, expressive, gentle shadings of light and color, giving the room warmth for all its airiness.

Ianni, as promised, had brought Yarden to meet Gerdes, and once the conversation had begun, excused herself so the two could talk alone. Gerdes did most of the talking, and Yarden thrilled to be in the older woman's presence, because Gerdes, teacher of dance, was unlike anyone Yarden had ever met, and certainly unlike anyone she would have imagined as a dancer: thickset and short-limbed, with short, grizzled, gray hair and a ruddy face, small rosebud lips that turned down at the edges in a frown of motherly disapproval, frank hazel eyes that fairly sparkled with enthusiasm and intelligence. Her manner was gruff, but her tone patient and caring.

But it was not her appearance or her manner that Yarden found so fascinating—it was the extraordinary things she said. Yarden had never heard such words, such ideas. Gerdes talked about art, about creating beauty, and the way she spoke was beautiful too. Yarden glimpsed possibilities of expression she had never known existed; whole worlds of wonder opened up to her as the woman spoke. She saw herself poised for a plunge into a shimmering sea of promise. How she would emerge, she could not say, but she would be changed and the change would be wonderful.

"I understand," said Yarden softly.

Gerdes looked at her closely. "Do you? Do you really understand? It is not easy to be pure. It is hard work. The hardest. The discipline required of an artist is enormous. Many people—most, it seems—simply do not have such discipline, such single-mindedness of purpose and patience. It takes years to develop a craft; years of painstaking, difficult work. The discipline is beyond all but the most dedicated."

"What about talent?" asked Yarden. "Doesn't that count for something?"

"Oh yes, talent is good. Talent is commendable, for it makes the discipline easier to endure, and the dedication comes more naturally. But talent alone isn't the answer. Talent is raw; it is a beast, wild and untamed. Talent must be mastered; it must be trained so that it can be used with wisdom and purpose. It must be pruned like a tree so it will bear only the best fruit." Gerdes paused to shake her head slowly as she paced before Yarden. "No, talent without discipline is only an empty promise—the glitter of an unworked crystal. It is nothing of itself."

Gerdes returned to her chair opposite Yarden. She sat down and leaned back, placing her hands on the arms of the chair. The older woman studied Yarden for a moment, searching her eyes. Yarden gazed back hopefully, confidently, knowing herself to be in the presence of a wise and powerful teacher. "Tell me, daughter," Gerdes said at last, "why have you come to me?"

Now that they had finally come to the reason for Yarden's visit, Yarden found her voice had dried up. She forced the words out: "I want to dance. That is, I want to learn to be a dancer."

Gerdes peered at her and nodded absently. "Stand, please. Walk for me." She made a back-and-forth motion in the air with her hand.

Yarden stood and walked slowly, passing before Gerdes once, twice, and then again, conscious of the woman's sharp appraisal. "Yes," said Gerdes, "that's enough. You may sit."

Yarden returned to her seat. "Will you teach me?"

Gerdes nodded slowly, keeping her eyes on Yarden's face. "I'll teach you—but not to dance."

Yarden's smile disappeared instantly. "I don't understand. Why not, may I ask?"

Gerdes leaned forward, reaching out a hand to touch Yarden's knee. "You move well. There is grace and ease in your step. No doubt you have great natural abilities—talent, yes. But, daughter, you are too *old*."

This pronouncement shocked Yarden. She'd never been told she was too old for anything in her life. Why, she had at least a hundred and fifty good, productive years left, probably many more than that. How could she be too old? "Are you sure?" asked Yarden.

"I know what you are thinking," replied Gerdes. "Ianni has told me that your lifespan is not like ours. You will live long, many times longer than will I. In this you are like the Ancients of our own people. This is what you are thinking, yes?"

Yarden nodded silently.

"Of course. But the dancers that you saw yesterday, that filled you with such longing to dance, have been working at their craft since they were small children. Their bodies have been adapted to the dance, formed by it; their minds think in terms of movement and rhythm. Everything they think and do is dance."

"You don't think I could learn?" asked Yarden, disappointment making her petulant.

Gerdes simply shook her head. "No," she said, and then quickly explained. "Oh, you could learn the steps, the movement. You could dance, probably very well, I imagine. But never well enough to suit yourself, or the Fieri standards of excellence either, for that matter. If you danced, you would always be reminded just how inferior your craft remained. You would see children dance with greater skill and proficiency than you would ever achieve, and you would envy them.

"In time, your envy would turn bitter—you would hate yourself for not being better than you can ever be. This hate would destroy your craft and art. It would destroy your heart, your soul. In the end it would destroy *you*. Rather than being a blessing, dance would become a curse."

Yarden was amazed by what she heard. Never had anyone

spoken like this to her. "But—you said you would teach me," she replied, shaking her head in confusion.

Gerdes patted her knee and then leaned back once more, smiling. "Yes, I'll teach you. But not to dance. I'll teach you to paint."

"To paint?" The idea had never occurred to her.

Gerdes laughed. "You would be surprised to learn how close the two are to one another. There is much movement and rhythm in painting—it is dance of another kind, and more. I will teach you to paint, if you are willing."

Yarden blinked back, bewildered. "I don't know what to say."

"No one can decide for you. But I will tell you this: you have the heart of an artist; you are sensitive, you feel things very deeply in your soul. You long to create beauty and to share it. These things are good and necessary.

"What is more, painting is an art that requires a special kind of intelligence. I sense in you that intelligence—wise, intuitive, loving. This is important. If you lacked it, there would be no way to learn it, and neither I nor anyone else could give it to you." Gerdes gazed levelly at Yarden. "But think about it. When you have decided, come to me. I will be here."

Their meeting at an end, Yarden stood slowly and took Gerdes' hand. "Thank you for talking to me. I'll need some time to think about all you've said."

"There is no hurry, daughter. Come back when you have chosen."

Yarden nodded and thanked her host again, then left, stepping out into the sunlit day. She walked along the wide, tree-lined boulevard back to Ianni's house. Ianni lived some distance away, and the walk gave Yarden a chance to think about all she and Gerdes had discussed. By the time she reached home, she had made up her mind. Please, she thought, let me be an artist.

"Did you enjoy your talk?" asked Ianni as Yarden entered, glancing up from her work of cutting vegetables for a meal.

"It was—" she began, and then changed the subject. "Ianni, you *knew* that I could never be a dancer, didn't you? That's why you took me to Gerdes. You knew what she would tell me."

Ianni ducked her head to hide a smile and began putting

the sliced vegetables in bowls. "I suspected, yes. But you were so full of the wonder of the dance, I could not spoil it for you. What you felt was good and true, and I did not want to discourage you in any way. I knew Gerdes would know how to tell you. Hers is a wise spirit." She raised her head slightly. "You're not angry with me?"

"No, not angry. You were right. I am glad to have met Gerdes. And—" She hesitated, finding the title a little presumptuous, but then plunged in anyway. "I'm going to be an artist. A painter. More than anything, that's what I want to do."

Treet stared into the utter blackness of his cold rock cell. Huddled in a corner, he sat with his knees drawn up against his chest and waited for the reorientation to begin, knowing that it would be, could not be anything other than, disagreeable in the extreme.

He'd read about prisoners in one of Earth's senseless wars being forced to undergo what they called *brainwashing*—a cruel form of mental abuse designed to destroy a person's will, among other things. Some prisoners of war, though, came through the experience with their faculties intact. These men were mentally tough to begin with, but they also used a few basic survival tactics to counteract the brainwashing. They recognized that the pointless cruelty practiced upon them had no rational basis other than to wear down their mental defenses; all the meaningless tasks and contradictory orders and physical harassment and verbal abuse was an attempt to weaken the inner man and break the mind.

Just recognizing this went a long way toward defusing its effectiveness. Once a prisoner knew what he was up against, he could take steps to counteract it. The survivors, forced to give up control of the major aspects of their lives, learned to regain control in other, subtler ways, thereby retaining a degree of independence and a sense of personal freedom. Maintaining this control, however limited, was the key: a determined man with even a tiny amount of personal autonomy could not be broken. He might be killed, but not broken. And almost to a person, the survivors Treet had read about had vowed they would die before giving in.

The general idea of survival was to beat the enemy at their own game, to control them while they were controlling you. When taken for interrogation and ordered to sit down, the prisoner went to the chair and moved it slightly so that he sat, at least symbolically, where he chose; when captors came to his cell, he invited them in and directed them to places on his mat, subtly showing that he controlled the terms of the visit; when dragged from his cell at dawn and ordered to dig his own grave, the survivor determined where to dig, thereby exerting control in the choosing of his own plot; and when at noon he was ordered to refill the grave, he planted a seed or a clump of grass so that his work would have symbolic value, rather than, as intended, remain just another meaningless exercise meant to unhinge him.

Treet steeled himself with these thoughts and planned strategies to meet whatever barrages they threw at him. His overall plan was to make an outward show of resistance early on in the game and then give the appearance of having succumbed to the reorientation so that when he was released he would still have his head in one piece. He didn't know if he could pull it off, but it was his only chance—as long as they didn't use drugs. Against drugs—like the amnesiant they'd used on him the first time—there was little he could do.

He sat in his cell for hours—perhaps much longer, he couldn't tell—waiting for something to happen. When something finally did happen, it surprised him with its mildness: lights hidden in the rock ceiling came on, shining dimly, and with them a sound like that of an ocean washing over a pebbled shore. Nothing more.

Not too bad, thought Treet. I can handle this. He closed his eyes and went to sleep.

Some time later he was awakened by a pinging sound, like a small hammer tapping a scrap of steel plate at regular intervals. This pinging sound had been added to the ocean sound, and he noticed, too, that the lights were brighter. Clearly, they meant to hammer at him with sound and light for a while—in the manner of cooking a live frog: toss the frog into a pot of cold water and then gradually bring up the heat until the pot boils; the frog will never know what's happening until it's too late to hop away.

"This frog is wise to their tricks," Treet told himself, and unzipped the front of his singleton and began worrying an inner pocket, which he eventually succeeded in tearing off. He took the pocket and tore it in half, rolled up the halves, and stuck one in each ear. His improvised earplugs worked quite well and he curled up and went to sleep once more. Better to sleep now while he could, and conserve his strength. There was no telling what might come later.

When Treet awoke, the sound had stopped and the lights

were dim again. On the floor of the cell before the unidor lay a tray with a bowl and a jar. The bowl contained boiled beans—tough little legumes that tasted like leatherbound cardboard pellets; the jar contained water, tepid but fresh. He drank the water and tossed down a handful of beans before remembering that the food and water could well be drugged. He sniffed the bowl and tasted another bean, but could detect nothing out of the ordinary. He replaced the bowl. Hungry though he was, he did not want to risk drugging himself so early in the game.

The sound came on once more, louder this time. The ocean rolled, and the hammer pinged more insistently. Treet could see how that sound could get on a person's nerves after a while. He replaced his earplugs and closed his eyes, grateful for the escape of sleep.

A sharp, stinging pain on the side of his head brought Treet out of his slumber. His eyes flew open to see a Nilokerus guard standing over him with a stiff rod. "Get up," said the guard. Treet moved to get up, quickly removing his homemade earplugs and stuffing them in his pocket. The guard didn't appear to notice; he turned on his heel and walked out. Treet followed him, not knowing whether to feel apprehensive or hopeful. Were they releasing him, or getting down to business at last?

The guard led him through the cell block back to the central admitting area where he had come in. A different guard sat at the console, and this one looked particularly put out about something. Without preamble, he told Treet what was upsetting him. "I'm missing the funeral because of you," he growled.

"There's been a mistake," offered Treet—as if he'd gladly clear up the misunderstanding so the guard could toddle off to the funeral. "I think it can be worked out."

"Oh, it has been worked out," said the administrator, reaching out to tap a few keys into the console. "You are to be made an example of." He glanced at the Nilokerus standing behind Treet, slapping the rod against his hand. "Take him to the conditioning tank."

"No, wait! You're making a mistake. Let me go. I won't cause you any trouble. Please!"

The guard prodded him with the end of the rod, pushing him away from the console. The administrator glared at him and said, "Director Hladik has ordered this himself. Perhaps you'd care to discuss it with him?" He laughed as if he'd made the perfect joke, and Treet was steered down another of the rock-cut corridors radiating from the central room like the arms of an octopus.

The conditioning tank was an enormous transparent six-sided aquarium filled with green fluid. It looked like a jumbo nutrient bath; however, Treet strongly doubted its designers had any such benevolent purpose in mind. Several harnesses of webbing and electrical wire dangled from a gridwork suspended above the tank. There was no one in the tank at present, and only one other person in the hexagonal room—a rather stout toad of a man with a mashed-in, wrinkled face. Hair stuck out of his red-striped yos at the neckline, and his hands looked as if he wore fur gloves. He grunted when Treet and his guard entered the room.

"Here's one for you, Skank," said the guard with the rod, shoving Treet forward. "Take good care of him. Hladik wants him undamaged."

The one called Skank grunted again and shuffled over to Treet, appraising him with his eyes as if he were being asked to bid on a piece of spoiled merchandise. "Undamaged," snorted Skank, prodding Treet with hairy fingers. Treet was aware of a sour smell, like stale sweat or urine or both, and something else. Saltwater? He looked at the giant aquarium; there appeared to be algae growing in the water—which explained its charming green color, no doubt.

Treet stood passively and allowed himself to be poked. Skank turned him around and pounded him on the back, looked into his mouth, and felt him under the armpits. The guard watched this inspection idly and then turned to leave. "Where do you think you're going?" hollered Skank. "Get back here and help me put him in the soak."

The guard huffed and rolled his eyes, but did not speak. Very likely, he knew any protest would be lost on Skank, who was now grumbling and shuffling off to a small pedestal where he flicked a few switches. There came a grinding sound, and the metal grid began descending from the ceiling. "Take off your clothes," said Skank, returning with a large brown ball of waxy substance in his hands.

Treet undressed slowly, saying, "You're all making a big mistake."

"Save your breath," grunted Skank, grabbing the nearest harness as it came down. "You're headed for the tank."

The guard lifted Treet's arms and held them out at shoulder level while Skank fastened a band around Treet's chest and passed two straps between his legs. Next, webbing was wrapped around his torso and snugged down. His hands were bound loosely to his side; he could move his arms in shallow arcs, but could not touch his face or any other part of his body. The electrical wires, each with a flat electrode on the end, were attached to his skin at various points: over his heart, on his throat below his right jaw, on each temple and cheek, at the base of his spine, on his abdomen.

Treet submitted to this strange indignity, trying to appear far more calm and unconcerned than he felt. His stomach fluttered, but that might just have been emptiness; and his palms sweated, but it was quite humid in the room. He knew his act of aplomb was unconvincing when, as Skank's back was turned, the guard leaned close and whispered, "Don't fight it. Just relax. It will go easier for you if you don't resist."

Skank turned back, and Treet saw that he had fashioned a sort of mask out of the waxy ball. The mask had a mouth plug into which Skank inserted another electrode, and two protruding mounds where Treet's ears would be. The keeper of the tank glanced at Treet's face and made some small adjustments on the wax mask in his hands. Lifting the mask, he pressed it onto Treet's face with both hands. "Trabant take you! Open your mouth!"

Treet opened his mouth, and the was plug slid in like a tongue. The mask was pressed tight to his face, sealing ears and eyes and mouth. A panicky moment came when the mask closed off his nostrils and he couldn't breathe. "Hold your breath," said the guard; Treet heard his voice muted by the wax plugs in his ears. "It won't last."

At almost the same instant, Treet felt himself lifted off the floor in his harness, dangling like a doll on a rope. Still holding his breath, he began to worry about what was to happen next. Surely they didn't mean to drown him—what purpose would that serve? Yet, there had been no provision made for getting air to him underwater.

These thoughts ricocheted around in his brain as he felt his toes touch the water. He drew back in shock, but forced himself to relax and, as he dropped lower, swirled the water, making swimming motions with his feet. The water closed over him . . . now to his thighs . . . and now his hips . . . his waist . . . chest . . . neck . . .

The water was neither warm nor cold, but exactly skin temperature. Within moments of entering the tank, he could no longer feel whether he was wet or dry. In fact, he couldn't feel anything at all. He moved his hands, but could not even tell he moved them. The liquid was like water, but heavier, bulkier, more elastic. It did not register on his skin at all.

Sensory deprivation, Treet knew, used such heavier-than-water fluids to cut off sensation to the brain. He also knew such techniques were highly effective, that if left very long in isolation the subject could expect aural and visual hallucinations, as well as a host of mental experiences bordering on the psychotic. Insanity was an almost guaranteed side effect for anyone left too long in a deprivation chamber. At least with brainwashing he knew what to expect and had a survival plan. If anyone had ever found a way to beat a SD tank, Treet had yet to hear about it.

A more immediate concern, however, was the fact that he could not breathe. He knew he could hold his breath for six minutes. Six minutes was a good long time . . . but it was not forever.

ELEVEN

Threl Square in Saecaraz was draped in red: red banners hung from wires across the square, red streamers hung from every tree, red bunting wrapped the imposing columns of the Threl Chambers entrance. Everywhere one looked was red, the color of death and mourning. Tvrdy slipped through the standing crowds already thronging the square and moved toward the section designated for Tanais dignitaries. His Subdirector would already be there, along with as many other Tanais of stent that could be crammed into the numbered space.

Moving among the populace of Empyrion, he gauged the mood as one of restrained festivity—subdued now because of the nature of the ceremony about to be enacted. But later all restraint would give way to revelry, dead leader or no. Tvrdy knew that Jamrog had foreseen this—knew what effect this sort of celebration would produce. The masses were too easily won by simple pomp, and once won, too easily led.

It was the great irony of leadership, he thought, that in order to be a good leader, one had to give everything to a people unworthy of the sacrifice. He sighed; perhaps it was always so.

He pressed his way through the quickly coagulating crowds, and eventually arrived at the designated section to squeeze in among his Hagemen. Subdirector Danelka snapped to attention and handed the bhuj to his superior, whispering, "I was beginning to think you would miss the ceremony."

"So did I. But today of all days I suspect Jamrog's surveillance to be lax. There would never be a better chance of reaching them." To Danelka's unspoken question, Tvrdy said, "Yes, it went well. We are allies as of this morning."

Danelka grimaced and replied, "I know I should be pleased, Director, but . . ."

"Don't worry. I do not expect anyone to relish our arrangement, although it might be helpful if we learned to mask our true feelings for the Dhogs. Revulsion and resentment cannot help our cause. Besides, I think we will come to value them greatly."

Danelka shook his head doubtfully, but said nothing more.

"Did anyone suspect I was missing?" Tvrdy pulled his hood closer and turned the bhuj in his hands to display the Tanais face.

"I don't see how," answered his Subdirector. "I carried the bhuj and remained hooded the whole trip. The boatmen paid no attention to our boarding, and the Saecaraz who met us at the square's entrance merely inquired about the number, but did not count us themselves."

Tvrdy grinned suddenly. "Jamrog's laxity will be his undoing yet. He does not have the stamina to rule as he should. He is sloppy, Danelka. Sloppy and lazy."

"And dangerous," added Danelka.

Just then a blattering of horns sounded. When the blast died away, and with it the commotion of the vast crowd, a single large drum could be heard emanating from within the Threl Chambers. The booming drumbeat grew louder, and a Saecaraz Hage priest appeared between the pillars at the entrance, an enormous drum preceding him. The drum was affixed to long poles which were carried by four underpriests.

Behind the drum-beating priest came a whole regiment of Hage priests, each with a silver horn shaped like a crescent. As soon as these reached the steps below the pillars, they raised the horns to their lips and blew the long, low ringing note that had commenced the ceremony. Saecaraz Hagemen followed the priests: Jamrog came first, walking alone, wearing a red mourning cloak over his black-and-silver yos; he was followed by row on row of assorted Hage functionaries.

In the midst of the ranks of Saecaraz came Rohee's bier, borne up on the shoulders of his Hagemen. The red-shrouded coffin seemed to float above the heads of the crowd, making its slow, circuitous way around the square, pausing before each official Hage delegation to allow the Hage Leaders to pay their official respects—which they did by tossing black and silver paper streamers, symbolically representing Sirin Rohee's long life, over the pale, ashen gray body.

When the bier stopped before Tanais, Tvrdy flung his streamer over the body too, surreptitiously tearing a short length off one end—privately stating his suspicion that Rohee's life was cut short. No one else saw the gesture, and the severed length of streamer fell to the stone flagging unobserved.

The procession moved on, and when the last Hage had paid its respects, the priests began the funeral chant, calling on Great Trabant to ease Rohee's passage through the Two Houses, Ekante and Shikroth, and to send sympathetic Seraphic Spheres to guide him. They asked the Oversouls to remember Rohee's long life and account his deeds with greatness. On and on the chanting went while the bier circled again and again. Finally, after nearly two hours, the chanting stopped and the casket was placed in the center of the square.

"What's this?" Tvrdy nudged Danelka. A ramp was being pushed through the crowd to the bier; at the end of the ramp was a red-draped platform. The ramp stopped with the platform directly above the bier. Jamrog appeared at one end of the ramp and moved slowly up to take his place on the platform. The assembly, restless after the long ranting of the priests, fell silent once more as, stone-faced and regal, Jamrog ascended.

"I heard nothing about anything like this," whispered Danelka. "Most unusual."

Jamrog raised his hands for silence, although the throng was already hushed and every eye was on him. He stared out at the great crowd, assuring himself of their utmost attention. He drew the moment out, opened his mouth to speak, but did not, then slowly lowered his hands to indicate poor dead Rohee beneath him. He raised his face, and a cry of grief came from him: "Rohee-e-e!"

A thrill tingled through the vast audience. What was the new Supreme Director doing? Why was the body not being consigned to the flames?

"Ro-hee-e-e-e!" came the cry again. Silence followed as Jamrog looked about dolefully. A full minute elapsed as the Director gazed with sorrowful eyes across the sea of faces. When the tension reached its peak, he said in a loud voice, "Our leader is fallen! He is dead! Dead!" The word was a shout, followed by a softer echo. "Dead."

Jamrog drew a deep breath and began to speak more softly, so the crowds had to strain forward to hear him. "Our beloved leader of so many years has fallen to the sleep of death, and will never rise again. Farewell, Sirin Rohee. Your people salute you and mourn your passing." Gazing intently at the body, Jamrog raised a hand in farewell. The gesture was simple and touching.

"I almost believe he means it," whispered Danelka.

"Shh!" replied Tvrdy. "I want to hear what the liar says."

Jamrog continued: "Look, my people, look long on the body of your dead leader. Remember him always. Remember him in noble death. Remember him . . ." He spread his hands wide over the body. "Look and remember."

"Remember how he raped the Hages!" said Danelka under his breath. Tvrdy gave him a threatening glance, as Jamrog went on to recite a long catalog of Rohee's benevolent achievements, most of which, it seemed to Tvrdy, centered on the old cutthroat not maiming an opponent worse than he might have, and not crushing the people with any more impossible regulations than they could absolutely bear.

"Sirin Rohee was a man born to greatness, and that greatness will not be diminished in death," Jamrog went on. "I will not allow his body to be consumed by flames or corruption. Even though he is dead, I will see to it that he remains with us: his body will be embalmed in crystal and laid in Threl Chambers, where a special mausoleum will be prepared. Then, you, his beloved people, will come to look upon him and honor his memory. He will be with us always!"

Jamrog had so drawn his listeners along, carefully building the drama and emotion of his words, that no sooner had his last words been uttered than the amassed mourners loosed a tremendous, bone-shaking cheer. The great shout echoed through the empty streets of Empyrion, ascending to the dome's crystalline shell far above.

The crowd surged forward and seized the platform on which Jamrog stood, tearing it away from the ramp. The severed platform—with Jamrog standing placidly in the center of it, hands outstretched—was lifted high and borne through the square to ringing shouts of acclaim.

As Tanais Hagemen of lower stent streamed past him to join the melee, Tvrdy turned away from the spectacle. Danelka caught up with him as he stomped from the square. "So that's his trick," muttered Tvrdy. "I should have guessed. He has given them a show they will never forget. Already he is greater than Rohee ever was—and far more deadly."

Subdirector Danelka asked, "What do you want me to do?"

"Stay with the delegation. I'm going back to my kraam.

Come to me later and tell me what has happened." He looked at Danelka wearily. "I'm tired . . . tired." With that he slipped away through the clamorous crowd and disappeared.

• • • • • •

Talus and Mathiax strolled the path through the long grove of fan trees behind the Clerk of the College of Mentors' shore-side home. The air of Fierra was soft and warm, as always, and lightly scented with the fan tree's aromatic resin. An edge of gray cloud worked the upper atmosphere, drawing a light overcast across the great shining face of Prindahl from the North, giving the midday sun the appearance of white gold.

"It's going to rain," observed Mathiax to himself.

"Too early," Talus grunted absently, and the two walked on.

At length they stopped and faced one another. "We have been negligent," said Mathiax. "There is no denying it. We should not have let him go without first making some provision for communication."

"What could we do? The Preceptor's ban—"

Mathiax dismissed the thought with a quick shake of his head. "I'm not suggesting we should have gone with him—only that we should have found some way to allow him to reach us in need."

Talus frowned and rubbed his curly beard with the back of a broad hand. "The woman—Yarden—she told us she was a sympath. She could reach him."

"She won't." At Talus' sharp glance, Mathiax answered, "I already tried. I asked Ianni to bring the subject up when Bohm returned."

"And?"

"Ianni tried, but she refused to discuss it. It appears the two quarreled, and now she will have nothing to do with him."

"Something between lovers?"

Mathiax nodded. "Ianni says Yarden warned him not to return to Dome, and since he insisted on going she severed their relationship."

"I wish I had known that. Still, she may change her mind."

"Yarden is a strong person. Hers is a most formidable will and not easily influenced. We could grow old waiting for her to change her mind in this matter."

"I don't know what else to tell you, Mathiax. We did all we could do for him without violating the Preceptor's ban. As it is, we came very close."

"We believed he was right," pointed out Mathiax sternly.

"Of course. But even so, we must follow the Infinite Father's leading. War is an abhorrence to him. The Fieri will never lift a hand against—"

With an impatient wave of his hand Mathiax turned and began walking again. "You are right to remind me of our most holy precept. But I am uneasy, Talus. I tell you the truth: I cannot rest, thinking about Orion Treet. I think of him and feel a deep foreboding. It is a rare sensation with me, and one I do not like."

"What can we do? It is out of our hands, Mathiax. He is in the Sustainer's care now."

Mathiax nodded solemnly. "Yes. Yes, of course. But my foreboding may also be of divine origin, Talus."

Just then a large, glistening drop of water fell on the path between them, splattering heavily and sending up a little puff of dust. Talus looked up and saw that the cloud cover had thickened as lower-lying rainclouds had formed beneath the high leading edge. Another drop landed close to the first, and the sound of still other drops could be heard as they fell among the leaves of grass and trees close by.

Talus looked at the dark damp spots on the ground and then back at his friend. "I do not dismiss what you say, Mathiax." He indicated the heavy drops falling all around them now. "After all, you were right about the rain."

TWELVE

The rain fell in slanting sheets upon the roof of the Blue Forest, striking the natural thatch of closely interwoven leaves to trickle slowly down to the smaller trees and plants of the forest floor far below. Crocker heard the rain as a subdued roar overhead, and felt the heavy, moisture-laden air cool as the water seeped down from above, drip by drip. The forest—so loud with its exuberance of life only moments before the rain—now lay still, deserted as its creatures sought shelter from the damp.

Crocker, naked except for a broad waistband torn from his tattered jumpsuit and wrapped around his middle to form a pouch in which to carry the utility knife and a few other small articles he required, huddled under a low, spreading tree whose broad, waxy leaves shed the drops that were now coming more quickly as the forest canopy became saturated. He looked placidly around him, alert but unconcerned. His senses were becoming attuned to the forest's living awareness, that invisible web of consciousness formed by the combined mental activity of all forest dwellers.

He could now detect subtle pulses of communication humming through the webwork, but could not as yet decipher them. Still, knowing that all around him the forest continually spoke to itself gave him a secure feeling. He belonged here and in time would learn to speak the language of the web, and then would become one with all the other creatures.

The rain percolated down to the forest floor, soaking into the thick, dark soil. Trails became trickling runnels, bubbling over root and vine, carrying water away to hidden pools and larger streams. The smell of rain-damp earth and foliage filled the air as vaporous wisps rose like ghostly snakes to writhe and disappear on unseen currents. Crocker had settled back in his little shelter and was listening to the tick and dribble of the rain when suddenly an earsplitting scream shivered the air.

The shattering cry sounded like the fighting scream of an enraged cat—only the cat that had made this sound must have been the size of an elephant. This fearful cry was followed by an answering call—a booming bellow, like that of a buffalo four stories tall—a sound that actually shook the earth where Crocker sat.

The next thing the human heard was the sharp crack of splintering trees and the groan of bushes uprooted as the two mighty beasts closed on one another. There were tremendous thrashings and crashings, and he could hear branches being stripped from trees. The ground shook under the pummeling of the animals' huge feet.

Cringing back deeper into the shadows of his rain shelter, Crocker listened, his heart pounding wildly. He was helpless should one of those prodigious creatures come for him—or even if, in turning to flee the scene of battle, it should run over him. And from the nearness of the sounds, he guessed the clash to be taking place just beyond the curtain of vine hanging from the lower branches of the pillarlike trees directly in front of him.

It was over in seconds, and the last cries echoing through the forest shook the rain from the leaves of Crocker's bush. Straining into the silence that followed the brutal encounter, Crocker listened and at last heard ponderous footsteps moving away slowly, bulling through the underbrush. This he imagined was the buffalo creature. Of the cat, he could not detect a sound.

Very likely, the buffalo-thing had killed the cat-creature and now lumbered off to lick its wounds, which were certain to be grievous. The cat-creature surely lay dead or dying, its lifeblood pouring out through its mangled body.

After a time, the rain ceased, though the drip, drip, drip of the leaves would continue for a long time as water filtered down from above. Only when Crocker was certain he could hear nothing at all of either of the animals did he creep from hiding. Crouching, he crawled out, senses keen and wary, muscles tense, ready to flee. He pushed silently through the undergrowth, passing between the twin columns of two forest giants, ducking beneath the shroud of vines. He expected to find the bloodsoaked battlefield before him, but instead saw only more underbrush and more trees. A trail led through the tangle, so Crocker took it and began walking—warily, lest he meet up with a wounded creature out of its mind with pain.

He walked far longer than he estimated he would have to

before he came to the scene of the titanic battle. It was a clearing in the forest where a stream flattened and formed a shallow pool hemmed in by trees and thick brush. He stood and looked long and hard, scouring every inch of the clearing for movement, before stepping into it.

There was no dead cat-creature in the clearing, and no wounded buffalo-thing gasping out its last breath, either. But all around were signs of the monumental conflict: branches stripped from trees three meters off the ground, bushes squashed and flattened out of shape or uprooted altogether, smaller trees toppled and larger trees broken like twigs, the earth ripped into open furrows, mud from the pool bottom splattered over everything, depressions sunk ankle-deep in the forest floor.

The creatures that wreaked the destruction, he saw, must be the very lords of the Blue Forest. He stood alone looking at the gaping holes in the earth, the roots dangling in the air, the broken tree limbs strewn over the battlefield, and felt his bowels squirm inside him. There were creatures abroad in this world that dwarfed anything he could imagine. This realization made him feel small and vulnerable.

A weapon! He mouthed the word to himself and understood its meaning. He would find a suitable weapon, and then he would be safe. Other creatures would fear, but he would not.

He turned at once and began walking back to his hidden pool. Tomorrow he would begin searching for his weapon. And then . . . and then he would hunt down one of the great creatures and prove himself a forest lord.

• • • • • •

It had been three minutes, Treet estimated, since he had entered the tank. He still dangled from the harness, but could no longer feel it. In fact, he could not feel anything: all sensory stimulation had ceased. He could will his arms and legs and hands to move, but whether they moved as directed, he couldn't tell. It felt as if he no longer had a body at all, that he was a mind adrift, cut off from all physical attributes—except hunger, which still gnawed at him, more insistently now than ever.

Approaching four minutes, Treet began to worry. Surely

they would pull him up soon. What good would it do to drown him? And if that's what they intended, why go to all the trouble to truss him up like a turkey? Nothing made sense. But, rational or not, he would have to breathe soon. His lungs were beginning to ache.

Come on, pull me up! thought Treet desperately. Pull me up!

He fought down the impulse to swim for the surface. Thrashing around in the water would use up air too fast, and he could not be certain of swimming in the right direction—he might just as easily swim to the bottom of the tank as the top. It was best just to remain calm and wait. *Wait.*

Treet put his mind to work, concentrating on his keeper, holding the man's squat image on his mental screen, willing him to punch the button that would bring the harness up.

Push the button! Treet screamed mentally, putting every atom of his will behind it. Push the button—NOW!

The ache had become a burning, searing flame. His lungs felt as if they would burst.

Ordinarily he would expel some of the air, and this would allow him to stay submerged a little longer. But with the wax mask plastered on his face, and the wax plug between his teeth, he could not exhale. The pressure in his lungs increased.

He reached out with his mind and attempted to touch the mind of his keeper. Push the button! he screamed with his brain. Push it, damn you!

His lungs at the point of rupture, Treet knew that his captors had no intention of bringing him up. They intended letting him die. With this thought came a desperate plan: blow the mask off! Perhaps the force of his breath could tear the wax mask from his face; then he could see the surface and swim for it.

With this thought came the decision to do it—the two were simultaneous. He had nothing to lose.

The exhausted air burst from his mouth with as much force as he could put behind it. The result astonished him: the stream of air bubbles passed right through the mask! It was as if it wasn't there at all. His ears remained stoppered and the plug remained in his mouth, so the mask was still in place.

Panic seized him and wrung him. I can't breathe! I'll suffocate!

He thrashed his head from side to side in an effort to dislodge the mask, but could not tell if he were actually thrashing at all, or only imagining his thrashings. His lungs convulsed in agony.

Air! I must have air!

The vacuum in his lungs became too great. He could not hold back any longer. He had to inhale, even though the mask stayed on. His mind presented him with a picture of himself trying to suck air through a plastic bag, suffocating, the plastic molded to his features, cutting off his life.

A split second later moist air was streaming into his lungs. Treet had been so busy fighting it that when the involuntary impulse to draw air took over, he did not even notice. The quick inrush of air shocked and confused him—maybe it was water. Maybe this was what it was like to drown.

But no. He drew oxygen deep into his lungs and expelled it experimentally. The air seemed thicker, heavier than ordinary air, and damp—as if he were breathing through a wet sponge— but not at all like water. No, he was not drowning—at least he didn't think so. Somehow, he was breathing, and for that he was thankful.

He took a few slow, calming breaths. Obviously, the mask was some sort of oxygen-permeable membrane that allowed an air breather to breathe underwater. It held, still tightly plastered to his face, but from what he could feel of the plug in his mouth, the wax substance had changed consistency: it was soft and glutinous, molding to his features like dough.

Slowly Treet relaxed, his speeding heartbeat calmed, muscles unknotted and slackened. Whatever else happened to him in the tank, at least he wouldn't drown. That was a small comfort.

He drew oxygen through the membrane and tried to think about how he would survive the ordeal before him. His own mind was his greatest enemy in this struggle. Without the stimulation of data from his sense organs, his brain would begin to manufacture its own data in the form of hallucinations. He would begin to hear sounds and see images; he'd feel and smell things that were not there.

And as much as he would tell himself the hallucinations weren't real, there would come a time when he wouldn't be able to tell illusions from reality. Then the terror would start. He would experience the horror of his own nightmares, and he would not be able to stop them. His brain, like a runaway computer caught in an endless program loop, would run on and on and on. Cut off from his physical sensations, his brain would, like a prisoner too long deprived of sunlight and food, begin devouring itself in the darkness.

In the end he'd be nothing but a mindless shell of a man, demented, blithering. Unless . . . unless Hladik had other ideas. He had not considered that before, but considered it now. Of course, they had a purpose for him. He would be no use to them insane; therefore, his conditioning would likely stop short of that.

The question was, could he hold out?

Grimly, as Treet assessed his predicament, the thought came to him that, one way or another, he would find out.

THIRTEEN

izzle watched the rain sweep in undulating curtains across the flat, beaten-iron face of Prindahl. The fresh sea scent filled his nostrils, and he sighed contentedly, thinking about Starla and their long, dreamy evening. Never had he met a more engaging woman: warm, responsive, caring, a joy to behold and to be with.

The wind off the lake stirred the curtains of his room, and he turned away from the vista of rain-swept water to go in search of Jaire. He found her, auburn hair upswept and tied in a gold ribbon, lighting candles in the smaller dining room; the long table was already set.

"Can I help?" he asked.

"Thank you, Asquith. Yes, if you like. Over there you'll find goblets. Fill them from the pitcher, please."

He went to a tray on the sideboard and took up the crystal pitcher, carefully pouring the contents into the goblets on the round tray and wondering how to pose the question he was itching to ask.

"Did you enjoy the concert last night?" Jaire asked, favoring him with a bright smile.

Pizzle, trying not to reveal too much about his current emotional state, steadied his hand and replied in a matter-of-fact tone, "It was all right. Nice."

Jaire blew out the long wick with which she was lighting the tapers. "I'm glad you liked it. Did you find Starla an amiable companion?"

At the mention of her name, Pizzle gulped; a muscle in his eyelid twitched. He cleared his throat. "Oh, fine, I guess."

"She was *nice,* too?"

"Yeah, she's a nice lady, I—" He forgot what he was going to say next.

Jaire stood looking at him. If he hadn't been so flustered, he would have noticed the amused expression on her face and the knowing sparkle in her gold-flecked eyes. "I'll be sure to tell her that," replied Jaire, laughing.

Pizzle colored; his ears became crimson flags. "Does it—ah, show so much as all that?" he asked.

Jaire came to him and took his hand. She led him into the next room and to a cushioned chair where they sat down together. "You were out all night—it was nearly dawn when you came back."

"You waited up for me?"

"No, I was at the hospital, remember? I returned home only moments before you. I heard you come in."

"Uhh, hmmm. I see." Pizzle's features scrunched into a frown. "Did I violate some kind of a social taboo?"

Jaire blinked back at him. "A what?"

"You know, etiquette. Good manners, ethics, propriety—that sort of thing."

"Not that I am aware of. Did you?"

He almost leapt from his seat. "I—we, that is, didn't do anything improper, if that's what you mean."

"It *was* very late."

Pizzle nodded morosely. "Look, Jaire, I'm new here. I don't know what's proper and what isn't for courting a Fieri." He realized what he had just said and blanched.

"Courting?" Jaire tilted her head and peered at him, humor twitching at the corners of her lips. "That is a word I have never heard."

"It means . . . well, when two people, a man and a woman, like each other, see . . . well, they court. I mean the man courts the woman—he sees her."

"Sees her?"

"You know, they spend time together . . ."

"Ah, yes. I see what you mean."

"Well, what do you call it?"

"We call it pairing."

"Oh."

Pizzle looked so confused that Jaire laughed and put a hand on his arm. "Is that what you were doing?"

"I don't know. It wasn't like that—I mean, I didn't plan to stay out all night. It just happened."

"You do find Starla attractive?" It was more a statement of obvious fact than a question.

He nodded. "More attractive than anyone I've ever met. I

only—" He stopped, swallowing hard, and went on. "I only hope she likes me, too."

"Maybe you can ask her tonight."

"Ask her?" Pizzle glanced up sharply, his expression equal parts hope and terror. "Tonight?"

"Talus and Dania are away this evening, and Preben is dining with friends. I thought you might enjoy meeting some others. I've asked some of my friends to join us, Starla among them."

Now Pizzle did jump up. "I've got to get ready. What time is she coming?"

"They will begin arriving within the hour. You have time to—"

"Barely." He cut her off as he dashed away. She watched him fly back to his room on the upper story of the great house, smiled, and went back to her preparations.

• • • • • •

The Dhogs had gathered to celebrate the passing of Supreme Director Sirin Rohee. From throughout the Old Section they had come, each of the sixteen families represented in force. Giloon Bogney sat on a three-legged stool with his bhuj in his hand, the very picture of the revered tribal chief accepting the homage of his people. In fact, the gifts were donations of food and beverage that each family brought with them to provision the celebration.

Giloon smiled and nodded, rising now and then to embrace an especially worthy family head, exchanging jokes about the Surpreme Director's demise while the mound of foodstuffs and libation grew. From the look of the pile, there would be a fine feast tonight, and enough brew to produce a pleasant brain-numbing buzz for one and all.

Some of the Dhogs brought with them livestock—bakis (a variety of plump scavenger fowl) and prudos (the porcine equivalent of an ambulatory fertilizer factory). Dhog livestock had been bred for the ability to turn almost any organic substance into nourishment. The beasts, like their human masters, could survive on dry husks and chaff, and thrive on a meal of rinds and scraps. Both the bakis and the more substantial prudos would be butchered and roasted on spits around the bonfire to be lit at dusk.

As soon as they had heard that Rohee was dead, the Dhogs had begun collecting combustibles and had a large heap of flammable material amassed in the center of the dilapidated New America Square in the heart of the derelict section of Dome.

The Old Section had been, a little over three thousand years before, the site of the original Cynetics colony ship's landing. It was over New America Square that the first temporary dome had been erected on sterilized ground, and there the first Earthmen touched alien soil. But that was long, long ago—so long ago the current inhabitants could not even imagine that their crumbling ruin of a home had not always existed.

The Old Section had had a succession of names: Empyrion Base, Colony Administration, Plague Central, Fieri Ghetto, Dome Project Headquarters. As each name implied, the uses for the sprawling section, with its structures in ranks radiating from the central square, had been varied. Now it might have been called, simply, Sanctuary, for that was its current function— providing a home for Dome's nonbeings, the unfortunates who had, through one transgression or another, forfeited both Hage and stent, whose poak had been erased and their names expunged from the Hage priest's official rolls.

A Hageman who suddenly found himself without Hage or poak had only two choices: suicide or the Old Section. Most chose to join the Dhogs, accepting an existence—it could scarcely be called a life—of continual want amidst almost unimaginable squalor. To be a Dhog, the lowest of the low, was to be a nonentity, neither alive nor dead, but somewhere between the two, waiting for either to happen.

It was impossible to reach the Old Section from the Hages unless one knew the secret entrances and exits maintained by the Dhogs. Since no one did know—not even guides whose psi entities stubbornly refused to cooperate where the Old Section was concerned—new nonbeings were forced to wait until the Dhogs made one of their infrequent visits to the Hage refuse pits. The wretch who managed to convince the Dhogs to take him in was assigned to one of the sixteen families which were responsible for caring for their own members. The families worked to raise livestock and make any articles the family needed for survival.

Raw materials were scavenged from the Hage refuse pits—always a chancy enterprise since any Dhog caught in Hage was subject to the harshest abuse: torture always, and often death. So hated were they among the Hages that Dhogs risked life and limb simply by setting foot in Hage; hence they tended to move about only at night, and then only in twos and threes.

Though the refuse pits were their primary targets on their scavenging forays, anything not nailed down or too big to carry off was fair game for a Dhog: tools, vessels of various types, unattended cargo—these were the most highly sought rewards for a night's work. The Dhogs were careful never to take too much, or make their theft blatant, for they feared retaliation—against which they would be virtually defenseless. Even more, they feared making the Hages wary and overcautious, preferring a little carelessness on the part of their providers. If a tool that had been forgotten and left out disappeared, that was one thing. But if an entire tool bin were ransacked, that would force tighter security and stricter policing of all Hage goods, and that was one additional hardship the Dhogs definitely did not care to precipitate.

Therefore, their thefts were always judicious and cunning. Though it hurt terribly sometimes, they would leave a great haul untouched—a stack of ipumn bales left overnight on the wharf, or Hyrgo grain sacks waiting outside the granary—making off with just a single item so suspicion would not fall to them.

Giloon Bogney ruled his people with a genius composed equally of shrewdness and common sense, keeping order and dispensing rough justice, holding the reins of power with a firm, if filthy hand. Cleanliness was not a Dhog attribute. Water was to drink, not to wash in. The water teams had a hard enough time keeping up with their families' needs without worrying about providing wash water. People washed only when the opportunity presented itself, which was seldom.

When the last of the family heads had been formally greeted by their leader, Giloon signaled for the foodstuffs to be taken away and readied on tables provided for the purpose. Moments later, the squawks and squalls of the prudos and bakis rose above the festive commotion. A cry went up from the throng, numbering close to fifteen thousand by Giloon's estimation, for nearly every Dhog who could walk, hobble, or crawl had come: "The fire! The fire! Light the fire!"

Giloon cast an eye toward the dome far above; the last light of day glimmered weakly on the sectioned panes. He shrugged and called for the fire team to bring a brand. A runner was dispatched at once and returned moments later, threading his way through the crowds, firebrand lifted high.

The flaming torch was presented to Giloon, who, with exaggerated pomp and ceremony, took it and moved to the center of the square and the large mound of combustibles there. The Dhogs parted and formed an immense ring around the pile, their dark eyes and grimy faces keen in the torchlight.

Giloon raised the torch in his pudgy hand and said in a loud, ironic voice: "The Big Man be dead!"

"Better him than us!" shouted someone from the crowd, and everyone laughed.

"And it's being no too soon!" Giloon continued. "We knowing he liking the Afterworld—he sending so many of our people there always."

"He maybe gets a Dhog welcome," added the voice from the crowd.

"And maybe gets a Dhog Oversoul to lead him," shouted another wag. More laughter came as Giloon lowered the torch to the pile. The bundled rags used for kindling leapt to the flame, and the bonfire blazed. Freshly butchered carcasses were brought forth on spits by the dozen and set all around the perimeter of the blaze as closely as possible. Soon the aroma of roasting meat mingled with the varied scent of the burning rubbish.

Games and music began—both rude and uncouth to a more civilized observer, but spirited nonetheless. Tall, standing torches were lit throughout the square, and lines began forming at the beverage and food tables. Every face wore a carefree expression, for tonight of all nights there would be plenty to eat and drink for everyone, young and old alike.

Giloon, with his personal entourage, strolled the square, talking to his people, sharing their merriment, and receiving mock condolences as well as genuine toasts to his own health and longevity. As a leader, Giloon was appreciated and honored by the Dhogs, who admired his legendary shrewdness.

His feats of stealth and guile were remembered and told as

exemplars to the young. Like the time he had diverted a whole shipment of rice from Hyrgo Hage to the refuse pits simply by switching destination tags. The rice was sitting on the Hyrgo docks awaiting transportation to Saecaraz. He had scoured the Saecaraz refuse pits for the tags and then affixed them to the grain sacks. It had taken all night, but he had only to collect the sacks from Saecaraz the next night. The reward for that one exploit was over a thousand kils of rice, and everlasting glory.

When he finished making his rounds, the Dhog leader retired to a platform that had been set up overlooking the square. There, in the company of his closest friends, he entertained the heads of the Dhog families and watched over the festivities. It was a wild revelry: raucous, gluttonous, riotous.

The celebration lasted far into the night with dancing, singing, eating, and drinking until not a single Dhog was left standing. Children and older adults huddled in impromptu heaps; young people paired off and crept away for more intimate sleeping arrangements. The bonfire dwindled and died as dawn tinted the smudgy carapace of Dome overhead. Sirin Rohee was dead, and the Dhogs had celebrated. It would be the last celebration for many of them.

FOURTEEN

"It was grotesque," said Cejka, grimacing in distaste. "I have never seen anything so . . . so *bestial* in all my life. Not even at Trabantonna! Whole Hages swarming in drunken madness! Seven Jamuna were killed when Chryse torch dancers accidently set a draped pylon afire and the crowd surged away; three were trampled and four crushed against a rimwall. And theirs won't be the only bodies found tomorrow, I fear. Rohee's funeral is a death orgy! You were wise to leave when you did, Tvrdy. I am still shaking from it." The Rumon Director held out his hand to show how it trembled.

"At least it's over," replied Tvrdy, pouring out two glasses of souile and handing one to his friend. "A drink will calm you."

"But it's *not* over, as you well know." Cejka took up his glass, saluted Tvrdy, and took a sip. He sat back with a sigh. "This is quality souile, Director," he observed. "In memory of Sirin Rohee?"

Tvrdy gave Cejka a dark look. "Sorry, a bad joke," Cejka admitted, taking another sip.

"We drink not to Rohee's memory, but to our own," said Tvrdy. "And because I mean to deplete my stock. Once the Purge has begun, all will be confiscated, no doubt. I, for one, would rather see it poured into the cesspit than allow even one bottle to fall into Jamrog's hands."

Cejka looked stricken. "Don't talk so! Even if you are joking—and I think you are not—it produces bad ether. We must not even think of a Purge."

"You said it yourself just now: it's not over yet. In fact, today was only a beginning. The funeral was a signal to any keen enough to see it. Jamrog means to eliminate all opposition to his total authority."

"As he did away with Rohee? He can't do it. The Threl will not allow it. If he moves against even one of us, the rest will—"

"Will what?" Tvrdy snapped. "Stand by and watch him do it? Yes. Don't lie to me, Cejka, and most of all don't lie to yourself. Even if we all opposed him—which would never happen—he'd disband the Threl. If we sought to overthrow him, he'd have us executed as traitors. Jamrog will make himself answerable to no one."

Cejka stared into his drink. "Your words are harsh, but true. You speak my fears and I do not like it, but I know you are right."

"We are dead men, Cejka. We have no hope." Tvrdy's tone caused Cejka to look up sharply. He'd never heard the Tanais Director so depressed.

"No hope? This is souile talking, not my old friend."

"It is reality! Jamrog was more powerful from the start than we ever suspected. He hid it well. We put too much trust in Rohee's ability to guard his own selfish interests, and not enough in Jamrog's ability to use those interests for his own ends."

"You overestimate him and underestimate yourself," pointed out Cejka.

"He *murdered* Rohee, by Trabant! And no one has breathed a word against him. Wake up, Cejka. We have lost."

Cejka rose stiffly, drawing himself up full height. "I will not stay here and listen to you rave, Tvrdy. You are no coward. Why do you talk so?" Tvrdy made a weak gesture, but Cejka continued. "We have been through too much together for me to believe you mean what you say. Go to sleep, Tvrdy. It has been a long day. Tomorrow will look different to you."

"Yes," replied Tvrdy morosely, "tomorrow will look different. It will look worse!" He shook his head sadly. "Sit down, Cejka. At least let us enjoy this fine souile like good friends. It may be the last time we drink together."

"I think I should go," said Cejka quietly. "You need rest. You are exhausted. You must sleep."

"We'll have plenty of time to sleep, Cejka—once we've joined Rohee."

Cejka turned away and strode toward the lift tube on the opposite side of the room. "Good night, Tvrdy. I will talk to you again when you are sensible." With that, he left.

Tvrdy poured the last of the souile into his glass and drank deeply, then got up and walked to his balcony to watch a pink dawn tint the planes of Dome's crystal shell. He tilted his head back and drained the glass, held it for a moment, and then hurled it from the balcony. "That's one treasure you won't get, Supreme Director Jamrog," he said and went to find his bed.

• • • • • •

Yarden was up at first light, excited to begin her new life as an artist. Since her talk with Gerdes, it was all she could think about. She imagined all the wonderful paintings and drawings she would create—whole rooms full of beauty. She would dedicate herself heart and soul to art, and would pursue it with everything in her. She would learn all Gerdes could teach her and study the great Fieri masters; she would develop the talent she had been given and, in time, become a master herself.

Yarden dressed in a sand-colored chinti, which was what the Fieri called the suit of blouse and loose, knee-length trousers they all wore. She pulled on soft boots a shade or two darker and crept quietly down the stairs to the kitchen on the first level of the small house. There she set about making breakfast.

When Ianni joined her a little while later, the sun was up and bright in the trees in the garden just off the open kitchen. Fieri architecture revered open spaces, so that their homes always had at least one entire wall exposed to the outdoors— usually overlooking some restful scene: a garden, the lakeshore, a park. Ianni's kitchen was arranged so she and her guests could eat in the garden when the weather permitted. Given Empyrion's paradisiacal climate, this was nearly every day of the year.

"Good morning," said Yarden cheerfully as Ianni entered the room. "I thought we'd have fruit this morning. I've already set our places outside."

Ianni gave her a look of approval and said, "Now I know you feel at home here. This is the first day you have fixed breakfast."

"Have I been an inconsiderate guest? Believe me, Ianni, I didn't mean to be. Really, I never thought—"

The Fieri woman shushed her. "I didn't say that for you to chide yourself. I am happy to serve you. But when you start serving me, you are no longer a guest. You are family."

Yarden smiled at the compliment. "Thank you, Ianni. You have done so much for me, I'll never be able to repay you."

"It is not to be repaid. What I did for you, I did for the Infinite."

"I understand," said Yarden. "But I still want to express my gratitude for all you've shown me and taught me. And most of all, for introducing me to Gerdes."

"Were you not even a little disappointed when she said you would never be a dancer?" asked Ianni as Yarden handed her a plate of fruit. They walked out into the garden to the table and chairs surrounded by shrubs flowing with cascades of scarlet flowers. Little fuzzy insects, like tiny balls of lint, toiled in the blossoms, spreading fragrant pollen from flower to flower.

"Disappointed? Maybe I was, but only for an instant. Gerdes told me the truth and I accepted it," Yarden explained as they began to eat. "She also gave me hope that I could become an artist of a different kind. And since she had told me the truth about my dancing, I could trust her about painting."

Ianni nodded, chewing thoughtfully. "You are anxious to begin, I know, but I wonder if you might consider delaying your study for a time?"

"Delay it? Why?"

"It's just an idea," Ianni said as she speared another piece of sweet, succulent ameang, a pulpy tree-grown fruit with tender white flesh. "I thought perhaps you might like to come with us to the Bay of Talking Fish."

Yarden laughed at the name. "Talking fish? Are you serious?"

"The name comes from before the Burning, so I suppose it does sound strange to you."

"Strange yes, but more fanciful—whimsical, I should say. I'm fascinated; tell me about it."

Ianni put down her fork and began telling Yarden about the wonderful creatures of the bay. "In the Far North country, in the region of the Light Mountains, there is a great ocean inlet that forms a bay—a body of water much bigger than Prindahl."

"The fish live there?" asked Yarden, her eyes dancing, picturing this magical place.

"No, the fish live far out in the deep ocean. But once every seven years they return to birth their young in the gentle waters of the bay." Ianni paused, remembering with a look of quiet rapture on her face. Presently she came to herself and continued, "It's a long trip; we travel by river through the mountains, and it takes several weeks."

"It must be quite an experience—the way you speak of it."

"The Preceptor could tell you better than I—I don't have the words. But yes, it's utterly exalting. We go, as many as can make the jouney, and arrive at the bay a few days before the fish arrive. We wait for them. Then they come. You can see their tail fins riding high in the water as they enter the bay. They know we will be waiting for them, and they begin to leap and play." Ianni's eyes lit up as she told about the fish. "It's the most beautiful sight: thousands of blue fins shining in the silver water as they come. The leaders bring the school right into the shallows, and we wade out to greet them."

"Do they actually talk?" Yarden had some idea that the noise the fish made sounded like talking. Ianni's answer surprised her.

"Not the way you mean. They talk yes, but not with words—it's more the way you do, when you choose to. We talk to them in our minds and hearts."

"Really!" Yarden looked at her host in wonder. "The fish communicate sympathically?"

"It's very similar, I believe. Mathiax could tell you more about it."

"Unbelievable!" The more she heard, the more fanciful Ianni's story seemed. "But, you—that is, the Fieri don't use mind-speech ordinarily. You have not developed it among yourselves."

"True," admitted Ianni, "but with the fish, it's different. We can speak to them, and they speak to us. Oh, it's wonderful, Yarden! I want you to come with us."

"I will! I want to very much—if it's as you say, I wouldn't want to miss it. When do you leave?"

"Very soon. Preparations are already being made."

Yarden's sympathic awareness caught Ianni's sense of awe and excitement; she definitely wanted to go, yet felt slightly disappointed in delaying her study. "But what will I tell Gerdes? I had planned to begin studying today."

"Gerdes will understand, I'm sure. She'll urge you to go. You can begin your studies when you return."

FIFTEEN

In the darkness of the blackest night he'd ever known, Treet felt the cold, wet kisses of snowflakes alighting and melting on his skin. The wind howled miserably, sending the flakes swirling over him. He felt their fleeting stings as they found him, spinning out of the vast, hollow emptiness to caress him and vanish.

Then the darkness began to pulse, convulsing in rhythmic shudders as cataclysmic tremors pounded through the black emptiness. Gradually the darkness changed, fading to deep red, as if a terrible sunrise trembled on some lost horizon. And the snow changed, too, becoming tiny biting insects—midges that swarmed and stung the skin where they touched. In an instant, Treet's hide was covered with minute swelling bumps. He cried out—not so much in pain, as in torment. The insects continued to swarm, and he was powerless to stop them.

The deep red grew brighter and the ponderous convulsions more regular and pronounced. Pounding, pounding, pounding, each pulse reverberated in his brain. Treet's insides quivered with every tremor as the vacuum grew brighter still, turning blood crimson. The insects changed in turn. They were insects no longer, but oblong cells floating in slow motion all around him, surging and subsiding with every booming thump of the drumming pulse.

Treet knew then where he was. Somehow he had become trapped inside his own heart!

The resounding tremor was his heart beating with laborious regularity; the tiny cells swimming around him were his own blood cells and platelets, surging with the tide of his blood through the chambers of his heart. And he was caught there with no idea of how to get out. He would drown in his own blood.

Instantly, as if reacting to this morbid thought, the heartbeat quickened, lurching rapidly and wildly. The blood fluids tugged erratically at him, pulling him first this way and then another. The cells and platelets assailed him, driven on by the wash of blood through his heart. Now he could see the walls of his heart constricting. The organ was shrinking with every beat!

Treet watched in horror as the fleshy walls of muscle closed around him. He opened his mouth wide and screamed.

The heart squeezed down, harder and harder, clamping him in a death grip. His heart beat faster now, grasping him tighter and tighter. He would be crushed to death by his own body. The insanity of it made his brain squirm. He screamed again for it to stop.

The heart stopped beating.

The blood, surging violently around him an instant before, stopped. The thunderous thumping stopped. Everything ceased.

My heart has stopped, he thought; I'm saved! The implication of this struck Treet even as relief overtook him: that means I'm dead!

The irrationality of this paradoxical event shocked Treet. Whoever heard of anyone dying in order to live? Preposterous! I can't be dead, he thought. And yet, if I'm not dead why can't I see? Or hear? Or breathe?

No, there is nothing wrong with me. I'm just sleeping. I'm all right. I will survive. I'll make it. I won't let a little nightmare unhinge me.

The terror, so real only moments before, quickly faded, and a sense of expanding euphoria took its place. Treet drifted in the warmth of the feeling until he realized that it was remarkably similar to another sensation: hunger. This roused him. He had not eaten in some time, except for the handful of beans and the sip of water he'd had in his cell, and who knew how long ago that had been?

Fully awake now, floating in the thick soup of the conditioning tank, Treet decided to again try an experiment he'd been conducting from the moment he'd been lowered into the tank: an experiment in sympathic awareness. Something Yarden had once told him had come back to him—probably in light of his futile attempt at swaying the tank operator to push the button on the console that would bring him up.

"Are you a sympath?" she had asked him aboard the *Zephyros*. "Some people are natural adepts and do not know it, Mr. Treet. You could be one of them."

The idea that he might be a sympath had unsettled him for a while after that, though he could not at the time think why.

He'd chalked it up to an ambiguous fear of disorder—a man of clear-eyed logic and cold rationality worshiped order and sense. The sympathic awareness and its sense-defying tendencies frightened him. Treet had always figured that a man needed a firm anchor in reality to survive all the insanity the modern world threw at him.

And so he did. But all of Treet's logic and rationality had not saved him. Here on Empyrion, these things were of little consequence or value, apparently. Therefore, lacking any better weapons, Treet had decided to fight back with the only tool he had—his own mind.

He had intermittently been sending Yarden messages of his demise. Without knowing precisely how the sympathic awareness worked, he had no real hope that he would be able to receive actual messages from Yarden, but he thought he might be able to nudge her consciousness somehow or otherwise make himself known to her. Once alerted, she would be able to receive his "thought impressions"—to use her term. Then it was up to Yarden.

He could not believe that she would be so cold to his plight that she would ignore him. She would come with help . . . wouldn't she?

The thought of Yarden coming to him made his heart ache with emptiness. He wished he'd been able to persuade her to return with him. Return to what? he wondered. To this? To capture and mental torture at the hands of their enemies?

No, it was better this way. At least she was free. Even if he had to pay the ultimate price for his foolishness, at least she would be spared joining him. She would never know what became of him.

Hard on this thought came the sobering realization, not for the first time, that if he failed, he would not be the only victim. Unless he found a way to alter the course of events, the relentless flow would carry the Fieri to death and destruction once more. Nuclear holocaust would be repeated as Dome in its unfathomable hatred and stupidity turned against the loving Fieri again—for the second time in fifteen hundred years. If that happened, as he was sure it would, none of his friends would live through it.

More and more, it appeared he would be the first casualty of the hostility. No, sadly, not the first—merely the latest in a long, long crowded line stretching back nearly three millennia.

The futility of his situation stung him. His helplessness mocked him bitterly. So much depended on him, and there was absolutely nothing he could do. Nothing but wait, hold out as long as he could, and hope.

• • • • • •

Far from the cells of Cavern level, Jamrog strolled the secluded pathways of Rohee's private pleasure ground high above Threl Chambers. Mrukk walked beside his master, hands clasped behind him, dressed in the light gray yos the Invisibles wore when in Hage. When prowling through Dome, the Invisibles took the colors of whichever Hage they happened to be passing through, blending in with the Hagemen at will. An easy trick, but always effective.

"What did you observe, Commander?" asked Jamrog placidly. The day before had been the triumph he'd hoped for and more. He'd slept well, after an evening spent entertaining two female companions, and risen early, eager to begin his rule by removing the first obstacles to his total authority.

Mrukk, a brooding hulk of a man, gave a quick sideways flick of his keen eyes—more out of habit than suspicion—and answered in a low voice. "The Directors were all in attendance, as you no doubt have been informed by your Hage priests. The Hages were well represented, and no overt signs of disapproval have been observed or reported."

Jamrog turned to him. "You don't sound convinced of that. Why?"

"There is an unsubstantiated report that Tvrdy was seen leaving Threl Square alone just after your speech."

"Hmmm." Jamrog's eyes narrowed. "Who saw him?"

"One of the Hage priests recognized him and reported it to Nilokerus security. By the time the report reached us, it could not be confirmed. However, his presence was noted when the Tanais returned to Hage, so perhaps the priest was mistaken."

Jamrog nodded slowly. "It doesn't matter. I do not care to trap the Tanais so easily; I have better plans for him. When I am finished with Tvrdy, his own Hagemen will deny they ever knew him." Jamrog chuckled easily. He was well on his way to becoming invincible, and after so many years biding his time, waiting in Rohee's shadow, it was a very heady feeling.

Mrukk said nothing; his cold gray eyes stared ahead impassively. The fearsome commander of the Mors Ultima knew Jamrog well and knew how quickly the man's mood could change. But he knew also that he was more than a match for his master. His ruthlessness and cold brutality had been rewarded time and again as he advanced through the ranks to become leader of the elite force of the Invisibles. There was nothing he would not do for his master, true, but his loyalty had its price. He wondered sometimes how much Jamrog was willing to pay.

They walked a little further together, Jamrog frowned in concentration, clenching and unclenching his fists absently, his soft-shod feet whispering on the paving stones. "Commander," he said after a time, "I want you to see to it that the Invisibles are rewarded for their service yesterday."

"Of course, Supreme Director. Did you have a sum in mind, or should I use my own discretion?"

"Five hundred shares."

"Five hundred is very generous, Director," Mrukk said slyly. "Perhaps a lesser amount would serve as well. Some of the men may not know what to do with so much, seh?"

"Five hundred," said Jamrog decisively, glancing up quickly. "And make certain they know it is a reward for service. Instruct them that they can expect such rewards from now on—for good service, of course. Poor service will be punished in like manner."

"I understand, Supreme Director. It will be done immediately."

"Good," replied Jamrog. "You may return to your duties. Oh, there is one more detail. Do you remember the discussion we had some time ago about Hladik's usefulness?"

Mrukk's eyes narrowed; a thin smile twitched the corners of his cruel lips. "Of course."

"I have reason to doubt the Nilokerus Director's sincerity of late."

"Would you like me to have him watched by one of my men?"

"I think it best. It would not do to begin my rule with anything less than the total confidence and loyalty of all my

Directors." Jamrog dismissed the commander with a gesture and walked on by himself, musing on his various schemes, letting his feet wander where they would among the trimmed hedgeways and flowered paths.

This very pleasure ground was where Rohee had met his death in the form of a cordial, laced with a special poison which Jamrog had concocted.

Sirin Rohee in his last years, weary of ruling and of the spoils of his handsomely exploited position, had taken to spending long hours in his private pleasure grounds—a garden park planted with miniature trees and fragrant flowering shrubbery of every type produced by Hyrgo Hage. It was his habit to spend the afternoon hours walking off his meal amidst the greenery of his park, often with a nubile Hagemate (of either sex; it made no difference at all to Rohee).

He also enjoyed a cordial made from sweetened cherimoyas and distilled souile, which he sipped as he took his daily tour of his gardens—changed continually by Hyrgo growers so that the Supreme Director would not become bored with his favorite pastime. It had been a simple matter to drop the poison into the old man's drink. Jamrog had merely arrived to discuss a bit of business and slipped the powder into the bottle. He'd had his talk and then left.

Later that night, the news of Rohee's unfortunate demise had reached the ambitious Jamrog. The poison, slow acting, though excruciating in its irreversible final stages, had taken effect, and the Supreme Director had died screaming in his bed in the middle of the night, frightening his Hagemate out of her wits. Jamrog had been summoned at once, but it was by then too late. Sirin Rohee was dead. The girl swore no one had been near the old man all day and that he had eaten nothing that she herself had not eaten.

It was not especially important to Jamrog that he remain above suspicion in Rohee's death, merely convenient. The Hage priests would cooperate more readily if they did not have cause to accuse him of muddying the ethereal realms with the negative energy produced by murder. He needed the Hage priests for a special program he planned to institute soon, and their cooperation would be most helpful.

Therefore, when he had examined the problem from all possible angles and had decided that he had no further use for

Rohee, he poisoned his old master and established himself in his place. Exactly as he'd planned from the beginning.

Jamrog gave a great sigh of contentment. It was good, and the best was yet to come.

SIXTEEN

*P*izzle lay in bed, having just passed one of the most baffling nights in his relatively brief but confusing life. In utter chagrin he reviewed the events of the previous evening one by one, examining each moment as it unfolded in his brain, trying to perceive where he'd gone wrong.

Jaire's guests had arrived and he'd been introduced. To his dismay, Starla had not been among them. A few of the guests had expressed interest in Pizzle's impressions of Fierra, and others wanted to hear about his journey. Surprisingly, no one seemed interested in hearing about Dome, or about Earth either. At least these topics were avoided in open discussion. The reason, Pizzle guessed, was because Dome, and Earth also for all he knew, held negative associations for the Fieri.

It wasn't that they forbade hearing about such things, or made it a rule to avoid them, but more that they did not wish to entertain anything of a negative nature for any length of time. This was why the facts of their arrival on Empyrion and their sojourn in Dome had been described only once—at an appropriate time before the assembled Mentors. Nothing more was said after that. There was no inquisition, no endless sessions of debriefing, no covert poking and prodding into the visitor's intentions or motives in coming.

This was the real corker for Pizzle. He'd expected a completely different response. On Earth, alien space travelers would have been instantly quarantined and subjected to endless inquiry and study. It was like Treet had said: "Our reception at Dome made more sense."

The Fieri were not fainthearted, Pizzle thought. And they didn't appear prudish in their approach to life. They just weren't interested in hearing about Dome. As it had been expressed to him by Mathiax one day, "What good can come of contemplating darkness?"

For the Fieri, darkness was a force always active, always encroaching on the light, and therefore always to be resisted in whatever form it took at the moment. Not ordinarily given to strong conviction himself, Pizzle nevertheless found himself admiring the Fieri devotion. But the way he felt now, it was hard *not* to admire everything about the race that had produced his beloved. If for no other reason, Pizzle would have adored the Fieri *en masse* for the one noble achievement of rearing a daughter so fair.

While he related the facts of his desert journey and consequent rescue by a Fieri airship—aided, of course, by his own ingenious signal device and his heroic actions, which he never failed to mention—he watched the room's entrance for Starla's appearance. She did not appear. Nor did she arrive during his monologue about his impressions of their amazing city.

Jaire had called them to the table, and the gathering drifted leisurely to the dining room. Pizzle, frankly disappointed, had decided to make the best of it by seating himself between two charming Fieri women. He had just settled in his chair and turned to the dinner companion on his left and . . . there, in the arched doorway, stood Starla, talking to a young man who was holding her tightly by the hand.

Pizzle's heart lurched; he felt as if he were a gourd that had just had its insides scooped out. He turned his eyes away quickly and sat down before she saw him looking at her, then clamped his mouth shut so hard his jaws ached. His eyesight blurred and he sat through the entire meal without looking to his left, where *she* sat toward the end of the table. He could hear her voice, now and again, talking in intimate tones with her escort. His ears burned, and his mind seethed.

Jaire served the meal—smiling, gracious, oblivious to his pain. He longed for the torture to be over so he could flee to the solace of his room and take up once more his foreordained solitary existence. Starla had obviously deceived him, leading him on with no intention of following through. Probably she thought the whole thing a great joke at his expense, a game to satisfy her idle curiosity. Sure, that's all he meant to her: an oddity from another planet, a freak, a conversation piece, something to tell her grandchildren about: My date with a Space Geek.

Pizzle sank lower in his chair as his heart sank lower into melancholy. He cursed his blind foolishness and wallowed in wave after wave of self-pity that rolled over him. By the meal's third course, he was so deep in his despair that he became frantic and began talking loudly and volubly to those around him. His two dinner companions exchanged looks of bewilderment. What had gotten into this foreigner? Silent as a stone through the first half of the meal, he was now boisterous to the point of hysterics.

Pizzle did not see the looks exchanged around the table. He did not see the stricken expression on Starla's face as he proceeded to make a monumental ass of himself, capping his performance by spilling his glass into the lap of the guest next to him. Jaire attempted intervention, trying her best to calm him, but to no avail.

Finally Pizzle, fearing some greater humiliation, excused himself and walked out into the canopied courtyard. The sunshield was drawn back, and the stars looked down in icy disapproval of his behavior at the table. Pizzle sighed morosely and shuffled over to a seat, slumped down, and closed his eyes in misery.

Some time later, an hour perhaps, he became aware of a perfumed presence. He opened his eyes and, with his slightly fuzzy vision, saw a dream drifting toward him. Starla came to stand before him, a look of hurt and disappointment on her lovely face. Pizzle needed no explanation to know what she was feeling, for her expression fairly well mirrored his own. But *why* she should feel this way he couldn't figure.

"May I sit down?" she asked.

"It's a free country," sniffed Pizzle. She gave him a questioning glance. "It's an expression—it means go ahead, nobody's going to stop you."

"You wish someone would stop me from sitting with you?"

"No, I didn't mean that. I meant—look, just do what you want, okay?"

Starla sat down in a woven chair across from him, crisp in her blue chinti. She looked at him with her large, dark eyes, liquid in the starlight. "I thought you'd be glad to see me," she said softly. "I thought we were friends."

"Yeah, I thought so, too," grumped Pizzle. "And I *was* glad to see you—until I saw you were with someone else."

"I brought Vanon to meet you."

"Great. I love meeting a girl's boyfriends."

"I do not understand you, Pizzy. Explain yourself please."

She was asking for it, was she? Very well, he'd give her both barrels. "I'll explain myself. I was hoping to see you tonight—I waited and waited for you to show up, and when you finally do it's on the arm of some bozo you say you want to introduce me to. Why? You want my blessing or what? I'm sure you'll both be very happy together. How's that? Now why don't you run back inside before he comes out here looking for you. One thing I don't need is to see you leave with him."

A shocked expression replaced the hurt look on Starla's face. "What's the matter?" asked Pizzle. "Didn't anybody ever talk like that to you before?"

Mute, Starla shook her head.

"Too bad," snarled Pizzle. "People talk like that to me all the time. You get used to it."

"I came looking for you—" she began.

"So you could rub it in? Don't bother."

"I wanted . . . to be with you." Her voice quavered as she stood to leave.

Now Pizzle felt like a prize jerk. Why couldn't he just leave well enough alone? Why did he always have to push a thing too far? Because I'm a pin-headed stupido, he thought, kicking himself. "Look, you're not going to cry or anything, are you?" he said weakly.

Starla shook her head again and looked away momentarily. Pizzle thought he saw the glint of a tear on her lashes. "You're angry with me," Starla observed. "But I don't know why."

"I'm not angry with you. I mean, I *was,* but not now. Sit back down a minute."

Starla sat stiffly, folding her hands in her lap, glanced up at him, and said, "Vanon is my brother. He's my only family."

Pizzle groaned and slid down in his chair. "Somebody shoot me."

"If my bringing him here to meet you was wrong, I am sorry. I did not wish to hurt you."

It was, Pizzle reflected, probably genetically impossible for a Fieri to willfully hurt another human being. What a blundering, self-centered, gravel-headed dizzard I've been! What a toad! "I—It's just—I can't—" He stumbled over the words. "I'm sorry, Starla, I thought . . . I don't know what I thought."

"You thought I didn't want to be with you tonight?"

"Yeah, that's what I thought all right," Pizzle admitted. "I've got mashed potatoes for brains sometimes. I'm sorry. I should have trusted you." He swallowed hard. "You'll forgive me?"

"I forgive you, Asquith," she said.

He leaned closer to her and caught her scent in the warm night air. "Back on Earth there's a custom," he said softly, his heart pounding, "that when lovers quarrel and make up, they kiss."

She gazed steadily back at him and replied, "We have the same custom."

The next thing Pizzle knew, Starla was in his arms and he was kissing her, his heart bumping so loudly in his chest he thought he was having a heart attack, but didn't mind in the least.

"I love you, Starla," he said when he came up for air, astonishing himself with his declaration. He'd scarcely admitted it to himself. What am I doing? he wondered. Why can't I control myself?

Starla drew away from him, looked at him calmly, and said, "I love you, too, Asquith. I have from the first night when you told me all about *The Hobbit.*"

"You did?" Pizzle stared. This is terrible! What am I going to do now? She's in love with me! I've really done it this time. "You really did?"

She nodded and reached for his hand, took it, and held it. Pizzle entered the seventh dimension—a place where time stood still and flashed by at incredible speed simultaneously. His head swam, and his feet perspired. His throat tightened, and his eyes spun in his head.

"I . . . Starla, I've hardly ever—that is, never—loved anyone before." His tongue grew thick and unwieldy in his mouth. "Not really."

She looked at him strangely. "Was there never a woman for you?"

"Oh, sure, lots of women—but none of them would ever have anything to do with me. I am, I guess you might say, just not what every woman looks for first in a man. Let's face it, I'm no holovision star."

Starla puzzled over his words. "I still do not understand many of the things you say. But I see into your heart, and I know you are a gentle spirit."

Pizzle could only stare. No one had ever said anything like

that to him before, and he didn't know how to respond. He simply sat holding her hand very tightly. A few minutes passed this way before either one spoke. Finally Pizzle broke the silence by saying, "Well, what do we do now—get married?"

The words were out of his mouth before he knew what he was saying. To her credit Starla did not leap up and run screaming into the night. She sat beside him, gazing at him intently, the starlight shimmering in her hair. She acted as if what he had said had some basis in logical possibility, as if she were actually considering it.

"I must introduce you to my brother first. Among Fieri, marriage is not entered lightly," was all she said.

"Oh, right. But maybe I shouldn't—I mean, what I said just now . . . well, that was . . . Sure, let's go meet your brother." Pizzle stood abruptly, before any more ludicrous words could cross his lips, and together they went back inside to rejoin Jaire's dinner party.

The rest of the evening went pinwheeling by in a blur. Pizzle, reeling from the implications of his hasty suggestion, wandered dazed through the introduction to Vanon, Starla's brother. At some point the party was over. The guests departed, Starla disappeared, and he found himself standing before the open end of his room, staring unseeing out upon Prindahl's calm, starlit face.

Eventually he found his bed and lay down in it, not to sleep, but to toss restlessly as his mind wrestled with the idea of marriage . . . MARRIAGE!

Now, as he lay contemplating his probable fate, Pizzle had regained most of his wits and composure. As dawn's pearly light streamed into his room, he remembered more clearly what had transpired last night in the courtyard. Starla had not said they *would* get married, only that marriage was not entered into lightly.

Feeling like a prisoner granted a surprise reprieve, Pizzle rose, ready to face the day. With any luck at all Starla would not even recall their conversation.

SEVENTEEN

The tree Crocker found was perfect: about six centimeters in diameter and arrow straight. Although merely a sapling, its trunk was tall and strong, its wood dense. Using his small utility knife, he trimmed off the few inconsequential upper branches and then proceeded to cut off the trunk near the roots, patiently shaving away the wood layer by layer in a tapering cone shape. It took him many long hours, but when he finished, he had a sturdy javelin as tall as he was.

He spent the next hours sharpening his weapon, whittling the cone into an elongated pyramid shape—four lethal triangles for strength. Once finished he began practicing with it, studying its balance and attitude of flight. It took much shaving of the shaft to get it properly balanced, but as he worked and practiced he discovered he could throw his spear nearly thirty meters with accuracy.

He had not heard or seen any traces of the behemoth lords since the titanic struggle overheard several days ago. The thought that such creatures existed and moved through the forest both frightened and thrilled Crocker. Whenever he happened to recall the terrible clash a twitch in his gut, a physical memory of fear, reminded him of the exquisite thrill he'd experienced in those dreadful moments when he believed the creatures would discover him.

Crocker spent the next several days ranging the forest for small game, traipsing only as far as he could go and still return to his secluded bower by nightfall. He still slept by the little pool and swam there. He had eaten on the carcass of the plump animal he'd killed until the meat had begun to rot. But that had been days ago, and no more animals had visited his pool to drink. He was hungry again, and anxious to try his weapon in earnest.

The Blue Forest abounded in wildlife of all kinds—most of it, unfortunately, inhabiting the upper regions of the leaf canopy, well above the reach of his spear. Birds and small mammalian creatures watched him pass along the forest pathways far below.

But there were larger, less wary animals to be found as well. He saw their spoor and occasionally caught a glimpse of a sleek hide gliding into the brush just ahead.

As hunger became more acute, his stealth improved in direct proportion. By the third day, he crept through the verdant byways as silently as the creatures he stalked. Although much of his human awareness was gone, Crocker still possessed a superior animal cunning. And if he neither knew nor remembered anything of his former life, at least certain latent portions of his mentality were responding vigorously to the stimulus of life in the forest. In place of memory, for example, he was developing an extraordinary patience and perseverance, allowing him to sit unmoving in a single spot or slog along a promising path for hours on end without complaint or exhaustion.

Of these things he was ignorant, however, for not a speck of consciousness remained. His life was governed by the most basic of forces: day and night, hunger and thirst.

He wandered the Blue Forest unaware of who he was or where he had come from, simply reacting to his needs of the moment, thinking no further ahead than the next meal. The robo-carrier did not accompany him on these forays, for the soft whirr of its motors and the shush of its treads as it passed through the brush made too much noise. Crocker had carved a tunnel for it to enter his secluded bower: once there, he switched the machine off.

Crouching atop a moss-covered rock overhang from which he could survey the trail below, he sat with his javelin resting loosely in his hands, waiting for an animal to pass beneath him. Several hours had gone by, and he was just about to give up his vigil and move on when he heard a rustling of dry leaves. He had placed a fallen vine across the path a little way up the trail. Something was coming!

Instantly alert, Crocker's grasp on the spear tightened. His muscles tensed. He leaned forward, rising on the balls of his feet. The rustling persisted. Not one animal only, but many.

Just then the first creature appeared on the trail below. It was smaller than he'd hoped, with stringy red-brown hair over a barrel-shaped body supported by four spindly legs that looked too delicate to support it. Its narrow head sported a longish, semiflexible snout which waved in all directions, searching the becalmed air of the forest for scent traces. Crocker, keen to kill, would have let fly with his spear, but some recently awakened instinct stayed in his hand. *Wait!* this newfound voice cautioned. *Larger prey is coming. Wait.*

He paused, and shortly the first animal moved on, snuffling at the ground with its floppy proboscis. Immediately behind it came another, slightly larger version of the same animal. Crocker raised the spear once more.

No, came the voice again. *Be patient. This is not the one. You will know it when you see it.*

Crocker obeyed the instruction, lowering the weapon slightly, biding his time. Two more creatures scuttled by on the trail below—neither one acceptable. He waited and was about to give chase when he heard again the rustling of the vine. This time the animal that passed beneath his gaze was slower and much more stout—its belly nearly dragged the path as it walked along, snout writhing, sampling the leaves of all the plants it passed.

Now! cried the voice in his head. *Strike now and you will eat well tonight!*

Crocker's reaction was instantaneous. He felt a tension in his arm as he drew back the spear and sighted down its length. Teeth clenched, he heaved the shaft forward with a rolling motion of his shoulder.

The spear flashed through the air. A frightened squeal shattered the stillness. The animal dodged. It tried to run, but its body would not move—the beast was pierced through its thick neck and pinioned to the earth.

It struggled feebly and then expired. Crocker scrambled down from his rock and raced to his kill. He let out a whoop as he stood shivering with excitement over his handiwork. The spear flew true, its sharp point easily penetrating hide and muscle. His aim had been good, and the animal died quickly.

Good. You have brought down a leaf-eater. Their flesh is tender and warms the stomach.

He bent to retrieve his weapon and noticed a shadow moving toward him along the trail to his left. He whipped the spear around as an enormous black feline sauntered up, its midnight fur glistening in the patchy light, large golden eyes watching him keenly.

Crocker's hands stiffened on his spear. *Do not move,* his

inner voice cautioned. *Your spear is useless against a wevicat. Do nothing.*

On huge silent paws the beast padded forward, the nostrils of its great muzzle twitching. It gave the man a look of intense curiosity and then yawned mightily, revealing a grooved pink tongue and very sharp, very white triangular teeth lining wide jaws in a double row.

The man gave ground, backing away slowly, keeping the spear ready should the enormous feline charge. The cat blinked unconcernedly at him, yawned again, and nuzzled the fallen beast.

Crocker stood motionless and watched the cat rip into the carcass of the leaf-eater. He rebelled at losing his kill, and though he feared the wevicat, he would not be robbed of the meal he'd worked so hard for. The wevicat glanced up from its work, snorted in his direction as if to dismiss him, and went back to delicately peeling the hide from the haunches of the dead animal.

Rage leapt up in the man as he watched the wevicat nonchalantly stealing his food. Hands shaking, he tightened his grip on the spear and raised it above his head, bringing it down square on the wevicat's big head. Thwack!

The huge black beast spun, ears flattened to its skull, snarling. Crocker stood erect, challenging, the spear leveled at the spitting cat. *His claws scream for your blood, foolish one.* The voice was a terse whisper in his brain. *Your life is his.*

Crocker thrust the spear forward into the big cat's face. Quick as a blink the wevicat lifted a paw and swiped the spear aside, but Crocker, still shaking with rage and fear, brought the spear back. The cat's muscles rippled beneath its glistening coat, its golden eyes narrowed to vicious slits.

For a long tense moment the two glared at each other, neither backing down. *The smell of fear fills his nostrils,* said the disembodied voice inside the man's brain. *Flee and you will surely die.* The prospect of the hairless beast challenging him for the prey seemed to perplex the cat. It relaxed and sat back, gazing at the man warily. Here was something new—a creature of obvious weakness that did not run when threatened. The wevicat shook its great black head.

Crocker lowered the spear and tapped its tip on the side of

the dead animal's neck where the wevicat had begun to feed. The cat looked from the prey to the man, seemed to consider for a moment, then placed a paw on the side of the dead animal. *He says there is enough meat,* whispered the voice. *The wevicat respects you now. You will not sleep hungry this night.*

The cat returned to the kill and began stripping great chunks of meat from the carcass and devouring them whole. Crocker hunkered down to wait and watched the choicest pieces disappear into the wevicat's gaping maw. In time, however, the cat stood, licked its muzzle, yawned, and sauntered off a few paces. It lazily dropped onto its side, stretched out, and went to sleep.

Crocker crept forward and looked at what the cat had left for him: the stringy meat along the ribs and backbone and a portion of the forequarters between the front legs. Crocker took his small knife from his rag pouch and began cutting the meat into strips, chewing the still-warm meat slowly. From time to time, he glanced over at the wevicat to see if it might wake up. But the animal's sides rose and fell rhythmically in deep sleep, so Crocker went on with his meal.

He gorged himself on the sweet flesh, and soon the forest sounds buzzed in his ears and his head felt heavy. Tucking a last morsel into his mouth, Crocker pushed himself away from the decimated carcass, stumbled along the trail, and curled up under a bristle bush.

"An excellent idea!" replied Gerdes when Yarden told her she'd like to postpone the beginning of her studies so she could go on the trip to see the talking fish. "I will go, too. It has been too long since I last saw them. I'll invite some of my other students, and we can work along the way."

Yarden was quick to second the idea. "It's the perfect solution, Gerdes. Still, I can't wait to begin."

"We won't wait," said Gerdes, smiling. "We will begin as planned. Are you ready?"

"Begin now? Certainly. I'm ready." Yarden glanced quickly around the bare room in which Gerdes conducted her instruction. "But I don't see any paint or brushes or surfaces."

Gerdes smiled. "Nor will you for a very long time. Painting does not begin with the paint, but with the *painter!* We must first explore Yarden and find out who she is and what kind of artist she may become. We will begin with movement."

"Dance movement?"

"You remember what I said, good." Gerdes nodded approvingly. "Yes, I told you painting and dance had much in common. To paint well, you must move well and understand movement and rhythm. You will learn it by learning to move rhythmically." Gerdes moved to a near wall where a crystal was mounted on a panel with a row of colored tabs beneath it.

These triangular crystals, Yarden had learned, were employed by the Fieri in various tasks of communication. Evidently the crystals could both transmit and receive vibrations which could be used to carry signals. Exactly how this was accomplished, Yarden did not understand, but she had seen the devices often enough. Mentors like Talus and Mathiax were rarely without one affixed to their clothing.

Gerdes touched a colored tab, and the room filled with music: soft, lilting music, gentle and evocative. "Close your eyes, daughter. Listen for a moment. Concentrate. Let the music seep into you; let it fill you up until you cannot hold it any longer."

Yarden did as instructed, closing her eyes as she stood in

the center of the room. Gerdes' voice became softer, remote. Yarden listened to the music, letting it touch every part of her. She felt it in her fingers and arms and legs first.

"Drink it in as if you were very dry and the sound was cool water for your thirst. Feel it in every muscle, every fiber of your body." Gerdes went on talking, slowly, softly, speaking in time with the music.

Yarden allowed the music to fill up all the places within her that she could think of—shoulders, neck, stomach, chest, hips, thighs . . . everywhere.

"When you cannot contain it any longer, let the music overflow in movement. Make your body a vessel for the music to flow through, and become yourself that motion. Let it carry you as you carry it."

Yarden hesitated, uncertain how to interpret Gerdes' last instruction.

"Don't think about it, don't try to make too much sense of it. Just do what you feel. Hear the music, let it fill you and overflow in motion. Move with it."

Feeling awkward and uncertain, Yarden began to move—tentatively, jerkily. She lifted an arm, dropped it. Stepped forward, stopped. She glanced at Gerdes. "Keep your eyes closed. I know it feels clumsy. That's because you're thinking too much. Don't think about it, just do it. Let your body interpret the music, not your brain."

So, feeling very awkward and not a little self-conscious, Yarden began to move, slowly, haltingly at first. Arms outspread, legs taking hesitant steps, she turned in a tight circle.

"That's right," said Gerdes. "Feel the music. Translate the sound into motion. Good . . . good." With this encouragement, Yarden began to take bigger steps and move her arms in circles around her body, approximating the circles the melody made as it circled through the song.

"Relax," soothed Gerdes, "There are no steps to this dance except those you make yourself; so there is nothing to be afraid of. Fear makes you stiff. The music is fluid; you must become fluid, too."

It was true—Yarden was afraid of looking foolish before her teacher, afraid of making an awkward movement. She slowed her turning steps and concentrated on relaxing her body. Gerdes noticed the difference at once.

"That's better," she said. "Let go of your fear. See? The tension is leaving your shoulders. Now, let your backbone bend—it is not made of wood, it will become supple if you allow it. The music will show you."

Yarden stopped. "I can't. It's too—"

"Shh. Don't speak. Don't think. Begin again." Gerdes came close and put her hands on Yarden's shoulders lightly. "You're trying too hard. Don't fight what is already within you. Your body knows what to do, but your mind intrudes. Relax. Let your body do what it knows. Begin again."

Yarden closed her eyes once more and began to move, forcing herself not to think about anything. Instead, she willed her consciousness into the music, emptied herself into it, let it cover her and pull her along in its smooth, gently unfolding rhythms. She was surprised to find that her body was already responding. Slowly, but with increasing confidence, she moved, not arms and legs only, but torso and shoulders and hips and neck.

It felt good to move with such freedom. Burrowing deeper into the music, she allowed the music to dictate the motion. For once she had succeeded in silencing that sharply self-critical voice that judged and reported her every action. That was the trick—to divorce the judging self from the feeling self, to remove the bothersome self-awareness altogether so it could not intrude on the pure emotional response, allowing the body to move freely.

"Yes, yes," said Gerdes with obvious satisfaction. "Much better. You're feeling the music now. Go deeper into it; let it fill all the empty places. Take it in, and transform it into motion."

Eyes closed, Yarden moved to the music, her motions growing ever more sure. Gerdes brought her along with softly uttered encouragement until she could feel the music deep inside her as it coiled and spun and flowed like rippling water from the well of her soul. She became the music, entering into it completely, merging with it, taking it in and letting it out again as pure, free-form motion.

She did not notice when the song changed and the tempo became faster, but merely felt the rhythm undulate more quickly, demanding more of her willingness to give herself to it. Gerdes' words intoned in her ears, but she did not hear them as much as she felt their presence. In fact, she was aware of nothing but the transmutation of music into motion that was taking place in her body.

When the music finally stopped, dwindling away like a whisper on the wind, Yarden felt her limbs slow and sag and knew the dance was over. She stood motionless for a moment and savored the warmth the exercise had generated. Exhaustion and exultation mingled, producing in her a pleasure close to ecstasy.

She opened her eyes to see Gerdes holding out a cloth to her and watching her with a quizzical expression. Yarden rubbed the soft cloth over her sweating face and neck, not ready yet to break the spell of the moment. Finally she could bear Gerdes' silence no longer; she had to know what her teacher thought of her exercise. "Did I do well?" she asked, somewhat timidly.

Gerdes gazed at her pupil intently. "That is a question you must answer for yourself, daughter. What does your body tell you?"

Yarden shook her head and felt sweat-damp curls slap against the back of her neck. "I scarcely know. I feel . . . almost dizzy with delight. It's the most wonderful feeling." At that, her words tumbled out in a rush. "Gerdes, I became the song—I was inside the music. I felt it throughout my body, inside me as I was inside it. I've never experienced anything so strange and wonderful."

The older woman gave her an appraising look and led her to a grouping of soft-cushioned chairs. They sat, and Yarden leaned back and felt the delicious looseness of a body totally relaxed. Gerdes said nothing, but continued to watch her student with the same thoughtful, questioning expression on her face.

Yarden sensed sympathically that there was something more than curiosity in her instructor's mind. She sensed something else. Fear? No, not fear, but close. Awe. This puzzled Yarden. She would have pursued the matter using her sympathic abilities—Gerdes would likely be compatible—but refrained. She did not want to know anything her teacher did not choose to say to her directly. Still, she could not help sensing the force of Gerdes' mental and emotional reaction.

The two sat for a long time until Gerdes finally arrived at what she wanted to say. Looking at Yarden directly, she placed her hands together and began, saying, "We are all given gifts freely from the hand of the All-Gracious Giver, who gives to all as He will. In my years I have seen many whose gifts shine bright as sunstone within them—and many of lesser endowment whose best efforts are nevertheless worthy enough to adorn the Preceptor's palace.

"Though I've seen gifts great and small in the most unlikely places, I've never seen any like yours. You, my daughter, are the bearer of a rare and special gift."

"Are you certain?" asked Yarden. The Fieri woman's words filled her with a mixture of apprehension and delight.

"Perhaps I was wrong about you becoming a dancer," intoned Gerdes, speaking mostly to herself. "I believe you have the ability and could be trained. But dance, I think, would use only part of the gift. There is something deeper there—I could see it when you forgot yourself and entered into the music. I could see it, but I don't know what it is."

"I felt it, too," replied Yarden. "I've felt it before, but never as strongly as I felt it today. I can't describe how it was, but I seem to have stepped outside myself. I was not conscious of what I was doing—each movement flowed through me, dictated from some other, greater source." She smiled suddenly. "Oh, Gerdes, it felt so good, so free and pure."

Gerdes nodded thoughtfully. "Yes, that is the body responding to the inner gift. The body knows how to move—it's made for movement after all. We have no need to teach it what it already knows."

"Liberating the body to do what it knows how to do—is that it?"

"Yes," agreed Gerdes. "You learn quickly."

Yarden jumped up. "I want to do it again. Please? Right now. I don't want to forget the feeling. I want to remember exactly how I did it."

"Very well," said Gerdes, rising slowly and making her way to the panel on the wall. "Ready yourself."

In a moment the music drifted into the room and Yarden, poised, ready to receive it, heard the first wispy notes and began to sway, guiding herself into the music and away from the critical awareness of her movements. It was easier this time, now that she knew what she was attempting. In no time at all she had entered into that state where her mind soared up through the dreamy, many-toned layers of sound, leaving her body free to respond in its own way.

The session left Yarden exhausted, but flushed with triumph and eager for her next lesson. "Thank you, Gerdes," she said, a little reluctant to leave. "I intend to practice every moment until I return. To think I had this—this wonderful gift inside me all this time and never knew it. I'll never be able to thank you enough for showing it to me."

"Your joy is thanks enough," Gerdes replied. "But you must not think that it will always be so easy. We have much hard work ahead of us, and yes, some pain as well. Tears are as much a part of creation as joy."

"I know that, Gerdes."

The older woman shook her head gently. "No, you don't. But it's all right. We will take it as it comes. Good-bye now."

Yarden said good-bye and walked home, luxuriating in the deep, warm, languorous feeling of physical exhaustion and the knowledge that her special gift had only begun to be explored. There were much finer things awaiting her, she knew; she thrilled to think what they might be.

NINETEEN

It seemed to Treet that he floated in space wrapped in cloud-soft vapors that curled around him, enveloping him and bearing him through endless corridors of darkness. He had floated this way from time immemorial, eternally traveling, yet never really going anywhere at all.

This celestial voyage was perpetually interrupted by vivid hallucinations: the one where he became trapped inside his own heart was a favorite torment, but there were others equally grotesque and frightening. One of them concerned being swallowed by a great transparent eel and enduring a living death inside its hideous stomach. Another saw him entombed inside a coffin-sized slab of crystal, frozen forever, unable to move or cry out, while all around him people moved and lived and breathed, oblivious to his torture.

In his lucid moments, Treet still knew himself to be suspended by wires in a tank of buoyant liquid, undergoing the process of conditioning. He knew this and told himself over and over in what had become for him a litany: *I will survive. . . I will survive . . . I will survive . . . I will . . . survive . . .*

But the periods of lucidity were shrinking, and the boundaries between consciousness and the nightmare region grew ever more amorphous. And his litany of resolve sounded more like naive optimism, cheap and mocking in his own ears.

Still, he would not give in to the creeping despair he could feel gathering around him, and instead continued to fight for his clarity of mind. Yet, to give himself over to the insanity of his weird visions would be far easier than constantly maintaining such a scrupulously tight rein on his mental processes. What did it matter whether he thought he was inside a giant eel? What did it matter what he thought about anything? He was never going to leave the tank with his head intact. In many ways it would be easier on him to simply give in, accept whatever insanity presented itself, and be done with it. Then at least he'd be released. The longer he held out, the longer he'd remain in the conditioning tank and the longer the torture would continue. Better to give in and regain freedom as quickly as possible.

A lesser man would have given in, as untold hundreds of Hladik's victims had. Here, however, Treet's innate stubbornness and frugality came to his aid. As a man who had lived the better part of a century with little more than the price of the next meal in his pocket at any one time, he simply could not allow himself to give up anything that had taken so much precious effort to accumulate in the first place. His mental acuity was a hard-won possession, arrived at only after years of painful and painstaking effort. It was, Treet had learned during the course of his life, no small achievement to be completely sane.

Mental clarity required such tremendous expenditures of discipline, vigilance, and perseverance that Treet was awed to think he had succeeded where so many, many others had utterly failed. He did not fault those who had failed. Theirs was a fate he had come too close to sharing for him to find any wide margin of comfort in his success.

But little by little, despite Treet's heroic efforts, the machinery of the conditioning tank worked on its victim. He found his sane moments fewer and more tenuous and the hallucinations fiercer, more frequent, relentless. He felt his grip on reality eroding bit by bit; the plunge could not be far off.

Nevertheless, striving to hold off the inevitable a little longer, Treet undertook yet another of his experiments in sympathic communication. Thus far these efforts had produced nothing of benefit, save giving him something to do. As he had done many times before, he began by sending his thoughts like hands outstretched, feeling, like radar waves spreading out, searching.

Only this time, instead of his mental radar streaming out into the endless void, something came back. Like the echoed ping of sonar bouncing back from a solid object, Treet sensed something moving at the farthest edge of his awareness. Something massive. He felt like one of those oceanic divers who, in the cold, dark depths of an arctic sea, feels the turbulence of the giant humpback's flukes as the creature glides silently, invisibly past.

The contact shocked Treet so much, his fragile concentration shattered. What was that? Another hallucination? Had he begun hallucinating that he was lucid and receiving impulses from his mental experiments? Or had it really happened?

Cautiously, Treet flung out his mental net once again. He caught nothing, so forced himself to concentrate, to stretch the

strands to the utmost. The effort was taxing; the hair-fine filaments of consciousness trembled with exhaustion. He was about
to collapse the tenuous net when he felt the mysterious shudder
again, and stronger this time.

There was no mistake. He was not imagining it. It was
there.

A presence, an intelligence that was not his own, hovered
nearby, watching him, regarding him with keen interest, dwarf-
ing him like the whale dwarfs the deep sea diver. Yet, he had
nothing to fear from the leviathan his net had snagged. This he
sensed intuitively even as his net shrank reflexively from the
contact. Whatever he had attracted with his feeble efforts meant
him no harm. That much came through instantaneously.

Treet attempted another probe, but could not sustain the
effort and withdrew to puzzle over his surprising discovery.
There was something out there—he had imagined his mental
universe as space, infinite and empty . . . until now. Now, there
was a presence lurking out there on the rim of his imagined
universe. Something or someone.

Could it be Yarden? Treet wondered. He dismissed the
possibility at once. Yarden, he reasoned, would feel familiar to
him somehow. Her presence would be colored by her personality, and he would know her. This thing, this entity was no one
he knew. Perhaps it wasn't even human. Perhaps it was something entirely indigenous to Empyrion, an alien intelligence
drawn by his puny experiments. Of course, it could easily have
nothing at all to do with Empyrion—a being of pure mental
energy inhabiting a separate plane of existence, perhaps.

The possibilities were endless. He simply did not have
enough information to know what he was dealing with, and
until he did it was useless to speculate. So Treet put the matter
aside for the time being and determined to rest up for another
attempt at contact later. He wanted his next effort to be his
best. He did not know if he'd have another chance.

· · · · · ·

The Nilokerus glanced up quickly from his work as his
superior came in. He stiffened and made a hasty salute. "Forgive
me, Director, you were not announced."

"Does order and efficiency exist only when I am announced?" The scowl on Hladik's face made it clear that no answer would be sufficient and none was wanted. The Hageman kept his mouth wisely shut. "Where's Fertig? I want him."

The Nilokerus glanced around the stone-cut room quickly, as if the Subdirector might be found crouching in one of the corners. "He has not been seen, Director."

"Find him. I want to see the new prisoner. Where is he?"

"Skank—"

Hladik turned abruptly and started for the conditioning chamber. "Find Fertig and send him to me. I want to see him immediately," he called over his shoulder as he marched into the narrow corridor of cells leading to the room where the conditioning tanks were kept. It had been a sour day for the Nilokerus Director, a day for distractions and irritations. He had the uneasy feeling that things were imperceptibly going wrong, that his authority was crumbling under his feet and he could not see it. He'd soon put it right, however.

He'd crack a few skulls to demonstrate his displeasure, and soon his organization would be back to normal. It was all this business of Rohee's death and Jamrog's funereal spectacle that had made everything lax. A demonstration was needed. Fertig would make a good example. Where was the man? He'd been noticeably scarce since—well, since the Fieri escape. That long ago?

Hladik snorted. Fertig would have some explaining to do. Perhaps it was time to designate a new Subdirector. Yes, that might do. Fertig's demise would serve as a handsome warning to any Nilokerus tempted to slough their duties or allow zeal to flag.

He arrived at the conditioning chamber and entered. The room was dimly lit, the only illumination coming from the tank itself, which had two bodies suspended in it. Strange thought Hladik, I was aware of only one prisoner. Where had the other come from? What is going on here?

He spun on his heel. "Skank!" he shouted in his best outraged Director's tone. "Present yourself! Skank!"

His summons was rewarded by a shuffling sound from the adjoining room as the lumpy bulk of Skank came lumbering into view. The man gave Hladik a look of frank disapproval, which the Director ignored as he did the stench of the place. "Where have you been?" Skank opened his mouth to answer, but Hladik threw a hand toward the tank. "Why are there two prisoners in the tank? I come to see one and find two. Under whose order was this done?"

Skank peered at his leader with open contempt, spat on the floor, and said, "Two, did you say?"

"Yes, two! Are you blind as well as stupid? Look!" Hladik whirled around and gestured at the tank and at the single figure floating there. Stunned, he sputtered in protest. "Th-there were two just now. I saw them clearly with my own eyes. Two men in the tank. I saw them."

Skank spat and shrugged. "There's but one now."

The Director clenched his fists and would have struck the insolent Skank, but remembered what he'd come to do. "Yes, there is but one now. I want a report."

"The prisoner is as you see."

"His mental status?"

"Heavy alpha and beta activity. This one has stamina, Director. He resists with force."

"Then increase the stimulus. I want him broken."

Skank rolled a foul eye at his master. "My orders were to keep him undamaged."

"I give the orders, Skank. Do as you are told, or I will find someone who will." Hladik stepped close to the tank and peered at the captive suspended motionless inside. Was there something familiar about this one? Hard to tell—they all looked alike after a while.

He turned away. "Send word as soon as he is ready to receive the theta key." He fixed Skank with an ominous stare and marched from the stinking chamber, pausing to steal a final glance at the tank. Strange, he thought, I distinctly saw two.

TWENTY

Fertig stole a last look around his kraam. Had he forgotten anything? No, he had checked and checked again. He had all he could take with him in the bundle beneath his yos. It was time to go. Now. Before he was missed, before Hladik sent Invisibles to find him.

The day the Fieri had escaped, Fertig had chosen his course. To save his life he had only one hope: making his way to the Old Section to join the Dhogs—if they would have him. To help persuade the Dhogs that he was a valuable asset, Fertig had spent the last weeks searching for information of likely use to the nonbeings. Now, armed with an assortment of facts—enough, he hoped, to buy himself a place among them—Fertig was ready to depart.

Hladik had not mentioned the Fieri debacle since that day, but Fertig knew the Hage Leader had not forgotten. The Subdirector had time and time again seen Hladik pull out from his formidable memory long lists of past transgressions to indict a victim. Fertig knew Hladik had not forgotten his presence in the room the day he and Jamrog had ordered the Mors Ultima to strike another Director. And he knew it was only a matter of time before his role in the escape of the Fieri was discovered and his death warrant issued.

He had considered joining Tvrdy, but contacting the Tanais Director was too risky. Jamrog now had Invisibles seeded throughout Hage Tanais, and Tvrdy was under closest observation. Fertig strongly doubted he could reach Tvrdy without being recognized and reported the moment he set foot on Tanais soil. Besides, time was running out for Tvrdy too. Jamrog was closing for the kill. Thus, the only path left Fertig led to the Old Section.

Desperate as he was, Fertig found no comfort in the prospect of joining the Dhogs. If even a fraction of the tales were true, life among them was certain to be raw misery. But Fertig feared death more than discomfort—and death was certain if he stayed. Already Jamrog's instability was manifest for anyone with eyes to see it. Empyrion was spinning into a chaos of blood and destruction. Who would be left alive when the smoke cleared?

The Nilokerus Subdirector walked to the unidor, put his hand on the switchplate, and stared at the open portal as if it were the gate into the netherworld, which in a way it was. He shifted the bundle beneath his yos, took a deep breath, and departed.

• • • • • •

The first word back from the men he'd sent to Giloon Bogney put Tvrdy in a better frame of mind than he'd been in for many days. The message had come during the night: contact successful . . . Dhogs well organized . . . cooperation complete . . . ready for supplies . . . send second contingent . . . more weapons needed . . .

Tvrdy read the decoded message once more, wadded the flimsy sheet into a tight ball, swallowed it, and smiled. The men he'd sent to the Old Section had made it. Giloon had lived up to his word. Here was a glimmer of hope at last: a most remote chance, but a chance nonetheless, that Jamrog could be stopped. He was not fooling himself; there was a staggering amount of work to be done before Jamrog could even be challenged, let alone unseated, but now at least there was a place to stand. That's all Tvrdy needed.

"Is anything wrong, Director?" Danelka, Tvrdy's industrious Subdirector, watched his leader casually.

"No, nothing." Tvrdy glanced up quickly. How long had the man been standing there? He cringed from the thought; it was unworthy. That's what came of suspecting everyone. Danelka was one of Tvrdy's five most trusted Hagemen, a man of unquestioned loyalty. "I want you to call them now. It is time."

"Of course. Is that all?"

"For the moment."

The man left to carry out his errand, and Tvrdy dropped into a chair. He had put off the decision long enough. It had to be today, while he could still control the circumstances of his decision. He would go on his own terms, and not on Jamrog's. Danelka would become Director, and one of the four underdirectors must be chosen to take Danelka's place as Subdirector. Over the years Tvrdy had groomed his men carefully; he knew each one and knew there was not a traitor among them. But now one must be raised over the others to a position of utmost sensitivity. The future of Empyrion might well depend on the choice. Which one would it be?

Within minutes, the first of the candidates had arrived. When all were assembled, he joined them, meeting their eager glances with keen appraisal. "You will have guessed, I think, why you are here," Tvrdy began.

Some of the men nodded; all stood mute and tense. The chance of a lifetime had come. To be advanced to the position of Subdirector meant high Hage stent—almost the highest. The tension was almost more than they could bear. "I won't waste words," the Director was saying. Had he already chosen then?

"I am leaving. Danelka will become acting Director. Which one of you will serve him?" The underdirectors looked levelly ahead. No one answered.

"You see how it is," Tvrdy gently intoned. He stood slowly. "This is one decision I will not make. It might be well for Danelka to choose, but as the one chosen will come under Jamrog's intense scrutiny. . ." He looked at them and spread his hands. "*You* will decide who it is to be." The underdirectors appeared shocked, so Tvrdy repeated himself. "You will choose among yourselves which it is to be. That way, you will all be satisfied with the choice."

The foremost of the candidates, a young man named Egrem, spoke up. "How will we choose, Director?"

"That is up to you. Decide however you like, but I must have an answer today. Any other questions?"

The underdirectors made no reply. Several glanced sideways at their companions as Tvrdy turned and left the room, saying, "I will be waiting in my kraam. Bring me your answer."

The Tanais Director was resting on his suspension bed when the signal sounded from the terminal across the room. He got up and stabbed a lighted tab, allowing the lift to come up from below. He went to greet the new Subdirector and was surprised to find all four tumbling out of the small lift.

"Well?" he asked when they had assembled themselves.

Illim stepped forward. "But if it pleases you, Director, I wish to make an explanation."

"Yes?"

"We have a condition among us, Director."

"Which means you require my assent."

"Yes."

"What is the condition?"

"We have agreed that the one chosen must forfeit—" The assistant halted, unable to make himself say the rest.

But Tvrdy had already surmised the agreement. "Will forfeit any claim to a possible future Directorship should Danelka and I be killed—is that it?"

Illim nodded.

Tvrdy smiled to himself. Yes, it was an admirable solution. That way the one chosen would not diminish the others' chances. They could still serve with hope in their hearts, and the chosen one would not have to fear their ambition. It was a solution worthy of the Tanais. Tvrdy made a show of turning the idea over in his mind before answering.

At last he said, "Am I to understand that the one chosen to serve the Hage is the one with the least ambition among you?"

The underdirectors looked abashed at the suggestion. Egrem said, "Send us all away if you think that, Director."

Tvrdy smiled and allowed his underlings to see his pleasure. "No, it is well done. I was right in trusting you. It was a hard decision. No one knows that better than I." He paused, then snapped back to business once more. "All right, I agree to the condition. Illim, present yourself." Illim stepped forward solemnly. "Illim will become Subdirector, but will forfeit his chance at a Director's kraam in the future. It is done."

"I will serve the Hage well, Hage Leader."

"I do not doubt it, Illim," said Tvrdy. "As for the rest of you, I have given Danelka orders to increase your poak by eighty shares each. Your loyalty is to be rewarded." The underdirectors could not conceal their happiness at this news. Eighty shares! They'd be almost as rich as magicians.

Tvrdy brought them quickly back to reality. "You will earn your increase, Hagemen. The lines of force are drawn. Already Jamrog plots against the Threl. I believe he will attempt to have each Director removed. If he cannot do it outright by assassination—as he did with Sirin Rohee—he will work among those closest to the Director. Make no mistake—he will try to turn you to his side."

The underdirectors darted defiance from their glances, but Tvrdy continued. "He will promise you wealth and power in exchange for treachery. He will make it easy for you to accept, impossible for you to refuse. But you must be strong. Do not believe his lies, and do not give in to him.

"Our only hope of survival is to remain steadfast. Report any contacts to Danelka at once. We must be strong or Jamrog will not be stopped.

"For your own protection," Tvrdy continued, "you will not know where I have gone, or when. Only Danelka has been briefed. He is to be the only contact between the Hage and myself from now on. He will pass only the information I instruct him to share with you. This also is for your protection."

The underdirectors had never heard their leader speak this way; certainly he had never addressed them so candidly. They were flattered, gratified by his confidence in them, and left pledging their strength and loyalty to Tvrdy, to the Hage, and to one another.

TWENTY
ONE

Hladik pushed away his hagemate's hand, but the tickling sensation that had roused him from sleep did not stop. "Enough," he muttered thickly. "No more tonight. Go to sleep."

Still the tickling continued. He opened his eyes. It was dark in the sleep chamber, but he sensed someone else in the room. "Who is it?" he said softly. "Who's there? Bremot?"

He put his hand out and touched the lamp next to the suspension bed. The globe came on, glowing softly. Hladik's eyes went wide with horror as he saw the bloody pool thickening beneath his hagemate's body. Her eyes stared emptily upward, a thin red line sliced across her lovely white throat.

There was a movement at the foot of the bed, and a figure emerged from the shadow. "Mrukk!" Hladik moved to get up. "What have you done?"

The assassin moved close, the blade glittering darkly in his hand. "You will approve, Director. I am removing a traitor from our midst."

"What do you mean?" He threw a frightened glance at his bed partner. "She—"

"Not her, Director . . . you!" Mrukk's eyes glinted as they narrowed to evil slits.

Hladik struggled to get up. Only then did he notice the dark stain spreading across his own bedclothes. The tickle that had awakened him had suddenly become a fiery burn. With a strangled cry he threw back the thin sheet and stared in disbelief at the deep cleft running from pubic bone to sternum. "Jam—rog-g . . ." he gasped, the name gurgling in his throat.

The Nilokerus Director clutched at his stomach, and lurched to his feet; he staggered two steps before his strength gave out, and collapsed at his assassin's feet. Mrukk's lips drew back in a sneer as he stooped to wipe his blade in his victim's hair; he had expected more courage from his former superior. Hladik moaned weakly as his limbs convulsed in death spasms.

"Jamrog, yes. Your benefactor, Director. I'll tell him you

thought to thank him for his last gift." Mrukk gave the body a shove with his toe. The mass of flesh jiggled and lay still. Replacing the knife in its sheath beneath his black yos, Mrukk stepped over the body of Hladik's guide and stole from the kraam, silent as the dead he left behind.

· · · · · ·

The last few days had been a happy blur to Pizzle—his daylight hours filled with pleasant, if exhausting, labor as he worked side-by-side with the Fieri readying the ships that would make the long trip to the Bay of Talking Fish. By night he and Starla met to be together and share the details of their day. Neither mentioned marriage again, much to Pizzle's relief. Apparently Starla had forgotten that the word ever passed between them—which was exactly what he had hoped would happen.

There was so much to be done before they could set out on the journey. Pizzle had been intrigued by the notion of talking fish, and volunteered immediately when Jaire's brother, Preben, had told him about it. "Come with us," Preben invited. "It is an experience never forgotten."

"Gee, I'd like to," replied Pizzle. "Could I? You'd really let me?"

"Certainly," laughed Preben. Pizzle's eagerness was so childlike. "Anyone may go who cares to. Many hundreds will make the journey. And as I am to command one of the ships, you can travel with me."

"Great!" shouted Pizzle. "This is fantastic! Wait till Starla hears about this . . . How soon do we leave? Can I do anything? Do they really talk?"

"We will leave within a month, before the beginning of the next solar period."

Pizzle counted the days on his fingers. Based on what he was learning about Fieri timekeeping it worked out to—"That's less than three weeks away."

"The Preceptor will choose the appropriate day. We must be ready to leave at her signal. And since you ask, you *can* help me. I want our ship to be among the first. The Preceptor may choose ours to carry her, which would be a great honor."

So Pizzle had thrown himself into the preparations, helping

Preben's crew gather and stow supplies, scrape and repaint the ship top to bottom, check lifesaving gear, and freshen every one of the several dozen sleeping compartments below the wide, flat deck. The days sped by, each full of activity and anticipation.

One evening Pizzle went to meet Starla at their prearranged rendezvous—a secluded hill overlooking a cove on the shore of Prindahl. The sun still lit the twilight sky, though the first stars had emerged to take their places in the cloud-spattered heavens. He arrived early and waited, stretched out on the grassy turf, breathing the night air fresh off the great, dark water soughing gently on the shore below.

This is paradise, thought Pizzle idly. He had never been more happy, more satisfied, more at peace with himself. He wanted nothing else but for life to go on and on and on just the way it was. If only it could last forever. The Fieri actually believed that it would go on forever, that the Infinite Father had made them for eternity.

It was a notion Pizzle had always found quaint and somewhat ridiculous before. Now he saw it as profound wisdom. This kind of life, this heaven, made sense. For the first time in his life, he had begun to suspect that one lifetime may not be enough.

Then, quite without warning, a swift and poignant sadness rushed over him and he began to weep. Big, salty tears rolled from his eyes.

It would end. His life would end. He would die one day and it would be over, finished, no more. He would leave Starla behind and descend into dissolution and dust. And that would be that. Death at this tender moment seemed bitterly cruel and perverse, an outrage. To take away all this . . . this happiness, to be cut off so suddenly, so completely and finally was, Pizzle now considered, a monstrous and tragic injustice.

He lay on his back, staring blindly at the sky as the tears slid quietly down his cheeks. Starla found him that way. He heard her approach and sat up quickly, blotting his eyes with the heels of his hands. "What's wrong, my love?" she asked, settling down beside him.

He felt her cool hands on his face and produced a bleary-eyed smile for her benefit. "Nothing," he said. "I—uh, just got a little wrapped up in something I was thinking."

"Sad thoughts?"

"Not particularly." He tried to laugh. "No, not sad." He drew a long shaky breath and fell silent as he turned and gazed out on the water.

"What was it? Tell me, Asquith. I want to know." Starla's hand found his and clasped it warmly.

The nearness of her, the love and warmth that flowed from her to him, he found, in his present frame of mind, unbearable. The tears began again. He bent his head and let them fall.

"Darling . . ." Starla gathered him in her arms. "What is it?"

It was a long time before Pizzle could speak. At last he sat up and wiped his face on his sleeve. "I'm sorry," he said, "I'm not handling this very well. It's just that you're the most beautiful woman I've ever known. I don't deserve to be with—I don't deserve you."

"Shhh, don't talk so—" she began.

"It's true. I'm nothing—less than nothing. If you had known me on Earth, you wouldn't've given me the time of day. Please. Don't say anything," he said and looked away quickly again. "But by some miracle I'm here. I accept that. It's a dream. I know I don't deserve any of this, but here I am and I love it. I love you, I love Fierra, I love my life.

"I know this probably sounds dopey to you, but for the first time in my life I love my life."

He was silent for a moment, then sniffed and continued. "This—" He waved a hand to take in all Empyrion. "All this just overwhelmed me is all. I know it can't last, but . . . you don't know how much I wish it *could* last."

"It *will* last," said Starla softly. "It will last forever."

"I wish I could believe that."

"Believe it, Asquith. It's true."

"Yeah."

"Why do you doubt?"

Pizzle lifted his shoulders heavily. "You don't know how much I'd like to believe." He sighed heavily. "If I thought it could be true . . ."

"What you felt tonight was the voice of the Searcher calling you to Him, as He calls each of us. The Gatherer is reaching out for you, Asquith. Go to Him. Accept Him."

"I wish I could," Pizzle said sincerely. "There's just so much I have to sort out first."

"I understand," Starla said and snuggled closer. They talked of the approaching journey and the preparations to be made. Then they grew silent and simply drank in one another's company. At last they rose and made their way back down to their waiting evees, kissed good-night, and parted. The melancholy which lay heavily on Pizzle's heart stayed with him through the night. He went to his room at Liamoge and sat staring out at the deep, star-flecked water for a long time before slipping off into a light, restless sleep.

"Hladik's ashes and those of his hagemate will be entombed in the Hall of Directors in Nilokerus Hage," Jamrog said stiffly. His expression was bland and unreadable; his eyes shifted continually around the ring of Directors. The Threl took the news of Hladik's death in shocked silence. There was not a man among them who believed Jamrog's story of the incident. But the Supreme Director pushed the charade further, saying, "Subdirector Fertig will be apprehended. Even now the Invisibles are closing on his trail. He will face justice, Hage Leaders. This abominable deed will not go long unpunished, I can assure you."

Threl High Chambers were silent; each Director had understood Jamrog's implicit message: do not interfere with my plans or you will suffer the same fate as Hladik.

Into this tense silence came the tapping of a bhuj on the floor. "You wish to offer condolences, Rumon?" asked Jamrog sweetly.

"Condolences, yes," said Cejka. "But I would also ask the other members of the Threl to note our leader's remarkable fortitude in the face of this unimaginable tragedy. Hladik was, I believe, your closest friend and ally, was he not?"

There was nothing but innocence in Cejka's tone. Still, Jamrog watched him suspiciously, his eyes flicking between Tvrdy and Cejka. "It is true, I am deeply grieved by Director Hladik's unfortunate death," said Jamrog. "He was my friend and the ally of us all. To be sure, we will all feel the loss."

"Most unfortunate," agreed Chryse Director Dey. "I am saddened and outraged."

"As are we all," put in Bouc, offering a doleful smile of sympathy.

"Murder," said Tvrdy sternly, "is always a cause for outrage."

There were murmurs of assent all around. "May I suggest that Subdirector Fertig stand before the Threl and answer for his crimes?" added Cejka. "I, for one, would hear his confession from his own lips."

The others tapped their bhujes on the floor in agreement.

"Thank you, Directors, for your concern and sympathy," said Jamrog tersely. "I will give the order that Fertig is not to be harmed. He will be made to stand before this body and give his confession." He stood abruptly and slammed his bhuj down. "This emergency assembly is dismissed. I am in mourning."

With that Jamrog fled the chambers, his face set in a fierce scowl. When he had gone, the others left quietly, avoiding one another's eyes. Tvrdy passed a secret signal to Cejka as they filed from the room. They met a little while later in one of the disused corridors of the Threl meeting place.

"That was a dangerous game you were playing," said Tvrdy once their guides were positioned to afford them privacy. "Why did you do it?"

"The monster!" Cejka blurted. "I could not sit there and hear him speak his lies any longer. I wanted the others to know I did not fear him."

"You would risk all our work for a show of bravado? Everyone knows what happened last night."

"Bouc and Dey—they make my stomach turn. Did you see them? Even after what happened to Hladik, they still try to worm their way into Jamrog's confidence." Cejka made a face of gross distaste.

"Forget them; they have chosen their destruction. I have news."

"Bogney?"

Tvrdy nodded. "He has lived up to his word."

"Amazing."

"We are to send more men and supplies as soon as possible. When can you be ready?"

Cejka smiled. "I am ready now. They will leave tonight."

"Good. I am ready, too. The sooner we join them, the better." Tvrdy looked at the Tanais bhuj in his hand. "The day has come when it is too dangerous to hold one of these." He let the ceremonial weapon clatter to the floor where it lay among broken bits of tile.

"You think there will be a Purge?"

"Cejka, open your eyes. The Purge has begun!"

• • • • • •

The machinery ground into operation, and the wires suspending Treet in the conditioning tank tightened. Skank watched as the body was slowly lifted, adjusting the levers to swing it over the tank's rim and drop it to the floor where it lay limp in a puddle of reeking fluid.

"Unstrap him," said the Nilokerus officer, pointing at the unmoving body. "Get him out of here."

"Unstrap him yourself," replied Skank, spitting on the floor. "I received no such order."

"Hladik is dead. Killed in his sleep last night by Subdirector Fertig. Now I am responsible for Cavern level, and I will not answer for this."

"And I received no order for his release!"

"Shut up! Don't you understand? There is no Threl authorization. This was another of Hladik's secrets. Who knows what the Director intended? There will be a new Hage Leader selected soon. What if the new Director finds out I kept one of Hladik's experiments? How am I to explain? What if the Threl finds out? I would be held responsible, and I will not sacrifice myself for Hladik's memory."

"Ahh," said Skank, winking slyly, "what if they find out you released him?"

"With Hladik's death he disappears. That's all I know."

Skank spat. "Take him then. I never saw him." He turned and lumbered away.

The Nilokerus stood looking at the huddled mass of inert flesh before him, then stooped and began tugging at the straps and wires, freeing Hladik's last captive.

· · · · · ·

Treet felt nothing. No sensation of movement signaled his release. Cut off from all external stimulation, his senses had long ago ceased to function, his muscles to respond. In his mind he floated, drifting on endless waves or through endless corridors of empty space.

The fearful hallucinations had diminished along with his own dwindling consciousness. Until the last, he had kept up his effort to contact the alien intelligence he had attracted with his mental experiments. Each time he tried, the contact was strong-

er than the last. Although no thoughts were exchanged directly, Treet had the distinct impression that the entity allowed itself
to be brought nearer, revealed more of itself to him. Treet had
begun to suspect that in some way the mysterious presence had
initiated the contact in the first place.

Treet's concentration waned as his mental energies depleted
themselves. He lapsed into unconsciousness for longer periods,
emerging only with great effort. The last time he regained awareness, the presence had been there with him, waiting for him.
Treet had wanted very much to reach out to the entity—he
sensed it was somehow very close to him—but it was all he
could do to keep from sliding back into oblivion.

So he had merely held himself out to it, allowing the entity
to behold him in whatever way it could. Here I am, Treet
thought. I'm yours. To Treet's amazement, the presence had
entered his mental space—simply merging with his awareness,
but without violating him in any way. The effect was intensely
comforting to Treet, who could not have prevented such an
invasion in any case.

The exhilaration Treet felt when the entity entered his consciousness was electric. It inundated him, swallowed him, overwhelmed him like a tidal wave washing over a pebble on a storm-
tossed beach. Even so, he sensed that the entity was holding back
so that he would not receive the full force of the contact.

Treet accepted this and derived comfort from it, though he
did not try to understand. There was something there with him,
close to him, comforting him—that's all he understood. That,
and that this entity was many times more immense than he
could imagine.

These had been among Orion Treet's last conscious
thoughts. Soon after the contact he had slipped into unconsciousness—though not before he had received a very strong
sensation of calmness and assurance from the alien intelligence,
a sensation designed to tell him that there was nothing to fear—
a strange concept to communicate since there were certainly any
number of things to fear, and with more than ample reason.

Treet accepted this offered assurance in the same way that
he accepted the fact of the alien entity's existence—simply and
without question. He did not have the strength for questions.

Treet had succumbed then, and the clouds he had labored
to hold off descended, covered him, and bore him away.

S ome time later, Treet became aware of a pressure on his chest and, of all places, his left cheek. He put up with the annoyance as long as he could and then squirmed. The shock of his hand smacking against a solid surface sent spasms rippling through his long-neglected muscles. The seizure left him exhausted, but simply aware that his environment had been altered; it now had hard surfaces.

This discovery roused Treet slightly. Light streamed into his brain, and he realized his eyes were open. He could see! The hideous wax mask was gone, and he could see. The pressure in his lungs reminded him that he could also breathe. He took a breath and immediately choked. Green liquid came gushing out of his nose and mouth. He vomited the vile stuff, aspirated it, and choked again.

When his lungs and stomach were finally empty, he drew a ragged breath and felt the cool air sear like a firebrand into the tissues. The pain brought him around. He perceived himself to be lying on the floor of one of the cells, more dead than alive. But alive nonetheless.

For that he was thankful, though he still wondered a little ungratefully what his next torture would be. Not eager to find out, Treet closed his eyes again and devoted himself to the luxury of sleep—a luxury soon interrupted by the arrival of a Nilokerus guard with a harsh voice that boomed in his sensory-deprived brain like the report of a cannon.

Throwing his hands over his ears, Treet writhed on the floor, then felt hands on him, lifting him, jerking him roughly upright.

"Get these on," the guard said, shoving a bundle at him. Treet's eyes fluttered in his head, and his skull vibrated with the noise of the guard's proximity. The room bucked and swayed. "Make it quick if you want to get out of here."

Treet could make no sense of the words. The man's mouth moved, his voice grated inside Treet's brain, but the words were gibberish.

The guard stared at Treet and then turned around and

stomped out. Treet staggered back, collapsed against the wall of his cell, and slid to the floor, still clutching the package that had been thrust into his hands.

Moments later the guard came back with another dressed in the red and white of the Nilokerus. "We'll have to dress him. He doesn't know where he is," the first explained.

"Can he walk?" asked his companion doubtfully.

"No, we'll have to drag him."

"Why can't we just leave him here?"

"Uri wants him gone right away. You heard about Hladik?"

The other said nothing, but frowned and nodded.

"That's why we've got to get rid of him."

"What'll we do with him?"

"I've got an idea. You'll see."

They pulled the yos over Treet's head and stuffed his legs into the trousers. "I'll get an em—it will be quicker that way," said the first guard. "Wait here."

The Nilokerus looked at Treet distastefully, as if he were a hunk of meat that had spoiled. Treet closed his eyes again and tried to marshal his meager resources. If only they would leave me alone, he thought, and recognized that it was a coherent thought. The brain cells were starting to warm up again.

A few minutes later the other guard was back, and Treet was pulled up and slung between them and dragged out into the corridor where he tried to swim to the waiting em, swinging his arms and legs in random order. The Nilokerus barked at him to be still and dumped him in the back of the vehicle.

Treet's next impression was of speeding through a snaking pipeline: rising, twisting, turning, falling, looping around and around and around endlessly until at last they came to a halt. Treet was hauled from the back of the em and dragged across an empty expanse. His head happened to flop back, and he saw stars gleaming through the transparent panes of Dome's crystal roof far above.

He was propelled up a short flight of steps by the guards, who were by now cursing their duty, and at last flung down before an arched doorway. He heard his captors exchange a few mumbled words and then the sound of their footsteps retreating back down the steps and across the empty square. He was left alone, whimpering, limbs quivering, bewildered brain buzzing with sensory overload.

That was how two third-order Nilokerus physicians found him a few hours later.

• • • • • •

The big cat had followed Crocker for several days, padding along on huge, silent paws, a dark, fluid wave in motion. At first this unnerved the man, but he soon grew accustomed to glancing back over his shoulder and seeing the enormous feline creature a few meters behind him on the trail.

After their shared meal, Crocker had slept and then crept away, leaving the wevicat stretched out beside the carcass. When he happened to stop along the trail an hour or so later, he realized he was being followed. It was near sundown, the dense green of the forest was deepening to indigo all around, and the trails were becoming shadowed canyons. The cat was difficult to see, but Crocker knew it was there. His voice told him, *The cat's still back there. Go slowly. It has eaten, so it is not hunting. The creature is just curious.*

Crocker obeyed the voice and went on slowly, pausing now and then to look back, sensing the cat by the prickled hair of his scalp. When he reached his hedge-protected pool, he hesitated. Should he go in? Or find somewhere else to spend the night? A high tree?

Go in, his voice told him. *The wevicat will not follow you.*

The man obeyed and passed through the hedge. He dropped the meat scraps he carried and went down to the pool's edge to drink and wash himself, then returned to where the robot stood, placed his spear in the carrier, and lay down on the spongy turf to sleep.

The next morning, when Crocker left his bower the animal was waiting for him, tail curled around forefeet, great golden eyes gleaming with ferocious curiosity. They stood looking at one another for a long time, Crocker frozen with indecision over the presence of the beast, until his voice rescued him by saying, *The creature means to follow you. Show it that you accept it. It will not harm you.*

Crocker put down his spear and stepped forward. The cat yawned, came to the man, and pressed itself against him, knocking him to the ground. The huge furrowed tongue came out and licked the whole side of Crocker's head in one wet flick. The friendship was sealed. From then on, the wevicat had followed the man more or less continually—sometimes disappearing into the bush for a few hours on errands of its own, but always bounding into view again just when the man thought the beast had finally lost interest and had gone off to seek a new diversion.

The next night the wevicat joined Crocker in his lair, and the following morning they hunted together. They caught another of the slow bush cattle, and though the cat still claimed the kill, it left a slightly better portion for its human companion.

They ate and slept and took their time returning to their shared lair. The day had been sticky and hot, and now, as he neared the hedgewall, the man thought of the pool beyond and remembered how good a swim would feel on his sweaty skin.

Slipping through the hedge, Crocker stowed his spear in the carrier, stripped off the loinpouch, walked to the water's edge, paused to gaze into the cool depths, and dove in. The wevicat heard the splash and jumped to the edge of the pool where it crouched, ready to spring.

Crocker's head broke the surface. He gulped air and let himself slide under the water again. He came up splashing a moment later, shaking himself with pure, animal pleasure. The wevicat took one look at the man's head bobbing in the water and, with a lightning snap of its tail, leaped. The cat's body flashed through the air in a graceful arc and plunged in feet first almost on top of the man.

The next thing Crocker knew he was being hauled bodily out of the pool, his entire right shoulder and much of his right side wedged firmly in the wevicat's mouth. The cat dropped him on the springy turf and stood dripping over him, looking gaunt and skeletal in its sopping coat.

Crocker's round-eyed fright gave way to laughter when—after he'd checked himself to make sure he was not bleeding from several score puncture wounds—he realized the wevicat had not attacked him. Rather, it had rescued him. *It thought you were drowning,* explained the voice. He shuddered involuntarily, thinking about all those razor-tipped teeth piercing his soft flesh. But the animal had been extremely gentle, cradling him as it would one of its own cubs.

He climbed to his feet and looped his arms around the big

cat's neck and pushed against it with all his might. The beast stepped backwards, and they both tumbled into the pool where Crocker began whooping and splashing, kicking up the water and flinging handfuls into the wevicat's face.

The cat growled lightly and slapped out at the man with huge paws, pouncing and rolling, knocking him down or trying to catch him as he dove. Once Crocker climbed on the creature's back, and the wevicat spun in circles trying to dislodge him. Crocker noticed, however, that the animal was careful to keep its ebony claws sheathed.

After their watery rollick, the two dragged themselves from the pool and flopped down on the bank. The air was a thick blanket, causing skin and fur to dry slowly. They lay side by side and listened to the night sounds creep into the evening stillness as the twilight chorus limbered its voice. Some of the sounds Crocker could identify: the eerie, echoing howls belonged to fat flightless birds high in the upper levels of the forest; the gnawing chatters and barks were those of fuzzy tree rats; the gurgling squeaks and coos were tiny, wide-eyed lemurlike primates. The rest of the pips, croaks, hoots, gabbles, snorts, and startling yelps belonged to a large assortment of unseen mammalian throats of various sizes.

Crocker listened to the sounds as he had each night, and for the first time felt totally secure among them. Peace seemed to flow directly from the imperturbable presence of the great cat beside him. A bond had formed between them; they had hunted together, shared meat, and played together. An emptiness he had not even known existed had been filled in the man. He put out his hand and felt the sleek warmth of the beast beside him and stroked it gently; the cat loosed a deep, resonant purr that droned sleepy contentment. Night closed its fist around them, and they slept.

TWENTY
FOUR

Fourteen ships lay at anchor on the glass-smooth sea. Prindahl's mirrored face reflected the long, low hulls of blue and white and green. The sun's first rays stained the early morning sky watery blue. The day was but a promise; yet scores of Fieri already lined the shore, and more streamed down to the water's edge with the approach of dawn.

Yarden was among the first. Having found it impossible to sleep, she and Ianni had come to the shore to await the Preceptor's arrival. They joined those who had held vigil, marking the occasion with laughter and song through the night. The eve of leave-taking was a festive time, a time of keen anticipation and fond remembrance.

Flickering campfires dotted the shoreline, illuminating the ring of excited faces around each one. In between songs and stories, baskets of food were shared to keep up the reveler's strength.

The jovial mood reminded Yarden of Christmases she had known as a youngster, when the house had filled with relatives and friends, and the children had been allowed to stay awake late into the night to welcome the joyous day with gifts and games. This observation made Yarden pensive; it had been a long time since she had thought about her Earth life, a life that was now, quite literally, light-years away.

It was still early when the Preceptor appeared; clothed in her sky-blue travel garb and attended by three Mentors, she greeted her people as she passed slowly among them, accepting their best wishes for the journey. Yarden watched as the regal figure made her way to the foremost of the tethered boats, expecting a ceremony of some sort—a speech perhaps, or a christening. At very least, a prayer offered up for safe passage.

Instead, the Preceptor and her party merely boarded the vessel and took their places on deck. This was a signal to all the others who were waiting to go aboard. Instantly the crowd surged forward, and each of the fourteen ships rocked as their wide decks filled with passengers.

Yarden was swept forward with all the others and found herself standing in shallow water gazing up at a mast pointing skyward, its furled red sails bright against the new sky. Ianni, who had been right beside her only moments before, was nowhere in sight. Fieri clamored around her and called to their friends finding places on deck. She was trapped among a happy host and for a moment feared she would miss boarding altogether.

"Ianni!" she called. "Ianni, where are you?"

A voice sounded above her. "Yarden, what are you doing down there? Are you coming with us?"

She turned and looked up to see Pizzle's elfin grin beaming down at her over the rail. Next to him stood a young woman who smiled prettily. "You're Yarden?" she asked. "One of the Travelers?"

Yarden nodded and said, "I'm looking for my friend, Ianni. We were to board together, but I seem to have taken a wrong turn somewhere."

"Here, hold on," said Pizzle. "I'll get you aboard."

"What about Ianni—" began Yarden, but Pizzle had disappeared already. She sighed and ducked back into the crowd in an attempt to force her way to the gangplank, lost her footing, and fell backward with a splash. She was hauled onto her feet by nearby Fieri, who took her predicament in such good humor that it was difficult for Yarden not to laugh too.

"Now what are you doing?" Pizzle found her squeezing water from her clothes and hair. "Come on." He led her through the throng and pushed her up the gangplank. "What did you say your friend's name was?"

"Ianni," said Yarden. "I'm not sure if this is the boat we're supposed to be on or not . . ."

"Not to worry—I'm sort of second-in-command here, unofficially. I'll find you a place." He dashed back through the press around the gangplank and pulled Yarden along in his wake. People were eager yet considerate despite the excitement, and let them pass.

"We were supposed to meet Gerdes, my teacher, here," Yarden explained as they stepped off the gangplank and onto the deck. "I'll never find them now."

"Your teacher?"

"I'm studying painting. That is, I'm going to start."

"Going to be an artist, huh? Real nice," remarked Pizzle. "Let's talk about it later. I'm helping Preben—he's got command of this boat, and we're second in line. We've got to make ready to cast off."

"Wait! What about Ianni and Gerdes?"

Pizzle darted into the milling throng on deck and called back, "Later—we'll find them later."

Yarden sighed and looked around helplessly, hoping to spot one or the other of her friends. She fluffed her wet clothes and wished she could start the day over.

"Yarden?"

She turned and saw the woman who had been standing next to Pizzle at the rail. "I'm Starla," the stranger said. "Please don't be concerned for your friends. You'll find them."

"But how? I don't see them anywhere. They'll be looking for me."

"They'll find you." The young woman smiled again, and Yarden felt some of the tension leave her.

"I suppose you're right," Yarden admitted, relaxing just a little.

"It's a very long journey. We'll stop often along the way. If they are not on this boat, you'll find them on one of the others."

"Yes, of course." Yarden smiled at her own silliness. "I wasn't thinking. I can join them later." She noticed the young woman studying her intently and grew suddenly self-conscious.

"Forgive my forwardness," said Starla simply. "But you are very beautiful and I—"

Yarden guessed what the young Fieri woman was trying to say. She had encountered it elsewhere. "You are curious about what a female Traveler would look like?"

"Yes. And there is another reason . . ." Starla hesitated and then, when she saw that Yarden really wanted to know, said, "Asquith has said he finds me beautiful—"

"As you are," Yarden assured her.

"And he has described you as a very beautiful woman. I merely wanted to see . . ." She hesitated, glancing up at Yarden from under her long lashes.

"To see his definition? And I must look a sight—standing here dripping all over the deck." To Starla's puzzled look she added, "Never mind, I understand."

"I hope I have not offended you."

Yarden smiled warmly. "How could I be offended? It seems Pizzle has a good eye. We should both feel complimented."

"You are very kind. I can find you some dry clothes."

Just then Pizzle returned. "Hey, you've met. Great! Yarden, I've got it fixed for you. We're a little jammed up—all the ships are full to capacity. But you can share with Starla until you get back in touch with your friends. Okay?"

"Fine. Starla has explained already."

"Come on, let's get a place at the rail. Look—" He cast an eye to the top of the mast where a thin red banner fluttered in the rising breeze. "We're about to cast off. You won't want to miss this."

"What is it?" Yarden followed them to the rail and found a place next to Pizzle.

"It's the send-off. Preben told me about it."

The barge ahead of them had unfurled its great triangular sail of royal blue. It fluttered lightly and then puffed. The boat began to draw slowly away from the shore, turning out into deeper water.

A rippling of fabric sounded above them; Yarden turned to see a crimson sail shaking itself out and filling with the breeze. Then they were gliding away, taking a position behind and a little to one side of the first boat. The third vessel came on in its turn and all the rest, one by one, until all were under sail.

They passed along the shoreline and came to a place where rounded hills tumbled gently to deep water. The boats came close to the steep banks, and Yarden saw that the hills were lined with people. Fieri in small groups scattered over the hills from the heights right down to the water's edge, stood watching them quietly. The passengers aboard the barges fell silent. Yarden felt her pulse quicken with expectation.

Then, as if on signal, the multitude gathered on the hillsides began swaying slowly and singing, lifting their arms and waving. Some had bright squares of cloth which they held aloft in the breeze as they moved. Their song was a simple, rising, falling, melodic chant, sung slowly, over and over, as the hillside host swayed, some with linked arms and others with outspread arms, and all facing the rising sun and the ships moving slowly away.

The Fieri song sounded clear over the still water:

With peace we send
  you on your way;
In peace your journey wend.
Protector lend
  fair wind this day,
And joy to your journey's end.

The words were simple, but together with the plaintive melody—sung over and over in the style of a round, one hillside
starting the tune and the next picking it up and beginning
again when the first reached the end of the stanza, repeated
again and again, from hillside to hillside—altogether it created a
beautifully evocative and moving ceremony: the colorful ships
plying slowly along green-cloaked hills asway with Fieri, faces
bright in the rising sun, singing their loved ones away with a
gentle blessing.

Yarden listened, enchanted by the simple beauty of it,
drinking in every nuance of the experience. When she looked
along the rail, she saw more than a few eyes shining with tears
and noticed her own misting over as well. "It kind of gets to
you," Pizzle sniffed.

The boats slid away from the hills; and although many of
the singers followed along the shore, they were soon out-
distanced and the song faded on the morning wind. "Wonderful," sighed Yarden; she felt as if she were coming out of a
dream. "I wouldn't have missed this for the world."

"These people grow on you," said Pizzle. Yarden noted the
way he stared at Starla when he spoke. "There's no doubt about
it. This is going to be some trip."

• • • • • •

Morning came to the Starwatch level of Nilokerus Hage,
although Treet, in his sense-numbed stupor, did not comprehend
the gray lightening of the great crystal panes above him. He did
understand that the floor he lay upon was cold and hard and
that his body ached in as many places as it was possible for a
human body to hurt.

He had lain here all his life, it seemed. He could not

remember a time when his body had not ached and he had not huddled on the cold stone of a strange doorway. This being the case, he saw little sense in moving. And anyway, moving might make the pain worse.

He drowsed and woke and drowsed again. He dreamed that some Nilokerus guards came and trundled him off to their distant torture chambers, glad for another chance at tormenting him. In his dream he heard the crackle of electricity as they tuned their instruments of torture. Faces drifted in and out of his dream—one face in particular: round and lightly wrinkled, with concern in lively green eyes. A woman's face. How odd.

Treet puzzled over this endlessly. It was to him the riddle of the universe. Why a woman's face? Who was she? Where had she come from? What did she want? Why had she joined his torturers?

There were voices, too. *Rest . . . rest,* they said. *You are safe . . . safe . . . nothing can happen . . . happen . . . to you . . . safe . . . sleep . . . sleep . . .*

There was comfort in these voices, reverberating as they did inside his head. Treet grasped the comfort and hugged it to him. Such solace was difficult to find in this world and must not be shunned. Cast it roughly aside and it might never return.

Treet hung for the longest time lightly suspended between the conscious world and the unconscious, sometimes more in one than the other, but never totally in either. Thoughts came infrequently into his mental never-never land, and those that did were flimsy, awkward things, insubstantial as phantom butter-flies.

He thought about a dark-haired woman with a face made of rain; a great, troubling hole in the ground filled with broken glass; a thundering, yellow sky that burned and burned forever; a man who wore a turtle's shell on his back and hid from the sun. These and other whimsical images floated through his lazy awareness.

Far back in the further recess of his mind throbbed a sense of urgency: a charge had been given him; he had a duty to perform. Time was slipping away. The sense was anesthetized, the urgency dulled. But it was there, a clockwork, muffled and slowed though still ticking . . . ticking . . . ticking.

"Tell me, Mrukk, what did Hladik say when he died?" Jamrog reclined lazily in his chair, features slack, eyes half-lidded from the effects of the flash he'd been sampling all day. His hagerobe was carelessly draped over his lean frame. A young woman heated souile in an enameled jar over a small brazier.

The chief of the Mors Ultima studied the Supreme Director carefully, wondering, not for the first time, what kind of man his master was. Certainly he showed little of the restraint or discipline that had helped propel him into the Supreme Director's kraam; he had given in to his vices so quickly. That showed weakness. Mrukk detested weakness in any form.

"He invoked your name, Hage Leader," replied Mrukk.

"How considerate," smirked Jamrog. "To think of me at the moment of his demise." He giggled obscenely at his joke, his head lolling from side to side as his body shook. "I did not know I inspired such devotion."

Mrukk stood stiffly, eyes narrowed as his cold heart calculated: a quick blade thrust between the ribs—what would be the outcome of such an action?

"Here, Mrukk," said Jamrog, offering a souile cup from the lacquered tray held by his nubile companion. "A drink to Hladik's memory. Our loss is Trabant's gain, seh?"

Mrukk took the cup, held it between two fingers, and lifted it to his lips as Jamrog did. The warm liquor touched the tip of his tongue and no more. He replaced the cup on the tray. Jamrog lifted himself to his feet, swayed, and gathered his robe around him. "Come, Mrukk, walk with me."

They turned, moved out from under the multicolored canopy, and strolled into the Supreme Director's garden. "I have another task for you, Commander," said Jamrog when they were out of eavesdropping range. "One of the Directors challenged me before the Threl yesterday—as much as insinuated that I had no right to take Hladik's life." He paused, but Mrukk said nothing, so he continued. "I cannot countenance such flagrant impertinence. If left unchecked, it soon renders the office of Supreme Director impotent. I will not be made impotent, Mrukk, do you understand me?"

"I understand. Which traitor challenged you?"

"Rumon." Jamrog said the word as if tasting his revenge in the sound of it. "I think a lesson similar to Hladik's would be instructive. See to it, Mrukk."

"As you will, Supreme Director." The fierce Mrukk stopped and faced his master. "Is that all?"

"Yes, for the time being. However, I expect you will be very busy in the days to come. To tell you the truth, I suspect a plot against me by members of the Threl. You will inform me when the Invisibles have gathered the proper evidence. No doubt your men welcome the opportunity to prove their loyalty and express gratitude to their Hage Leader for his recent generosity."

Mrukk said nothing, merely inclining his head in mute assent. He turned and stalked away. Jamrog watched him go and then called his Hagemate to him, pulled her close, and kissed her violently. "More souile!" he shouted, pushing her away. "I must celebrate. More souile!"

• • • • • •

Giloon Bogney strode through the ruined Hageblock. His cloak—the cloak Tvrdy had given him—was thrown across his shoulders to sweep along behind him like a wing. His nasty face was matched with an equally nasty frown. The diminutive ruler liked the appearance of enhanced power which the strangers gave him before his people. But dealing with the loathsome interlopers was beginning to wear on his goodwill. The Old Section positively reeked with their presence.

It was one thing to tolerate them, but quite another to have to suffer their incessant badgering. Tvrdy's men were at best a continual pain in the lower belly. The Dhog was beginning to wonder why he had agreed to the arrangement in the first place.

"Why Giloon not knowing more Tanais and Rumon coming?" he demanded, bursting through the doorless arch of the ground-floor room he had given the Tanais as a command post.

The leader of the Tanais contingent, an exact man named

Kopetch, was as unbending and precise as the levels and plumb lines he'd handled most of his life. His engineer's love for accuracy had made him a formidable disciplinarian: implacable and unforgiving. Tvrdy had assigned him the unenviable task of creating some kind of order within the Old Section, readying the place for its coming transformation into an armed camp—the first step necessary to begin forming the Dhog rabble into something resembling a fighting unit.

If he was unbending and unforgiving, he was also fair. And not easily shaken or roused. He moved with an inexorable and patient logic in all matters of heart and mind. Glancing up unconcernedly as the Dhog leader flew into the room, he said, in words measured and sure, "If you care to explain what you are talking about, I will be happy to listen to you. If you go on gibbering, I will ignore you. There are important arrangements to be made this morning—I assume it *is* morning."

Bogney ground his teeth and fumed, his face livid through the grime. "Things happening and Giloon not told."

"As you are speaking of them now, I assume you must have been told about them. Therefore, your anger is irrational."

The Dhog leader stomped toward the Tanais engineer menacingly, who turned to regard the threat with a calm, equable expression. "Dhogs not needing you, Tanais. You go away!"

"And how would that help the Dhogs become a Hage?"

"Grrr-rrr!" Bogney ground his teeth at the man. "Trabant take you!"

"To answer your initial question, you were not informed because there was no time for advance warning. Rather than waste precious time sending messages back and forth—messages which could have been intercepted by Invisibles—the Tanais and Rumon came directly upon receiving our all-clear." Kopetch paused and, out of concern for his mission, offered, "If this disturbs you in some way, accept my apologies."

"Giloon say who coming to Old Section."

"They came on Tvrdy's order. Would you countermand his order?"

"Giloon Bogney not under Tanais hand."

"We are *both* under Director Tvrdy's authority—as are the Rumon—until the Purge is over."

The Dhog glared at his erect and unperturbed adversary. He was not used to being talked to this way. It stung and rankled. Bogney was still searching his vocabulary for a suitable expletive when the Tanais said, "Our leader has sent you a special gift. I was about to have it brought to you. As you are here, perhaps you'd like to have it now."

"A gift for Giloon?" His eyes swept the room crammed with supplies and weaponry.

Tvrdy was right, thought Kopetch. The Dhogs *were* like children still in creche. "He thought this might be of use to you." The Tanais reached into a fold in his yos and brought out a slim, tubular object with a flat handle.

Bogney reached out and took the metallic thing, pleased with its dull, blue-black color and its cool weight in his hand. He hefted it and then took it by the handle, which just fitted the palm of his hand. He waved it around, pointing, aiming. "This weapon?"

"A projectile thrower. Very old, but still lethal."

"Tanais sending this to Giloon?" The Dhog smiled happily, eyes glittering at the sight of his new prize. No one else he knew of had ever possessed such a thing.

"He thought you might have need for it one day soon and wanted you to have it."

"Giloon accepting Tanais gift, but Director talks to Director, not to underman."

"That might be sooner than you think," replied Kopetch, moving back to his work. "The Tanais bring word that the Purge has begun. The Directors may not remain in Hage much longer. Also, Hyrgo may be joining us soon."

"Hyrgo!" Giloon was about to protest the further invasion of his realm by yet another disagreeable horde.

Kopetch headed him off by suggesting, "Of course, with your permission, they will want to begin setting up hydroponics and food processing centers."

"Food," said Giloon, rubbing his filthy beard.

"We must become self-sufficient as soon as possible."

"Dhogs making Old Section good place for growers. Giloon seeing to that."

"You are steps ahead of me," replied Kopetch, picking up a map from the stack of papers on the table. "If I might suggest this area here . . ." He pointed to a place on the map. "Donner Heights I think it's called."

Bogney squinted and studied the map, fingering it with his

greasy fingers. "This place ruined," he announced at length, shoving the map back. "Old map."

"Yes, so I assumed. But since we have so little time, and the Hyrgo will need a place to begin food production . . ."

Bogney thumped his chest. "Giloon seeing to it. No making noisy guts on that."

"I knew you would see the potential," said Kopetch dryly. "Was there anything else, Director?"

At the engineer's use of the title, the Dhog leader felt a shiver of delight quiver through him. He smiled importantly, eyes round and gleaming. "Much to do. You be wasting good light talking." With that he swept from the room, leaving only a lingering odor in the air to suggest that he had been there.

Kopetch returned to his work of reordering the Old Section. When his Hage Leader arrived, he wanted everything to be ready. Now, having placated the loathsome Dhog for the time being, it appeared he would have a good chance of getting something accomplished.

Still, he had to wonder whether there was no other way— to join the Dhogs of all things! Who would have imagined it? All they needed now was time. The best plans took time. Patience and time—they would need plenty of both.

TWENTY
SIX

The day slid by easily as the ship carved the smooth water, tugged along by the steady breeze. They lost sight of land a little past midmorning; silver water shimmered on every side, broken only occasionally by shoals of leaping fish, whose bright fins burst through the surface, scattering light in shining fragments. The sky remained clean and cloudless and remote in its blue solitude.

To Yarden it was a magical day. The send-off, as Pizzle called it, provided by the Fieri had cast its spell over her heart, and she felt enchanted still. She strolled the decks wrapped in the gentle glow of a soft inner radiance that made everything she saw seem new-made and charmed. She felt as if this day, this very instant, her life was beginning, that all that had passed before was merely a prelude to this moment.

The other ships—twelve of them stretching out in a staggered line behind, the last one almost too distant to see clearly—plied Prindahl's deeper waters with solemn majesty, sails puffing proudly, painted hulls glistening, graceful outriggers slicing the low waves. Yarden thrilled to the sight; the procession reminded her of something out of the *Arabian Nights* or the *Tales of Sinbad,* and she found herself time and again, on one of her rounds of the deck, simply standing, staring out at the long string of boats sliding over the platinum sea.

Pizzle found her standing at the aft rail, her hair streaming in the breeze, eyes glazed in wonder. "I've been looking for you," he said.

"Umm," was all she said.

"Haven't seen much of you—I thought we might talk."

With an effort she turned her eyes away. "What about?" she asked dreamily.

"If you're busy, I can come back."

"Busy?"

"You want to be alone?"

She shook her head and took a deep breath. "The air is so

fresh!" She gazed back out at the colorful sails of the trailing barges. "So beautiful."

"I'll come back."

"How have you been, Pizzle?" she asked absently. "I haven't seen much of you lately."

"Is that so?"

She turned to him again with a questioning glance. "What did you say?"

"Nothing. It's just that you seem a little preoccupied right now. I guess you're thinking about Treet, huh?"

"Who?" She appeared genuinely puzzled.

"Orion Treet? A friend of ours—yours. Tall guy with lots of hair everywhere, likable, if a little poached topside. Remember him?"

"Treet . . ." A look of sharp vexation crossed her features. "I don't want to remember—to talk about him, I mean."

"Huh? I thought you two were real close." Pizzle wagged his head in amazement at female fickleness. "What happened? Lover's tiff?"

"I don't want to talk about it."

Pizzle was quiet for a moment, and Yarden thought he had gotten the message. "I guess he was probably too bullheaded for his own good," he said after a while. "Imagine, him going back there—back to Dome, I mean. I can't figure it. I didn't think he'd really do it."

"How dare you inflict him on me!" Yarden snapped. "I told you I don't want to talk about him. You're ruining everything. Just leave me alone."

"Hey, I'm sorry. I didn't know you two had scrapped it up. I was just wondering, okay?"

"Go away. Just . . . go away." Yarden turned abruptly, setting her jaw.

"Right, I'll see you later," said Pizzle, shuffling off.

Curse that Pizzle, she thought. Everything was beautiful until he'd mentioned Treet. I don't want to remember. I *won't* remember him. She pushed herself forcefully away from the rail—as if she were shoving away his memory. She continued her stroll once more around the deck, determined to regain the magical mood that had, like dew in the desert sun, evaporated at the drop of Treet's name.

• • • • • •

"I told you that he was not to be left alone—not even for a moment," said Ernina, raising an accusing finger at the slacker. "Where were you? Answer me."

"I just stepped out for—"

"I don't care. I don't want excuses, I want obedience. Someone is to be with him at all times. Understand?"

The first-order physician nodded ruefully.

"All right." The flinty old healer softened somewhat. "I know you are tired; I will send someone to relieve you soon." She studied her newest patient as she placed the fingers of her right hand against his throat. "I don't want anything to happen to him," she muttered.

"Is he someone important?" asked the young man.

Ernina delivered her answer with a look of reprimand in her quick, green eyes. "*Everyone* who needs our help is important."

"More important, I mean?"

The old woman evaded the question. "He has a mental disorder which requires constant attention. Should he awake, I wish to be notified at once." She turned on the young physician again. "When was the last time you read his aura?"

"Green, stabilized," he answered at once, "some shrinkage in the red, passing to yellow. His blue is still well below range."

Ernina nodded. "Any black showing?"

"Transient flares—nothing stable." He paused and looked thoughtfully at the man in the suspended bed. "He speaks aloud."

"It's to be expected."

"He speaks of his mishon. What is a mishon?"

Ernina shrugged. "Perhaps he will tell us when he is again in his right mind. Anything else?"

"Just muttering—nothing coherent."

She nodded and said, "I'll send your relief at once." Ernina left the room. This patient had a good chance to recover if his will to live was strong enough. Time would tell. She had done all she could for the moment.

How he had come to appear at her door, she didn't know. But she recognized Hladik's handiwork readily enough. The tortured man was a Fieri—that she also knew the moment she had seen him lying there shivering. Now that he was here, she was determined to protect him at all costs.

The news of Hladik's assassination had shaken the Hage. Not that she cared for the licentious Director, but his death augured ill for the future. Jamrog was, if possible, a worse tyrant than Sirin Rohee. And if, as the rumor messengers suggested, Hladik's death was the beginning of a Purge, her choice was clear.

Her patient could not be moved now—maybe not for a long while. But as soon as he was able . . .

In the meantime, there was so much to be done, so much to get ready before that eventuality.

She smiled grimly to herself; she had been given another chance to save the life of a Fieri. I lost the first one, she thought. One that I pledged to protect. I will *not* lose this one.

• • • • • •

Cejka climbed the steps of the communications tower which rose like a spearhead from the center of Rumon Hage. He paused to look out over his domain, peaceful in the hazy midday light. Clumps of trees in a long sinuous line marked the banks of Kyan; low, blue-tinted Hageblocks, scattered among green quadrangles, stepped up from the river's edge.

Rumon was not large, but its people were fiercely loyal—a fact Cejka had always appreciated and never abused. Within Rumon's neat borders, Hagemen came and went without fear and spoke their minds freely, for Rumon priests were not given to greed and petty malice as were most others. Cejka saw to that, keeping the bloated priesthood in check just as he kept his rumor messengers quick and subtle.

Under Cejka's leadership rumor messengers had become the main, often the only, source of reliable information for the common Hageman. Consequently, there was not a single Hageblock in all of Empyrion where a Rumon rumor messenger was not welcome. The swiftness of the network contributed to the messengers' high stent among the people of the various Hages, who for the most part considered rumor messengers on a level with magicians, so quickly did they appear and vanish.

The Rumon Director was now grateful for the speed and efficiency of his beloved network. He had known within seconds the precise moment that Mrukk had set foot in Rumon. Even though the Mors Ultima commander had appeared in disguise as a Rumon Hageman, he was instantly recognized and reported, his movements since then carefully observed.

There could only be one reason for the assassin's sudden appearance, and Cejka knew what it was: Jamrog had ordered his death, no doubt in retaliation for his remarks in the Threl session the day before. Now Cejka had two choices and a decision to be made quickly.

Reluctantly he turned his eyes away from the deceptively calm landscape before him. Death waited out there. He hurried inside the tower and rode the lift to the top, where he had established the heart of the rumor network. Subdirector Covol was waiting for him when he entered.

"Where is he?" Cejka came into the large, machine-crammed room. As always it was humming with activity, but today there was an edge to the excitement. Hagemen glanced up briefly as the Director walked by and then returned to their tasks, many of them staring into glowing screens or speaking softly into microphones; others, their heads encased in remote viewer helmets, sat motionless, their fingers twitching on the lighted panels before them. And everywhere magicians scurried, tending the machinery, keeping it going.

"Still on Riverwalk level," answered Covol. "He appears to be working his way toward Hage center, slowly; he is in no hurry."

"Has he attempted to contact any of the known Invisibles within Hage?"

"We have detected no contact. None of the Invisibles are near him at present." Covol regarded his chief. "What is your decision? Should we try to apprehend him?"

Cejka clasped his hands and bowed his head. When he raised his face again he said, "No."

"He is alone. We can take him."

"It would be too difficult and the loss of life too great. If we fail, we will have shown Jamrog the strength of our network."

"We can take him," insisted Covol. To Cejka's quick dismissal he said, "At least let us kill him. We can have him surrounded by weapons carriers within two minutes."

Cejka considered this. It was tempting. Yes, they could have Rumon snipers within range in minutes, and at least one enemy would be eliminated. But it wouldn't stop Jamrog. Losing his prime assassin would drive the Supreme Director into a killing frenzy; he would order a massive strike on the Hage, and thousands would die.

"No," he said.

Covol heard the finality in his leader's voice and despaired. "Do you propose to do nothing to protect yourself?"

"Where I am going, Covol, I will be well protected." The Subdirector stared. "What's wrong? We have planned for this day. The time has come, sooner than expected perhaps, but it has not caught us unaware. Are you ready to assume the Directorship?"

"You'll still be Director," pointed out Covol.

Cejka nodded. "Yes, yes, but since I will not be here to take care of them, our Hagemen will look to you for leadership. Jamrog may even have you formally installed." He silenced a quick protest. "You know what to do. We have agreed on the plan, and we will follow it."

"Yes, Director." Covol squared his shoulders.

"Good. I will leave with the Hyrgo tonight. Now, alert Tvrdy; he must be informed of my plans at once." Cejka took a last look around the busy command center he had worked so hard to create. It was possible that he'd never see the place again.

He pushed the thought from him. The Purge was just beginning; many decisive battles remained to be fought, and Cejka meant to see Jamrog's head on a bhuj in Threl High Chambers before it was over. That, he considered as he disappeared into his private rooms, was a prospect worth further contemplation.

TWENTY
SEVEN

Near sundown on the fifth day the Fieri sailboats reached the northernmost shores of Prindahl. The sails were furled as the first ships slid into a sand-rimmed cove and anchored in the clear, shallow water. The passengers disembarked to make camp on dry land for the night. The cove had been used by the Fieri as a stopping-place for generations; there were open-air pavilions and fresh-water wells scattered among the cool groves of flat-leafed shade trees lining the cove just above the sand line.

No one seemed to mind that they had to wade ashore, and the festive atmosphere was quickly rekindled among the convivial travelers. Yarden sloshed through the warm, knee-deep water, and would have given in to a swim—as many of the Fieri were doing—if not for the fact that she wanted to find Ianni and Gerdes as soon as possible. She looked among the laughing, splashing bathers from the first boat for her friends, but didn't see them.

On the beach, she wandered along the fine, white sand, stopping at each boat to search among the passengers in the water and coming ashore. The fifth ship, spring green sails with a bright yellow hull, was just gliding in when Yarden arrived. She waited as the anchor dropped with a splash and the gangplank was thrust out into the water. The first passengers off were youngsters who dove off the gangplank and into the turquoise shallows like seals too long pent-up for comfort. Amidst their happy squeals, the other passengers filed off. Among the first was Ianni.

"Over here!" Yarden cried, waving an arm above her head.

Ianni glanced up, smiled, and waved. "So you found a berth after all," she said as she joined Yarden on the beach. "I knew you would, or else I would have come back to look for you. I'm sorry, I guess I should have warned you about the boarding."

"It doesn't matter. I've enjoyed every minute of the trip so far, and I'll enjoy the rest even more now that we're together. Where is Gerdes?" Yarden asked, searching the oncoming throng for her teacher.

"She'll be along. I saw her earlier this afternoon," replied Ianni. "I know she's eager to get her pupils together. You're not the only one to get separated from her."

They began walking along the sand, listening to the laughter ringing in the still air. "As much as I love sailing," said Yarden, "it's good to feel solid ground beneath my feet." She fell silent then and was quiet so long that Ianni turned her head to study Yarden from the corner of her eye.

"Something is troubling you," observed Ianni. She stopped and drew Yarden down beside her, stretching out her long legs as she reclined.

Yarden's first impulse was to deny her friend's assertion. But it was true. Off and on the last few days she had been moody. "I'm . . . I don't know—I feel restless, unsettled."

Ianni said nothing, but merely waited for Yarden to continue. The sun touched the flat, metallic surface of the lake and spread white fire across the far horizon and long shadows on the beach. Yarden sat with her legs drawn up, arms folded on her knees, eyes closed in searching thought. Finally she lowered her head onto her arms. "It's Treet," she said.

"Go on."

Yarden sighed heavily. "I thought I could forget him. I nearly did—at least I thought so. Until that stupid Pizzle . . ."

"It wasn't Pizzle," Ianni said softly.

Yarden lifted her head. "No, I suppose not. Not really."

She fell silent again, watching the sun slide into the water. The remaining boats had slid into the cove, and their passengers now strolled the beach or swam, their voices clear as light in the air. There were tears in her eyes when she turned to Ianni. "I didn't want this to happen. I wanted to be free of him. I wanted to start a new life. It isn't fair. Why should he have this hold on me?"

"Are you certain it's Treet?"

Yarden nodded. "Who else?"

"The Seeker has His ways."

Pondering this, Yarden said, "I have been faithful to my call. I have sought the Infinite's leading. I have asked to be shown how to grow in belief and understanding. I have—"

"You have cut Treet from your life," Ianni pointed out gently. "And closed that part of your life to the Teacher."

"But I don't see how that matters."

"The Infinite requires an open heart, Yarden, and an open life. All of life is to be shared with Him. You ask Him to help you grow, yet set limits to that growth."

"But Treet—I want to give him up to follow the faith."

"I know. But perhaps the Infinite requires something different from you."

Yarden didn't like this. "You're saying I'm stuck with Treet? No matter what I happen to think or feel about it?"

Ianni laughed. "No, I didn't mean it like that. I only meant that there is obviously something to be accomplished between you. The Seeker has been prodding you to see this. Your rejection of Treet is unhealthy; it has made you unhappy, restless."

"What am I supposed to do? He's God knows where, doing God knows what, and I'm here. Just what am I supposed to do?"

"I can't answer that, Yarden. Nor, I think, could the Preceptor. This you must discover for yourself."

Yarden frowned unhappily. "I'll think about it."

"Yes, think about it. But don't think too long."

• • • • • •

The sumptuous Supreme Director's kraam had been stripped of its fine furniture and art objects and transformed into a palatial banqueting hall—complete with a bubbling fountain and pool with live fish near the entrance. Miniature trees had been placed around the perimeter of the room, and a circle of tables erected in the center. Behind screens and in secluded clusters conveniently hidden by hanging plants were soft couches and mounds of cushions for the assignations of his guests. Braziers on tall tripods lit the room with yellow flames that burned day and night, flickering before glistening Bolbe hangings of the very best quality.

The Supreme Director was entertaining with increasing frequency; he was busy cultivating a coterie of sycophants, stooges who would do his bidding without qualm or question and never dream of challenging his authority.

Jamrog entered the kraam, surrounded by his Mors Ultima bodyguard. Since Cejka and Tvrdy vanished, the Supreme Director had taken to moving about in public in the company of handpicked Invisibles. Subdirector Osmas, his Saecaraz successor, and a thin, sunken-eyed Nilokerus—one of Hladik's underdirectors, elevated to the Directorship following Fertig's disappearance—stood waiting with several Chryse and Bolbe artisans.

"Splendid!" Jamrog clapped his hands when he saw them. "You have something for me?"

The toady Osmas squirmed forward, rubbing his hands. "I have reviewed the work myself, Supreme Director. I think you will like the results."

Jamrog, eyes gleaming in anticipation, observed the dour Nilokerus. The man, though young, had sunken cheeks and a deathly pallor, suggesting a wasting disease. "What about you, Diltz? What do you think?"

The voice that answered was forceful enough, but had something of the tenor of the tomb. "You will be pleased, Supreme Director."

Jamrog made stirring motions with his hands. "Let's see it then, by all means." Osmas ushered the artisans forward. With some trepidation they produced a huge length of cloth and unrolled it on the floor, stretching it between them. As the folds were carefully shaken out, there appeared a gigantic image of the Supreme Director with ceremonial bhuj in uplifted hand painted on cloth of Saecaraz silver with black edging.

Jamrog studied the likeness carefully, striding right into the center of the cloth to stare down at his own portrait. The artists glanced at one another fearfully. But slowly the mercurial leader smiled and looked up. "I am pleased," he announced. "Well pleased. You have rendered my likeness admirably, and for that you will receive a thousand shares each."

"A thousand shares!" gasped one of the Bolbe. He clamped a hand over his mouth and, abashed, shrank back behind the others.

"What, not enough?" mocked Jamrog, turning on the man. "Two thousand then—but you'll have to earn it, greedy Bolbe."

The artisans were stunned; they'd never heard of such sums. However, one enterprising Chryse found his voice and asked, "How may we further serve you, Supreme Director?"

"I want a thousand just like this," Jamrog said, tapping the long-handled bhuj on the portrait beneath his feet.

"A thousand!" sputtered the Chryse in disbelief.

"Two thousand for one thousand," smiled Jamrog sweetly. "I want them ready for the Trabantonna."

Seeing the artisans quail at the request, Osmas stepped forward. "The Feast of the Departed is nearly upon us, Supreme Director," he interceded. "Or did we misunderstand?"

"No, you understand completely. I will have my image displayed on every Hageblock in every Hage and at every feast site. This will remind all Empyrion of their leader's thoughtfulness for them." He looked around him for any to gainsay the plan.

"Of course, Threl Leader," replied the Chryse spokesman. "It can be done."

"You see, Osmas? No misunderstanding." To Diltz he said, "The Nilokerus will see that the banners are hung to best effect in each Hage. When I make my appearances at the Trabantonna feasts, I want to see my image well represented."

The Nilokerus Director assented silently. "Excellent!" Jamrog said, tapping the image with the bhuj again. "Correct me if I am wrong, Directors, but I think this sort of thing helps our Hagemen tremendously. It focuses their attention, you see, makes them continually aware of me as I am of them."

"Oh, undoubtedly, Hage Leader," gushed Osmas.

"All the more reason to proceed with haste," offered Jamrog helpfully. "We have our Hagemen to think of in this matter."

The artisans dismissed themselves and were whisked away by several of the ever-attentive Invisibles. "Now then," snapped Jamrog when the others had gone, "what of the fugitives?"

"Latest reports are not encouraging, Supreme Director," explained the Saecaraz Subdirector. "There has been no sign of them."

Jamrog whirled on Diltz. "What about your security forces?"

"As I have explained, Supreme Director, we do not have checkpoints at all Hage borders—"

"Establish them at once," Jamrog ordered. "I want those traitors found."

Osmas attempted to soothe his leader. "Certainly you can have no serious thoughts for them now. They mean nothing."

"Tvrdy is a cunning enemy, and Cejka is no fool. Together they are twice the threat. The longer they are free, the more impudent they will become. All opposition to my leadership must be silenced. Traitors like Tvrdy and his puppet Cejka encourage other weak-willed malcontents to harbor treason in their hearts." He stepped close to Diltz and thrust a finger in his face. The man did not flinch. "The Nilokerus will begin a Hage by Hage search for the two enemies. Any help will be generously rewarded—five thousand shares if we find them. Publicize it."

"As you wish," Osmas replied. Diltz merely offered his silent acquiescence.

The Supreme Director sighed with satisfaction. "Ah, I'm hungry. Have my guests arrived?"

"They are waiting in the anteroom, Hage Leader."

"Let them come in. Bring me a hagerobe, and send the food at once." He dismissed Osmas to carry out his orders, and stood with his legs wide apart, gazing at his enormous image on the cloth beneath his feet. "It *is* a good likeness," he said. "Think—it will hang in every place of prominence. My reign, Diltz, my reign is the beginning of a glorious age, the like of which Empyrion has never seen!"

"Undoubtedly," intoned Diltz in his sepulchral voice, a spidery smile twitching his lips.

Jamrog put his arm around the man's bony shoulders, threw back his head, and laughed.

TWENTY EIGHT

He would live. There was no doubt in his mind about that. Neither was there any doubt that he was changed. Subtly perhaps, but definitely changed. Treet knew this, knew it in his heart and bones. He was simply not the same anymore.

At first he thought the conditioning had done its abominable work. But the more he thought about it—and he had a lot of time to do absolutely nothing but think—the more he was inclined to discount the idea. The way he had been yanked from the tank and dumped on the physicians' doorstep suggested that the process had been aborted. Secondly, the conditioning, he reasoned, was designed to remove, replace, or at least alter one's personal awareness, not heighten it.

This last fact was what strengthened his conviction that he had miraculously escaped before the procedure was completed, for Treet's awareness had clearly, decisively, unmistakably been boosted. He felt himself tingling with the sense that he *knew* something—some radical insight had been granted him, or some hidden inner secret of the universe had been revealed to him.

True, he didn't know what his secret revelation was—hadn't a clue—but the inner thrill of *knowing* was as unshakable as it was irrational. Treet delighted in a keenness of perception that had no object. And though he could hardly lift head from pillow, he felt strong and invincible, as if he could part oceans with a word.

The physical sensations did not stop there. His scalp prickled and his face, especially around the eyes and forehead, felt as if it were radioactive, as if he had stood too close to an atomic blast.

This was, however, not an entirely disagreeable feeling; nothing like a sunburn, for instance. He thought it could be an aftereffect of the wax mask he had worn in the tank, but the skin surface itself was not at all sensitive to the touch. The warmth seemed to emanate from inside, radiating heat outward. He imagined that his face might glow in the dark.

Combined with this burning-face phenomenon, there was a lightness in the pit of his stomach—like hunger only softer, more diffuse. He felt buoyant, as if his body were made of a less dense material: air perhaps, or light.

Absurdly, it seemed to Treet that he was floating inside himself. When he closed his eyes, he could feel himself drifting upward, or rising rapidly on invisible currents, streaming toward an unknown destination.

Taken together, these sensations might have alarmed him, or at least frightened him a little. Treet, however, experienced not a second's apprehension over any of his bizarre symptoms. This lack of concern was due to a continuing awareness of the alien presence he had contacted while in Hladik's torture tank.

The entity remained near him, unintrusive but present. As close as thought—as if a part of Treet's consciousness had been permeated by this other, but in such a way that increased rather than diminished his personal awareness—which accounted for his heightened sensitivity, no doubt. If consciousness were pictured as a great miasmic sphere inside which self-awareness dwelt, then a portion of Treet's sphere had been gently interfused with the alien entity's sphere. As a result, he was more himself rather than less.

Curiously, Treet found this pervasion a benign and wholesome affair, completing in him areas of previously unrealized deficiency, as if hidden gaps had been cemented, or wounds healed. He felt centered: a runaway planet that had been captured, stabilized, and pulled into useful orbit around a life-giving sun.

This was how he knew he would live, and how he knew he had changed.

The change, Treet knew in all his being—for the knowledge continually coursed through him like blood through his arteries—was toward life and away from death. There was a certainty, an inevitability to his life now that had been absent before. What is more, he knew that his life would be forever changed. No one, he reasoned, could undergo such an infusion of (there was no other word for it) goodness and remain indifferent or unchanged.

• • • • • •

The wevicat padded silently through the forest, stopping occasionally to sniff at a new scent as it crossed the trail. Crocker followed, loping easily along behind, content to have the cat lead the way back to the lair. They had been hunting again that afternoon and had caught nothing but three of the plump, flightless birds. They had surprised the hapless creatures on the ground, making their slow way to new trees and better feeding. A flurry of feathers, squawks, and a quick wevicat nip on their short necks, and supper was assured. Now, late in the afternoon, the ground mist already starting to curl around root and bole, they were returning with their catch.

Cook the birds over a fire, the voice in Crocker's head had suggested. *You could make a fire. The meat would taste good that way.*

Crocker was puzzling over the word *fire* when he saw the wevicat freeze. The man stopped and stood rock-still, eyes and ears instantly alert. The great cat's nostrils twitched; the tip of his tail quivered.

A scent on the air, his voice cautioned.

Crocker detected nothing save the ordinary earth smells of the deep forest, but knew the cat's senses were infinitely more keen than his own. Something stopped the animal in its tracks. Game? An enemy?

The wevicat jerked its head around and looked at its human companion, then sprang forward, bounding headlong down the trail. Crocker leaped ahead too, and came flying into a clearing a few meters away—just in time to see the enormous cat clawing its way up a stout tree that emerged from a pile of moss-bedecked rock at the far end of the clearing.

Gripping his spear in one hand, the man began following the cat's example, but much more slowly and with greater care, standing on a rock to reach the first branch a good two meters off the ground. He had cleared the second branch and was reaching for the third when he heard bushes rustling and branches snapping—together with a horrendous snuffling sound like that of a rooting hog amplified fifty times—on the trail behind him. He froze as the beast making the sound lumbered into the clearing.

The first glimpse of the creature almost knocked Crocker from his precarious perch. The thing was perfectly enormous—

big enough to make the awesome wevicat appear insignificant.

Crocker recognized instantly that here was one of the lords of the forest he had heard that rainy day when he had hid quivering under a bush, fearing for his life, feeling the very ground tremble beneath their unseen combat, hoping against hope that he would not be discovered by the titanic warriors.

The beast lumbering into the clearing below had a smooth, almost hairless hide, thick and blubbery, bulging around its sturdy limbs and around its neck and the hump of his massive shoulders. It walked on four legs—the first two a good deal shorter than the thick-muscled rear limbs—and held a horn-plated, knob-ended fleshy tail out almost perpendicular to the ground as it moved. Its head, balanced by the knobby tail at the other end, lolled this way and that, showing the tiny glints of black eyes squeezed nearly shut by the puffy flesh surrounding them. The head was round with the tag ends of ears sticking out oddly atop the expansive hillock of a cranium.

The animal moved slowly, slogging forward in an absurd rolling gait—an earthquake in motion. The behemoth was a mottled two-tone: a dusty reddish color above, gray-brown below. Much of its pitted hide was slick with greasy effluence. There were scars criss-crossing its back, pink and new, attesting to its contentious nature. It paused as it came directly into the center of the clearing, filling the closed space with its bulk.

Crocker shrank back. It was almost close enough to touch.

The creature snuffled the ground and, to the man's horror, reared back on its tremendous hind legs and raised its head, eyeing the tree hungrily. The monstrous face was split in half by two hanging lip flaps beneath wavering nostrils like convulsing tunnels. The gross flaps spread as the jaws opened to reveal flat-crowned, green-stained teeth and a prodigious, questing tongue. The stench of rotting meat and vegetation filled the air.

The man's heart thumped wildly in his chest. Above him, the cat tensed. The grotesque head wobbled closer, nudging leaves, then drawing a whole branch into its sinkhole of a mouth with the prehensile tongue to be crushed to pulp by the grinding teeth. The tree shook as the branch snapped off. The wevicat teetered, claws digging for a better hold.

The next bite nearly yanked the man out of the tree. The beast seized the very branch Crocker was hanging on to with his free hand, causing him to drop the spear and scrabble for a new handhold. The spear fell, slid into the animal's terrific maw, lodged sideways.

The monster worked its mouth up and down in an effort to dislodge the irritant, but succeeded only in wedging the spear further. Crocker struggled for a better handhold, slipped and plunged, catching himself at the last instant to scramble higher into the tree.

The behemoth just below heard the commotion caused by the man's fall and stopped. The head came up slowly until its eye was staring right into Crocker's terrified face.

TWENTY NINE

The beast let out a snort that nearly blew Crocker out of the tree. Then, as the man fought to regain his foothold, the great elastic tongue thrust out and wrapped itself around his thigh, yanking him closer to the cavernous mouth.

Tightening his grip on the branch, he felt his arm and shoulder muscles stretch as his leg was wrenched and pulled closer to the behemoth's grinding stumps of teeth. One hand gave way. Crocker screamed.

The monstrous tongue pulled him closer. The lip flaps parted to receive him. Crocker shrieked as, with a jerk of the beast's head, his hand was torn from the branch and he swung into the creature's mouth.

The teeth ground together, and Crocker felt himself crushed between them. The air rushed from his body. But something prevented the teeth from closing on him completely. He looked and saw his spear sticking into the side of the animal's fleshy jaw.

Twisting his body sideways, he squirmed to the spear. The teeth came down again. He cried out as the tremendous pressure ground into his bones. His hands closed on the spear, and he held on.

The teeth parted again. Crocker thrust the spear up, jamming the weapon further into the soft tissue. The behemoth grunted. The spear bent, splintered, snapped in two.

Crocker felt himself sliding into the tremendous gullet. The huge teeth came down over him.

Just then he heard a sound that jellied the marrow in his bones: the blood-thinning battle cry of an enraged cat. The wevicat leaped from its perch in the upper branches straight for the behemoth's face, claws extended like curved steel scimitars. One swipe of its massive paw and the behemoth lost an eye.

The startled beast roared with fright, and Crocker felt himself momentarily free. The animal's mouth opened and he was expelled, falling to the ground, where he landed on the rocks beneath the tree.

Bruised, bleeding, slimy with the beast's saliva, the man scrambled for safety among the rocks as the fight commenced above him, the cat spitting, raking its lethal claws at will over its enemy's head as the monster lurched ineffectually here and there, trying to dislodge the angry wevicat, bellowing with a sound that shook the very stones in the ground.

The huge cat dug in and held on. The behemoth shook its head ponderously and flailed with its knob-ended tail, tearing great gaping rents in the earth and flinging clumps of soil skyward with its feet. In desperation the behemoth drove straight toward the tree where the man was hiding.

Crocker flung himself to the side as the tree groaned, leaning toward him. The cat leaped lightly onto the monster's back, sinking its fearsome teeth into the bulging shoulder hump.

The behemoth bawled as the pain fought to its brain. The clublike tail smashed limbs from the tree as the beast whirled in torment. It lowered its head and lurched toward the tree.

There was a popping sound deep in the earth as roots snapped. The tree tilted and fell, black roots showering dirt into the air. The wevicat sprang with compact grace from the behemoth's back. Landing on its feet, it spun and reared, ears flat against its skull, paws spread wide. The behemoth lowered its huge ugly head, and, with a roar that rattled Crocker's teeth, whirled, whipping its thick tail through the air with surprising speed.

The wevicat was faster, leaping straight up into the air. The horn-plated tail struck the earth, carving a deep slash in the turf. The cat came down snarling and slashing the behemoth's blubbery hide, laying open the skin in ragged pink gashes. Blood bubbled from the horrendous wounds. The cat was covered with it.

Twice more the behemoth's tail plowed the ground, to no avail. The agile cat moved like caged lightning, always just out of range of the deadly tail. Crocker hunkered behind the fallen tree, shivering with shock and fright, breath coming in shallow gasps, pulse pounding in his ears.

Then, just as the behemoth's tail recoiled for another strike, the beast turned and staggered away, leaving the field to the victorious wevicat. As the crashing, thrashing sounds of the behemoth's retreat died away, Crocker crept from his hiding place and went to the cat. Its fur was spiked and sticky with blood, but it was unharmed.

The man put his hand on the cat's back; the cat snarled, jumped up, and spun toward him, then recognized him and sat down. *The cat has saved your life,* Crocker's internal voice told him.

"Saved my life," Crocker repeated aloud, his voice small in the clearing where the sounds of ferocious battle still hung in the air. He went to the animal and put his arms around its neck, hugging the creature as it calmly began licking its fur. Then, dusk swallowing the forest clearing, both man and cat rose and padded silently back to their lair.

· · · · · ·

"Well, let's have it," said Tvrdy. "I can see by your expression that it isn't good."

"Not good at all," said Cejka. "Covol says Jamrog is offering five thousand shares for information leading to our capture."

Tvrdy nodded, frowning.

"Five thousand," Piipo snorted. "The fool."

"There's more. The Nilokerus are setting up checkpoints in every Hage—all entry and exit points, as well as internal junctions. They are to be manned day and night."

"This is sooner than I expected. I did not think Jamrog would act to control Hage movement so quickly. What do they check?"

"Poak—for now. Covol belives they will soon issue identity cards and travel writs."

"Messy," said Tvrdy unhappily. "This could cut our supply lines completely."

"Director, if I may—" began Kopetch. He had been silent during the briefing.

"Yes, speak freely."

With a nod of deference to his superiors, he said, "I believe this unfortunate circumstance could work in our favor. Once these cards and writs are issued we can obtain them, alter them, or duplicate them. We can then travel at will without fear of discovery—with the proper precautions, of course. They will come to rely on the documents and not on their own eyes and ears. As long as we hold the documents, we will not be suspected."

"An ingenious suggestion worthy of a master strategist!" Tvrdy smiled with approval. It was the first time he'd smiled in many days. His escape from the Hage had been much sooner than he'd planned, and although it had been accomplished without incident, he was still anxious over the way he'd left his organization. And despite Cejka's repeated assurances and messages from Danelka that the escape had caused no unforeseen repercussions, the Tanais leader remained uneasy, feeling that some detail had been overlooked.

Now he relaxed a little. Men like Kopetch—and his organization was built on such—could be counted on. Somehow, they would find a way to meet each new challenge as it presented itself. "Pradim could not have done better himself," Tvrdy said.

"Excellent!" Cejka beamed. "We can issue our own cards and writs. If we could get a poak imprinter, we could even create identities for the Dhogs. Why, there's no limit to what we could do. Think of it! Think of the confusion we could cause."

"Tell Covol to obtain the documents as soon as possible— and any machinery necessary to duplicate or alter them." Tvrdy paused, his expression soured momentarily. "There is one other thing. Bogney insists that he be allowed to attend the briefing sessions. I think we must agree, although I see nothing but trouble from it."

"I don't like it any more than you, Tvrdy," Piipo said, "but we must begin treating the Dhogs as equals. Soon we will be asking them to die for us."

"I might suggest maintaining our nightly briefings in secret," put in Kopetch. "Bogney and one or two of his men could attend a morning session."

"Two briefings." Cejka chuckled. "Tvrdy, I think we have found Pradim's successor."

"Is there anything else tonight? No? All right. I will inform Bogney of our decision to have him join the briefing sessions. We will set the first for tomorrow morning before drills, but will meet together as usual tomorrow night—no, make that one hour later from now on."

With that Tvrdy dismissed the meeting, and they all filed

out of the fire-gutted building which had been hastily designated as a meeting place, occupying as it did a central location within the Blazedon district of the Old Section, overlooking a flat, rectangular desolation formerly known as Moscow Square.

Tvrdy returned to his rooms in the Tanais Hageblock and entered to find Giloon Bogney waiting for him. "Is courtesy not observed in a man's absence?" he asked, confronting the Dhog leader directly.

Bogney waved the objection aside with an impatient flick of the bhuj. "Giloon not liking Director talking big plans and him not hearing." He glared acidly at the Tanais Director, defying him to push the point.

Instead Tvrdy replied, "I understand. That is why I have decided to ask you to join us. The briefings are becoming too important not to have the leader of the Dhogs present. Will you join us?"

Bogney stroked his greasy mat of a beard, satisfaction gleaming in his bright little eyes. "So? Giloon joining Directors, seh?"

"I think it best."

"Giloon be joining. Night meetings?"

"No. Tomorrow morning at first light. Bring one or two of your men with you, but you must warn them: the matters discussed are to remain secret. If we discover any leaks—"

"Be saving your threats, Tanais. Dhogs knowing how to keep secrets."

"I'm sure you do." Tvrdy looked at the disgusting creature before him. "Was there anything else?"

"Giloon talking it tomorrow." Bogney screwed up his face into a grotesque smile. "Giloon being Director soon."

"You think it will be easy, do you?"

"We fight. We win."

"There will be fighting, yes—but not for a good long time, I hope. We're not ready yet. We don't have the supplies necessary to sustain a prolonged battle against Jamrog's Invisibles, much less win one. But the time will come."

"Giloon being there tomorrow." He gathered his cloak— the cloak Tvrdy had given him—around his sloping shoulders and waddled from the room.

Tvrdy restrained the impulse to slam the door after him, but the relic would probably have shattered into glassy fragments. He looked around the room, but nothing had been touched. He went to a ramshackle table that had been put in one corner, scanned the orderly rows of reports he had collected since his arrival in the Old Section, and, picking up a nearby reader, retired to his bed, popped the cartridge into the reader, and began to scan the contents.

With any luck at all, and no further interruptions, he'd finish before morning, and have an hour or two for a nap.

Treet swayed as the floor tilted up under his feet. He pitched forward, toward the bed, but the physician's hands held him up. "You're doing well," coaxed the young man. "Don't stop now."

"I—uh . . ." Treet puffed. "I—need to . . . lie down . . ."

"Just a little more and you can rest. You need to move your legs."

"Ohhhhhh!" Treet groaned. "Let me die in peace!"

"Die is just what you will not do." Treet glanced up as Ernina swept in with a tray in her hands. She had a habit of showing up when least expected.

"Just a little sickroom humor," offered Treet. "Nothing against my wonderful nursemaid here." He grimaced at the first-order physician and painfully kept moving. He completed one more circuit around the bed and then collapsed gratefully upon it. The suspension bed bounced in the air with his weight, righted itself, and hung steady. "Ahhh, that's better."

"That *is* better," replied Ernina. "Better in every way. You'll be able to move about on your own soon." She handed Treet a cup of steaming liquid and told him to sip it, then signaled to the physician, indicating that she wished to be left with the patient. When they were alone she said, "I think you are well enough now to talk."

Treet gazed calmly at the woman whom he had come to think of as his savior, and guessed what was coming. And although he had thought about it a great deal since regaining consciousness, he still did not know precisely what he would say to her.

He'd learned from his nursemaids, as he called them, that he'd been left on the healing center's doorstep, which meant, he guessed, that he was still somewhere in Nilokerus Hage. He had also found out that Hladik had been assassinated, and suspected his release had something to do with that. As for the rest, he didn't know how much anyone knew about him. At any rate, it was too late to invent anything now. He'd have to play it by ear. He waited for her to begin.

She did not waste any words. "I know who you are." This was accompanied by one of her most direct, probing gazes.

"You do?" gulped Treet, dashing down some of the hot herb mixture.

"You need not fear me. I have pledged my life to help you."

"You have?" This was not at all what Treet had expected.

Ernina glanced cautiously around, as if checking that the room was still empty. "I know that you are a Fieri." She sat back, satisfaction glowing in her brilliant green eyes.

Treet sipped the medicinal tea through pursed lips. "How long have you known?"

"From the first."

"I see."

"No one else suspects. To my staff you are simply another patient—one of Hladik's victims. We have seen many of those. Only I know the truth, and I have kept your secret."

"Why?" asked Treet. He needed to know how far he could trust her.

"It is difficult to explain, but I will try. Some time ago I was summoned to Cavern level to resuscitate a dying prisoner—another victim of Hladik's conditioning, I thought. And so he was, but when I examined him closely, I discovered the secret: he was a Fieri." Ernina said the ancient word, and her eyes shone with the wonder of it.

Treet nodded; it had to be Crocker she was talking about. So that's what had happened to him. "I know all about conditioning," replied Treet.

"The priests say that the Fieri don't exist anymore—maybe never did. But there are old, old stories, and many Hagemen still believe. The nonbeings are said to know how to find them. They—"

"Nonbeings?"

"The Shadow People, the Dhogs. They are Hage outcasts whose poak has been erased and stent forfeited. They live in the Old Section, it is believed, though no one ever sees them. They exist, but do not exist."

"Why are they called Dhogs?"

Ernina lifted her shoulders in an eloquent shrug. "No one knows."

Treet was silent for a moment—something the woman had

said . . . what was it? "Go on with what you were saying—about the other Fieri."

"I vowed to save him and, eventually, to help him escape. But Hladik came for him—took him from his bed before he was completely healed." She added sadly, "I never learned what became of him."

Better you don't know, thought Treet.

"But I will *not* let those murderers succeed a second time." She smacked a tight fist into her palm. "I have made plans. Hladik is dead. They say Subdirector Fertig is responsible, but I smell Jamrog's handiwork in it. And that isn't all: rumor messengers have been saying that a Purge is beginning. Two Threl Leaders have disappeared."

Treet groaned. "Not Tvrdy and Cejka?"

The physician nodded gravely. "Tanais and Rumon, yes. You know them?"

"I—ah . . ." He paused to rephrase what he'd been about to say. "Yes, I was helping them—we were trying to prevent the Purge. But then Hladik caught me."

"He won't catch you again, nor will anyone else. I will see to that." She stood and took his cup, then placed an experienced hand against his throat. Treet felt comfort in the gesture. "Rest now. We will talk again soon and make plans. You are safe here for now. Rest and grow strong."

"All right, I'm all yours," he said. He was tired of talking anyway, and she had given him more than enough to think about for a while. Treet settled back and closed his eyes.

· · · · · ·

In the room adjoining Treet's, the young physician replaced the broken tile near the floor and crept from behind the multicolored Bolbe hanging. His breath was shallow and his feet unsteady as he moved off. A Fieri! his mind shrieked. The patient was a *Fieri!*

No one, not even the Nilokerus who contacted him and persuaded him to become a lipreader, could have guessed he would discover anything this important. His Nilokerus instructor would be pleased. But should he tell?

Yes, that is what his training had been for. And think of the shares he would earn. But who would pay the most for this information? The priests? The Hage Leader? The Supreme Director himself?

· · · · · ·

The boats lay motionless, the water making little licking sounds as it lapped between the hulls. Laughter echoed from the rafters of the pavilions scattered around the bay as stories were remembered and recounted. Firelight glittered through the clustered groves, and music sighed on the soft night air.

The white sand beneath his feet shone blue in the starlight as Pizzle wandered the beach, lost in the enchantment of the night. Starla walked beside him, humming now and then as snatches of tune caught her fancy. The Empyrion sky was alive with stars, and their winking faces were mirrored in the calm deep of the lake, and in Starla's eyes.

"Tomorrow we start upriver," said Pizzle absently.

"Taleraan," replied Starla just as absently.

"What?"

"The river's name—"

"Right. Preben told me." They walked on in silence a while longer. "Too bad Jaire couldn't come along."

"She chose to remain at the hospital with the children."

"I know." He put an arm around Starla's shoulders and drew her to him. "I'm glad you're here, though. I wouldn't have wanted to experience this without you."

"I have spoken to my brother," she said.

"That's nice," said Pizzle absently. "What did he say?"

"He said he trusted me to make a wise decision."

"I'm sure you will."

"I've decided to ask the Preceptor."

"Good."

"She will know how to advise us."

"Advise us?" Pizzle replayed their conversation back in his mind. "Starla, what are we talking about exactly? What did you ask your brother?"

"About our marriage."

Pizzle stopped and held her out at arm's length. "You what? Marriage?"

"Out of respect for her parents, a woman seeks their wisdom regarding her marriage. But my parents are with the Infinite Father. Therefore, I asked my brother. Vanon likes you. He still talks about the story you told him—what was it?"

"*The Rune Readers of Ptolemy X*," sighed Pizzle. "It was one of Z. Z. Papoon's best efforts." He wondered what ol' Z. Z. would have said to the notion that the plot of one of his novels would endear a woman's family to the idea of marriage to an alien on a world eleven light-years from his home in Mussle Head, Massachusetts.

"Yes, that was it," continued Starla. "He allowed me to make my own decision. I think, though, it would be wise to ask the Preceptor to advise us."

"In case there's a regulation against someone marrying an alien, huh?"

"The Preceptor would know."

Pizzle reflected on this for a moment. "Are you saying you *want* to marry me?"

"You spoke of marriage. You haven't forgotten?"

"I haven't forgotten. But I thought you had." Now what was he going to do? He looked at her standing before him in the starlight, watching him expectantly. She was beautiful, desirable, a joy to be with and behold—what was he waiting for? Still, there was something holding him back, and he knew what it was. How could he tell her? Well, see, Starla, it's nothing really major, it's just that I'm from another planet and all.

"What's wrong, Asquith?" she asked softly.

"N-nothing . . . well, it's just that . . . we're different."

"I know that. I love you, Asquith. I believe you love me, too."

Pizzle looked at her and melted. "Oh, I do, Starla, believe me I do." He drew her close and held her for a long time.

· · · · · ·

Yarden sat alone, her back against a tree, watching the firelight shift the shadows of those gathered around the campfire, enjoying its warmth and light. She heard the songs and stories, heard the laughter, but felt herself slipping further and further away from those convivial sounds into a barren and lonely place.

And it was all because of Treet.

One way or another, Treet was behind her unhappiness. Therefore, one way or another, he was responsible.

Yarden had never been one to show any dependence upon men. Why all of a sudden she should be mumbling and fretting over someone she didn't even particularly like, confused and upset her more than she cared to admit.

Sure, there had been a time when she thought she was in love with Treet. But likely as not, that had merely been a physical infatuation: two people surviving a harrowing experience, glad to be alive and eager to show it—that sort of thing. Had she, in her heart of hearts, ever had any genuine feelings for Orion Treet? At all?

Well, maybe. But whatever she felt—if anything—had flown right out the door the day Treet decided to go traipsing back to Dome on his lunatic crusade.

She still believed that she had been right to cut off their relationship right then and there. To sever it cleanly, once and for all. That was the best way. The only way. She wouldn't live with the anxiety of not knowing where he was, what he was doing, whether he was in trouble or hurt, alive or not—any of a jillion things a lover could find to worry about.

But we *aren't* lovers, Yarden insisted to herself. Not now. Not ever.

No.

She would *not* change her mind. In spite of everything Ianni might say, she had chosen her course and Treet had chosen his. There was nothing she could do about him anyway. He was back in *Dome*—the very word filled her with sick dread. There was no way she would go back there, and nothing could make her. Yarden had felt the evil of Dome, felt it most powerfully. She knew it for what it was. And because she knew, she would not go back lest the same power seize and overtake her as it very nearly had the first time.

If no one else could understand that, too bad. No one— not Ianni, not the Preceptor, not the Infinite Father himself— was going to make her change her mind.

THIRTY
ONE

Saecaraz Subdirector Osmas stared at the two Nilokerus before him. Two Saecaraz underdirectors, their faces pursed into identical scowls of authority usurped, stood behind. "What do you mean coming here like this?" he demanded. "Application must be made—"

"A matter of utmost urgency, Hage Leader," replied the more intrepid of the two. The other, a young man, hung back with an expression mingling awe and fright on his beardless face.

"It must be if you expect me to disturb the Supreme Director at this most inconvenient hour," Osmas growled. "What is it?"

"That, I think, we must wait to tell the Supreme Director."

"Wait you will—he sees no one at this hour."

The Nilokerus looked at one another. The brave one said, "Tell him that it—" He hesitated, choosing his words carefully. "That it concerns an escaped Fieri."

Osmas eyed the two suspiciously. "What are you saying? Explain yourself!"

The Nilokerus only shook his head slowly.

"I can have your poak erased." The Subdirector's voice was taut, but the threat brought no response from the Nilokerus. "You insist on meeting with the Supreme Director? All right, I warned you. Wait over there." Osmas pointed to a long bench against one wall of the anteroom, turned, and disappeared into the convoluted corridor leading to the cluster of kraams and chambers making up the Hage administration center beneath Threl High Chambers.

The Subdirector returned a few minutes later, bothered and anxious. "Come with me," he said and led them back into the cluster, where they entered a lift and rode up several levels to the Threl Chambers. Osmas said nothing, but his dark glances let the two Nilokerus know that he was not at all pleased with this development. Without ceremony he ushered them into the cylindrical meeting room and brought them to stand before a disheveled-looking man flopped in the Supreme Director's chair who frowned drowsily at them and demanded, "What's this about an escaped Fieri?"

Osmas nodded to the foremost Nilokerus, who stepped forward cautiously.

"Well? You have dragged me from my well-deserved sleep to hear this lie—" He yawned. "Let's hear it."

"I am a Nilokerus trainer, security section—" the man began.

"Yes, yes, we know all that. What about this Fieri?"

The Nilokerus turned to his young companion and said, "Tell him what you told me."

The young man crept forward timidly, although the Supreme Director appeared more sleepy than fierce. "There is a patient in Hage who claims to be a Fieri—I've seen him myself . . ."

Jamrog glanced at his Subdirector. "You brought me here for this?"

Osmas sputtered. The first Nilokerus spoke. "He's nervous, Supreme Director. I can speak for him."

"Then do so!"

"He is a lipreader—a first-order physician on Starwatch level." The young man nodded to authenticate the detail. "Yesterday he discovered that one of the patients in their care was a Fieri spy—escaped, apparently—who had come seeking help from the physicians."

"Escaped?"

"Apparently."

"How? Escaped from where?" These questions were directed to the physician.

The young Nilokerus plucked up his courage and said, "We found him one morning—many days ago now. He was wearing a Nilokerus yos, but was unconscious, unable to move. Believing him to be one of Hlad—" A terrified expression blossomed upon the young man's face as he realized what he was about to say.

"One of Hladik's prisoners?" Jamrog supplied the words equably.

"We took him in," the physician continued, "and stabilized him. He improved. Yesterday Ernina came to talk to him. She was the one who discovered he was a Fieri. She told him she knew—he didn't deny it. She told him she has vowed to protect him."

"Protect him from what?"

The young man glanced at his companion, who winced. "I don't know," he answered hesitantly.

The Supreme Director's eyes narrowed. He clasped his hands and leaned forward. "A Fieri among Nilokerus physicians," he said thoughtfully. Yes, it came back to him now. The fugitive caught in the Archives—thinking him one of Tvrdy's agents, Hladik had wanted to condition him. A Fieri?

According to Mrukk the Fieri had all escaped—aided, of course, by Tvrdy. Jamrog remembered the debacle well. It was Rohee's handling of the Fieri fiasco that had convinced Jamrog the time had come for him to seize power. If I had been in control then, considered Jamrog, the matter would have been handled differently. Huh! It would be just like Hladik to bungle the conditioning. Luckily this lipreader had some sense. Perhaps now he would have another chance to discover the truth about these Fieri agitators.

His head snapped up. "I would see this Fieri, Osmas. Send for Mrukk."

The Subdirector hurried away to summon the chief of the Invisibles. Jamrog sat nodding in his chair. "I suppose you think you deserve a reward?"

"It has been said that the new Supreme Director is most generous," replied the Nilokerus instructor uncertainly.

Jamrog sneered, his lips drawing back from his teeth. "Most generous." He staggered from his chair, clutching his wrinkled hagerobe. "Go now. Wait below, and I will have Osmas bring your reward." The Supreme Director lurched off, leaving the two Nilokerus gaping.

They found their way back to the lift, dropped down to the main level, and returned to the bench they had occupied before, there to wait in squirming anticipation.

At the sight of the Subdirector both men leapt to their feet. How much would it be? A thousand shares? Two thousand?

Osmas came toward the waiting men, Mrukk treading softly beside him. "I have brought your reward," he announced when they had drawn close to the waiting Nilokerus.

The instructor flashed a quick, greedy smile at his pupil. "Our thanks, Subdirector."

"Three thousand apiece." Osmas produced a poak imprinter from his yos and raised its glowing point. "The Supreme Director wishes to demonstrate his unquestionable generosity to those who aid Empyrion. Tell your Hagemen."

He held the stylus up and took the first Nilokerus by the arm.

"Allow me," said Mrukk, suddenly stepping close.

No one noticed the naked blade as his hand flicked out and up.

Blood cascaded down the Nilokerus' yos, and a look of astonishment appeared on his face. His mouth worked, and his hands fluttered to his neck, trying to rejoin the rent in his throat as he toppled to the floor.

The young lipreader cried out and turned to flee. He dashed a few steps and stopped, arms twisting backward, hands grasping, clawing at a spot between his shoulderblades where Mrukk's knife had suddenly appeared, buried to the hilt in his flesh.

Osmas stared at the carnage, horrified. "What have you done?"

The chief of the Invisibles stooped to retrieve his weapon, and wiped it casually on the clothing of his victim. "I have saved the Saecaraz treasury six thousand shares."

"When Jamrog finds out about this—"

Mrukk laughed. "You think he doesn't know?"

"But the reward . . ."

"Keep it for yourself. A bonus."

"I couldn't."

"Then give it to someone who knows what to do with it." Mrukk laughed again and pushed up the sleeve of his yos. Grimly, Osmas set the imprinter and pressed it to Mrukk's muscled arm. "Now then," said Mrukk, stepping over the body of the Nilokerus at his feet, "let's go find this Fieri."

• • • • • •

Just a little east of the tranquil bay, pastel green hills slanted up from the northern shore of Prindahl, to march away into the shimmering blue distance. The hillsides were covered by small round trees with leaves so dark they appeared blue in the morning light, making the hillsides look dotted with minature balons ready to take flight on the first breeze. Through these hills wound the deep waters of Taleraan, upon whose broad back the Fieri boats would embark this day.

The glass-smooth lake reflected a high, cloudless sky of chromium blue and a sun rising white into a new day. The ships floated in the crystalline water, painted hulls gleaming, rigging glinting like silver tracery in the sunlight. Atop the tall masts several rakkes had taken residence, holding their wings out to warm in the new sun.

On shore, the travelers awoke to breakfasts of fresh fruit, tea, and flat loaves of sweet bread. They talked excitedly while they ate, some of the younger Fieri slipping off to swim one last time before boarding. In all, it was a leisurely start to the day. Although everyone expressed eagerness to depart, no one appeared in any hurry to leave—a fact Pizzle found slightly maddening. Even if no one else cared to start, he was ready—had been ready for hours before sunrise. In fact, he had not actually slept the night before: he'd been too excited.

After saying good-night to Starla (a process that took well over an hour), he had wandered the beach aimlessly, his head filled with thoughts of love and marriage and family. Then he'd scooped a shallow depression in the warm sand and laid out under the stars contemplating the harmony of the universe.

Now he was anxious to be off, but first he had to locate the Preceptor and request an audience. He lingered near the first ship, the one in which she traveled, hoping to be in the right place at the right time when she appeared. He was not disappointed.

Pizzle was standing at the water's edge, looking hungrily at the happy breakfasters in a nearby pavilion when he turned and found the Preceptor standing on the deck of the boat behind him, watching him.

"Good morning, Preceptor," he called. "Have you had breakfast?"

"Good morning, Traveler Pizzle," came her reply. "I have just come from my devotions and have not eaten yet. Will you join me? I would like to speak to you."

"Sure, whatever you say." He waded out to the gangplank

to meet the Fieri leader. She had changed her white chinti for one of amber yellow, and her hair was braided and tied in a sheer yellow scarf. She came gracefully down the gangplank and entered the water. Pizzle met her and offered a hand which she accepted regally, allowing herself to be escorted to the beach.

A place was made for them at the table inside the pavilion and food served at once. Most of the Fieri were finished eating and vanished discreetly. "Actually," Pizzle said after the Preceptor had asked a blessing over the food and they began to eat, "I wanted to speak to you, too. I would like to have an audience."

"Oh, yes?" The Preceptor looked at him curiously, her amethyst eyes bright with interest.

Pizzle nodded, picked up a small, red plumlike fruit, and bit into it. Juice ran down his arm. "Yesh," he said with his mouth full. He swallowed and then added, "If it's not too much trouble. It's for myself and Starla."

"I see." The Preceptor continued to gaze at him—for such a long time that Pizzle became uncomfortable.

"Is there something wrong?" he asked.

The question was met with a smile. "Please, think no negative thought. I was asking the Teacher for leading."

"Oh." Pizzle picked up another plum fruit and ate it thoughtfully.

"I am happy to give you an audience," the Preceptor said. "Would this evening suit you?"

"That would be perfect." Pizzle grinned happily.

"You are much changed since you came to us," the Preceptor observed.

"Was that what you wanted to talk to me about?"

"Yes, and to ask you if you are happy here."

Pizzle grew solemn. "I've never been happier in my whole entire life. I never knew anyone as happy as I am—I didn't even know it was possible to be this happy," he declared. "Really."

"Have you discovered your purpose among us, Asquith?"

"My purpose?"

"Everyone has a purpose given them by the Infinite Father. In order to find true happiness, it is necessary to fulfill your purpose."

Pizzle thought about this for a moment and had to admit that he didn't know what his purpose was.

"There is time to discover it, Asquith," said the Preceptor

gently, humor shining in her eyes. "But it does not do to put off the search too long."

Pizzle nodded. "I'll do my best."

The Preceptor rose. "I'll be waiting for you." She smiled lightly. "Until this evening, then."

"This evening," confirmed Pizzle. He got up slowly, and the Preceptor moved off to greet her people, many of whom had gathered to wait for her. He watched her move among them, giving and receiving blessings, and sharing with them the joy of the day.

Presently he came to himself. Hey! I've got to find Starla and tell her! He grabbed a loaf of the sweet bread and trotted off down the beach.

THIRTY
TWO

The Invisibles appeared so suddenly, there was no time for Ernina to put her plan into action. No time for anything except quick thinking and a desperate hope.

One moment she had been bending over Treet. The next, Mrukk and three of his Mors Ultima were standing in the doorway. She stepped around the bed to meet them. "It took you long enough to get here," she said angrily. "What kept you?"

Mrukk's eyes flicked from the man in the bed to the flinty old physician. She did not wait for a reply. "Didn't my Hageman tell you it was urgent?"

The Mors Ultima chief regarded her suspiciously. "No."

"What *did* he tell you?" Ernina demanded, hands on hips.

"Out of the way, woman." Mrukk made move to push past her. She put her hands on his chest and held him back.

"I sent him to tell the Supreme Director. I found the Fieri. The reward is mine. What did he tell you?"

"You sent him?" Mrukk glared at the immovable woman, and signaled to his men to go ahead with the abduction. They went to the bed and pulled Treet from it. He awoke startled, saw the shimmering black yoses, and hollered. He was dragged from the bed kicking and screaming.

Ernina did not risk so much as a backward glance. "Well? Answer me."

"The Nilokerus and the Hageman with him said he was a lipreader. They said you had vowed to protect the Fieri—" Mrukk glared at her fiercely.

"Protect the Fieri! Trabant take him!" she shouted, her face livid.

"Ernina!" Treet yelled as he was jerked through the doorway. "What are you doing? For God's sake, help me!"

"Don't you see what they have done? They have cheated me out of my reward. I intend to see the Supreme Director about this. The Fieri was mine! The reward is mine!" she screamed shrilly. "It's mine!"

Mrukk backed away a step. "I know nothing about the reward."

"Liar!" Ernina advanced toward him.

Treet's cries echoed in the corridor beyond—confused, enraged, helpless.

"The reward is mine. I'm going to the Supreme Director."

"Do it. I have what I came for. I don't care what you do."
With that, Mrukk spun on his heel and disappeared.

Ernina fell back on the bed, stunned. So it had been Uissal.
She had guessed the moment the Invisibles appeared, mentally
cursing herself for being so blind. It was all there for her to see:
the young physician's absence that day, his habit of lurking
nearby whenever she spoke privately with a patient, his perpetually guilty expression . . .

She jumped to her feet. There was no time now for that.
She had to move at once. She swept through the medical cluster
to her own chambers, gathered up a large bundle from her table,
and stood a moment looking at her beloved ancient books,
running her hand along their disintegrating spines. Then she
swung the bundle over her shoulder and departed.

• • • • • •

Tvrdy watched the drills from the wrecked tower of twisted metal that had once served as the outer stairway to a Hageblock long ago reduced to rubble. In the dirt-covered field below, ranks of Dhogs labored to become soldiers: moving here and there in ragged packs, running, diving, lunging, shouting, flailing arms and legs at imaginary enemies under the tutelage of Tanais and Rumon instructors.

The resulting display was so miserable that Tvrdy's frown had passed directly from anger to despair. The Dhogs were a hopeless rabble—dirty, ill-clothed, and ignorant. Even under tight Tanais discipline, they could not be organized; confusion reigned on the drill field. After he'd seen enough, Tvrdy descended from the tower and called one of his lieutenants from the field for a consultation.

"What is going on out there?"

The Tanais, sweating, his face dark with frustration, answered readily. "The Dhogs cannot be taught. They are too stupid for even simple exercises."

"Do they accept your leadership?"

"It isn't that. These nonbeings, Hage leader, they think with their stomachs only. They say they are hungry."

"Are they?"

The man shrugged. "They're always hungry. We all are."

Tvrdy folded his arms across his chest, lowered his head for a moment in thought. "All right, continue as best you can. But tell them that tomorrow, and from now on, before drills they will be given a meal. Also at night. See that they understand."

The Tanais instructor nodded to his superior. "As you say, Hage Leader." He didn't ask where the food was going to come from, although he wondered.

Tvrdy turned and walked from the drill field. How could men think when their bellies were empty? How could they work without food?

The Tanais Director walked briskly across the field to the Hageblock opposite, where Piipo had set up the Hyrgo headquarters in order to be near the Directors' command posts, although the growing fields were being established on the Old Section's outer ring much further away.

"Ahh, Tvrdy!" The Hyrgo leader looked up as Tvrdy entered the ramshackle room. He stood with several Hagemen who were holding transparent sacks of soil for his inspection. "I did not expect to see you again so soon this morning." To his men he said, "Begin revitalization. I'll join you in the fields."

They trooped out and Piipo came over to Tvrdy, dusting his hands. "The soil is dreadful—still, not so bad as I expected. We'll be able to work with it."

Tvrdy noticed a keenness in the Hyrgo's glance and tone. He said, "I believe you are enjoying this, Piipo."

"It's true. I can't explain it, but I find this all very stimulating." He noticed the gravity in Tvrdy's tone and asked, "What is it, Hageman?"

"How close are we to feeding ourselves?"

The question took Piipo aback. "You're serious?"

"Always."

"Tvrdy, we have not even planted. It will be months. The soil . . . the water . . . four or five months at least. I told you at the first briefing."

"Yes, I know. How long can we sustain ourselves on the supplies we brought with us?"

"At the present consumption level—until the first crops come in. This I also explained during the briefing. Why are you asking me these things?"

"I want to begin feeding the Dhogs."

"Feeding nonbeings?" Piipo's expression showed pure astonishment.

"They have no food. They are so hungry they cannot complete even simple maneuvers. We have to build them up if we are ever to make fighters of them. It's that simple."

"Starvation is also simple. We feed the Dhogs and our supplies vanish overnight. We can starve right along with the rest—what will that accomplish?"

"I don't propose to starve, Piipo."

"Then you must propose to bring in more supplies, because I can't make the seeds sprout any faster."

"What word from your Hage?"

"Subdirector Gorov is to be installed as Director pending an investigation of my disappearance. He says the Hage is in full production. The Purge has not touched the Hyrgo yet."

"This is good." Tvrdy tugged on his lower lip thoughtfully.

"What are you thinking?"

"I think we must bring in more supplies."

"Of course, but how can we do that? Jamrog's checkpoints—"

"Not through the supply route," said Tvrdy. "We must visit your granaries, Piipo."

"Raid the granaries!"

"It's the only way. We don't have the equipment yet to issue the travel writs and identification. But with Gorov's help, we should be able to get in and out unnoticed."

"It's dangerous."

"Of course."

Piipo was silent for a long time. Finally he said, "I don't like it, but it could be done. Unfortunately, Hage Nilokerus abuts. If anything went wrong, it would not take them long to get to us."

"Us? You'll stay here, Piipo. We need your expertise."

"No, I must go with you. Who knows the Hage better than its Director?"

"We'll take one of your underdirectors."

"No. I'm going."

Tvrdy saw it was no use arguing with the Hrygo, so he

said, "Meet me at the briefing kraam in an hour. We will all sit down and plan the raid. Then Cejka will arrange to get instructions to Gorov at once."

"When will the raid take place?"

"Tonight."

THIRTY
THREE

The pale green hills drifted slowly by the ships which stretched out in a long, snaking train along Taleraan's undulating curves. The boats kept to the center of the wide channel and the deepest part of the river, forging upstream against the slow current. The sails were furled, for now the ships were driven by the crystal-powered engines carried in the outrigged pods which had been attached to either side of the boat. These propelled the ships cleanly and quietly upriver.

Bemused hill creatures inhabiting the thickets and groves along the wide banks halted their foraging to watch the grand procession pass. The Fieri hailed the animals, watching the banks and pointing out each new species to one another. Yarden hung over the rail with the rest, enjoying the scenery and the fauna, quite forgetting her agitation of the night before in the beauty of the day.

At first glance desolate, the hills were actually swarming with wildlife once one learned how and where to look for them. There were creatures that looked like fluffy, long-legged antelopes, floating like tawny clouds as they grazed the rolling hillsides in scattered herds. Lower, among the frilly trees along the riverbanks, scuttled small orange bearlike animals with shaggy golden manes. Larger, darker shapes moved among the shadowed backgrounds, and stout gray-blue water beasts with long necks and rotund bodies plied the shallows, diving and surfacing with water pods in their toothless jaws.

Besides the ubiquitous rakkes, there were avian battalions of swooping, diving fishers with pointed beaks and brilliant green and red banded wings that sliced the air in sharp maneuvers to the delight of their captivated audiences, snatching tiny striped fish out of the water on the fly. Their less pretentious cousins strolled the river's edge on pink stilt legs, stepping carefully through the turquoise forests of long-bladed watergrass, their bright yellow heads cocked, great round eyes scanning the silted bottom for the jade-colored lizards on which they fed.

Yarden was enthralled with all she saw, and never tired of

looking as each new bend in the river revealed a panorama of fresh beauty. The slow, steady progress of the boats, marked by a lulling chorus of bird and animal calls, worked on Yarden like a delicious elixir, and she drank in every brilliant moment.

Gerdes also inspired her, too, but in a different way. Each afternoon the Fieri teacher gathered her brood of eager young artists beneath the ocher canopy on the aft deck of the barge. There she led them through exercises. "A limber body is often the companion of a limber mind," she told them. "The body is the bridge between the mind and the emotions, just as the emotions are the bridge between the mind and spirit."

Of the eight students Gerdes had gathered for the journey, Yarden was the oldest by far, and found herself slightly envious of their youth, wishing she had embarked upon her career earlier. An absurd thought, she told herself on reflection, since there was no way she could have come to Empyrion any sooner, and in her other life—her life as an executive administrator to one of the most powerful men in the known universe—the idea of becoming an artist had never occurred to her. Seriously, that is. She had sometimes felt artistic yearnings within her, and thought she might like to do something creative, but always dismissed the urges as inappropriate or impractical.

But here on Empyrion all things were possible. She was not subject to the tyranny of the practical. In fact, her previous life seemed to her now to have been largely a waste of precious time. A waste she would have resented if it did not now seem so remote and inconsequential. In fact, she had to think very hard about it in order to remember her life with Cynetics at all.

Together the eight would-be artists and their instructor filled the afternoon hours with exercises in body awareness and movement, and sessions of mental conditioning. Through all of the exercises, Gerdes imparted nuggets of her artistic philosophy: "Art is thought as well as feeling. An artist's abilities, mind, and spirit are brought to the act of creation."

"Why do we spend so much time in movement exercises?" asked one of the Fieri, a stocky young man with black curly hair and a ruddy complexion, full of exuberance and high spirits, but definitely not inclined to patience.

"Because, Luarco, my restless one," Gerdes said, and the other Fieri laughed, "we already know how to think. We think all the time. The mind controls all we do, sometimes inhibiting motion. The body was made to move, not to think; therefore, we must learn to free the body to do what it knows how to do."

"But doesn't that contradict what you just said about the role of the artist's mind in the act of creation?" asked a young woman sitting next to Yarden.

"Ahh, Taniani, you are always running far ahead. I was coming to that. Once we have learned to move freely, without unnecessary restriction, we can reintroduce the mental aspect in its proper place. Here is the key: *balance*. In art there must be a balance of the physical, mental, emotional, and spiritual."

"The Preceptor calls that the key to life," Luarco pointed out—with just a touch of belligerence, Yarden thought.

"Oh, it is, Luarco, it is. It is also the key to great art. Think now! What is the most important component of the work?"

"Skill," replied a young man sprawled out full-length on the deck, his sandy hair ruffled in the breeze.

"I'm not surprised you would say that, Gheorgi. Your skill is admirable." Gerdes asked the others, "Is he right?"

"No," said the girl next to him. "Technical skill by itself means nothing. The thought the artist is trying to communicate is the most important. If the artist has nothing to say, it doesn't matter how great his skill."

"It's the artist's *expression,*" said another. "Without the right expression nothing is communicated, no matter how well conceived or executed."

Gerdes smiled with self-satisfaction. "Do you hear yourselves? You have proven my point. Who sees it?" Her gaze swept the group. "Yarden?"

Yarden had been engrossed in the discussion, and was startled to hear her name called. "Because," she said slowly, "any element elevated to the exclusion of the others . . . ah, works against the piece."

"Precisely!" Gerdes crowed. "Do you see it? Balance! As in life, all elements are equally important. It is self-evident: exclude one and the work is flawed. Without the physical, there is no substance; without the emotional, it has no heart; without the mind, it has no direction; and without the spiritual, the work has no soul. All elements are necessary. All must be maintained in balance."

The rippling of water and the clear keening of the rakkes punctuated the silence as the students turned these things over in their heads. At last Gerdes said, "Make this a part of your meditations for tonight. We will begin with brush and ink tomorrow."

Noting Luarco's pained expression, Gerdes added, "Yes, *black* ink, Luarco. Color will come later. First, I want to see your brush strokes live."

The students broke up, most drifting off along the decks in pairs, continuing the discussion; others stretched out beneath the canopy, now golden with the afternoon sun full on it. Yarden got up to leave and Gerdes came to her, taking her arm and steering her toward the stern.

Fieri sat on benches along the rail, quietly talking, or napped in colored cloth deckchairs. Several youngsters had made paper boats which they floated from the ends of long strings. It was, Yarden thought, a typical tourboat scene from the last century. They found a place on a nearby bench and sat down together. "A very perceptive answer, Yarden," began Gerdes.

Yarden smiled, but shrugged off the compliment. "You said yourself it was self-evident."

"Certainly, but we do not always see the obvious—rarely, in fact. Anyway, it showed you were thinking."

"I am doing a lot of that lately, it seems."

Gerdes' kind face puckered in concern. "Not all of it about painting, I would guess."

She gave her teacher a sideways glance. "I know, think no negative thought. But—well, I just . . . I've had a lot to think about. I didn't know it showed."

"When the heart is troubled, the body responds in its own way. I noticed your exercises were stiff, tentative. You were not centered in yourself."

"It's true. I did feel awkward this afternoon. But I'll do better tomorrow."

Gerdes smiled gently and took her hand. "Dear Yarden, do you really suppose that's why I wanted to talk to you? I care about you far more than I care about your lessons. I merely thought that if something was troubling you, and if talking would help, we could talk."

"Thank you, Gerdes; you're kind and thoughtful. But this is something I need to work out alone."

"You're sure?"

Yarden nodded, and squeezed her teacher's hand.

"As you say. Still, if you think it might help—"

"I'll remember."

Gerdes rose and moved off. Yarden remained by herself on the bench. What am I going to do? she wondered. Just when I think I've made some progress, someone comes along and tells me I'm unhappy. I've got to pull myself together.

• • • • • •

The rain pattered down upon the forest floor, filtering through layer upon layer of leaves until it percolated down to the ground to soak the fertile soil and transform forest pathways into gurgling brooks. The man and his great dark feline companion waited out the rain, listening to the water sounds and napping beneath a low, umbrella-shaped bush whose broad, frilly leaves kept them perfectly dry.

The bond between the man and the wevicat had deepened since the combat with the behemoth, and Crocker had begun talking to the cat, haltingly at first, but with increasing fluency. The cat gazed at the man with golden calm in its great eyes, now and then licking its paws with its deeply grooved tongue, prepared to listen to the man-sounds indefinitely.

"Rain, rain, go away," muttered the man.

The wevicat rolled over on its side and laid its head down on the dry leaves. In a moment a rumble like mountain thunder sounded as the animal began to purr. It was the sound of pure contentment and soon Crocker, too, had stretched out, his head resting against the cat's warm flank. "Rain, rain, go away," he said again, like a child enthralled with the sound of its own voice. "Crocker come back another day."

Jamrog was beside himself. "He doesn't look like much. Are
you certain this is the Fieri? Perhaps you have captured a
Jamuna wastehandler by mistake." The Supreme Director
walked slowly around his prisoner, prodding him roughly with
the butt of the bhuj. Diltz and Mrukk looked on. "Why, he
looks just like an ordinary Hageman. I must say I'm very disappointed, Mrukk. I expected much more."

"Look at his teeth, Hage Leader," suggested Diltz.

"Open your mouth, Fieri," commanded Jamrog, grabbing
Treet by the chin. Treet did not cooperate, so the Supreme
Director called the Mors Ultima standing at attention nearby.
"Open his mouth," he ordered.

Treet's jaws were forced open. Jamrog came close and
poked a finger inside his mouth. "Ah, yes! I see what you mean,
Diltz. Those teeth have never been touched by Nilokerus physicians. They are perfect. But can he speak with those perfect
teeth in his mouth?"

Treet said nothing. His initial shock at being apprehended
had worn off, and now he was simply sullen. Oddly, he was not
at all afraid. Instead, much to his own surprise, he was merely
disgruntled by the necessity of having to deal with the inconve-
nience of being a prisoner once more.

He had not yet worked out in his own mind how he was
going to respond to the situation. There were a number of
options: he could become the indignant emissary and make
subtle threats; he could remain unresponsive, refuse to play
along; or he could put on a harmless demeanor, pretend he was
friend to one and all.

None of the options appealed to him. For one thing, he
didn't like Jamrog. The man was creeping slime from what Treet
could see. Sirin Rohee had been different; at least with Rohee
there had been a scrap of humanity in the old man that Treet
felt he could appeal to. Though he'd never met Jamrog, he'd
heard from Tvrdy that the man was filth, and dangerous filth at

that. The moment he set eyes on the new Supreme Director, Treet knew Tvrdy's assessment had been only too accurate.

The heavy, bulging forehead; the dull, empty eyes and lusterless complexion; the full, sensual lips curled in a perpetual sneer; the easy, open stance that spoke of indulgence and authority; the smooth, milk-fed flesh: all combined to create a portrait of cool, malignant debauchery.

Treet recognized Jamrog for what he was, and shrank away from the recognition. Not from fear did he recoil, but from revulsion. The reaction was so strong, it surprised him. Treet, a man of tolerance, a man accustomed to taking life as he found it and witholding judgment, felt a genuine and powerful disgust for the man mocking him. And he felt something else as well: pity.

He saw Jamrog as a petty, pathetic poser, drunk on power and sinking beneath his own ballooning megalomania even as his appetite for greater and greater atrocity grew. Treet looked at him and saw a poor, crabbed creature, stunted and shriveled. A being with a soul so wasted it could no longer be called human, could no longer even be feared, merely pitied.

He had no doubt whatsoever that Jamrog should be stamped out. But there was no vengeance in the thought, just a little sadness—as much as a man might feel upon realizing that a rabid dog has to be put out of its misery.

These were new thoughts for Treet, new sensations. He seemed to be seeing all before him with unaccustomed clarity— a trick he chalked up to his heightened awareness. It was as if he were viewing events through new eyes.

"The question now is what to do with him. Any suggestions?" Jamrog babbled on. "We could let him go, I suppose. But what mischief would that cause? No, too risky." He rumpled his brow in mock thoughtfulness. "I know," he said gaily. "We could persuade him to divulge the secrets of the ages." He put his face close to Treet's. "What do *you* say, Fieri? What should we do with you?"

Treet made no move.

"Your refusal to speak wearies me. Speak, Fieri. What do you think we should do with you?"

Treet returned the Supreme Director's gaze calmly.

"Answer me!" Jamrog screamed, a thick vein standing out on his forehead.

"You won't like what I have to say," said Treet, who didn't really know yet what he had to say.

"See? I told you, Mrukk, he does talk. What's more, I understood every word." He leaned close, placing a hand on Treet's shoulder. "I'm not your enemy, Fieri. I can help you. Yes, I want to help you."

"Then let me go."

"But I want you to be my guest here and stay with me. You'd like that. I could make you very comfortable. I could take good care of you."

"Like you took care of Sirin Rohee?"

That rocked the Supreme Director back. "You must not listen to idle Hage gossip while among us, Fieri." He darted a glance at the chief of the Invisibles. "Mrukk, take him. Reason with him, and bring him back in a more receptive mood."

With that, Treet was hauled from the kraam and marched off into the convoluted heart of Threl High Chambers.

• • • • • •

The Preceptor met them at the door to her stateroom below deck. The early evening sky still held the afternoon light. Pizzle entered first, remembered his manners, and pulled Starla from behind him, ushered her ahead, then came in himself, closing the door.

"I'm glad you could see us so soon, Preceptor," Starla said, completely at ease.

"Yeah, it's real great of you," remarked Pizzle. He walked like a puppet whose strings were fouled.

"Let's sit down here." The Preceptor directed them to three cushioned chairs. They sat, and there followed a moment of thoughtful silence into which Pizzle blurted, "This is a real nice room you have here, Preceptor. Looks very cozy."

She smiled graciously. "I am very comfortable here. Are you enjoying the journey?"

"It's outrageous, it really is. I mean it's simply fantastic. Super-fantastic! Did you see those gazelle-things? And those fuzzy orange lion-bears? Incredible." Pizzle realized he was making a fool of himself, but was unable to stop. His face felt tight.

His hands were flying all over the place, and his voice cracked with excitement. He forced himself to take a deep breath. "Yes," he said as he exhaled, "I guess you could say I'm enjoying the trip very much."

Starla came to his rescue. "Asquith and I need your guidance, Preceptor."

"How may I help you, Starla?"

Starla turned to Pizzle with encouragement in her glance. "We are thinking—that is, Starla and myself want to know if you can tell us if . . . is there any reason that we ought to know about . . . I mean, is it all right with you for us to get married?"

The Preceptor did not smile this time. She studied both of them for a moment before replying. When she spoke, her voice was gentle but firm. "I have known since the beginning that this question would arise. Now that it is here, I must speak frankly."

"Please do, Preceptor," said Starla. Pizzle, whose mouth had suddenly gone dry, bobbed his head.

"You may find my words hard to accept." She looked from one to the other of them. Pizzle licked his lips.

"We wish to hear them, Preceptor," Starla said and turned to Pizzle.

"Right! Sure. Oh, yeah," he managed to say.

The Preceptor placed her fingertips together and raised them to her chin. "It is my opinion that marriage would not be beneficial for you."

Pizzle saw the light go out of Starla's eyes, felt his heart go lumpy in his chest. A startled "What?" passed his lips.

Starla regrouped quickly. "Could you explain, Preceptor, so we may better understand?"

"As you wish." The Preceptor inclined her head. Turning to address Pizzle directly, she said, "Empyrion has not yet traveled one-half of its solar cycle during the time you have been with us. That is very little time when one is considering the commitment of a lifetime. There are differences between your people and ours, Asquith—"

"I appreciate those differences," put in Pizzle.

"Perhaps in time you may come to appreciate them. The distance between your race and ours is not measured in billions of kilometers; it is a distance of hearts and minds, which in its own way is just as profound as the distance between our stars."

Pizzle could not speak; he did not have the words to counter this unexpected argument. He turned hopeless eyes on his beloved.

"Forgive me, Preceptor, are you saying that we should not be married?" Starla asked, her voice tense and quiet.

"You have come to me for my advice. I have thought about this matter for a long time, and I am persuaded that a marriage between you would be a sad, perhaps tragic, mistake." The Preceptor regarded them both lovingly. From the open porthole came the gentle sounds of the river at play against the hull and the cry of the rakkes as they soared overhead.

Pizzle was still trying to make himself understand what he had heard when Starla rose to her feet. "Thank you for your guidance, Preceptor. We will abide by your decision."

"Wait a minute!" Pizzle was on his feet. "Is that all? Can't we talk about this? I mean, really. Huh?"

Starla looked stricken. She'd never heard anyone speak to the Preceptor so. "Asquith! Please, don't—"

The Preceptor accepted Pizzle's outburst with aplomb. "Speak, Traveler Pizzle."

Pizzle ran a hand through his hair and began to pace. "It's just that . . . I mean . . . Look, is this advice of yours final, the last word? I mean, can't we do anything about it? It seems to me we ought to have the chance anyway."

"What would you do if granted such a chance?" the Preceptor asked, her violet eyes keen in the fading light of the stateroom.

"Make you change your mind."

"How would you do that?"

"Well, shoot, I don't know. What would it take?" He nodded vigorously, his ears waggling. "Name it, I'll do it—we both will. Anything! Just you name it."

The Preceptor rose from her chair and came to stand before them. "It will be a most difficult trial for you. Are you willing?" Both nodded silently, looking at each other for encouragement. "You must not see one another again until the end of the solar cycle."

"Not at all?" Pizzle's voice whined.

"In the presence of others only; you must not be alone together."

Starla nodded, her expression grim. Pizzle frowned, but nodded too. "That's all?" he asked.

The Preceptor held up a long finger. "I also ask that you, Asquith, undertake a period of instruction from one of the Mentors."

"Sure. No problem. That's it? Then you'll change your mind?"

"We will see what time brings; then we will talk again."

THIRTY
FIVE

"Let the Fieri go, Mrukk," a strangely muffled voice commanded from the shadows. The Invisibles halted at the sound. They were two levels below Threl chambers in a dark and disused corridor, leading their prisoner to one of the many kraams throughout Dome that the Invisibles had recently converted for special interrogations.

The Mors Ultima commander whirled toward the sound, his hand already on his knife. "Show yourself."

A dark mass moved within the darkness of a blacked-out entryway leading to a connecting tunnel.

Treet peered into the darkness and recognized the bulky shape.

So did Mrukk, who barked a sharp laugh. "We don't need you yet, physician."

"Let him go now if you care for your lives." Again the muffled voice, as if the speaker were wearing a mask.

Mrukk took a step closer to where Ernina stood. "Come, we will talk. I'll share the reward with you."

There came a tiny pinging sound, and Mrukk stopped. "What was that?"

To Treet it sounded like a glass bead dropped onto concrete.

"Release the Fieri now." Another ping. A small round pellet dropped to the floor, bounced and rolled into the darkness.

"We could ta—" began Mrukk.

Another pellet dropped. Treet stood still, relaxed but ready to dive toward the tunnel instantly.

"What are you doing?" Mrukk demanded.

"Send the Fieri to me now!" At that, two more pellets fell and bounced.

"Stop it!" ordered Mrukk. "What is that?"

"Release him." A whole handful of pellets rattled onto the floor. Treet saw them bounce and scatter like marbles.

Mrukk signaled one of the Invisibles to advance on the

physician. He inched forward as if he were walking on live coals.

A few more pellets cascaded onto the floor of the darkened corridor, each ping echoing in the empty corridor.

"Do not step on one of those capsules," warned Ernina.

"Get her!" shouted Mrukk. The Invisible took one more step. There was a hollow crunching sound, as if he had stepped on a light bulb.

In the darkness Treet saw the man raise his foot to take another step, totter, and stagger back gasping for breath. He made a gurgling sound in his throat as he pitched forward onto his face. A second later Treet tasted almonds on his lips: cyanide.

"You will die for this, you stupid old mother!" swore Mrukk.

A whole hailstorm of pellets fell, pinging and bouncing into the corridor, some of them rolling to the Invisibles' feet. Everyone stood paralyzed. The odor of almonds was strong in the corridor now. The Invisible holding Treet coughed. "I could kill him right here!" Mrukk growled.

Ernina's reply, though muted, was calm. "What would Jamrog say about that?"

Mrukk ground his teeth and spun on Treet. In the dim green light of the single overhead globe, Treet could see Mrukk's face twisted into a snarl of impotent rage. "When Jamrog is finished with you, Fieri, you are mine! I will have you both before the day is out."

Then he turned to where Ernina stood in the darkened tunnelway. He laughed and said, "Take him, old mother. I give him to you. Let's see how far he gets."

"Come forward, Orion," she said. "Carefully."

Treet raised his foot and lowered it as if expecting the floor to explode. He felt nothing beneath his foot, so trusted his weight to it. He took another equally nerve-stretching step, and then another.

He was now three steps from Mrukk, and one from the Invisible collapsed on the floor. This was certainly the slowest getaway in the combined history of two planets. He doubted whether anyone had ever escaped from the Mors Ultima less speedily.

"Stop there," instructed Ernina. "I'm going to throw you something." She moved to make the throw.

Treet heard a rustle of cloth behind him. "Down, Ernina!"

The knife whizzed by his head, and he heard it clatter in the tunnel beyond, followed by Mrukk's stifled curse.

Treet straightened. "I'm ready." A moment later he felt something rubbery land in his outstretched hands.

"Put it on," said Ernina. "You'll be safe."

"I'll find you!" shouted Mrukk, his voice raw with hate.

Treet turned the floppy object over in his hands several times before he found the opening and pulled the mask over his head. The mask fit snugly over nose and mouth, but left eyes and ears free. He could breathe easily, but the air tasted flat and heavily metallic.

He took an experimental step and crunched a pellet under his heel. He smelled and tasted nothing but the stale, filtered air of his mask. Treet dashed forward quickly, his feet scattering pellets and crunching them willy-nilly. Then he was standing before Ernina and felt her hands on his arm, tugging him back into the tunnel.

"Follow us if you will," called Ernina over her shoulder, as she dumped still more pellets into the tunnel.

Gasps and coughing filled the corridor as they dashed off. They came at once to a turn, and Ernina pulled Treet around the corner. She paused to scatter another handful of the mysterious pellets. "Pray to Cynetics that these will slow them down," said Ernina into her mask, and they hurried on.

• • • • • •

Tvrdy did not like yielding to Bogney in the matter of planning the raid, but knew that the Dhog leader was his only hope of getting in and out of Hyrgo Hage undetected. Bogney had taken Tvrdy's decision with great good humor, roaring at the invitation to lead the sortie. "Tanais needs the Dhogs. Giloon not being useless, seh?"

"No one ever said you were useless," replied Tvrdy. "We all have our expertise. Moving through Hage unnoticed is your expertise. We must all learn from each other."

Bogney roared still louder. "You watching then and learn, Tanais. Giloon be teaching you good."

The plan had been discussed from all angles and the route, including two alternate escape routes, approved by all. Then, as soon as darkness had come to the Old Section, they set off, moving into the complex labyrinth of long abandoned corridors and tunnels known as the Isedon Zone.

The Dhogs knew this mazework intimately, knew every turn and every blind avenue, knew each tunnel junction and intersection. Many of the streets they passed through were choked with rubble but for a narrow footpath winding around the debris. Most of the tunnels had collapsed completely, or had been filled in—whether by the Dhogs or by Hagemen, Tvrdy couldn't say. Bogney led the party expertly, keeping a good pace, even through the worst of the ruin.

Tvrdy marveled at the speed with which the Dhogs could move—never hesitating, never making a wrong turn—covering the same distance in minutes that had taken him hours to navigate that first day. But then this was, after all, the Dhogs' domain, and much of their protection lay in their ability to move quickly and quietly. As they went along, Tvrdy began to feel he'd been right to include Bogney when he had.

The raiding party, thirty-five men in all, made its way along the Isedon Zone toward the border between Chryse and Hage Jamuna. There, the Kyan swung out nearest the Zone, and they could pick their way carefully to the river and along the River-walk to the boat Rumon had left for them. By boat they would follow the river through Jamuna and into Hyrgo Hage.

The trip was accomplished without incident, although they had to skirt a checkpoint on the Chryse border which they had not known about. Once in Hyrgo, Piipo took charge, saying, "Now I'll show you Hyrgo efficiency."

To Tvrdy's surprise, Bogney merely shrugged and fell back to wait at the head of his Dhog troops. Tvrdy had expected a confrontation, and was glad he did not have to intervene. He began to feel that the raid would succeed without incident.

Piipo ordered the boat into a small cove just west of the granary wharf, and the party disembarked. With movements just as certain and decisive as the Dhogs had shown in the Zone, Piipo led them directly to the great ribbed mounds of the Hyrgo granaries, avoiding open areas and the Nilokerus checkpoints.

"There is a door on the third level," Piipo explained as they gathered outside the granary nearest the river. "The climb is not difficult, and the door will be open. Wait here until you hear the signal. I'll need help opening the doors."

"You're not to go," protested Tvrdy. "That isn't in our plan."

"No one is going to plunder this storehouse but me."

"Piipo, think what you're doing."

"Wait. I will return in a moment."

Tvrdy didn't like this development, but allowed Piipo to go without further comment. In a few minutes the party, huddled outside the huge granary doors, heard a distinct clank, a pause, and then three solid knocks on the fibersteel doors. Grabbing the rings, the Dhogs hauled the doors open and then stood staring at the wealth of food stacked within.

"Move, Dhogs!" whispered Bogney urgently. "Drool later." He pushed by them and ran inside to where Piipo's Subdirector, Gorov, had arranged the granary stock to make it easier for the raiders to load onto the waiting warehouse wagons.

Piipo smiled broadly when he saw that and said, "See? The Tanais and Rumon are not the only ones who know how to plan."

The Dhogs leaped to the bulging grain sacks, a dozen to a stack, and began heaving them onto the first wagon. When it was full, they began hauling it out of the warehouse. Ordinarily tractor ems were used to pull the wagons, but these were too noisy. So the wagons had to be disengaged from their tracks and pushed to the boat.

The first wagonload arrived at the boat and was stowed on board within minutes. The plan was working perfectly. But Giloon Bogney commented, "This being too slow. Wharf being near for fast big loading."

"We follow the plan." Tvrdy's tone left no room for discussion.

On the second trip to the boat, two teams of Dhogs disappeared and Bogney as well. Tvrdy, arriving at the boat with the third load, discovered the second wagon waiting at the cove, still loaded. "Where are they?" he demanded of the Tanais he'd left to guard the boat.

"I tried to stop them, Director," said the man, none too happy himself. "They brought the wagons and then left. I thought to signal you, but I did not want to jeopardize the operation."

Tvrdy smashed his hand against a grain sack. Whap! When

he could speak again he said, "Did they say where they were going?"

"No, but they went that way," replied the Tanais, pointing toward the wharf.

"I'm going after them." He turned to those behind him. "Start unloading the wagons. When the next wagon gets here, empty it and then get the wagons on board. Tell Piipo if I do not return by the time the wagons are aboard, he is to leave without me. Understand?"

The Tanais mumbled and began unloading the wagons. Tvrdy turned and followed the Riverwalk to the wharf. The walk was dark most of the way, and he covered the distance quickly, arriving at the waterfront just in time to hear a startled cry.

Tvrdy ducked down beside the Riverwalk wall and crept forward in a crouch, keeping out of sight of the Nilokerus checkpoint. There, directly ahead in the center of the waterfront where the wharf and the Riverwalk met, he saw three Nilokerus struggling, their weapons flashing dully in the ring of lights around a checkpoint booth swarming with Dhogs.

They were deep in Saecaraz, somewhere in the confusion of galleries and passages below Threl High Chambers. They rounded a corner; Treet felt cool fresh air on his face, and a moment later they were standing at a rimwall overlooking the great barren expanse of Threl Square on their flight to the river. Pressing a hand to his side, and wheezing like a leaky bellows, he gasped, "I—ha-ave to . . . rest . . ."

Ernina halted and pulled her mask off and Treet's as well. "Is the pain bad?"

"N-no . . . I can make it," Treet gulped, head down. "Just need . . . rest a minute."

"Over here is better," she said, leading Treet to a clump of flat, fan-shaped trees growing at the edge of the rimwalk. "Take shallow breaths. Relax. The pain will go." She looked behind them and saw the globe-lit rimwalk bending away out of sight into the darkness. "We must hurry on soon."

In a moment Treet was indeed breathing easier. "Thanks for coming back for me. What were they—cyanide pellets?"

Ernina's sober face wrinkled in a smile. "No, just an anesthetic—and fear. The Invisibles are so used to such cruelty, they easily imagine the worst. Their own fear paralyzed them."

"You had me fooled," replied Treet. "Where did you get those things?"

"I have been making these," she dug into a bag at her side and held up a pellet the size of a marble, "since Hladik took my first Fieri. I foresaw the day when I might need an escape."

"It worked, and I'm glad. But you had me going for a while."

"I'm not proud of that. I hope you weren't distressed."

"When I calmed down, I figured that it was just an act. Hollering about your reward—that was good." Treet straightened; the pain in his ribs had eased. "Where do we go from here?"

"We must get to the river. There is an entrance to the Old Section between Jamuna and Chryse." She appraised Treet with a practiced eye. "Can you make it?"

"I'm not staying here. You know where this entrance is?"

Ernina looked grave. "I don't. But some of Hladik's prisoners I have treated over the years have told me about it. I'm no guide, but perhaps we can find it."

"Will the Dhogs take us in?"

"A physician is always welcome. And you, a Fieri, will be worshiped."

"Is that so?" Treet had to give her credit. She was made of stern stuff. Standing up to Mrukk like that, outwitting him, cutting him down to size with bluff and nerves alone—that took plenty of cool courage, and a good knowledge of the human psyche, as well as just plain old backwoods cunning. "Well, I'm ready. Let's get moving. I think we've worn out our welcome."

They hurried off again and were soon making their way across the dark expanse of Threl Square, two small figures scuttling over the stone flagging toward the line of spire-shaped trees marking Kyan in the distance. They had just reached the far side of the square when the shouts began. Treet threw a glance over his shoulder to see the black shapes of Mors Ultima boiling out into the square behind them.

· · · · · ·

Tvrdy could not believe his eyes. Unarmed Dhogs had attacked the Nilokerus checkpoint. Apparently their uncanny stealth had allowed them to get within striking distance, for the Nilokerus had not had time to draw their weapons. Perhaps the guards had been asleep. At any rate, the struggle was decidedly one-sided. The Dhogs, due to superior numbers, had the Nilokerus subdued in short order, and Tvrdy stepped out from hiding.

"Ah, Tanais!" cried Bogney when Tvrdy came up. "Now we loading faster, seh?"

Tvrdy did not strike the Dhog leader, but came very close. He fought down the impulse to lay into the grubby Bogney—causing the Dhog leader to lose face in front of his men would be a grave tactical error, especially at the moment of their first success. They *had* taken a checkpoint; that, for the Dhogs at least, was a real triumph.

"Take some men back to the boat. When you have finished

loading what is there, tell my man to bring the boat around. We will have the other wagons ready to load from the wharf." He cocked an eye skyward to the enormous vault of the dome, still showing the faint glimmer of stars in the firmament beyond its transparent panes. "We've got to hurry if we're going to make it back to the Zone before sunrise."

Bogney chose a few of his men, and the Dhogs raced silently away. Tvrdy looked at the Nilokerus unconscious at his feet and wondered what to do with them. He had not planned on taking any prisoners and hated the thought of killing them outright. But if they regained consciousness before the operation was finished, he'd have no choice. He stooped and retrieved the three Nilokerus weapons. "You stay here with them," he ordered the remaining Dhogs. "Do not let them get away, and do not let them signal for help."

Tvrdy made his way back to the granary, where two more wagons were ready to go. "Take them to the wharf," he told the men. "The boat will be there soon."

The wagons rolled out on their tracks and down the slight incline toward the wharf. "Come on, get moving!" Tvrdy yelled. "There are still two wagons left."

Piipo came up puffing. "What happened down there? I heard a shout."

"The Dhogs changed the plan. They attacked the check-point on the wharf."

"Anybody killed?"

"No. The Nilokerus must have been asleep. They didn't even get their weapons out. It was clean."

Piipo let out a sigh of relief. "Two more wagons and we're free. When the priests find this tomorrow, there will be Trabant to pay, of course. But Gorov will thunder and shout and demand an inventory. That should keep them busy. There's a chance Jamrog may not even hear about this."

"You're forgetting the Nilokerus down there. They'll talk."

"What do we do?"

"I don't know. Nothing, I guess. Jamrog will find out. We can't help that now."

"Then let's take the Nilokerus with us."

Tvrdy's eyebrows arched up. Piipo explained, "Of course, if we leave them they will talk; but if we take them, no one will know precisely what happened. They may even think the Nilokerus had something to do with it. Also, if we take them back with us, we can force them to tell us the arrangement of the checkpoints and how they are manned."

"Piipo, I underestimate you. Who knows, after they have told us what they know, they may even wish to join us—considering the alternatives."

A group of men came dashing up from the wharf just then, sweating from their night's exertion. "Just two more loads," Tvrdy told them, "and then we start back."

The men fell to, hefting up grain sacks and heaving them onto the wagons. They were joined by others up from the wharf, and the wagons were loaded in minutes and pushed out on the tracks down to the waiting boat, pausing at the checkpoint booth to pick up the groggy Nilokerus, who were tossed atop the load. Tvrdy and Piipo walked behind the last wagon to make certain nothing went wrong.

"We're going to make it," said Piipo as the last wagon, its wheels emitting a gritty squeal on the track, was pushed up to the side of the boat.

The words were no sooner out of his mouth than a bright, jagged tongue of flame streaked out of the night and the nearest grain sack exploded in a shower of bright orange sparks, flinging grain like tiny shrapnel in all directions. The next blast strafed the front of the boat, melting the fibersteel where it touched.

"Get aboard!" cried Tvrdy. "Leave the rest!" Piipo scrambled aboard, and Tvrdy climbed into the boat behind him. "Cast off! Let's go, you men! Get aboard or we'll leave you," he shouted to the Dhogs still heaving grain sacks over the rail.

He signaled to the pilot, and the engines growled. The boat slid backwards in the water. Still the Dhogs did not give up. They continued piling the grain sacks into the moving boat as the fire flashed around them, striking the dock, the boat, sending up steaming showers of water where a blast impacted on the surface of the river. Tvrdy shouted, "Leave the grain! Get aboard!"

He grabbed one of the Nilokerus weapons he'd confiscated and, jumping on top of the sizable pyramid of grain sacks, began returning fire. He was joined by two of his lieutenants, and the Nilokerus swarming down to the wharf from the granaries were momentarily shocked to find themselves exposed and under fire.

The boat pulled away from the wharf. The Dhogs, who had not so much as peeked over a shoulder during the attack, threw the last grain sack aboard and then flung themselves over the rail just as the boat swung into the bay. The last Dhog aboard was Giloon Bogney, who picked himself up and began pounding his men on the back.

"We got it all!" he crowed, grinning through his tangled mat of beard. The water around the boat erupted in steaming geysers as the Nilokerus on the wharf, having scrambled to cover, opened fire once more.

Tvrdy gave his weapon to one of his men and stomped back to Bogney. Towering over the shabby Dhog, he glared down and, with a voice as cold and sharp as ice, said, "Get your men below deck, and stay there with them. I don't want to see any of you until we reach Jamuna." He walked away, leaving the Dhog with a quickly fading grin on his greasy face.

THIRTY
SEVEN

"Head for that Hageblock," said Treet. "If we can outrun them we have a chance." There were, as near as Treet could count in the dark while running, only eight Invisibles pursuing them. But he had little doubt there would be more soon. Without a word Ernina took off; Treet followed on her heels.

Threl Square was bounded on all sides by a band of tree-lined greenspace. Saecaraz Hageblocks, squat gray slab-and-pillar structures, stood along this border. Treet and Ernina made for the nearest of these, flying over the darkened lawn, darting and dodging in an erratic batflight through the trees.

They reached the block and dashed into the first entrance they came upon. The block was built around a courtyard, and the fugitives fled through the open entry and into the yard. "It's blind!" Treet whispered harshly. There was not another exit to be seen.

"Hurry!" said Ernina. "Over there!" She pointed to a line of doorways facing the courtyard.

They ran across the yard, the footsteps of the Invisibles sounding in the short passage behind them. Ernina slipped into the fourth doorway; Treet followed her, and together they shrank into the shadowed depths. An instant later Invisibles pounded into the courtyard.

The Invisibles spread out and began combing the court-yard, those on the perimeter checking each door as they passed . . . the first door . . . the second door . . .

Treet heard the footsteps outside the doorway next to theirs. Silence. Then the footsteps paused outside their door. Treet held his breath and pressed himself flat against the rough wall, mentally readying himself to fight.

The Invisible stood framed in the doorway. He took a slow step forward.

Treet's hands balled into fists, his heart lunging against his ribs.

The Invisible advanced, and Treet, remembering the pellets

in Ernina's pouch, felt at his side. He found the pouch and pulled out a handful of pellets, took a deep breath and held it. Ernina did the same. The Invisible heard the movement and swung around, his weapon arcing toward them. Treet threw himself forward and put his hand into the Invisible's face, crunching the pellets in his fist in the same motion. The Invisible backpedaled, gasped, and then wobbled uncertainly on his feet. Treet kept his hand before the man's face, laid him down, and then tiptoed to the entryway to peer out across the courtyard. There was not an Invisible to be seen. Treet did not linger to analyze the situation, expelling his breath and tasting almonds on his tongue. "This is our chance," he said. Ernina staggered forward and Treet grabbed her, pulling her forward with him as he raced out into the courtyard once more.

They fled back through the entryway and into the greenspace beyond. Then, step by careful step, they worked their way through the trees and around toward the river once more. But between them and the river stood block upon block of Hage dwellings and, at the center of the main thoroughfare, directly ahead, a Nilokerus checkpoint.

"Well, what do we do now?" said Treet. He was tired. The exertion was beginning to tell on him. He felt limp and wrung out. "We can't go that way."

"We'll have to go around, but keep working toward the river." She raised a hand to his damp forehead. "How are you feeling?"

"Okay. Lead on," said Treet as he fell into step.

When they reached the first of the dwelling blocks, Treet gave a quick backward glance to see the dark shapes of Invisibles once again on course behind them. Although he didn't count them, it appeared that the original eight had picked up a few reinforcements along the way. From the way the Invisibles were approaching—slow and deliberate with a lot of side-to-side movement—Treet guessed they had not yet discovered them, but were stalking. "Our friends with the crummy sense of humor are back," whispered Treet.

He and Ernina ducked into the nearest entrance, a covered gallery leading into the interior of the block. The tunnel curved sharply to the right, and after passing dozens of kraams, each sealed with opaqued unidors, the gallery teminated at a plaza formed by the backs of the Hageblocks. In the center of the plaza, yellow lights blazing, sat another Nilokerus checkpoint.

Treet took one look at the booth, and his heart sank. There were five Nilokerus at attention talking to three Invisibles; each of the Invisibles wore the shimmery black yos of the Mors Ultima. "It doesn't take them long to—"

"Shh!" Ernina said sharply. "Listen."

In the distance came the pattering of footsteps in the gallery.

"We're in it now," Treet said. "Trapped."

"Perhaps we could work our way around the plaza."

"Not with the men in black out there."

The footsteps in the tunnel behind them grew louder.

"We've got to do something," Ernina pointed out.

"How many of those goofballs have you got left?"

"The anesthetic?"

"Yeah, how many?"

Ernina dug into the pouch and brought out a handful. "Not many. Two or three handfuls."

"That might do it. Give me a handful, and you take the rest."

"What are you going to do?"

"See if we can burn these bozos three times with one match."

Treet pointed Ernina back down the tunnel. "Scatter them evenly and then come back here." She nodded once and hurried away.

Treet crept to the mouth of the gallery and laid down the pellets one-by-one just inside the entrance. Then, stepping through the carefully arranged trap, he took a deep breath and stepped out into the plaza.

Treet proceeded along the side of the Hageblock. To his dismay, none of the Nilokerus or their Mors Ultima helpers saw him. A few steps ahead he saw a stack of metal rods leaning against the wall. Treet put his foot against the stack and shoved. The rods clattered to the ground and rolled.

Treet jumped back and looked surprised. The heads of the Nilokerus swiveled around. The Mors Ultima were already racing toward him. Treet pretended indecision and then flew back to the gallery and disappeared inside. He rounded the curve of the tunnel and nearly collided with Ernina. "Put this on," she said, thrusting the mask into his hands.

Pulling the mask on, Treet felt his stomach tighten into a hard lump—as if he'd swallowed a cast-iron grapefruit. Either his plan would work or they'd be captured right here. They waited.

There were a few sharp coughs, some gasps and a moan or two, and then silence.

"It worked!" Treet shouted, the mask garbling his voice.

They ran back to the plaza entrance to find bodies sprawled helter-skelter just inside. "Uh oh," said Treet, "there's one missing."

Ernina confirmed his body count as she stooped to retrieve several untrampled pellets. "Five Nilokerus and two Invisibles."

"The other Invisible's still out there someplace." Treet peered out into the plaza. "I don't see him anywhere."

"Maybe he went to signal the others."

"We can only hope." Treet paused and considered the alternatives and then shrugged. "Well, we can't stay here."

They picked up two of the Nilokerus weapons and left the tunnel, reaching the other side of the plaza moments later. There was still no sign of the missing Invisible, so they hurried on into the warrens of the Hageblocks, making their way to the river.

The Saecaraz Hageblocks were old and had been allowed to spread over the centuries as kraam was added to kraam and building thrust upon building until they resembled nothing so much as the ancient gypsy ghettos Treet had once visited in old Budapest. Picking their way through the narrow, winding streets and meandering boulevards crowded with kraams and market stalls and kiosks was slow work. Treet felt his strength going; he was light-headed and woozy.

At one point Ernina stopped beneath a yellow glow globe, turned to him, and placed her fingertips against the side of his throat. "Your pulse is fast." She gazed deeply into his eyes. "Treet, are you all right?"

"I'm a little tired," he admitted.

"Here—" The physician reached into her yos and pulled out a flat, puck-shaped biscuit. "Eat this—it'll give you strength."

Treet raised the biscuit to his mouth and nibbled. It was dry and tasted of herbs. "What is it?"

"It's a stimulant."

Treet chewed slowly, wishing he had something cold and

wet to wash it down. Ernina watched him for a moment and then said, "The river is just beyond here, I think. Saecaraz is very logical—not like Chryse or Rumon—and I've been here often enough on health inspections."

"And then?"

"There are boats along the waterfront."

"I wouldn't mind a ride."

They moved off, and Treet did begin to feel revived. The stimulant worked, but he wondered how long he could keep going. The deeper into the warren they went, the more twisted and convoluted their path became until it seemed as if they were following a meandering creek bed through stone canyons. They passed beneath towering cliffs of jumbled kraams and Hageworks stacked layer upon layer. Whenever there was a choice of direction, Ernina took the route that moved them closer to the river. Winding through the empty byways made Treet think of touring the bombed out shell of a city: any one of a dozen or so Irani-Syrian-Lebanese settlements gutted during the Middle East holocaust of the last century.

But these streets were empty, whereas any other city on Earth, no matter how desolated, literally crawled with life— beggars and scavengers certainly, wandering armies of orphan pickpockets usually, packs of yapping dogs and vermin if nothing else. In Saecaraz at least, the citizens were sealed tightly in their kraams until dawn's early light.

"It sure is empty," said Treet as they paused at a deserted crossroads to consider the best direction. "I've never seen a city shut down so completely."

Ernina raised her finger to her lips and looked around.

Treet heard the scuffle of a footfall. It stopped abruptly.

"Our tail is showing," said Treet.

"The missing Invisible," replied Ernina. "But the waterfront is just down there." She pointed through an open archway overgrown with hanging vines, orange in the light of a single globe. A stone pathway angled down through the arch into the darkness beyond.

They struck off for the arch, and the footsteps started again. At the arch Treet paused to listen; the shuffling steps paused, too. Treet ducked under the archway and stepped to the side. Ernina took up a position on the other side, and they waited. Treet did not intend on ambushing the Invisible—he doubted whether he could go hand-to-hand with one even if he were in peak condition, and he was far from being in the best of shape. He merely hoped that by hiding among the hanging vines they could throw the Invisible off their trail long enough to find a boat.

Long moments passed. Then, as Treet was about to risk peering around the corner to see what had become of their tracker, he heard the soft scuffing footfall again, closer. He froze.

The Invisible came through the arch and then hesitated. He stopped and looked around as if perplexed. Treet noticed that the Invisible was a good deal shorter than he was and slighter of build. Also, he wore the banded silver of the Saecaraz.

This was no Invisible. Treet decided to take a chance.

The man was only a step and a half away, and, even granted the element of surprise, Treet nearly lost him.

Treet stepped from his hiding place, and the vines rustled. The Saecaraz turned at the same instant, saw him, and bolted away. Treet stretched after him, snagged the corner of his yos, and held on. The grab yanked the stranger off his feet, and he landed with a thump and a whimper on the pavement where he squirmed, throwing his hands over his head to protect himself.

Ernina ran up and took one look at the Hageman cringing at Treet's feet and said, "Get up!" Her tone was authority itself, and the man jolted as if he'd been struck. But he lowered his hands and peered fearfully up at the two standing over him. A look of recognition lit Ernina's eyes.

Treet saw it and remarked, "You know this clown?"

Ernina bent to help the man to his feet. An expression of relief erased the fear from his pinched face. "I know him," said Ernina. "It's Nilokerus Subdirector Fertig!"

THIRTY EIGHT

"I am Fertig," the Hageman replied, "but no longer Subdirector."

"I gather there's a lot of that going around," offered Treet. "So what are you doing following us?"

"I have been hiding—many days it is now—trying to find the Old Section." He spread his hands wide. "But I can't find it. There is no entrance in Saecaraz—perhaps at one time, but it no longer exists. I decided to wait and watch for Dhogs to come into Hage and then follow them."

"You thought we were Dhogs?"

"No." Fertig shook his head, a wisp of a smile on his lips. "I knew you were not Dhogs, but when I saw the Invisibles chasing you, I guessed Jamrog was up to something. I decided to follow you."

"Can you get us out of here?"

"It depends on where you are going."

"Chryse," explained Ernina. "The entrance to the Old Section is in Chryse on the Jamuna border." To Fertig's look, she replied, "A physician of many years learns many things; not all concern medicine. Now we will need a boat."

Fertig shook his head. "An em would be better. Faster."

"Great! Where can we get one of those?" asked Treet.

"Rohee had many of them placed around the Hage. It fell to Hladik to maintain them. It is one of the things I was responsible for—making certain they were always ready. If Jamrog hasn't moved them . . ." He stared out into the mottled darkness, eyes scanning the shadowed jumble of the waterfront before them. Kyan lapped the pilings and riffled in the shallows. "This way," said Fertig, starting away. "I think there is one near here."

Treet and Ernina followed the former Subdirector along the waterfront and came to the Saecaraz dockyard. Row upon row of boats chained for the night to fibersteel rings set in the dock let Treet know that they would have had a very difficult time getting a boat here. But Fertig led them away from the dock, turning back toward the Hageblocks for a short distance until he came to a flat-roofed building with a double-wide unidor.

Fertig went to the door and pressed the code into the lighted tabs. The unidor snapped off with a crack as an interior light blinked on. There before them was a silver em with two rear seats. "Our spirit guides are with us tonight," called Fertig as he leaped into the driver seat. "This one Rohee used to take him to and from his boat."

The em rolled out of its nook on squashy tires. Ernina climbed into the seat beside Fertig, and Treet piled into the one behind. "Home, James," he said.

"Can you get us to Chryse?" asked Ernina.

"Yes. We could follow the riverwalk, but I know a better way."

"What about checkpoints? The Nilokerus have been alerted; they will be looking for us by now."

"Don't worry. There will be no checkpoints."

The em jerked away and they were off, rolling soundlessly along the riverwalk. Treet watched the blurred shapes of trees ripple past and the occasional light across the river dance over the silent water. The air in his face felt good; he slid down in the seat and closed his eyes.

He awoke again as the em jolted to a stop. They were sitting in a narrow street with tiered kraams pressing in on either side. Ahead was a deserted arcade with a few empty kiosks. The place had a gritty, stained appearance. Clearly, they were no longer in Saecaraz. "What is it?" asked Treet, his voice hoarse with sleep.

"Invisibles," whispered Fertig. "I saw three of them cross just ahead of us."

"Where are we?" He swiveled his head around. The dome overhead showed dull charcoal, and there were few stars showing. He had slept a good while then, but it seemed only an instant and he was still exhausted.

"We're in Jamuna Hage," replied Ernina, "near the border of Chryse. It's only a little way now."

Treet sat in the back and rubbed his face. He felt as if he had been pulled apart and reassembled backwards, every joint out of place and wrong. They waited a few minutes, and then Fertig said, "I think we can go now."

The em rolled out into the arcade and headed for a street

angling off into deep Hage. They reached the street and heard the shout simultaneously. A split second later a portion of the pavement sprouted flame, and rock splinters scattered. Fertig raced ahead and turned off the street at first opportunity. Treet, white-knuckling the handgrips and watching their rear, saw two Invisibles appear in the street behind them, raise weapons—and then they were taken from sight by Fertig's quick turn.

"We're at the border," said Fertig as they raced down narrow, twisting streets. "There is a checkpoint just ahead—"

"Go right on through," said Treet. "Don't even slow down."

"But—"

"They know we're here now. And it's close to dawn. We've got to find that entrance soon. I say run the checkpoint."

Fertig nodded and grimly pressed his foot to the floor. The em was not built for speed, and with three passengers it would never set any land speed records, but Fertig coaxed the little vehicle to a respectable pace and they whisked through the empty Jamuna streets and out into a section of terraced fields of brown sludge overset with dingy towers. "Oohh! Smell that," said Treet, tears rising to his eyes. "Ammonia!"

Past the fields rose a wall of stone brick topped by a high curtain of fibersteel panels. A great arch was cut in the wall allowing the road to pass through. Directly ahead was a Nilokerus checkpoint with a gate. Two Nilokerus stood by the gate and one inside the booth, all three apparently asleep on their feet.

The em whizzed toward the gate and the oblivious guards. The fugitives were barely ten meters away before the first guard awoke and sounded the alarm. The em crashed through the gate, shoving it into the booth as the two gate guards stood gaping. They yelled and then ran after the em, but it was too fast, and they stopped. As an afterthought they pulled out their weapons to fire halfheartedly at the receding vehicle.

"We did it!" crowed Treet. Fertig grinned glassily, his hands tight on the steering bar. "Masterful job, Fertig old stick! We're rolling now."

They were rolling, but not for long. The entire front end of the em started rattling, and then vibrating, and then shaking as if it would fly to pieces. Fertig allowed the machine to coast to a stop, got out, and stared at the left front tire.

"I knew it was too good to last," sighed Treet as he surveyed the flat tire. "We must have picked up part of the gate."

"It doesn't matter," replied Ernina gazing at the landscape. "The entrance is near."

Treet followed her gaze. Chryse was as different from Jamuna and Saecaraz as Fierra from Dome. Even in the gloom Treet could see that Hage Chryse had a symmetry of design that set it apart. He remembered his last and only visit to the Hage when Calin, his magician guide, had brought him here. A double-barbed pang of guilt and grief pierced him at the thought.

"We should get this thing off the road," said Treet.

Fertig climbed back in and drove away, limping down the hillside to a clump of droopy-limbed trees. He drove the em into the trees and emerged a moment later, hurrying back up to the road. Ernina strode away in the opposite direction, climbing the nearest hill. Treet and Fertig followed, and soon they were walking parallel to the towering border wall.

The dome above grew lighter, graying with the sunrise. The hills of outer Chryse took on shape and definition; color seeped into the landscape. White moundlike structures emerged out of the murk away to the left. On the right, green hemispheres of hills met the wall, which stretched in a long, slow curve toward deep Hage.

Ernina pressed ahead at a nimble pace, and soon they came to a place where the sculptured hills ended and Chryse Hageworks began. Picking their way among the scattered structures, the three paused often to allow Ernina to study their position. "They say there is an old air conduit beneath a broadcast antenna—from before the Old Section was abandoned," she said, gazing around her at the huddled conglomeration of buildings crammed together in the carved-out bowl of the hillside.

"Why was the Old Section abandoned?" wondered Treet.

"No one knows," said Ernina. "It was many Supreme Directors ago."

"Some say it was destroyed long ago and no longer exists," offered Fertig. "Others say it was taken over by the Fieri and they sealed it. They were left alone, and no one went there after that."

"Hmmm," Treet said. Doubtless there was something in what Fertig said, although most likely he had it reversed. The

Fieri were probably driven back or quarantined in the Old Section and the section sealed to prevent their escape or to keep them separated from the rest. Then again, the Old Section may have had some lingering bad associations with the Red Death and had become psychologically uninhabitable. "Are you sure this is the place? I don't see any antenna."

"Here somewhere, yes," replied Ernina. With that, she moved down the hill and entered the Hageworks, keeping the border wall to her left as she pushed deeper into the Hage. Chryse appeared as if it had been designed by inebriated gnome architects. Squat mushroom-shaped structures, large and small, sprang from the scooped-out grassy bowl. The streets were pink, paved footpaths winding through arches and walls and around the smooth, white-stuccoed buildings in almost whimsical fashion, making it difficult to proceed with any kind of haste. The dome grew brighter as dawn came on; the fugitives' efforts became more desperate.

"Maybe we should find a place to hide out," offered Treet at one point. "We could lay low until nightfall and take up the search again." He looked around at all the Hageblocks and imagined Chryse pouring out of them at any moment to start the day's work. "We don't want to be caught out here."

"It's near," insisted Ernina.

"Sure," agreed Treet. "But it might take a little more time to find than we dare spend right now. I still don't see anything that looks like an antenna. We should have seen it long ago if it was close by."

Fertig stood a little way off, listening. He broke in, saying, "Shh! Someone is coming."

Due to the ensnarled pattern of arches, pathways, and walls, it was difficult to tell where the sound was coming from, but Fertig was right: the shush of many feet on the pink stone pavement told them someone was coming quickly their way.

"Invisibles," muttered Treet. "We've got to get out of here."

"This way," said Fertig, leading them through the nearest archway into a narrow street lined with round kraam entrances like mouse holes.

There they waited, peering around the smooth white arch to see a ragged man, the tatters of his clothes flying as he came.

He paused, glanced around quickly, and then signaled to others behind him. Then there came a creaking sound, as if a heavy machine were being pulled along with leather straps.

. Presently a troop of men, each as disheveled as the next—like deserters of a bedraggled army—came into view pushing Hyrgo wagons loaded to bursting with sacks of grain. The wheels of the wagons were wrapped with sacking.

"Dhogs!" whispered Ernina, her eyes lighting up. "We can follow them."

Treet watched as one grain wagon disappeared down the next street, followed by another, and then another. With the fourth wagon came a rear guard—two Dhogs and two others. One of these turned toward them, and Treet jumped out from behind the arch. "Tvrdy!"

It was a foolish move. Instantly the procession froze. Weapons whipped around, and he would have been flash-fried if the quick-thinking Tanais Director had not intervened.

"Wait!" Tvrdy cried, throwing wide his hands.

Treet gulped. What have I done, he thought? I'm wearing Nilokerus colors. He doesn't recognize me.

Tvrdy approached. The Dhogs stared. No one moved.

The Tanais came to stand directly in front of Treet; he stared into his eyes. Recognition came slowly. "Traveler!" Tvrdy said, breaking into a wide grin. "You have returned at last. I thought you dead."

"It's good to see you, too," replied Treet.

Tvrdy turned and signaled to the others to move on quickly. "There are Invisibles after us," Tvrdy explained. "We cannot talk now. Come with us."

"We'd be glad for the escort. The Invisibles are after us, too. We're looking for the entrance to the Old Section."

"We?" A light leapt up in his eyes.

Treet motioned for Ernina and Fertig to come out of hiding. "It's all right," Treet said. "They're going our way."

The stocky physician stepped confidently out from behind the arch, followed by Fertig, looking none too certain about his reception. Tvrdy eyed them both, disappointed. "Ernina, sixth-order Nilokerus physician, I believe." She inclined her head, and Tvrdy glanced at Fertig slinking up. "Ah, another Nilokerus! Defection makes our numbers swell."

"They helped me," said Treet. "Ernina saved my life, and Fertig kept us out of reach of the Invisibles."

Tvrdy nodded curtly. "Perhaps he can do the same for us one day." He waved, and the wagon creaked into motion once more. Treet and the others fell in behind the wagon, and the Dhogs led them through the still silent streets. At one point, the procession surprised a Chryse, sleepy-eyed and yawning, who was just stumbling out of his kraam. The man stood gawking for a moment before it dawned on him that he was seeing something highly illicit, then closed his eyes and scuttled back into his kraam.

Before the raiding party could encounter any more Chryse, they reached the further edge of the bowl and a deserted district where a cluster of gutted shells of buildings formed a boundary to the Hageworks. And there, behind this boundary, lay the long, collapsed skeleton of the antenna.

They pushed between two of the empty hulks and found that the Dhogs had rolled their wagons up to the foot of the antenna, which at one time stood atop a low embankment. On one side of this embankment was a large oval louvre panel. As Treet watched, the panel was pried open and the first of the wagons hauled inside the giant air duct.

Ernina, Fertig, Treet, and Tvrdy were the last to go in. Fertig and Tvrdy tugged the louvre down and secured it from the inside. And then Tvrdy hurried to where Treet and the others waited in the darkness of the conduit. "A night's work done," he said. "I hope not wasted."

THIRTY NINE

For Yarden, the days settled into a routine of pleasure. She awoke to silver mornings of tranquil meditation and convivial breakfasts with her shipboard companions. Then she spent the next hours totally absorbed in her painting exercises, standing with her easel at the rail, face scrunched in concentration as she labored to achieve fluidity of motion in the controlled line. Her afternoons were taken with Gerdes' classes under the orange canopy on the aft deck of the ship. Evenings found her alone, watching night sweep over the fair landscape, talking with Ianni, or taking in Fieri entertainment under the bright Empyrion stars.

And always, the wide enchanting countryside slid by the rail: hills alive with exotic wildlife; thick, luxuriant vegetation blanketing the land and encroaching on the river's edge; mountains, blue-misted in the distance, rising up to crown the tumbling hills with cool supremacy. Empyrion was paradise—a vast, unspoiled paradise.

She slept well at night and emerged fresh in the morning to begin another day just like the one before. And each morning as she came on deck to greet the day, she felt born anew. Such was life among the Fieri. They were, Yarden was learning, not only gentle, peaceable people, but they were also nimble-witted, and possessed of an insatiable appetite for jokes and humorous stories of all kinds.

Still, their humor was just as gentle as they were themselves, never unbecoming, never cynical. Yarden began to believe that the Fieri did not have it in them to mock or jeer; cruelty of thought or word was as far beneath them as cruelty of action. There was joy and wisdom in their frivolity—a soaring lightheartedness that was an expression of genuine Fieri goodness. And it came through their humor as in everything they did.

Wherever two or more Fieri gathered for very long, there would be laughter, and Yarden found she could listen to the sound of it for hours, though at first she did not always understand the jokes—many of which depended on a clever observation of a world with which she was, in many ways, still unfamiliar. The stories, though, she understood well enough; and in the evenings, wrapped in starlight and the warmth of one another's company, the Fieri would cluster on deck to hear a tale.

Everyone told stories—the supply was apparently limitless. But the best Fieri stories were the province of certain designated storytellers—men and women who had gained reputations as skilled and inventive orators. Typically, the storyteller would have prepared a story for the evening, although tradition demanded that he be coaxed into telling it. The listeners would gather sometime after the evening meal and begin talking about how it was a beautiful night for a story (any night for the Fieri was a beautiful night for a story), and how they missed hearing the old stories, and how it had been such a long time since they had heard a really good tale (even though in all likelihood they had heard one just the night before), and how they longed for a storyteller like the storytellers of old . . .

The call would go up for a story, and the call would quickly become a chant. Then, to a crescendo of cheers and applause, the storyteller would stump up in feigned bewilderment, usually saying that he didn't know if his stories would please or not, but with the audience's indulgence, he'd try. The audience would draw close—children right down in front, their parents and other adults pressing in behind. When everyone was settled, the storyteller would climb up on his stool; when all was quiet, he'd begin. Some stories had set beginnings, but ordinarily the teller would start by connecting his tale to some recent event or an observation he'd made that very day.

This preamble would stretch out as long as he could sustain it, building tension while inexorably working toward the place where he'd say something like: "which reminds me of the time that. . . ," at which point the audible sigh of relief would go up from the audience and he'd be off on his tale.

Yarden enjoyed the stories as much as any Fieri child. The storytellers were as much actor and actress as tale-spinner, breathing life into their characters with vocal inflections, gestures, and facial expressions, especially at moments of high drama. The Fieri would sit and listen raptly, catching every nuance of the performance, savoring it, showing their approval with their "ohs" and "ahs" in the appropriate places. Each Fieri knew the stories so well that it was something of a game to try to catch the teller in a slip or omission. The tellers, on the other hand, knew their audience was waiting for a bungle, and kept them vigilant by refusing to tell their stories in precisely the same way as before.

Thus the stories were always the same, yet always different, and the stories had a fresh familiarity about them that Yarden found appealing and comforting—though she had not been among them long enough to have heard all the stories once, let alone twice.

When at last the evening's tale came to an end to universal acclaim, the group would disperse reluctantly or, in typical Fieri fashion, finish a singular entertainment with a time of singing.

Fieri songs were rich, mellifluous creations with innumerable verses and haunting melody lines that wandered, lapsing and recurring almost at will, Yarden thought—although every Fieri knew exactly where the tune went. The songs were difficult to learn, but a joy to hear, and Yarden would sit amidst the singers, arms wrapped around legs, chin on knees, drifting in delicious rapture. Fieri singing was exalting, stirring, and somehow always poignant—as if the music bubbled up from a fountain at whose deep roots seeped a sadness that mingled the music with traces of pain.

This pain, Yarden suspected, stemmed from the Burning— the nuclear holocaust visited on their noble race by the monsters of Dome centuries ago. It was a scar the Fieri bore, a pain that would never heal.

As playful as the Fieri could be, Yarden often wondered whether the humor was not alloyed of feelings of profound grief. She asked Ianni about this one evening, and Ianni's answer surprised her. "You are very perceptive, Yarden. Perhaps our merrymaking does spring from the hurt of the past."

"But wouldn't it be better to forget the past, to let it go so the wound can heal?"

"Time will not heal it; nothing can. The hurt is too deep."

Yarden didn't understand this, so pressed the question again. "But that doesn't make sense. You say the Infinite Father cares for you. Can't He do something?"

Ianni only smiled and shook her head. "You see, but do not see yet. Look around you, Yarden." She lifted a palm upward. "All of life is pain. We are born to pain and death, and there is no escape from it. Every living thing must bear the pain of life."

"That sounds very pessimistic," snapped Yarden. "What's wrong with you? You're the one who's always telling me, Trust, believe, have faith. What good is any of that if there is no escape from pain and death?"

"Ah, but we do not attempt to escape from the pain."

"No?"

"No. We know it for what it is; we embrace it. We take it to ourselves, and through the Infinite's love we transform it into something else. In the end we transcend it."

"What is the suffering transformed into?"

"Love, compassion, kindness, joy—all the holy virtues. Don't you see? As long as one tries to escape, the pain will consume and destroy. But if it is accepted, it can be transformed."

"I don't know if I want to accept it," said Yarden. "You make it sound so . . . so hopeless."

"Never hopeless. Hope is born of grief, Yarden. Without the suffering, there can be no striving for something better. Hope is the yearning for a better place where pain can no longer hurt."

"Is there such a place?"

"Only with the Infinite. He has promised us His presence in this life and the life to come. He helps us bear the pain of our creation—it is no less His pain, after all."

They spoke of other things after that, but Yarden remembered and thought about this part of their conversation often. It had affected her deeply, although she didn't know it at the time. The idea of hope springing from the basic pain of life was foreign to her. Not that Yarden was naive—she knew that life was tough, that one was born to hardship, that strife was the nature of things. But she had always believed that only through struggle could one overcome the pain and hardship.

The notion that pain must be embraced was difficult for her to accept. But the more she saw of the Fieri, the more she began to understand. The Fieri professed that the creation of the cosmos had cost the Infinite Father something; He had paid a tremendous toll to bring His beloved universe into existence. He had labored, and suffered the pain of His laboring. In this suffering, love itself was born.

"What else is love," Mathiax had asked her one day, "but

taking the pain of another as your own—especially when you are not obliged to?" Thus, pain was woven into the very fabric of the universe—because there could be no love without it, and because the Infinite Father had set love as the cornerstone of His creation.

These were heady thoughts, but Yarden found herself returning to them again and again as she tried to understand the Fieri and their God, whom she wanted very much to accept as her own.

So the trip upriver to the Bay of Talking Fish became for Yarden an inner pilgrimage as she wrestled with these thoughts and felt the struggle changing her, slowly, gently as understanding grew.

Each day the sweeping line of barges drew nearer the vast wrinkled highlands of the Light Mountain range, and at night the passengers could see the faint glow in the sky above the peaks—each night a little clearer than the night before. But earlier in the day the nautical procession had passed beyond the green-wrapped foothills and into steep-sided, red-rock canyons. Ahead lay the bare, wind-whipped crags and peaks of the Light Mountains.

This night, Yarden sat with Ianni and others on the foredeck watching the sky give forth a splendid display as the Light Mountains lit the heavens with a shifting aura of colors—an earthborn borealis, known to the Fieri as a sunshower.

The light began at dusk when the sunstone began giving up its stored solar energy, glowing brightly as the sky darkened. The colors were soft, opalescent blues and greens and golds with wisps of red and violet, corresponding to the various types of sunstone—the same sunstone used to build Fierra. The shifting color was brought about by a combination of common atmospheric conditions: minute sunstone particles in the air, turbulence caused by layers of warmer surface air rolling against cooler upper air, reflection off high clouds.

The effect was stunning. It was like watching slow motion fireworks, Yarden thought dreamily as she gazed up into the shimmering sky. The evanescent color formed softly spectral patterns—shifting ribbons of light, transparent streamers that lit up, swirling and blending, then vanishing, only to reappear again and again in continually changing shapes.

Yarden found herself mesmerized by the brilliant aerial

performance, transported beyond herself and into a realm of pure light and color. She looked at her surroundings as if gazing down upon the world from the rarefied heights of a region absolutely alive with peace and beauty and joy. All this she saw mirrored on the upturned faces of the Fieri gathered around her.

After a while one of the Fieri—a Mentor named Elson— got up and addressed the rapt watchers. Speaking softly, he said, "We are now following the way of our ancestors. In the Wandering our fathers found Taleraan and sailed long ships up the deep water into the Light Mountains. Perhaps they too lifted their eyes to the sky one night to see the first sunshower and discovered the secret of the shining stone.

"We do not know their thoughts, but we can imagine what they must have felt at that time of great discovery when, looking into the darkness, they saw the very rock of the mountains begin to glow with unaccustomed radiance.

"When the time of wandering came to an end, they built the bright cities with this same shining stone and named it sunstone. They lived in splendor both day and night . . ."

Although the recitation went on, Yarden's thoughts drifted in another direction. She remembered the Preceptor's words the night Treet had declared the growing danger from Dome. "On that day, our bright homeland became the Blighted Lands, a desert where no living thing could ever survive . . . All that we knew passed away; all that we loved died. The treasures of our great civilization fell into dust . . ."

All at once, Yarden felt the ache of that loss as she remembered those words and that night. She had just been reunited with Treet, and then he'd gone and made his ridiculous pronouncement: "The horror is starting again!"

And that had put an end to their burgeoning relationship. Rather, *she* had put an end to it by refusing to follow him back to Dome. For the first time since that night, the tiniest barb of doubt pricked her conscience: What if he was right?

FORTY

There was nothing to do but weather the storm and hope
to repair the damage later. The three members of the Supreme Director's inner circle stood stoically and took the
full brunt of their superior's fury. Jamrog was livid. Since the
night of the raid, information had been trickling in, and now he
could assess the full extent of the debacle. Which was not, as
first thought, one failure only, but a whole series of disasters—
apparently all linked together.

The ceremonial bhuj swung in short, swift, murderous arcs
as he paced, his teeth grinding between clipped words. "So! The
Fieri has escaped again—taken right out of your hands, Mrukk.
And with the help of one of your physicians, Diltz. Meanwhile,
checkpoints are overrun by force and guards carried off, never
to be seen again." He stopped to glare at his silent audience. The
Invisibles behind him kept their eyes riveted on the ceiling, not
daring to witness the dire proceedings. "Does anyone have an
explanation?" Jamrog challenged. He thrust the bhuj at Osmas.

The Saecaraz Subdirector swallowed hard and said, "The
Dhogs are becoming more brazen, Supreme Director. They—"

"Dhogs! Yes, surely, blame the Dhogs. But doesn't it seem
strange to you that Tvrdy and Cejka disappeared—and Piipo,
too, for all we know—and suddenly the Dhogs become more
brazen?"

Osmas winced at the bite of Jamrog's sarcasm.

"They were well organized," offered Mrukk. "The raid was
well planned and perfectly staged. There is little doubt it was
Tvrdy's doing."

"Thank you, Mrukk," Jamrog said sweetly. "I'm so glad for
your keen evaluation. You who had your captive stolen from you
by an old mother and failed to lift a finger to prevent it. None of
your men were killed? No? In fact, no one suffered so much as a
scratch, I believe.

"What about it, Diltz?" The bhuj swung toward the emaciated Director. "She was one of your physicians."

"Yes," he replied, his tone even more sepulchral than usual.
"She was a Nilokerus."

"That's all you have to say? She was a Nilokerus?"

Diltz remained silent.

Jamrog spun away angrily and continued pacing. "And this morning Hyrgo priests tell me there is grain missing from the stores. It seems they were reluctant to say anything about it before, but in light of the general disarray we find ourselves in these last days, they thought better to mention the incident in case something could be done about it."

"Supreme Director, how much grain is missing?" asked Mrukk.

"Oh, enough. Enough to feed a whole Hage for several weeks!"

"They had to have help," observed Osmas.

"What makes you say that? With guards asleep at checkpoints and Invisibles unable to follow even an old woman, they had all the help they required."

Jamrog spun the bhuj in his hands and with a swipe that indicted them all, he said, "I tell you, Hagemen, I will tolerate no more failure. Do you understand me? I find myself forced to take emergency measures for the good of Empyrion."

"Emergency measures?" asked Osmas.

"These will be announced shortly. I have convened a special session of the Threl this afternoon, and I will present my plan then." He paused and stared into the distance momentarily, then tapped the bhuj on the floor. "But I have something for you three, too, never fear. I want every Invisible involved in the fiasco punished. I want the guard doubled at each checkpoint. I want the entrance to the Old Section found, and I want the Dhogs routed out and slaughtered. I want Tvrdy and Cejka apprehended and brought before a Threl tribunal to answer for their crimes before they face execution."

His eyes narrowed as he gazed at his coterie. "Oh, yes, and I want the Fieri found. I want him found and brought back to me at once."

Diltz, ignoring the consequences of affronting the Supreme Director, asked, "Why is this Fieri so important to you? How do we know the Fieri even exist anymore?"

Jamrog allowed himself a fierce smile. "Don't you see it, Diltz? It should be obvious to all of you. The Fieri are behind the disruption we are experiencing. The Fieri are fomenting rebellion; they are inciting the Dhogs."

The three shifted uneasily.

Jamrog continued, "I imagine that when we get to the bottom of this, we will find the Fieri have been involved from the beginning. Rohee was a fool. He believed they had come in goodwill, believed he could learn something from them. But it's clear that they want only what they have always wanted: Empyrion's downfall.

"History repeats its lessons from time to time, Hagemen. We are witnessing the first attempts by the Fieri to establish themselves once more within our midst. This time, however, we will be ready. This time we will be vigilant. We will strike before they can gain their full strength. We will search them out and destroy them before they destroy us." Jamrog, who had been momentarily carried away by his speech, came to himself and concluded, "I want the Fieri found before he can do any more harm. I want him, Hagemen."

With that, Jamrog left the kraam, taking his bodyguard with him and leaving the three chastised followers glowering at one another.

Osmas was the first to speak. "This is your fault, Mrukk. If you—"

"Watch your tongue, little man."

Diltz spoke as if to himself. "These Fieri interest me. I must find out more about them."

"Fieri!" Osmas snorted. "There are no Fieri. They are something Rohee imagined in his dotage."

"You're wrong," said Mrukk. "I saw him. He was like us, but unlike us."

"A Dhog."

"No. He was no Dhog."

"One of Tvrdy's agents then, or Cejka's."

Mrukk shook his head. "I was there the day they arrived."

"They?" wondered Diltz.

"There were four. With my own eyes I saw the airship. I saw the scorch marks on the platform. I gave the order to take them."

"Airship?" wondered Osmas. "I never heard anything about a Fieri airship."

"Rohee demanded secrecy. He had the airship destroyed, and the Fieri were given psilobe to deaden their memories. Then he stupidly had them hidden in Hage—all except one. He kept one for himself."

"What happened then?" asked Diltz, fascinated.

"Tvrdy got them. He hoped to use them to take over the Threl. But Jamrog intervened, and we moved in before they could mount their attack. They were forced to retreat. They escaped through the Archives doors to the outside."

"Outside?" Osmas reeled in amazement.

"Extraordinary," said Diltz. "Where did they go?"

"To the southwest. We lost sight of them in the hills."

"You didn't pursue them?"

"What was the point? They had no weapons and were fleeing for their lives. They could do nothing."

"But now one of them, at least, has returned," said Diltz. "They seem most insistent."

Mrukk shrugged. "We will capture him again. And this time he will not escape."

. . . . . .

Treet's first impression of the Old Section was that he had entered a life-sized, three-dimensional representation of a Hieronymus Bosch painting: a chaotic postapocalypse world—fire-gutted and crumbling, vermin-infested ruins through which scrabbled half-naked creatures that may once have been human.

Refuse moldered in reeking mounds piled high in the center of the main square surrounded by charred and twisted trunks of trees. Pale, sickly weeds squeezed up through cracks in the wildly tilting paving stones. The air was rank and stale, the yellowed light weak. The few desolate facades still standing were blackened by soot and time.

The Old Section was clearly older than the rest of Dome. The architecture was different—more like contemporary utilitarian architecture back on Earth: permastone slabs and fibersteel girders, plastic sheathing over industrial foam—all of it arranged in the standard honeycomb fashion of interlocking square boxes. The only variation Treet could see was that here and there the design had been augmented by native stone. A few wrecks showed signs of a developing indigenous architecture quite different from the stark, no-nonsense constructions around them.

Treet realized he was seeing back in time to the earliest days of the Cynetics colony. He imagined the young colony alive and thriving, building a glorious future on a paradise planet. The hope these people must have felt, the dreams they must have had for themselves and their children were now ruined and sinking into filth. The ruins had the stink of age, that oppressive sour smell of a thing too long removed from fresh air and sunlight.

Here the Red Death had forever changed the destiny of the colony. No, he reminded himself, not the Red Death alone. That had been a factor certainly, but there were others. A massive failure of nerve perhaps chief among them. Where had the men of vision gone, the men of bold ideas? Why had the voices of wisdom and intelligence been silenced? What had become of the courageous women who with their gentle, steady hands anchor all around them against the chaos? Were there no young people burning with impatience and idealism to challenge the status quo?

The ruins knew, and Treet could guess. In a word: fear. Paradise had turned against the settlers—apparently through their own carelessness—and the resulting disaster had so demoralized the survivors that they were paralyzed by fear. They had become afraid to dream again, afraid to act, afraid to trust their own best instincts and those of their fellow survivors. Afraid to live again.

Empyrion's bright promise had faded, and darkness rushed in to crush out the trembling light forever.

Now all that remained of the original colony was a blasted shell inhabited by the subhuman nonbeings. As Treet passed through the Old Section, Dhogs, their tattered remnants of clothing fluttering like feathers, flitted among the refuse heaps like great scavenger birds scrounging for scraps and morsels. Scruffy, malnourished children bawled like stray animals, their tears making muddy rivulets down stained cheeks.

The Dhogs were a noisome bunch, and Treet could hardly stand to be near them. The odor was such that a few whiffs could make his stomach unsteady. He recoiled from contact with the Dhogs and tried to avoid them without giving offense, which was difficult because, as Ernina had predicted, among the Dhogs he was revered to the point of outright worship.

The first day the rumor had spread that a Fieri was among the newcomers. That night hundreds of Dhogs had gathered silently outside the building where he'd been given a room. The crowd waited all night, hoping for a glimpse of him.

The mad flight to the Old Section had sapped most of Treet's strength. It took a couple days of bedrest for him to recuperate enough to feel like getting up and moving around again. On his first venture out, he discovered the uncanny effect he had on the masses. People followed him wherever he went— politely, at a distance, murmuring to themselves. But if he stopped long enough, they would become bold and put their hands on him, touch his skin, pinch his flesh as if to reassure themselves of his corporeality.

As uncomfortable as that made Treet feel—being worshiped by a rabble of reeking scavengers—he accepted that it was necessary, even desirable for the time being. After his first encounter, Treet had spoken to Tvrdy about it. "Shouldn't we tell them I'm not a Fieri?" he had asked.

"Why? It does no harm, and it might be a useful thing when the time comes."

"When the time comes for what?"

"To stir these people to action."

"The Dhogs? You're not serious. You don't mean—"

"Mean to use them? Certainly I do."

"But they're hopeless. Look at them—they can hardly feed and clothe themselves. What could they do against Invisibles?"

"Don't misjudge them. They are shrewd and capable within certain limits. They have survived for centuries in this festering pesthole. Besides, we have begun training the more able-bodied—that is what the food is for. And soon we will begin feeding the rest."

"Fattening the lambs for the slaughter, is that it?"

Tvrdy did not understand the metaphor, so Treet explained, "I mean, I don't see how you can ask them to fight for you."

"Not for me, for themselves. Do you think Jamrog will forget what happened? For years he has been laying plans to attack the Old Section and exterminate the Dhogs. Now there is nothing to stop him. He will come. Sooner or later we will all have to defend ourselves or be killed." Here Tvrdy stopped and grinned unexpectedly; he placed a hand on Treet's shoulder. "Besides, I won't be the one to ask them to fight."

Treet stiffened. "Who then?" He already had a pretty good idea who.

"The Fieri will ask them."

So Treet had grudgingly become the resident Fieri, and tried to keep a low profile, staying out of sight as much as possible. But then something happened to make him more sensitive to his delicate position.

The morning of his fifth day among the Dhogs, he had attended the morning briefing session with Tvrdy and the others. There he and Ernina had been introduced to the mechanics of the rebellion; he had then related what had taken place on his mission to the Fieri. Although it hurt him to tell it, he had ended by saying, "We can expect no help from the Fieri. I tried very hard to convince them, but they are prevented by a sacred vow of nonaggression from entering this struggle—even for a good cause."

Treet did not say that this vow had come about because Dome had wiped out the Fieri cities with nuclear weapons, reducing their fair civilization to radioactive waste, and therefore the Fieri were understandably shy about involving themselves in the perverse machinations of Dome politics. He did not say that the *only* reason he himself had returned was to try to prevent it from happening again.

Treet's unhappy news had been greeted with calm acceptance, and he guessed that no one had really expected any help from the Fieri. It had been a long shot, after all. No one knew that better than Treet—just surviving the desert had been remarkable enough in the Dome dwellers' eyes.

After the briefing ended, a swarthy little hobgoblin had come up to Treet, thumped himself on the chest, and said, "Giloon Bogney."

"Orion Treet," he replied.

"Come, Giloon show you Old Section."

Tvrdy had been looking on and nodded his encouragement, so Treet had agreed. Bogney led him out, and they were quickly surrounded by Dhogs. The Dhog leader waded through his people, pulling Treet along with him, and they struck off across the refuse-piled New America Square. The tour became a parade—more people joining the procession as it wound through the jumbled, beaten-earth pathways.

They stopped from time to time for Bogney to point out some item of local interest. The Dhog's speech was so deteriorated that Treet caught scarcely any of what was said. He nodded a good deal and looked bemused. Finally they stopped before a wall—most of which was lying in collapsed sections under the low roof of dirt-and-smoke filmed crystal.

The wall was made of gray Empyrion stone, cut and fitted into place without mortar. It stood to just over Treet's head, though the top row of capstones was missing. In all it was fairly unremarkable, except for the feature Bogney indicated with his grubby hand.

Carved into the stone was the image of a winged man with his hair tied back in a long braid and wearing a flowing robe. The man's wings were stretched wide on either side of his body, with broad feathers radiating out behind him. A mysterious amulet hung on the thick chest. The head was in profile, and with a blinding shock of recognition, Treet remembered where he'd seen those same straight, angular features:

On a door nearly eleven light-years away, back on Earth, in Houston. The door to Chairman Neviss' office suite.

Treet gawked at the chiseled image. It was rather crudely done, but clearly recognizable and the subject so unique there could be no mistake. The artist whose hands had created the likeness had seen the very doors Treet had seen—three thousand years ago by Empyrion reckoning.

He reached a hand to the stone and traced the work with his fingertips, marveling at the mix of emotions roiling inside him: awe, despair, loneliness, and other feelings too obscure to decipher. I am the only one who knows what happened, he thought. I am the only one. He felt immensely old and burdened just then—as if the knowledge he held inside him was an enormous weight he had carried a lifetime.

He gazed at the carved image, and it occurred to Treet that both he and the nameless sculptor had stood in the same spot and admired the Chairman's doors back on Earth—a place Empyrion's present inhabitants did not even remember.

This seemed incredibly significant to Treet, until he thought about it. What did it mean really? What did it tell him that he did not already know?

In the end, nothing.

A sense of hopelessness stole over him. What was the use? Dome's problems were legion. What could one man do?

"Cynetix," said Bogney, fingering the image.

"Huh?" Treet stirred.

"Cynetix," Bogney repeated, and the Dhogs pressed closer, muttering the name softly.

Treet nodded. "Yes, Cynetics."

Bogney raised a hand and patted the air, as if to flatten it. The Dhogs understood the gesture and sat down on the ground. Pointing to the image once more, Bogney said, "Cynetix. Dhogs hearing Fieri man telling now." He then sat down cross-legged with the rest, and they all looked up expectantly at Treet.

Treet gazed around him. What can I tell them? he wondered. They think this winged man is Cynetics, a god. They think I'm a god of some sort. How would they ever understand?

Looking at their earnest eyes, Treet again felt the strange, burning-face sensation he'd felt in Ernina's hospital. The Infinite was still with him, within him. The presence stirred, and the hopelessness vanished. In its place appeared a word of comfort: It's not up to you to solve Dome's problems—only to do your part, and do it as well as you can.

Very well. Here then was one thing he could do. He could tell the Dhogs about their history and what was happening in the world outside the Old Section; he could sow the seeds of truth. He had no sooner framed the thought than the words began making their way to his tongue; so, adopting the mythical language of the storyteller, he began.

"In the old time there were giants who lived far away beyond the stars. The biggest giant of all was Cynetics, and he was very big. The world where he lived, Earth, grew too small for him, so he turned his eyes to the sky one night and he saw this world."

The Dhogs murmured at this and nodded, hunkering down like children to better hear the story. Treet didn't know how much they understood of his speech, but figured the sound of his voice was what mattered most anyway.

"Cynetics said to himself," Treet continued, "I will send my sons there to make a new place for me to live. So, riding in a— ah, sky em—the sons of Cynetics came to Empyrion and flew over the land until they came to this place, and they said, 'Here we will make our home.' And they built a city and named it Empyrion. They filled their city with people, and the city prospered.

"One day, when the city was still new, the Red Death came, and the sons of Cynetics died. Men and women, young and old alike, everyone died, for nothing could stop the Red Death. The people struggled; they fought for life and a few survived, but the city was broken." The Dhogs were hushed, taking in the story in awed silence. "The city was broken into two pieces. Both were Cynetics' children, but they quarreled over how to rebuild the city.

"In the heat of the quarrel, the sons who had taken the name Fieri were cast out. Those who remained here raised high walls and sealed the city with crystal, forever shutting out their brothers. They became Dome.

"The Fieri wandered the world and grew strong in the

open air. The day came when they stopped wandering and built their own city, called Fierra. It was a magnificent city, a city of wonders untold. And the Fieri grew great in the land.

"Many long years passed, and the people of Dome saw the greatness of the Fieri and grew jealous. Their jealousy turned to hate, and they rose up against the Fieri and killed them with a fire that burned even the stones.

"The dome dwellers rejoiced, believing they had rubbed out all the Fieri, but a few lived on, even as the Old Ones lived on after the Red Death. The Fieri who survived the all-consuming fire traveled far away and built another city by the sea—that is, a great water. They renamed their new city Fierra and said to themselves, 'Nevermore will we go to our brothers in Dome, for we will not forget what they have done to us.'

"In time, the Fieri grew strong once again and became very wise, and the new Fierra became greater even than the first city." Here Treet paused, uncertain of where to go with his tale. He looked out on the upturned faces, alert, intent. He saw the flicker of hope in the dull gray eyes and understood the power he now held. The Dhogs trusted him. Their trust gave him unquestioned authority over them. The next words he spoke would determine how he used that authority and power.

"Many long years have passed," said Treet slowly. "And once again the rulers of Dome are preparing to make war on the Fieri. I have come to try to stop them." He turned and regarded the winged man carved into the gray stone. "Cynetics is far away. He does not hear his sons anymore, and he cannot help us. It is up to us to help ourselves."

From the astonished stares of his hearers Treet saw the revolution these last words had stirred. He decided he'd said enough for the moment, so stepped from the wall and made his way through the crowd still seated on the ground.

• • • • • •

The afternoon light through Dome's great crystal panes shimmered over the green fields as, their day's work done, the Hyrgo began descending from the terraces to make their way back to their kraams. The workers wound down the zigzag path between the tiered fields leading to the broad boulevard at the bottom of the valley, heading back to deep Hage and their suppers, talking quietly among themselves in the slow, patient Hyrgo way.

A group of about thirty workers reached the lower field and proceeded along the boulevard. They had not gone more than a hundred meters when they were met by a band of Invisibles.

The Hyrgo fell silent, moving ahead hesitantly. As the first of the Hyrgo approached, the Invisibles fanned out across the boulevard. "Halt!" shouted the Invisibles' commander, a Mors Ultima in glistening black.

The Hyrgo stopped at once, looking fearfully at one another.

"What is the trouble, please?" asked the foremost Hyrgo, a fourth-order tender.

"Shut up!" yelled the Invisible. "Against the wall!" He shoved the foreman toward the rimwall.

Weapons appeared in the Invisibles' hands and the Hyrgo backed to the wall, eyes wide, mouths quivering in mute protest.

"What is this?" cried the Hyrgo foreman. "We have done nothing. We are field tenders."

The Mors Ultima stepped up and slashed the man across the mouth with the butt of the weapon in his hand. The Hyrgo workers gasped. Blood dribbled over the injured Hyrgo's chin and down the front of his yos. He fell back with a whimper.

"Get moving!" ordered the Invisible in charge. The stunned Hyrgo did not move, so his men leapt to action and began driving the Hagemen back along the boulevard.

"Where are you taking us?" demanded the Hyrgo foreman through bleeding lips.

The Mors Ultima stepped close and struck him against the side of the head with the weapon. The Hyrgo went down. Two Invisibles sprang forward, hauled him to his knees, and dragged him away. Other Hyrgo coming down from the fields appeared along the rimwall. "Go to your kraams," shouted the Mors Ultima, "or else follow your Hagemen to reorientation."

The frightened Hyrgo hurried away, letting their Hagemen go without a word.

At the Hyrgo checkpoint, the group was held until large multipassenger ems arrived; then they were pushed aboard, and the vehicles whisked them away to the reorientation center on

Cavern level deep in Hage Nilokerus. There, along with prisoners from other Hages—they saw the turquoise-and-silver of Chryse, the blue hood and hem of Bolbe, and the red stripes of Rumon—they were crowded into newly constructed holding pens. Women were crying hysterically and men stood dazed, wringing their hands and staring.

"What is happening here?" asked the Hyrgo foreman of a fourth-order Chryse.

"Reorientation," replied the Chryse flatly. "What else?"

"I don't understand. We were taken from the fields. We have done nothing."

The Chryse shook his head and spat. "Haven't you heard? The Supreme Director is angry with the Chryse and Hyrgo—you for letting the grain be stolen, us for letting the thieves pass through our Hage."

"But it was Dhogs. We had nothing to do with it."

The Chryse lifted his shoulders. "Does that matter?"

"I see Bolbe here—what of them?"

"I don't know. They claim they have done nothing, but it's clear they must have violated the Clear Way or they wouldn't be here."

Just then Nilokerus security guards came to the holding pen and began pulling people out—the Hyrgo foreman among them. He was taken into the central admitting area, a huge cylindrical room aswarm with people. He was made to stand in a long line before a desk behind which sat four hooded Nilokerus, their faces green in the light of data screens.

When his turn finally came, he was prodded to the desk by a guard with a long, flexible rod. "Name," said the Nilokerus at the terminal. He glanced up from the screen. "Give me your name."

"Grensil," replied the Hyrgo.

"Cell N-34K," said the Nilokerus. "Next."

"Wait!" shouted the Hyrgo. "What have I done? You must tell me what I have done."

"Take him away," grunted the guard. "Next!"

The rod jabbed him in the ribs, and the Hyrgo foreman was prodded into one of the long corridors radiating out from the central admitting area. The corridor was crowded with guards and prisoners, and they shoved their way through to the cell. When the unidor snapped off, the Hyrgo was pushed forward. He threw his hands out and gripped the stone, holding himself back. The rod smashed his fingers again and again until he let go and, to a chorus of curses, tumbled into the cell.

Inside there were six men—six men in a space designed for only one. No one could stand upright, and there was not room for them to sit down. So they squatted against one another, shifting their weight painfully and cursing. The air was foul with the odor of vomit and urine. One of the men, a Rumon, at the back of the cell was bleeding from facial wounds; he muttered incoherently, his head lolling back and forth.

Grensil settled into the crush of bodies and was elbowed sharply as he tried to fit himself into the too small space. Lightheaded, reeling with the horror of what was happening to him, the Hyrgo closed his eyes, muttering, "Trabant take me, I am dead."

FORTY TWO

The night's dispatch had brought a thick file of information. Upon arrival, Tvrdy had awakened to spend the early hours deciphering it. Now, as the others gathered for the morning briefing, the Tanais Director sat gray-faced, hair disheveled, dark circles under his eyes, waiting to begin.

Cejka was the first to arrive, followed by Piipo with two of his aides, and Kopetch. Treet shambled in, greeted everyone, and sat down in a corner by himself. Ernina arrived, spoke a few words to Tvrdy, and took her seat. Giloon Bogney strutted in last, two odious Dhogs on his heels. They sat down front and center, and Giloon craned his neck around, saying, "All here now. We begin."

Tvrdy raised himself slowly to his feet, passing a hand through his hair. "This came in during the night," he said, thumping the file reader in his hand. "It isn't good."

"Tell us everything," said Cejka. The others mumbled their assent.

"The retaliation is worse than we expected. At last count, upwards of eight hundred Hyrgo have been arrested and taken to reorientation—"

"No-o," Piipo groaned.

"Nearly as many Tanais," Tvrdy continued, "and about a hundred Bolbe have been taken as well."

"Rumon?" asked Cejka.

"There are two hundred Rumon missing—although no rumor messengers, so far. Seventy-five Chryse have been taken. Numbers are not available for the other Hages, but all are presumed to have been affected. There are reports of Nilokerus and Saecaraz being tortured—probably for failure to apprehend us in the raid. Also, Jamuna have been killed outright by Mors Ultima; Jamuna Director Bouc is in hiding. These are unsubstantiated reports at present, but it appears Jamrog is being very thorough in his retaliation."

"The monster," muttered Ernina. "How can he justify this—this outrage?"

"The official explanation," Tvrdy replied, "is that the Fieri have infiltrated Empyrion and are determined to seize power. This is what Jamrog has ordered the Directors to tell the Hages. Before the retaliation started, he convened a special session of the Threl and bullied them into approving his emergency security measures. The checkpoints have been strengthened and an official curfew imposed. Invisibles are patrolling the main entry and exit routes between Hages during curfew hours, and they have set up interrogation cells throughout.

"Also, he has granted priests authority to act as informants for reward. Predictably, they are quick to accuse and collect for any imagined crime."

"It isn't hard to see where this will lead," said Cejka. "No one will be safe from their greed."

"We could use that," pointed out Kopetch. "Don't we have a priest or two we might persuade?"

"Yes," confirmed Tvrdy. "See me after the briefing." He glanced down at the file reader and thumbed the scanner window. "Invisibles are searching Hage Chryse for the entrance to the Old Section. We'll have to seal that entrance and use the others from now on."

"That's to be expected," offered Cejka.

"Here is something unexpected: food rations are being cut, and work hours extended to meet increased production quotas. The Archives have been opened to Nilokerus and Saecaraz magicians—"

"I ran into them," put in Treet.

"What does it mean?" asked Piipo.

"Jamrog is readying himself for a fight," explained Kopetch. "He is attempting to create a surplus from which to stockpile supplies. When he feels he has enough to sustain a protracted battle, he will strike."

"But—the Archives?"

"They're searching for weapons," said Treet. "From the old time."

"He's probably right," affirmed Tvrdy. "They may succeed."

"We can't let that happen," said Cejka. "We would be defenseless."

"Obviously he is moving faster than we anticipated," said Tvrdy. "We're going to have to become active sooner than we planned."

"That, or use our Hage forces," said Kopetch.

"We must not endanger our Hagemen," said Piipo.

"They are already in danger," snapped Kopetch. "All of Empyrion is in danger."

"But if we don't anger Jamrog again," began Piipo, "perhaps—"

"Didn't you hear?" said Cejka, his voice shrill. "Eight hundred Hyrgo and Tanais—and who knows how many others! Jamuna killed and Saecaraz tortured! That's just the beginning."

Treet felt the tension rise in the room as fear frayed taut nerves and tempers escalated. He glanced at Tvrdy and saw that the Tanais Director felt it too. Tvrdy roused himself. "All right!" he shouted. The room fell silent. "Yes, we feel deeply for those who suffer Jamrog's wrath. But we must not let this divide us or draw us from our task. Let it instead provoke us to greater determination."

"He's right," said Cejka, and the tension dissipated at once.

The briefing resumed matter-of-factly, and Treet did not again sense the crippling fear. Tvrdy had, like the adroit leader he was, acted with quick efficiency to defuse a potentially disastrous situation. "Now then," Tvrdy continued, "in view of the information we have received, I suggest we begin planning another raid."

As the others turned this unexpected idea over in their heads, Kopetch leaped up. "Yes!" he said. "It is exactly what we need."

"Wait," said Piipo cautiously, "we should discuss this first."

"Of course." Tvrdy motioned for Kopetch to be seated. "I merely wished to put forth the suggestion. I have no specific plan at this time."

"But it makes sense," offered Cejka. "It will keep Jamrog off balance."

"Forgive me, but I am new to this way of thinking. What would be the aim of this raid?" asked Ernina.

"That remains to be determined. But the effect of the raid would be at least twofold: harassment, as Cejka has suggested; and a demonstration of our ability to move at will throughout Empyrion."

"This demonstration is important? Important enough to justify the probable loss of life?" asked the physician.

"I believe so. Jamrog must know that he is not in total control."

"Wouldn't this drive him to further atrocities?"

"Perhaps," answered Kopetch. "But his anger would also cloud his reason. An angry man makes mistakes—mistakes we could use to our benefit."

Ernina did not appear convinced by this line of reasoning, but said no more.

"I'm with Ernina," put in Treet. "I think it's a costly enterprise. Maybe too costly—unless the stakes were raised significantly." The blank looks of his listeners let Treet know he'd used an obscure figure of speech. "I mean, unless the aim of the raid were of greater importance."

Cejka joined in. "I agree. The purpose must justify the risk."

"Your concerns are mine, Hagemen, precisely," said Tvrdy.

"Would this raid take place soon?" wondered Piipo, who had been whispering to his aides.

"That I can answer with certainty," Tvrdy replied. "The Trabantonna—"

"The Feast of the Dead!" cried Piipo, "But that's—"

"Not much time," said Tvrdy calmly. "I know. But it must be during the Trabantonna feasts. We will not have a better chance. The confusion will be a natural cover for our movements."

"It's the perfect time," said Kopetch, "to work maximum havoc with minimum risk."

The briefing ended; the participants filed silently from the room, each preoccupied with private thoughts. Treet, who had promised to help Ernina begin setting up a medical center, watched as the others hurried away to their duties, one thought drumming in his brain: two thousand people are right now suffering for the rebels' actions, and the Fieri are being blamed!

I was right, Treet thought bitterly, seeing the cruel irony of the situation. I came back to try to save the Fieri, and it's through my actions that the Fieri have become involved.

How swiftly had the complexion of the struggle changed. It wasn't a question of personal survival anymore . . . it was war.

• • • • • •

Except for two brief and somewhat furtive meetings, Pizzle had not so much as set eyes on Starla for a week. The deprivation was killing him. He moped around the deck of the ship all day and grew distant and morose at night. When he wasn't talking to Anthon, his Mentor, Pizzle was absolutely disconsolate. Nothing short of the thought of an impending visit with his beloved could cheer him up. And since Starla had moved to another ship—ostensibly to keep from torturing Pizzle with her presence, although her absence tortured him just as much—Pizzle was miserable a good deal of the time.

Even the nightly spectacle of the sunshower failed to lift his spirits very much. He lost his appetite, his sense of humor, what little native dignity he'd possessed. He wallowed in his self-pity as if it were a balm to his forlorn soul.

Anthon chose not to notice Pizzle's misery, but diverted him as much as possible with stimulating monologues and discussions pertaining to Fieri life and thought. During these episodes, Pizzle was able to forget himself a little and enjoy the mental exercise. Mentor Anthon was a wise instructor. He spoke as one who contemplated life from a pinnacle of years, although in appearance he seemed only slightly older than Pizzle himself. And despite the sagacity of his thought, from under the dark ridges of his brows glittered bright brown eyes as quick as any delinquent youngster's. In all, he reminded Pizzle of Mishmac the Mahat, a character from Papoon's immortal *Orb of Odin* series.

Pizzle made the most of his opportunities to talk with his Mentor. And they enjoyed one another's company for hours on end. Still, as much time as Anthon gave him, there were too many empty hours. Preben, too, noticed Pizzle's predicament and tried to help by assigning him more duties aboard the ship. But try as he might, Pizzle could not muster more than a lackluster enthusiasm for sailing.

"You must think us very cruel," Anthon said one day when Pizzle came for his catechism.

"Cruel?" The word took Pizzle aback. He shook his head until his ears wobbled. "Never. No way. Why would you say that?"

"Separating you from your beloved is a painful charge."

"Yeah," Pizzle agreed. "I guess so."

Anthon looked at him for a long moment and then said, "Tell me the Prime Virtues in the order of their ascendancy."

So began the day's lesson, but at least Pizzle knew that his Mentor understood what he was going through. That helped a little. Seeing Starla helped more. Unfortunately, he could only see her when the boats made one of their infrequent landings, and the next one was not scheduled for another five days.

Early the next morning he found Yarden sitting by herself on deck, wrapped in a scarlet blanket. He slumped down beside her and put his hands behind his head, closing his eyes, feeling the warmth of the polished wood on his back. "I don't think I'm going to make it," he said glumly.

"Welcome to the club," she said.

Her reply was so uncharacteristic Pizzle jolted upright. "You, too?"

Yarden didn't answer. She gazed steadily out at the water and at the ragged roots of the mountains gliding by.

"You want to talk about it?" asked Pizzle.

She turned red-rimmed eyes on him. "If I wanted to talk about it, would I be sitting here by myself all night?"

"You sat here all night?"

She nodded, raising a hand to rub her eyes and smoothe back her hair.

"What's wrong?" Pizzle's misery had made him a shade more sensitive to others' feelings.

"Everything," she snapped. "I thought this trip would be something special. More and more, I'm sorry I came."

"You can say that again."

She gave him a look he could not read. "I heard about your little trial."

"You make it sound like I deserve it or something," Pizzle whined. "I didn't do anything to deserve the way I feel."

"Calm down. At least you still have Starla."

"Yeah, and last time I looked, you were all hot on this art stuff."

"Go away, Pizzle. I don't want to talk about it."

"Sheesh! Every time I come around it's 'Go away, Pizzle! Go away, Pizzle! I don't want to talk about this, I don't want to talk about that.' How come you're the only one on this planet that gets to have any private feelings? You're always delivering these ultimatums to everybody. Well, I for one am getting tired of it."

Yarden softened, smiled. "Your ears get pink when you're mad, you know that?"

"Hmmph!"

"I'm sorry, Pizzle. I apologize, okay?"

"Okay," Pizzle allowed grudgingly. "Us Earthlings ought to stick together."

"Fair enough," said Yarden. She was silent a moment, then sighed and said, "It's just that I'm afraid I've made the most dreadful mistake."

"Treet again?"

Yarden nodded, chin pulled in.

"Pshoo—" Pizzle let air whistle over his teeth. "I don't know what to tell you there."

"It's all right. I have to work this out for myself."

Pizzle didn't say anything. The two simply sat together and listened to the rippling water and the canyons echoing with the keening cries of the ever-present rakkes sailing the wind currents among the rock peaks high above. The white sunlight struck the angled cliffs, scattering silvery light off the rocks. The deck rocked gently as the boats, strung in a long, sweeping line, slid relentlessly upriver toward the bay.

"I should have gone with him," said Yarden softly. It was the first time she had admitted it to herself, but once the words were out she felt the truth in them.

Pizzle took his time responding. "How could you know? I mean, he was far from stable. It sounded so . . . so theatrical. Crackpot—you know? I liked the guy, and I still thought the idea was nutso."

"*Liked.* Past tense."

"Sorry, bad choice of words."

"You think he's dead, too."

"Dead?" Pizzle's head swiveled around. "Golly, Yarden, you shouldn't think anything like that."

"Why not? It's possible, isn't it?"

Pizzle swallowed hard. "Possible," he allowed cautiously, "but highly improbable."

"All too probable. Which is why none of us would go back with him."

"He knew the risks."

"Yes, he knew the risks and he still went back." Yarden

dropped her head to her updrawn knees. "I've been so incredibly selfish."

Pizzle watched her for a moment. "Preben says the bay is only a week away," he said, trying to change the subject. "The last few kilometers, however, are overland through the mountains. But there's a pass, so it's an easy climb."

"I've lived my whole life without regret," Yarden replied. "Now this."

"Would it help if you knew he was okay?"

"What are you suggesting?"

"Well, you could find out easy enough, couldn't you? I mean, with your mental thing you could find out." He studied her expression for a moment and added, "You never thought of that?"

"I—no, I couldn't do that to Treet."

"Why? Afraid of what you'll find?"

She dropped her eyes.

Pizzle climbed slowly to his feet. "I'm hungry. Are you? I smell something cooking below. Want to come down and get some breakfast with me?"

"Ah, no. No, thank you, Asquith." Yarden raised her head and smiled. "I appreciate what you're trying to do for me. Really. But this is going to take a little time."

"Sure." He turned and started away, then paused and turned back. "Look, if you want me for anything I'm here. I mean, if you should want to try contacting him or something. Okay?"

Yarden accepted Pizzle's offer. "Thanks, I won't forget. Us Earthlings ought to stick together."

"Darn right."

FORTY
THREE

"We can't do it this way. It's wrong." Treet was adamant.

Tvrdy gazed at him with an exasperated expression. "I don't understand you. Jamrog is our enemy—remove him and the Purge is over. It is as simple as that."

"It is never that simple," Treet retorted. He looked around the ring of grim faces, yellow in the foul light of a smoking lamp. They were going over the newly revealed details of the Trabantonna raid. It was late, and everyone was tired.

"It's a good plan," Cejka put in gently. "Tvrdy and Kopetch have spent every minute of the last two days working on it. It's brilliant."

"It was you," said Kopetch, "who insisted the purpose of the raid must justify the risk."

"I wasn't suggesting that we assassinate Jamrog."

"What else is there?" demanded Tvrdy. "We cannot fight the Invisibles and the Nilokerus security forces; we are not ready."

"It is most expedient," added Kopetch, fatigue making his voice sharp. "In terms of risk against feasibility and potential reward, it makes perfect sense. Besides, the timing is extremely advantageous."

"In the whole history of humankind, assassination has never solved anything. It just doesn't work." Treet growled. "I won't be a part of it."

"That cannot be helped," Tvrdy snapped. "The plan is set. Trabantonna begins in two days. Our Tanais and Rumon Hagemen have been informed. Everything is ready. Kopetch is right—it is the best chance we will have for a very long time. And it is the one thing Jamrog will not expect."

Treet clamped his mouth shut and sat down. The briefing continued, but he was no longer paying attention. There was something very wrong about the planned assassination. The trouble was, he couldn't articulate exactly what made it wrong. As Kopetch maintained, the plan made sense in several solid ways that made Treet's feeble objections seem grossly irrational.

It's a curse, thought Treet, to be suddenly afflicted with a good conscience so late in life. One felt the pangs of righteousness, but was unable to give proper voice to them for lack of the long history of careful, reasoned thought and self-examination necessary for persuasive argument. Without that, all one had left was the emotional discord caused by ruffled scruples.

What was so wrong, really? Removing one man made infinitely more sense than engaging in the slaughter of thousands. In terms of human suffering alone, it was no contest; given a choice between all-out war and the simple assassination of one depraved ruler, assassination won every time.

And yet the idea repulsed Treet. He found it morally repugnant. Assassination was a dirty business, the domain of terrorist subversives and scheming anarchists warped by ideological misanthropy and too cowardly to stand up in the light of day and support their beliefs, however perverse, in honest combat, intellectual or otherwise. No matter how well justified, assassination always tainted its practitioners with its own reeking corruption. And yet, in this particular case perhaps . . .

So he sat and fumed, furiously trying to determine why he felt the way he did, and how to put it into words. The effort came to nothing. And by the time the briefing was over, Treet was no nearer an answer.

"It is a good plan," Tvrdy said as the others trooped from the room. "We should all be united in its support."

"I know how you feel, Tvrdy. I'm sorry. I can't tell you why, but I know this is wrong. It won't solve anything."

Tvrdy appeared about to object, but changed his mind. "You will remain here with Ernina. The raid will take place as planned."

"Fine." Treet rose stiffly and stumped from the room.

In darkness, he walked across the bare compound toward the building where he had his room. As he was about to enter, he saw a light shining from the low semiruined structure Ernina had commandeered for a medical center, and where she planned to begin treating the Dhogs for parasites and toxicity as soon as she could get her hands on a few basic supplies.

Treet moved toward the light and entered the building to find the physician busily arranging large floppy mats on the floor by the light of a single lamp whose dirty flame produced more smoke than illumination. The smoke stank.

"The briefing is over?" She watched him with concern in her sharp green eyes.

"It's over."

Ernina laid the mat down and indicated for Treet to take a seat. He dropped onto a mat and leaned on his elbow. "You look terrible," she observed.

"I feel terrible."

"Perhaps you are not recovered fully from our escape. You were very weak. I feared you would not make it."

"It isn't that. It's the raid."

"Oh? You are not happy about the decision?"

"It's wrong. I don't know why, but it is."

The physician regarded Treet for a few moments. "I agree."

"You do?"

"That's why I did not come tonight. I will not come to any more briefings—I have no time for planning death."

"Even if it's an insane tyrant like Jamrog?"

She frowned. "I have enough to do trying to keep people alive."

"I tried to convince them to abandon the idea. I tried—" He looked at the physician's kind face earnestly. "But I don't have the words. I don't know what to say to them. Their reasons all make perfect sense. Kill Jamrog and the Purge will end. The insanity will stop. Thousands of people will be spared. The torture, the death—remove Jamrog and it will stop. And yet . . ."

"You don't believe it."

"No," answered Treet sadly. "It doesn't matter how I justify it, I can't make myself believe it. At first I thought I was just being squeamish, scared. I don't know—maybe I am just scared. I don't know what I expected."

"The suffering must stop."

"Yes, but not this way."

"There is a better way?"

"No. I don't know. There must be." Treet lay back and put his hands under his head. "It's just that this is so—so dirty, so cowardly, so cold."

"All the same, Jamrog does not shrink from it—it put him in power."

Treet stared at the physician for a moment, then jumped up. "That's it! Ernina, that's it exactly. If we use assassination we're no better than he is. Once we stoop to using our enemy's tactics, *we* become the enemy."

He reached out and took Ernina by the shoulders. "That's it! That's what's been gnawing at me. I've got to tell Tvrdy."

"Do you think he will listen?"

Treet stopped. "What he does about it is up to him, I guess. I have to tell him, though." He took Ernina's hand and gripped it tight. "Thanks for understanding." Then he was gone.

Treet found Tvrdy in his room, sitting on a cushion poring over the maps of the Old Section. He looked up as Treet came in. "It is amazing how many secrets the Dhogs have guarded over the years. I never guessed there were so many entrances and exits linking the Old Section to the Hages. We will be able to strike in four Hages at once! Think of that. The confusion will be complete."

"We can't do it," replied Treet. He sat down beside Tvrdy and tapped the map with a forefinger. "All the planning in the world won't make it right."

Tvrdy's features clouded with anger. "If you have come here to weary me further with your irrational misgivings, save your breath. I have more important things to do."

"Tvrdy, listen to me. Please, just listen, and then I'll go. If we assassinate Jamrog, we're no better than he is. Do you see that?"

Tvrdy turned away. "No."

"By taking our enemy's weapon and using it against him, we become *worse* than he is. Yes, worse; because we have a choice. We don't have to use it. If we do, we become the enemy—we perpetuate the evil. You can't fight evil with evil, Tvrdy. You must see that."

"Who is to say what is right and what is wrong? In war, good and evil have no meaning. You do what must be done to win. There are no rules. There is only expediency."

"You don't believe that. You can't."

"Unless we kill Jamrog first, he will kill us. That is a fact. Where is your good and evil then? If we lose, good will also die."

"What will that matter if we win and lose ourselves in the process? We will be just as bad as Jamrog."

Tvrdy stared at Treet, eyes hard, mouth pressed into an implacable line. "You argue nonsense," he said softly.

"I'm right, and you know it." Treet stood slowly. "I leave it with you, Tvrdy. I'm not going to say anything more about it." He walked to the doorway, paused, then added, "Think about what I've said. It's not too late to change the plan."

Tvrdy shook his head and returned to his maps. "It is too late. To change now would place our Hagemen in danger."

"Cancel. Call it off."

"The information has gone out. Using the network again before the raid would jeopardize the entire operation. I won't do that."

Treet turned and walked back to his room. I've done what I can, he thought. It's out of my hands.

FORTY FOUR

Danelka hurried across the plaza, skirting the lake. He entered the central tower and smiled to himself. All was in place for the coming raid. He'd seen to the last and most delicate details himself and sent the ready signal. No more communication would take place until after the Trabantonna . . . and then? And then there would be no need for stealth.

One more day . . . just one more day . . .

He dashed across the empty hall. Upon reaching the Director's lift, two figures stepped from a nearby alcove.

"What do you want?" Danelka said. The two men at the lift entrance wore Tanais gold.

"Please, we need your help." The man on the left stepped close, glancing quickly around to see if they were observed.

"Yes?"

"You must come with us."

Danelka looked at the men more closely. "Who are you? You're not Tanais."

The man on the right moved nearer. "There is a problem."

"What problem?"

"Only you can help."

"I don't understand. What sort of problem?"

"Security," answered the first man. He put a hand on Danelka's arm.

The Tanais shook off the stranger's hand. "I'm not going anywhere with you." He turned back to the lift.

"We have authorization." The first man raised his voice.

Danelka spun back around. "What sort of authorization?"

The second man pulled a packet from his yos. "Charges have been made."

"What sort of charges?" Danelka demanded angrily.

"Very serious charges," said the man with the packet.

"It's probably a mistake," replied the first. "But you must come and help us straighten it out."

"I'm not going anywhere until I know what this is all

about." Danelka glared at the two men and crossed his arms across his chest.

"We should go now," said the second man, the more reasonable of the two.

"What are these charges? If someone has been making accusations against me, I have a right to know what they are."

"You have been charged with treason," the first man told him.

Danelka blanched. "Let me see that!"

The man pulled the packet away. "It's probably a mistake," said the first man. "If you come with us, we can get it cleared up."

Danelka hesitated. "I'm going to call my Subdirector. He must be notified."

"It won't take long."

"Treason . . . that's ridiculous." A sick look skidded across his face.

"A mistake, surely," said the man on the left. "We will clear it up now, and you can return to your kraam and to your supper."

The man on the right took Danelka firmly by the arm and pulled him away from the lift. "Let's go quietly. It does not look good for a man of authority to cause trouble."

"It is a mistake," said Danelka harshly. "And you will soon regret your part in it, I promise you."

The interim Director was taken to an interrogation kraam in one of the Hageblocks near the Tanais border with Saecaraz. There he was made to stand before an Invisible who was sitting behind a portable data screen. The Invisible read a long list of charges, then looked up at the prisoner for the first time. "Do you confess to these charges?"

"Lies! All lies!" Danelka shouted. "I confess to nothing. I want to call my Subdirector."

The Invisible remained silent, but motioned to the two who had brought him in. Danelka resisted and was dragged bodily into the next room, where he was shoved into a large metal chair. His yos was stripped off, and loops of thin wire were fastened around his wrists and ankles and around his neck.

"You can't do this to me!" shouted Danelka. "I am the Tanais Director. I demand a Threl hearing."

The Invisibles left then, Danelka's angry shouts ringing in the empty room. A few moments later two more Invisibles entered the room. One took his place behind the console which controlled the chair, and the other came to stand before the prisoner. Danelka took one look at the Mors Ultima yos and quailed.

"We know you are in contact with your former Director," said Mrukk. "I can have the charges against you dropped now if you tell me where he is."

Danelka glared back at the Mors Ultima commander, but kept his mouth firmly shut.

"He will be caught and executed for the traitor he is." Mrukk put his face close to his victim's. "But you don't have to share his fate. You can go free. I can arrange it for you to continue as Director. I can even see to it that you are rewarded: ten thousand shares. It's all yours if you speak up now."

The Tanais Director pro-tem squirmed in the interrogation chair. The wire thongs bit into his flesh at wrists and ankles. "I won't be bought," he uttered through clenched teeth.

"Too bad," sighed Mrukk. "Ten thousand shares—a man could do something with ten thousand shares." He gave a nod to the Invisible behind the console, and the wire thongs jerked tight. Danelka stifled a scream. Sweat beaded up on his forehead and trickled from his armpits.

"Your loyalty is admirable," continued Mrukk as if nothing had happened. "But do you not have a greater loyalty to the Supreme Director? That's worth thinking about. Shall I leave you to think about it?"

Danelka stared at his blue, swollen hands. His feet felt as if they were about to burst. Sharp needles stabbed his flesh. "I will come back in a few hours to see if you have changed your mind."

"I won't tell you," Danelka hissed. "Kill me now."

"No, not yet," replied Mrukk, pressing his face close. "Already you ask for death, and we have just begun. It can get much worse. Believe me . . . much worse. You'll be amazed to discover how much you can take. I'll be back and we'll talk again."

"Trabant take you!"

Mrukk strode from the room and heard his victim's

screams sharp in the air. There was still much force behind the cries, but a few more hours under the wires would see them weaken.

When Mrukk returned, Danelka was unconscious, his flesh pasty and damp, his breath coming in shallow gasps. The Mors Ultima chief smiled to himself. It was too easy, really. These bloodless wretches had no stamina, no endurance. The first twinge of pain and they crumbled.

"Wake him up," Mrukk ordered. The Invisible monitoring the pain sensors stepped from behind the console with a probe in his hand. He applied the probe to the side of the victim's neck, and the body jerked spasmodically. Danelka's eyes fluttered open, and he moaned.

"Now then," said Mrukk, "this can stop at once. Tell me where your master is and what he plans, and I will release you."

Danelka made no reply. His head rolled limply on his chest. Mrukk leaned forward, grasped a handful of hair, and snapped the head up. He gazed into the clouded eyes.

Taking the probe from the Invisible standing by, Mrukk inserted the probe in the victim's mouth. A strangled scream tore from Danelka's throat; front teeth shattered as rigid jaw muscles clamped tight.

"That's better," observed Mrukk, peering into his victim's eyes again. The fresh pain had revived Danelka somewhat. "Now then, tell me and this will end. Where is Tvrdy?"

Danelka opened his mouth, hesitated. Mrukk brought the probe close once more. "N-n-o! I—I'll tell you."

"Tell me then."

"He is with the Dhogs in the Old Section."

"We already know that!" shouted Mrukk. "What are his plans?"

Anger shook the young man's frame. "Y-you said . . . only . . . where he is . . . you said—"

"That was before. But you've kept me waiting. I want more. What are his plans?"

"I don't know."

"You're lying." Mrukk placed the probe against the soft flesh of the Tanais Subdirector's belly. The man writhed in the chair, cords standing out on his neck, facial muscles etched in a rictus of agony.

"What are his plans?"

Danelka gasped. "I don't know."

Mrukk's hand flicked out from under his yos. He held the knife blade before Danelka's horrified face. "His plans?"

Danelka, sweat streaming from his face, shook his head weakly. The blade dropped, and the Subdirector's index finger tumbled onto the floor amidst a spray of blood.

Mrukk raised the stained knife blade again. "You have many other fingers, Hageman. We will try again. What are Tvrdy's plans?"

Danelka grimaced and spat out, "I don't know his plans. He did not tell me."

The blade slashed down, and another finger rolled to the floor. Mrukk stooped to retrieve it, held it up before Danelka's ghostly face. "Perhaps he did not tell you precisely what his plans were," he said, turning the severed finger around. "But he told you something. What did he tell you?"

Mrukk lowered the razor-sharp blade slowly onto Danelka's little finger. The hand, held firm by the wire at the wrist, twitched, but could not evade the knife. The blade pressed down.

"The Trabantonna!" Danelka yelled. "The Trabantonna . . ."

"What will happen?"

Danelka squeezed his eyes shut as tears streamed down his face. "Assassination."

Mrukk straightened, grimacing fiercely. "You stinking Tanais filth!"

Danelka's eyes flew open. "I—I told you . . . release me!"

Mrukk's hand blurred in the air, and the knife sliced through the soft flesh of his victim's neck. Danelka's scream died bubbling in his throat.

• • • • • •

Mrukk entered Jamrog's kraam, was met by Osmas, and passed quickly through to Jamrog's private bedchamber. There Mrukk found the Supreme Director in the company of three comely young Hagemates. The girls giggled as the Mors Ultima commander came in.

"Ah, Mrukk," said Jamrog, rolling out of bed. "I expected you much earlier and grew tired of waiting."

"The subject was quite unresponsive, Supreme Director. He required extensive convincing."

"And was he convinced?"

"In the end."

Jamrog laughed. "You can be most persuasive, Mrukk." He held out his arms for one of the girls to drape a hagerobe over him. "Leave us for the moment," he told them. The girls tittered, and Mrukk's eyes followed their easy movement as they flounced from the room. Jamrog saw the look and said, "Yes, they are beautiful, aren't they? But you don't like women, do you? What do you like, Mrukk? I wonder."

The Mors Ultima stiffened.

"Ah, well, what did your inquiries produce?"

"It is as we suspected, Supreme Director," Mrukk replied tersely. "Tvrdy and the others have fled to the Old Section. They have formed an alliance with the Dhogs."

Jamrog nodded, walked to a table, took the flask from the warming cradle, and poured two cups of souile. He handed one to Mrukk and downed his cup in a single swallow, poured another, and sipped slowly. "Yes, it is as we suspected. Continue."

Mrukk stared at the cup in his hand. "They are transferring information freely from the Hages to the Old Section."

"Yes, yes," said Jamrog impatiently, "do go on."

Mrukk glanced up and eyed the Supreme Director.

"What is it?" demanded Jamrog. "Why do you look at me like that?"

"There is to be an assassination."

"An attempt on my life? When?"

"During the Trabantonna."

"During the Trabantonna!" Jamrog cried. "Wonderful!"

"We don't know where."

Jamrog sipped the warm souile and said, "It doesn't matter. We'll be ready for them. This will be a triumph, Mrukk. A triumph!" Jamrog downed his cup in a gulp and poured another. "We must make special arrangements for our unexpected guests. You'll see to it, Mrukk."

The Mors Ultima nodded slowly. "I will see to it."

"Tvrdy has overreached himself at last, and will be destroyed!" Jamrog spun and smashed his cup down on the table. The cup shattered, and glass fragments scattered over the floor. Jamrog raised a bleeding finger to his mouth and sucked it. "I don't want him killed, Mrukk. Instruct your men; they can kill the others, but not Tvrdy."

"They will be instructed."

Mrukk turned and made his way to the door. "Remember," Jamrog called after him. "I want him alive. Alive!"

The night before Trabantonna the Hage priests hold vigil in the temples of Empyrion. Black tapers of rendered human fat with wicks made from the braided hair of children are burnt through the night, while the priests pour libations over themselves and submit their bodies for ritual cleansings.

As dawn draws near, the priestly revel reaches its climax as the Hage priests, having chosen the corpse of a recently deceased Hageman, strip the corpse, paint it red, and bind it to a thronelike chair. In an elaborate ceremony the cadaver is consecrated to Trabant Animus. The chair and its grotesque occupant are then lifted high and marched around the temple.

As morning's first light strikes Dome's massive crystal panes, the painted corpse emerges from the temple borne on the shoulders of the Hage priests. The procession is greeted by the people who have gathered before daybreak to await the spectacle. The priests push through the crowd and move slowly down the ramp and into the temple square now thronged with onlookers. Those closest to the priests press themselves closer still in an effort to touch the lifeless celebrant as the chair passes.

The chair is carried in this way to the center of the Hage where, in the largest square or plaza, it is established at the head of a table set up on a stage or scaffold. The corpse is officially welcomed and the title Chairman of the Feast conferred upon it. The populace then engages in rites of mourning: men shout and curse and pound the stones with their fists; women wail and throw themselves to the ground, tearing at their clothing and hair.

When the ritual mourning reaches a fevered emotional pitch, a Hage priest, dressed in a scarlet yos, moves through the crowd, scattering warm blood (from freshly killed sacrificial animals) over the mourners. Upon receiving the spattered blood on clothing, faces, and hands, the people leap up and begin dancing hysterically, throwing themselves into wild and unnatural contortions. They scratch themselves and claw at their flesh, they writhe and squirm, they shake with convulsions—all this to the accompaniment of a ghastly chorus of howls and shrieks.

The mad dance continues until exhaustion overcomes the participants. Gradually the screams die and the people lie still. The priests then move through the cataleptic throng touching the people on the back of the neck with a ceremonial bhuj. At the touch, each unmoving Hageman rises slowly and goes to the table where, taking up a bowl and filling it from the mounds of food piled in the center of the board, he sits down to eat.

So begins the Trabantonna, the Feast of the Dead.

· · · · · ·

Jamrog looked out on Hage Saecaraz from a rimwall overlooking Threl Square, where the Saecaraz Trabantonna celebration had just commenced. The squares, filled to overflowing with bellowing, gyrating Hagemen, were ringed with gigantic banners bearing the Supreme Director's likeness. Mrukk stood beside him, restless, wary, tense.

"Relax, Mrukk," Jamrog cooed. "It is early yet. The Feast is just begun. He will not strike so soon. He will wait until the evening, when the chaos is complete. Then Tvrdy will come. And then we will spring our trap."

"Underestimate Tvrdy today, Supreme Director," replied Mrukk stiffly, "and you will pay with your life."

"Have you no faith in your own Mors Ultima to protect me?" Jamrog's smile was fierce and rigid.

Mrukk did not answer. Instead he said, "I have posted men in every Hage. We will be in continual contact with them as we move from Hage to Hage. Any unusual activity today will be met with extreme force."

"Pity the celebrant who drinks too much souile and wanders off to puke in the river." Jamrog's laugh was a sharp bark.

"We are not playing tuebla. Let Tvrdy outsmart you and tomorrow Empyrion will have a new Supreme Director."

"You would like that, Mrukk, would you?" Jamrog laughed again and turned to gaze out over the square where the celebrants writhed and flailed, their screams ringing off the stone. "Listen, it's the music of misery," said Jamrog. "This will soon be Tvrdy's song as well."

"You wish to join the feast now?" asked Subdirector Osmas, deep lines of anxiety etched across his forehead. He and several underdirectors stood back among the Invisibles; they knew of the impending assassination attempt and were trying to remain inconspicuous.

Mrukk stood with arms folded across his chest, black yos glistening in the morning light, narrow eyes sweeping the scene below, watching for any unusual detail: a figure too aloof, an eye too watchful, a shadow out of place.

"It's a long day. There's no need to hurry it along. We can wait here a few more minutes. I will make my appearance when the feast has begun."

They watched as one by one the celebrants grew still. When all the square lay covered with unmoving bodies, the Saecaraz priests began moving among the silent populace, touching each celebrant on the neck and passing on. When all the people had been thus resurrected, Jamrog turned to Mrukk and said, "Now I will go down to them."

Jamrog turned and, with Mrukk at his right hand and his close bodyguard of handpicked Mors Ultima right behind, made his way down to the square. There, to the loud acclaim of his Hagemen, he climbed to the high table where the grinning corpse sat overlooking the feast. The Supreme Director gazed benevolently out upon the proceedings and spoke a few words of license to the revelers. He was presented with a bowl of food, which he accepted and immediately passed to one of his bodyguards. Jamrog then walked among the celebrants for a time.

So caught up was he in the drama of his own presence, Jamrog did not notice that their greetings were perfunctory and subdued—as if the people were afraid to address him at all, yet feared not addressing him even more.

When he had tired of the Saecaraz, Jamrog and his entourage left Threl Square, boarded waiting ems, and were whisked away to Hage Nilokerus. There they were greeted by Director Diltz, who welcomed them warmly and led them along to the feast site. "As you have ordered, Invisibles are scattered among the celebrants, and the perimeter is under hidden patrol. There have been no reports of anyone leaving the feast, and all who arrive are searched."

"Have you found anything?" asked Mrukk.

"Nothing."

"You won't find anything," said Jamrog. "Tvrdy will not attack here. He will choose a neutral place. Hage Nilokerus is too hostile for him. He needs a place where he can manuever more easily—Hyrgo, Rumon, or Tanais would suit him best."

"I'd say Tanais," offered Diltz. "There his network, if he has one, will be ready."

"It would suit Tvrdy's arrogance," said Osmas. He shrank back as soon as he had spoken, remembering his plan to stay out of sight.

"Enough," Jamrog said. "I have come to participate in a feast, not a funeral. We'll stay with our plan and trust to Mrukk's invincible efficiency."

Mrukk grunted, and they moved off. A few hours later the party moved on to Chryse Hage, arriving by boat. They disembarked and were greeted by Director Dey and his underlings, who escorted the growing entourage to the feast site where the Chryse, in an effort to outshine the other Hages in an extravagant show of loyalty, had constructed a huge, octagonal tower in the center of the feast square and scores of long poles around its perimeter. Each side of the tower, as well as every pole, wore Jamrog's huge portrait framed in Saecaraz red.

The gesture was not wasted on the Supreme Director. "I'm impressed, Director," he whispered. "I did not expect the Chryse to respond so warmly."

Dey caught the insinuated reference to the imprisonment of the seventy-five Chryse and replied, "My Hagemen would not have you think that all Chryse are suspect. They want you to know that they are forever loyal to their beloved Supreme Director. This . . ."—he gestured to the massive display—over a hundred gigantic banners in all—"is but a small token of Chryse sentiment."

"I'm sure it is," Jamrog replied. "I am flattered. What is more, such a demonstration requires a response of equal magnitude. Once their reorientation is completed, Director, I will personally see to it that your Hagemen are returned to Hage Chryse rather than being reassigned elsewhere."

"You are too gracious, Supreme Director," bubbled Dey. "But the Chryse seek no special favors. We are only happy to serve." He inclined his head toward Jamrog in a gesture of submission, but did not take his eyes from the Supreme Director's face.

"You have earned this favor, Dey. It is a feast day, and I can afford to be generous. And since I am in a generous mood, I invite you to join my party." Thus, several more bodies were added to the number surrounding the Supreme Director.

• • • • • •

As the afternoon drew on, and the Hage celebrations continued, Tvrdy, Cejka, Kopetch, Piipo, Bogney, and all those chosen to join the raid readied themselves and their equipment—most of it retrieved earlier from Tvrdy's private stockpile—for the trek through the Isedon Zone to the Hages they would strike. When all was ready, the leaders went through the details of the plan yet once more.

"This is the last time we do this," said Tvrdy gravely. "If there are questions, ask now." He looked at Bogney as he said this, but the Dhog leader did not respond. "All right, Cejka, you first. The Nilokerus temple is furthest from the feast site. That is where we will stage our first deception. Cejka, you must make certain the flames are seen before you leave. Sound the alarm yourself if you have to, but we must be certain that the Nilokerus know the temple is on fire. At the same time, four of your men will set fire to two Hageblocks," he pointed to the map, "here and here. They are enough distance from the temple that you will not have any trouble getting away safely. The temple is the crucial distraction; let them find the Hageblock fires on their own. It will produce more panic if discovered separately. Once the fires are lit, get away. Make your way to the rendezvous place in Isedon and wait for us. We will signal you if we need you."

Cejka nodded solemnly. "I understand."

Tvrdy swung to Piipo. "You and Bogney will go in with Cejka, but wait until the flames are sighted and the alarm given. You know where the Starwatch level is—" They both nodded. "So get there as quickly as possible. Ernina has given you a complete list of the supplies and equipment we need. Get what you can and get out. In the confusion, it will not be difficult to pass yourselves off as security. No one will question you if you shout orders and insults along the way. Meet Cejka at the rendezvous and wait with him. We will reclaim the supplies later." He paused. "I wish Pradim were here for this, but we don't have a guide, so you'll have to trust your own eyes and senses."

Piipo replied, "I have memorized the map; I believe I could find Starwatch in my sleep."

"It will look different—count on it. And don't be fooled." Tvrdy looked intently at Bogney. "Do you have any questions?"

The Dhog tapped his temple with a grubby finger. "Giloon understanding everything."

"Fine." Tvrdy turned to Kopetch. "Your mission in Tanais is of highest importance. Its execution must be perfect. Jamrog will visit Tanais last, and security will be tightest there. Mrukk will have Invisibles seeded throughout the Hage; they'll be alert for anything suspicious. It is imperative that you accomplish your goals without arousing the interest of the Invisibles. You'll be alone; there is no backup."

"I can do it," said Kopetch. "It will be a pleasure to outwit the Invisibles in plain sight."

"Just get close to Danelka. He'll tell you how Jamrog will be traveling back to Saecaraz." Tvrdy glanced at each of the others, drew a long breath. "That leaves the assassination itself."

"My rumor messengers are already in place. The weapons were hidden yesterday, and they only await Kopetch's signal."

"They'll have it in plenty of time."

"Nevertheless, use your shoulder set if you have to. The Invisibles will be monitoring all frequencies, so keep it short and in code. By the time Jamrog reaches Tanais, he will be informed of the fires in Nilokerus and will assume that we have bungled our plan. Or they will think it a distraction and expect the attack in Tanais. Either way, the Tanais visit will be perfunctory. He will be anxious to return to Saecaraz—this will help you, Kopetch."

Tvrdy continued, "Upon receiving the signal, I will get in place." His face lit briefly in a tense, tight smile. "Hagemen, I will not fail."

Cejka and his men crept from the disused drainpipe and made their way quickly, quietly through deserted streets, passing between the walls of Hageworks and blocks of kraams. Behind him, one minute later, came Piipo and Bogney with their team. Upon reaching the temple, Cejka and his three firestarters crouched in the growth at the edge of the temple square and waited until the second team had disappeared across the square and were well into the Hageblocks beyond.

"Now!" whispered Cejka. Instantly four figures were racing across the square, up the long ramp, and into the temple itself. The pyramid was empty, but the smutty black candles still burned. As they made their way to the altar at the front, each man lifted his yos and untied the bundle secured around his waist. Then each took up a candle and ran to the heavy hangings behind the altar.

Cejka took his bundle—a plastic bladder filled with a volatile liquid—and aimed the nozzle at the enormous hanging before him. He touched the candle to the damp spot, and the fabric burst into flames. In seconds fire streaked upward along the slanting ceiling. Then, walking backwards, Cejka began pouring the contents of the bladder over the floor. The others, candles in hand, went from one hanging to the next along the further aisles, igniting them as they went. All met at the temple's entrance and paused to view their handiwork.

Each floor-to-ceiling hanging had become a sheet of flames. Smoke rolled up in thick billows and spread like a black fog toward the entrance. All emptied the remaining contents of the plastic bladders in a pool at the door and tossed them aside. "Well done," said Cejka. "Now for the alarm."

They ran back across the temple square and hid once more in the dense growth at the edge of the square. There they waited. Smoke poured out of the open entrance, then flames, following the trail Cejka had left behind. Soon the temple square was lit up in garish orange. The sound of the fire became a roar, but there was no one around to hear it.

"Go back to the drainpipe. Wait for me there. If I do not

return, go back with Piipo and the others." The three crept away, and Cejka raced off toward the feast site.

He had not run far, however, when he was apprehended by two Invisibles on patrol. "Where are you running?" asked the nearest, weapon drawn.

"Fire!" Cejka bellowed as loud as he could. "Fire! The temple's on fire!"

The two Invisibles looked at him closely. "There have been no reports of a fire."

"Four men . . . just now," Cejka panted. "See for yourself." He turned and pointed behind him. "I must sound the alarm."

"Stop!" growled the first Invisible. He stepped close, and his hands played expertly over Cejka's body. "No weapons," he told his partner.

"Weapons?" gasped Cejka. "There's a fire! Go see for yourself if you don't believe me."

The two Invisibles hesitated, uncertain what to do. Cejka saw his chance. "I'll sound the alarm. You go see what you can do at the temple. Maybe you can catch them." He made to take off.

"Not so fast!" shouted one of the Invisibles. Cejka's heart faltered. Did they guess he was somehow involved? Should he try to get away?

He stopped, turned around. "All right," he said. "You go sound the alarm. I will stay here." The two Invisibles looked at one another. Just then there came a whoosh, and a brilliant red orange fireball lit up the night as it flashed skyward to flatten itself against the dome high above.

"Fire!" screamed Cejka again. "The temple's on fire!"

The two Invisibles dashed away, leaving Cejka alone. He wasted no time hurrying back the way he'd come. The quavering blare of a fire siren sounded as he reached the rendezvous point. "We've done our part," said a breathless Cejka as he hurried into the drainpipe to meet his men. "Let's hope the others succeed as well."

• • • • • •

True to his word, Piipo did not have any trouble finding the medical center on Starwatch level. He and Bogney and their team of ten encountered no one on the way and entered the physicians' domain unobserved. Once inside, they easily found the supply kraam and began filling the packs each one wore beneath a new Nilokerus yos with the articles Ernina had requested.

When all the packs were stuffed full, they went into the recovery kraam, where, to the astonished stares of the few Hagemen lying there, they took empty suspension beds, threw off the bedding, and began loading larger pieces of equipment onto the floating bed frames. The three physicians on duty heard the commotion and came running in. They were immediately seized, bound, gagged, and pushed into a corner.

The raiders took the beds and shoved them out of the kraam and into the corridors beyond, fleeing back down to the main level. When they reached the lower rimwall outside, they were met by a crowd of frightened Nilokerus Hagemen who had been stopped by security men. The Nilokerus security guards eyed the equipment suspiciously; the guard in charge barked an order, and weapons appeared. "The Hage is on fire!" someone shouted.

"Out of the way!" hollered Piipo, shoving people aside. "Can't you see we're physicians! We're needed elsewhere!"

The security men stepped back as Piipo pushed by. The others followed, and they rushed on. Bogney kept his head down and hurried along, not daring so much as a quick look around. By the time they slipped back into the drainpipe, the smell of smoke hung heavy in the air and flames could be seen darting above the trees in the distance.

"We did it!" cried Piipo when they reached the rendezvous point in Isedon. Cejka and his fireteams greeted them with jubilant hoots, and they all pounded one another on the back. "Anything from the others?" asked Piipo when the sound died down.

"Nothing," replied Cejka. "It's up to Kopetch and Tvrdy now."

• • • • • •

Tanais born, Kopetch had no trouble making his way unobserved to the place where Danelka would meet and offer an official greeting to the Supreme Director. The success of his assignment would depend on getting close enough to see Danelka's signal. If no signal were forthcoming, Danelka would lead the party close to the place where Kopetch waited, and a prearranged distraction—some souile-soaked Hagemen stumbling over one another, perhaps—would allow the agent to slip in unobserved.

Kopetch, secure under the protection of Jamrog's own Invisibles, would then go along with the official party until either Danelka found out Jamrog's return route or Kopetch himself discovered it by simple observation. Then he would relay the information to Tvrdy. His signal would allow Tvrdy to get into position for the kill.

He waited in the shadow of a boathouse near the wharf, listening to the cacophony of the feast from nearby Tanais square. The simple two-word Rumon signal he'd received earlier indicated that the Supreme Director left Hage Jamuna by boat, and that the official party had grown to nearly sixty people. With that number he would have little trouble blending in—*if* he could elude detection by the Mors Ultima.

The boat was late, but Kopetch, alert at his post, was soon rewarded by the sound of engines rumbling over the water. A few minutes later he could make out the craft, rounding a bend in the river, lights blazing.

I should be the one to do it, thought Kopetch. I could take him as he steps onto the dock. It would be suicide, but worth it for the privilege of killing the twisted tyrant. Why didn't we plan it that way?

Because, he told himself yet once more, if the attempt failed, the reprisals would destroy Empyrion; thousands of Hagemen would die. It was too chancy for a lone assassin. They had only one chance and had to maximize the possibilities for success. Yes, it was better that Tvrdy, backed up by two dozen Rumon, make the attempt. This way, they could manage more of the variables. By the time Jamrog returned to Saecaraz, they would know the exact place and time of his arrival. And, more importantly, Jamrog would believe himself safe from attack. Having visited each and every Hage without incident, he would think he had survived the day. At any rate, he would definitely not expect attack in his own Hage.

The boat came gliding into the Tanais cove. The engines

were cut as the heavy craft slid to the dock. Kopetch noticed that those aboard were strangely silent. Ordinarily, the Supreme Director's boat was the best place to enjoy the Trabantonna. In Sirin Rohee's time, those invited aboard were fed and entertained splendidly. But Jamrog's party was markedly subdued.

It is as Tvrdy said, Kopetch thought. Jamrog guesses something will happen here, as do all the rest. Their visit here will be cursory. The first passengers disembarked—Jamrog was not among them.

At the same moment the Tanais welcoming party arrived and proceeded to the boat.

What's this? wondered Kopetch. Only four? Where's the fifth? He looked closer.

Danelka! Where's Danelka? A jolt of fear quickened his pulse. Danelka was not with the Tanais party. There could be no signal.

Kopetch's mind whirled through his list of limited options and decided that to join the party in an effort to learn the information on his own would be dangerous without Danelka and his prearranged diversion, but possible.

He steeled himself for his task.

Jamrog was on the dock now, surrounded by his bodyguard. The Tanais were making him welcome. Now they were leading him into the Hage. The party—bodyguard and official guests included—gathered around the Supreme Director, and all moved off at once, leaving four Invisibles to guard the boat. The party went into Hage by a different way, passing far from where Kopetch waited.

Kopetch shrank back into the shadows, touched the switch at his side, and, turning his head to his shoulder, whispered, "Old mother, Trabant has taken our Hage Leader. Trabantonna proceeds without us."

FORTY
SEVEN

Kopetch's message was clear enough: Danelka had not appeared, and there had been no signal. Without Danelka to guide them along the prearranged route, Kopetch had not been able to join the party himself and now remained on the waterfront, awaiting further instructions.

Tvrdy had two choices: abort the operation, or take a chance on where Jamrog would reenter Saecaraz. If he guessed wrong, there would be no assassination. He had to decide now. In a few minutes Jamrog would be informed of the fires in Nilokerus, and he would leave Tanais.

The plan hinged on knowing ahead of time where Jamrog would arrive back in Saecaraz, because Tvrdy needed every possible second to get himself and his men into position or the attempt would never succeed. He had to know when Jamrog could be intercepted.

Danelka's part had been to supply that crucial bit of information sometime before the Supreme Director left the Hage. But all was not lost. If Kopetch remained in place, and if Jamrog left the Hage by boat, Kopetch would see and give the signal himself. On the other hand, if upon learning of the Nilokerus fire, Jamrog left by em, Kopetch would not know when or even where they had gone.

There were too many ifs in the equation to suit Tvrdy. To make any kind of intelligent guess, he'd have to have more information. He decided to risk another message. "Hagemate," he said into his shoulder mike, "can we cruise?"

There was a moment's silence, and then Kopetch's voice crackled, "No . . . too crowded on the dock."

Kopetch's answer meant that Invisibles guarded the Supreme Director's boat. Tvrdy made up his mind at once. Since the boat was guarded, there was a very good chance Jamrog meant to use it again. He was already on his way to the Saecaraz waterfront when he gave the signal to his backup team. "Hagemen, Trabant is thirsty."

• • • • • •

The Supreme Director, tired now from his long day of official duties, walked among the Tanais, bored by the wild revel around him. The orgiastic rite was now at its frenzied peak. Food and drink had long ago obliterated all normal inhibition, and the Hagemen, having given themselves over to the celebration, now indulged every desire. For Jamrog, however, the excess of the day had quickly jaded his experienced palate, and he longed for the piquant pleasures awaiting him back at his kraam.

Yawning, he reviewed the feast site and saw his magnified image displayed in every quarter. He shunned the Tanais delicacies prepared especially for him, but drank souile—which he had brought with him—with the underdirectors, who appeared anxious and ill-at-ease.

"I expected your Subdirector to meet me," said Jamrog as he sipped the warm liquor. "I hope he is not indisposed."

Underdirector Egrem heard the intentional slip. Danelka was pro-tem Director following Tvrdy's disappearance; his Directorship had not yet been ratified by the Threl, so technically he was still only the Subdirector. "He will regret missing your visit, Supreme Director," replied Egrem. "Too much food and drink have laid many low this day."

"Too much of anything when one is unused to it can be torture," Jamrog sniffed. "Oh, well, I am not one to hold the weaknesses of a man against him. Still, you strike me as one who could handle a Directorship."

Egrem blanched. Was Jamrog offering him, an underdirector, the Tanais Directorship? Here? Now? It didn't make sense unless, as they all suspected, Danelka was dead. "I count it an honor to be so highly considered, Supreme Director," Egrem answered.

"Yes," said Jamrog, as if thinking of it for the first time. "Come to me, and we will talk more about this. What with the trouble Tanais has had lately with its leadership, I believe a term of stability would greatly improve relations between Saecaraz and Tanais. Am I right?"

"Of course, Supreme Director. And I am flattered you think me capable of helping achieve this stability." Egrem smiled warmly, much more warmly than he felt. All the time thinking, So Danelka *is* dead; the Hage is without a Subdirector.

"Good," said Jamrog flatly.

Just then Mrukk, who had been conferring with one of the Mors Ultima in the bodyguard, interrupted saying, "A message, Supreme Director." Jamrog inclined his head, and Mrukk stepped close and whispered something into his ear.

Jamrog's smile transformed itself into a scowl. "When?" he asked sharply.

"Only minutes ago," Mrukk said.

The Supreme Director turned away from the Tanais delegation and spoke with the Mors Ultima commander. The official party stood looking on, whispering among themselves. When Jamrog turned back, he announced to the group, "Events take me elsewhere. I must return to Saecaraz at once. I'm sure you all understand." There were murmurs throughout the party. "My boat will return you to Saecaraz," he told his guests. To Egrem he said, "I require an em at once."

"Certainly, Supreme Director." Egrem nodded to one of the other underdirectors and the man disappeared, two Invisibles dogging his footsteps. Moments later the em appeared, moving slowly through the crowd, the Invisibles clearing a path for it through the mass of Tanais celebrants.

When the em arrived, Mrukk slid into the driver's seat with one of his Mors Ultima beside him; Jamrog climbed in the back with three more—one on either side and one behind, riding on the back of the vehicle. More Invisibles cleared the way in front of the em, and it rolled away. The remaining Invisibles then began herding what was left of the Supreme Director's party back to the waiting boat.

FORTY
EIGHT

"**I** don't like this," said Cejka. Piipo and Bogney nodded grimly in the torchlight, their teams of raiders sitting quietly along the curved sides of the conduit. "Kopetch should have responded by now."

The frequency monitor between them was silent. The last transmission had been the Nilokerus message to the Invisibles regarding the fire. They expected Kopetch's signal at any moment relaying Jamrog's movements to Tvrdy. The seconds, stretched by anxiety, ticked away slowly.

"Come on . . . come on," said Piipo under his breath.

Bogney stared at the monitor as if willing it to crackle to life. His lips remained pressed firmly into a straight line.

"Something's happened to him," Piipo said, his voice pinging off the fibersteel walls. "The Invisibles have—"

"Shh! Listen!" Cejka pressed his ear to the ancient machine's speaker. "There it is!" He held up his hand for silence. The others held their breath.

A row of tiny red lights on the monitor's control panel lit up. The speaker crackled. "Old mother, Trabant sails . . . but where is Trabant?"

Cejka's eyes flicked to Piipo, who stared at the monitor, a perplexed expression on his face. "What does it mean? 'Trabant sails, but where is Trabant' . . ." the Hyrgo said.

"It means," replied Cejka slowly, thinking, "that the boat left the Hage, but Kopetch did not see Jamrog."

"That must be it!" agreed Piipo, then looked stricken. "But this is not foreseen—what are we to do?"

"We go to Saecaraz." Bogney said it so matter-of-factly, the others blinked at him for a few seconds before understanding dawned.

"He's right," said Cejka at last. "We have to go to Saecaraz. Tvrdy may need help. We won't go into Hage unless we're needed, but we'll be there and ready."

He turned and described the situation to the waiting raiders, and they all hurried off together, Bogney and his Dhogs in the lead, guiding the way.

• • • • • •

Tvrdy received Kopetch's message halfway to the Saecaraz waterfront. He stopped and waited for the trailing Rumon to catch up with him. With lookouts posted, they huddled in an empty passageway, and he explained the problem: "We don't know whether Jamrog is on the boat or not. He might be, but Kopetch couldn't see him. We can't be sure."

The Rumon took in this information silently. "I think we should abort," Tvrdy continued. "If we strike and miss Jamrog, none of us will get out of Saecaraz alive."

"Director," said one of the Rumon, a slim young man with a cool, thoughtful gaze, "permit me to make a suggestion."

Tvrdy checked his first impulse to gainsay the suggestion at once without hearing it and instead answered, "Yes? You have something?"

"You have planned this operation well. It will still work. Only let us divide our number. Fifteen will go to the boat yard; the rest will go to the nearest border checkpoint."

The Cabal had originally considered doing just that—covering two or more Hage entrances—but had scrapped the plan as requiring too many people, people who had to be armed and moved through the Hage, thereby increasing the risk of discovery. Instead, they had opted for precise information. Now that had broken down.

"There are enough of us," added the Rumon, "to cover each place."

Tvrdy frowned.

The young Rumon pressed his argument. "If Jamrog comes by em, he cannot have his entire bodyguard with him. We could be at the checkpoint as planned. If he arrives, we take him and escape into Tanais."

"What you say is true," Tvrdy said slowly while his mind feverishly examined the idea from all angles. The only flaw that he could see was that dividing the force would leave those covering the dock shorthanded if Jamrog happened to be among his entourage after all—but not seriously shorthanded . . .

His head snapped up, eyes shining in the darkness. "It could work. We know that most of his bodyguard will be on that boat, even if he is not. All right . . ." The Director had made his decision. "We will do it."

• • • • • •

The em careened through Tanais Hage toward the border checkpoint. Mrukk coaxed the maximum speed from the vehicle, the headlights swinging right and left as they wound through empty streets and deserted roadways. But as they approached the checkpoint, Mrukk slowed, his killer instincts pricked by some sixth sense.

"What is it?" demanded Jamrog impatiently.

Mrukk made no answer, but his eyes narrowed as the booth came into view.

The em rolled closer.

The lights of the checkpoint booth shone brightly, creating an island of brilliant white light in the darkness. Five guards stood at attention around the booth. They turned casually as the em came toward them, one of the guards stepping into the center of the road, weapon leveled.

Mrukk coasted nearer.

"Tell them to let me through," said Jamrog. "I'm in a hurry."

The Mors Ultima commander touched the switch on his chest and spoke into his shoulder mike: "The Supreme Director will come through."

"Welcome, Supreme Director," came the reply. Ahead, the guard in the center of the road moved off to the right. The em proceeded, still losing speed.

"Well?" Jamrog waved them ahead. "They've cleared us."

Mrukk stared at the scene ahead, his senses quickened. Something was not right; he could feel it. Mrukk looked again and saw that each guard still had his weapon trained on the approaching vehicle . . . *after* having given clearance.

Mrukk suddenly jerked the wheel to the side and pulled on the brake, sending the em into a sideways skid, crying "Ambush!" at the same instant.

The air around the em convulsed as five thermal weapons discharged simultaneously. The heat-flash reached the skidding vehicle an instant later, blistering exposed flesh. But Mrukk's precise reflexes had saved them. The em took the full force of the blast, which lifted it and rolled it onto its side.

The Invisibles leaped from the still rolling em, weapons

drawn, firing, their clothing scorched and smoking. Mrukk threw himself from the vehicle and pulled Jamrog out, throwing him down on his face behind the em.

One Invisible racing for cover at the side of the road folded up in midstep and thudded to the pavement, his torso neatly creased in the middle. Another took a hit in the chest that flung him backward a few steps to drape himself over the side of the em, the front of his black yos sporting yellow flames.

The other two Invisibles reached cover and laid down a blanket of fire. The guard booth wilted under the blast and exploded, taking two raiders with it; another went down under Mrukk's expert marksmanship.

Mrukk touched the switch at his side and shouted, "Checkpoint under attack—Saecaraz/Tanais border! Supreme Director in danger!"

Shadows quaked and lightning sizzled around them while the air shuddered with a continuous ear-splitting shriek. Jamrog kept himself flattened to the pavement as blast after blast shook the burning em, rocking it back and back, raining sparks and hot metal debris down on the Supreme Director.

Then, just as suddenly as the firefight had begun, it stopped.

The two remaining Invisibles seized the chance and dashed forward. Mrukk jumped up. The raiders were nowhere to be seen.

"It's a trick!" Mrukk shouted.

But too late. The Mors Ultima were cut down before their commander's warning reached them. One moment they were sprinting for the flaming booth; an instant later they were tumbling through the air, bundles of blazing rags.

Mrukk, still standing in the open, marked the place where the raiders fired from, and directed a withering blast over the bodies of his men. The blast tore a flaming gash in the shrubbery; trees shriveled and burst into fireballs. At the same time a streaking bolt raked the ground at Mrukk's feet.

The Mors Ultima dove behind the burning em once more. "Do something!" cried Jamrog.

"Invisibles will be here any second."

"We'll be killed any second! Go after them! Kill them!"

A voice sounded over Mrukk's shoulder set. "Squad in position, Commander. Awaiting orders."

Mrukk turned his head and said, "They are in the ground cover to the left of the burning booth. I will draw their fire."

With that Mrukk jumped up, firing a bolt into the smoldering shrubs. Hot sparks showered over him as the expected return fire smashed into the nose of the em. He flung himself down again as his hidden Invisibles loosed a blazing volley into the roadside thicket.

There was a choked scream and then silence, save for the tick of hot metal. Moments later, the advancing Invisibles gave the all-clear. Mrukk stood and helped a shivering Jamrog to his feet. The Supreme Director—face blackened, hair and eyebrows singed—shook with fear and rage. His fine hagerobe hung in smoking tatters, full of holes where hot shrapnel had burned through. He looked as if he'd been set upon by incendiary moths. The air was sour with the smell of ozone.

"They meant to take us upon reentering the Hage," Mrukk growled.

"Tvrdy!" Jamrog spat, the word a curse on his tongue. "I will have his head—"

Before he could finish, Mrukk was barking orders into his radio. "Emergency! All Invisibles—Supreme Director's bodyguard will be attacked. Saecaraz boat yard! Emergency! Unit heads two, three, and four move your squads into cutoff position in sector eight. Unit heads five and six advance squads to the boat yard."

The Mors Ultima glanced up, smiling grimly. "We have him now. Tvrdy will not escape."

FORTY
NINE

The Supreme Director's boat was a floating bonfire. Bodies lay sprawled on the dock and floated in the flame-tinted water. Tvrdy's only thought was to disengage and retreat. He knew that within minutes more Invisibles would be swarming down on them.

They had been waiting for the boat, hidden among the boathouses and equipment on the dock near the Supreme Director's mooring place. A squad of Invisibles had appeared and begun searching the boat yard. The Invisibles were thorough. Moments after their arrival on the scene, one of the Rumon had been ferreted out and killed on the spot. Tvrdy knew then that their plan had been discovered, and he opened fire on the Invisibles.

The enemy squad was cut down in seconds. The raiders had then fled back toward the feast site and had been waylaid by another squad of Invisibles. Tvrdy lost six of his fighters before he managed to break away and flee back to the docks. They arrived just as the Supreme Director's boat came gliding in, canceling any hope of escape over the water. Overanxious, Jamrog's bodyguard opened fire on them—a foolish thing to do since the boat was such an easy target. Pinched between the river and the Hage, the raiders attacked the boat, easily destroying it.

But now they were pinned down on the docks, the blue-white bolts of thermal weapons searing the air around them.

"We cannot stay here," Tvrdy told his men. "There are more Invisibles on the way. We'll be surrounded. We've got to mount a counterattack at once. Concentrate your fire on the right—they appear weakest there. If we can break through, maybe we can reach Threl Square and lose ourselves in the celebration."

The raiders put their heads down and, under a withering barrage, advanced from the dock to the boat yard. Each meter they gained cost them, however, and upon reaching the boat yard the counterattack floundered. They simply could not break the Invisibles' line.

"This is it," said Tvrdy, panting. He and the five remaining Rumon crouched behind the overturned hulls of unfinished boats. "We dare not let them take us alive. We have two choices." He did not have to say what the choices were.

"I say we take as many with us as we can." The Rumon spoke with bold determination.

"I was about to suggest it," said Tvrdy. "We'll spread out, hold fire, and force them to come in and get us . . ." He paused and added, "You'll all know what to do."

"Director," said one of the Rumon, "you could get away." He nodded toward the river behind them. "We could cover your escape."

"No," replied Tvrdy. "I won't abandon you."

"The rebellion needs you," said another. "It is your duty to save yourself if you can."

"My Hagemen are right," put in a third. "Go now while you still can."

"We will die anyway, but our deaths will aid our Hagemen if they allow you to escape," added another.

Tvrdy looked at each of them. Yes, it would be most expedient. But something inside him struggled with the notion. "We can all escape," he said.

"If we all go, they'll catch us," replied the first Rumon. "But if you go alone, you have a chance." The others nodded their agreement, eyes hard, jaws set, faces earnest in the flickering light of the burning boat.

It's true, Tvrdy considered. There is a chance. What will happen to the rebellion without me?

"Old mother—" The voice startled Tvrdy. "Trabant is looking for you."

"Cejka!" He hit the switch. "Trabant has found us in the boat yard." He looked at his men. "We hit them as soon as Cejka opens fire. Be ready to move the instant the line breaks."

A long minute passed. Then another.

The Invisibles, suspicious of the lack of activity, began blasting the boat yard. The raiders hunkered down and covered their heads. "Hurry, Cejka," whispered Tvrdy.

The Invisibles, intent upon destroying the boat yard, did not see Cejka, Bogney, and the Dhogs slipping in behind them. The instant Cejka and his team attacked, Tvrdy and the Rumon opened fire. The Invisibles, crushed between the hammer and anvil of a dual attack, succumbed in seconds.

It happened so fast that it took Tvrdy and the Rumon a moment to understand that the way was clear. They crept cautiously from hiding and then scrambled over burning wreckage to join their comrades.

"Can we get back?" asked Tvrdy.

"I think so," answered Cejka, "if we hurry. There are more Invisibles on the way—we can count on it."

"Talk later," grunted Bogney.

They made their way slowly back to Threl Square using the escape route Tvrdy had designed, avoiding open areas and better-traveled byways. Bogney led the way, using his Dhog's finely honed sensitivity to detection. They saw no one until, skirting Threl Square, they encountered a Mors Ultima squad making a sweep through a row of Hageblocks.

"Deathmen coming this way," whispered Bogney.

"We'll have to leave our route, go around," Tvrdy replied. "Can you get us back on the other side?"

"Dhogs get Tanais and Rumon back." With that, he struck off in the opposite direction.

If not for the fact that the Dhog apparently possessed an uncanny sense of direction, Tvrdy would have said they were becoming hopelessly lost. But just when Tvrdy decided he must stop Bogney now before it was too late, the Dhog's unerring sense proved itself, and they emerged from an obscure passage into a close behind the Hageblock they'd been heading for when the Invisibles forced them off the path.

"Well done!" said Tvrdy, clapping the squat leader on his broad back.

They hurried off again, and eventually reached the Saecaraz refuse pits, which in times past had been built over the remains of the ductwork that at one time fed air to the Isedon section. At the bottom of one of the pits lay a grate which opened into the ancient duct.

The refuse pits were surrounded by a high fibersteel grid fence, which the Dhogs had long ago adapted to their own purposes. But between the Saecaraz wall and the fence lay a no-man's-land—a razed strip of moldering rubble.

The exhausted raiders stood in the mouth of a broken

sewer conduit and looked out across the strip. "We're almost there," said Tvrdy. "Cejka, you and your team go first. We'll cover you from here."

They struck off across the strip. Tvrdy and the others fanned out in front of the sewer conduit, scanning the surrounding Hageblocks and streets for any signs of approaching Invisibles. Cejka reached the refuse pits and gave the all-clear. "You're next," said Tvrdy to Bogney, and the Dhogs rushed out into the strip.

There must have been at least five squads of Invisibles already hidden in the rubble because lightning struck from every direction at once. The Dhogs, caught in the open, shriveled under the terrible blast, cut down as they ran.

Tvrdy attacked the Invisibles from behind, and Cejka's men, finding themselves suddenly exposed to hostile fire, scrambled for cover.

The Invisibles turned their attack on Tvrdy's team, now well hidden in the ruins around the sewer. The resulting fight was fierce and fast. The Invisibles, having divided up the raiders nicely, now sought to crush them by dint of superior numbers. They advanced without regard for life or limb, throwing themselves into the fight with a ferocity Tvrdy had never witnessed before.

The rebels fell one by one to the horrific onslaught. The Invisibles pressed the attack, bearing down relentlessly, forcing the rebels to give ground beneath a sheet of searing fire.

Tvrdy saw what was happening, and realized that if his men broke and ran, the Invisibles would butcher them in a killing frenzy. Their only hope was to stand against them and somehow withstand the force of the attack.

Above the shriek and crackle of the thermal weapons, the rebels heard a voice, Tvrdy's voice, crying, "Stand your ground! Stand! Stand!" And they saw their commander standing fast with his weapon on his hip, firing bolt after blistering bolt into the onrushing Invisibles.

Cejka's team, having survived the initial attack and regrouped, now laid into the Invisibles from behind the fibersteel grid of the refuse pits. The Invisibles' attack, broadsided even as they pressed for the kill, faltered.

Tvrdy saw the momentary confusion—the Invisibles' divide and conquer tactic had turned on them. He dashed forward, shouting, "Attack!" His men jumped up, and they ran to meet the Invisibles, screaming, weapons crackling, orange flames bursting the night into a million shadows. The Invisibles fell back upon themselves, stumbled, tripped over one another as the foremost ranks collided with those behind.

In seconds the Invisibles were reduced to chaos, and Tvrdy, still firing into the swarming ranks, broke off the attack and headed out across the strip. He reached the place where the Dhogs had gone down and found the few survivors struggling to pull their dead and dying out of the rubble.

"Leave them," shouted Tvrdy. "Save yourselves!"

"No leaving Dhogs behind," replied Bogney, swaying under the weight of a body slung across his shoulders.

There was no time to argue about it, so Tvrdy ordered his men to help get the casualties out while the Invisibles regrouped across the strip behind them, Cejka doing his best to hold them off. A moment later the raiders were fleeing to the refuse pits, the Invisibles charging hard after them.

The raiders reached the gridwork around the pits just as the Invisibles, seeing their prey escaping, rallied and broke out of Cejka's containment, their black shapes flying over the broken strip.

They came rushing in, heedless of the wilting return fire. Invisibles fell in clusters as Tvrdy's men labored to hold them off. But the Invisibles were too many and too quick. Their Mors Ultima commanders had decreed a suicide attack in a last-ditch effort to stop the rebels and, despite fearful casualties, were leveling the full force of their attack on Tvrdy's group, trapping them outside the grid fence.

Hemmed in on every side, men dropping all around, the rebel team made a desperate last stand—weapons blazing, throw-probes glowing white hot, overheated handgrips searing the hands of those who held them—and kept on firing.

The Invisibles bore down, wave after wave of raking fire strafing the stranded rebels. In seconds it would be all over.

Then, with a flash and a roar, the strip erupted, hurling debris and dirt high into the air as one long continuous explosion ripped the ground. The Invisibles, frozen in the terrible cataclysm, were blown back by the force of the explosion, their bodies broken and flung like so many bundles tossed through the air.

"Piipo!" Tvrdy cried, turning to see the Hyrgo and his squad racing to their aid, the blunt barrels of their old-fashioned weapons smoking.

"Get moving!" yelled Piipo. He waved the gun overhead. "We'll hold them off until you're inside."

The rebels scurried to safety, taking their casualties with them as they fled down into the refuse pits. Once inside, they passed the bodies of their comrades through the grate at the bottom of the pit and then followed them into the duct. More explosions thundered above, and then Piipo's team came pouring through a gaping hole in the grid fence and down into the pit.

"They'll . . . follow . . . us," said a breathless Tvrdy when Piipo had joined him. "Get the injured . . . out of here." His voice rang in the ductwork with a harsh metallic sound.

Cejka and his men were already dragging the injured and lifeless deeper into the great curving corridor. Piipo brandished his weapon. "I saved two rounds for them."

"Good," said Tvrdy. "Seal the duct. That will slow them down."

"We can never use this entrance again anyway," said Cejka. "Now they know about it."

"Give us as long as you can to get clear and then destroy it," ordered Tvrdy. He turned to leave, saying, "And give yourself plenty of time as well."

"Get going. I'll join you soon."

They hurried off down the snaking ductwork, hands pressed against the smooth metal sides, feeling their way in the darkness, for the old duct was lit only at rare intervals by smudge pots placed along the floor.

They felt the rumble of the detonation before the concussion pummeled them like a giant fist, laying them out in one devastating punch. The shockwave rattled the duct with a deafening clatter as the walls convulsed.

And then all was silent.

Tvrdy and Cejka picked themselves up, choking in the smoke and dust raised by the explosion. Both peered fearfully into the churning blackness behind them, "Piipo?" Cejka called. "Piipo!"

Hearing a cough and another and then footsteps staggering toward them, they reached out their hands and caught the floundering Piipo as he lurched toward them.

"Are you hurt?" asked Cejka.

Piipo looked at them with a dazed expression. "I'm all right," he shouted. "I can't hear so good."

They took him by the arms, and together the three threaded their way back to the Old Section.

FIFTY

"We heard on the monitor that you were in trouble," said Piipo, speaking slowly and a little overloud. He sat with his head in his hands, his right ear bandaged, both eyes black from the concussion of the bomb he'd used to seal the entrance. "When Cejka went to find you, he told us to stay there in case we were needed. I remembered the old weapons Tvrdy had showed us in the arsenal, and I thought they might be useful if the Invisibles found us. So I sent men back to get them."

"You sent men back?" wondered Tvrdy. "All the way back to the Old Section for those weapons?"

Piipo smiled proudly. "The Hyrgo are sturdy. It was nothing." Then he remembered the dead and added with a slow, sad shake of his head, "But we might have been quicker."

"You did well," said Tvrdy. "We all owe you our lives." He looked at Cejka. "And I thank you, too."

The mood in the briefing room was subdued. Treet had seen the raiders return, had seen the dead and dying carried into the Old Section, had seen the haggard, beaten expressions on the faces of the men . . . and knew that the raid had failed.

Now, a few brief hours later, Tvrdy was leading a much dejected group through an autopsy of the miscarried mission. "That is something at least," continued Tvrdy, "to still be alive this morning when so many are not."

The others in the room remained silent.

"I take responsibility for the failure of the raid," said Tvrdy, speaking softly. "It was my idea. I gave the order. I was wrong, and others paid for my mistake."

"Not your mistake," said Cejka. "We all agreed. We did what we thought right. Besides, the raid was not a total failure. We succeeded in every other objective. We wiped out Jamrog's bodyguard—the best of the Mors Ultima—and several squads of Invisibles." He raised a fist to shoulder level and smashed it into his palm. "And we would have had Jamrog, too, if not for Mrukk."

"The fact is," Tvrdy said, "that we did not meet our prima-

ry objective—to remove Jamrog. This morning he is alive, and
his hatred burns against us. We have succeeded only in making
him more furious than ever."

"Also a minor objective," Piipo reminded him.

Tvrdy gave a snort of displeasure. "But at what cost? Too
many men died for that success to have any value."

Treet remembered it was Kopetch who had suggested that
Jamrog's anger might be useful. He glanced around the room
and saw that Kopetch was not among them. Had he been killed,
too?

He also noticed that Bogney and his two Dhogs sat in
stony silence. Knowing the Dhogs had taken the brunt of the
beating at the refuse pits, he supposed they were hurt and angry
about the results, and were demonstrating as much by their
aloofness.

Fertig, who had stayed behind with Treet and Ernina, entered the room and took a seat. All eyes turned toward him.

"You might as well tell us now," said Tvrdy. "Waiting won't
make the news easier to hear."

"We lost forty-three in the raid," Fertig replied. "Seven
more died of their wounds during the night. Fifty altogether."

"The wounded?"

"Sixteen. Most should recover, but three or four may not.
Time will tell."

Tvrdy nodded. Treet had never seen him so despondent, so
beaten. "We have lost over half of our ready force."

"And the Invisibles now know one of our entrances,"
pointed out Cejka.

"It is sealed," offered Piipo.

"How long do you think that will stop them?"

"He's right," said Tvrdy. "We've got to destroy the rest of
the duct. We'll do it today."

"Not enough," said Bogney, speaking up. "Deathmen now
be coming for us here." He turned around again, away from the
others.

"We don't have enough supplies to hide here indefinitely,"
said Piipo.

"Getting our men back in fighting shape will take time,"
Cejka said.

"We weren't ready," replied Tvrdy, mostly to himself. "I
was too anxious . . . too arrogant . . ."

"We all wanted it as badly as you," Cejka said. "We couldn't know Danelka would be taken. We underestimated Mrukk."

"It will not happen again," said Tvrdy. "I can promise you that." He paused and drew a hand over his face. "We're all tired. I suggest we get some rest and meet back here tonight to begin picking up the pieces."

Treet shuffled out with the others, feeling particularly useless and overlooked. Is there nothing I can do to help the cause? he wondered. Why am I here?

• • • • • •

The forest had been thinning for two days, becoming less dense with every kilometer. The big cat walked easily beside the man, both as soundless as the shadows they passed through. They had awakened early a few days ago to a restlessness, a tingling sense of necessity to be moving, traveling. Taking up his spear, Crocker left the sheltered bower, following the cat, and they began walking.

They ate when hungry, satisfied their thirst in cool forest pools and muddy streams, slept when they grew tired. But hour by hour they pushed deeper into the forest, moving further westward, following the nameless urge.

With every step, a long-forgotten sense of anticipation quickened in Crocker. He felt as if he would see something very important around the next turn, or the next.

There was no frustration in the expectation when, as he rounded the next bend, only more blue forest presented itself to view. Instead, Crocker experienced a continual sense of assurance: when he reached his journey's end, he would be rewarded. It was not a thought, but a strong undercurrent of the same expectation. So he continued on, unhurriedly, even as the anticipation grew moment by moment.

From the jerk of the wevicat's tail, the man knew his feline companion sensed the growing anticipation, too. From time to time, as the cat ranged further ahead, it would stop and look back at the slower human, then watch him with large, luminous eyes full of sly intelligence as if to say: Hurry! There is little time. Something's going to happen. We must not miss it.

FIFTY
ONE

The boats reached the headwaters of the Taleraan at sunset. The Fieri disembarked to spend the night on shore—a rock shelf cut between two sheer canyons. Tomorrow they would make the journey by foot up through the mountain pass and down again to the lowlands and the Bay of Talking Fish, reaching it by dusk.

On shore Pizzle walked with his Mentor, Anthon, gazing at the canyon cliffs high above and at the sky beyond, taking on the color of iron. As they passed along the long line of boats moored in the shallows, Pizzle kept one eye peeled for a glimpse of Starla while Anthon instructed his charge in the protocol of approaching the talking fish.

"The fish really talk?" Pizzle inquired.

"Oh, yes," Anthon assured him. "But you must know how to listen, and you must be ready."

"How? How do you get ready?"

"Their speech is of a delicate, subtle kind—not really speech at all, since it has no words. Naturally, since this faculty is shared between two entirely different species, it is not at all strange to expect it to be so."

"But what do they say—however they say it?"

Anthon laughed. "They don't *say*, they *communicate*."

"Pure communication—is that what you're telling me?" Pizzle accepted Anthon's nod. "But communication must be about *something*, or it's not communication at all."

"Precisely, or we would never have called them talking fish." Anthon's brow wrinkled in an effort to put words to the enigma of the talking fish—something the Fieri had long ago given up trying to do, preferring simply to accept the phenomenon. "They communicate . . ." Anthon said, straining after words, "sense impressions; they communicate their experience of the world. The talking fish communicate themselves. That's why you have to know how to listen, or you'll never hear it."

Pizzle shook his head. "I still don't get it. What am I supposed to do? Meditate?"

"Precisely!" said Anthon. "You meditate, fill your heart with thoughts of goodness, of truth, of joy. You draw the fish to you by the quality of your thought. You prepare a place for the fish to come to you."

"I see. So I'm sitting there thinking all kinds of beautiful thoughts, and this fish swims up, and if he likes what he sees we have a chat. Is that it?"

Anthon laughed again. His laugh, like his manner, was gentle, understanding. "Yes, that's the sense of it."

"But do I say anything? Or do I just listen?"

"Whatever you feel," Anthon told him. "Most people prefer just to listen. That is enough."

"Hmmm." Pizzle frowned in concentration. "I think I'm getting it now. Forgive me, I'm not usually this dense."

"It's more difficult to explain than it is to do," admitted Anthon, placing a friendly hand on Pizzle's shoulder. "It's the same with so many things in life. We hinder ourselves with our fears and concerns when all that is needed is trust and faith."

"Believe that the fish will speak and they'll speak—something like that?"

"Something like that."

"When will the fish come? Will we have to wait long?"

"Not long. A day perhaps. At most, three." Anthon saw Pizzle's involuntary grimace and added, "But you won't mind waiting. The bay is beautiful. You will enjoy yourself. Besides, since everyone will be together on the beach, I don't see any reason why you and Starla should be apart."

"Terrific! You mean it? Wow, this is tremendous! Thanks, Anthon. You're aces!"

Anthon shook his head in bemusement. "The things you say, Asquith. Earth must be a very strange place indeed if everyone talks as you do."

They walked along a little further, and Pizzle gazed at the wide river stretching out before them, calm and deep, now shimmering with the reflected light of the sunstone cliffs, like captured sunset. The Fieri around them readied the evening meal, and smoke began drifting along the water's edge as music, light and tinkling like delicate cut glass, lifted into the darkening sky.

"It's so peaceful," remarked Pizzle. "I love this life."

Anthon heard the wistfulness in his voice. "Your life was very different on Earth?"

"*Very* different."

"Do you miss it?"

"Miss it?" Pizzle glanced at the Mentor quickly. "No, not at all. I never even think about it. Why would I? Back on Earth I was nothing—a cog in the corporate wheel, a nameless drone. All I did was shove printouts from one side of a plastic desk to the other, siphoning numbers off and putting them on other printouts. It was hell."

He sighed at the futility of it. "No, I don't miss it. Everything I ever dreamed of is here—it's paradise. I'm surprised you even understand an emotion like longing, you know?"

"How so? Are we so fullfilled we cannot long for ultimate perfection?"

Pizzle shrugged. "I don't miss it at all. Should I? I mean, I'm happier here than I ever was back there. Here . . . it's like a dream I never want to end, you know? I want it to go on and on forever."

"You speak of paradise," said Anthon. "This isn't paradise, Asquith. The life you speak of is found only in the Infinite Father. If Empyrion is good, its goodness is only a reflection of the greater goodness of the Creator."

"I don't care where it comes from," replied Pizzle. "I just know that's what I want." They were silent for a while. Upon reaching the last of the Fieri ships, they turned and started back. "Anthon?" said Pizzle. "Tell me something."

"Anything."

"Is it true—all you say about the Infinite Father?"

"There is a truth greater than we know, Asquith. This greater truth is the Infinite. We cannot know it; we can only get snatches, fleeting glimpses of it. But it is there. It exists. In fact, all that exists moves and lives in it." He paused, and added, "However, I can offer no proof for this assertion."

"I believe you," said Pizzle, "but not because of anything you could say."

"Oh?"

"No. That's all good stuff, you understand. But it makes sense to me because I know I'm a better person now, believing it, or trying to, than I ever was before. You know?"

Anthon put his arm around Pizzle's shoulders. "You have a freshness about you that does this old soul good. Yes, I know what you mean. Experience does often reflect its source. It is proof of a sort."

They walked back along the river and came to one of the large fires that had been made at intervals on the bank. Fish roasted on spits arched over the shimmering pyramid of flames. In the coals, wrapped in bundles of wet leaves, fresh-gathered vegetables steamed. The aroma melted into the air, piquant and tantalizing. Pizzle and Anthon sat down among the others gathered there as the first spit was taken down.

Pizzle ate, enjoying the close kinship of the Fieri, feeling very much a part of it himself. But after he had satisfied his hunger, he excused himself and got up to wander back to the boat.

There would be no sunshower tonight; the air was too clear and still. Instead, the Light Mountains gave forth a steady warm glow that reminded Pizzle of the lights of a city seen from a distance on a clear night.

He went up the gangplank and stretched out on the empty deck to watch the stars come out. Tomorrow they would reach the Bay of Talking Fish, and he would be with Starla. But tonight he wanted to be alone with his thoughts—to let himself wander in his mind toward the truth Anthon spoke of. This night he felt closer to it than ever before, and he wanted to savor that closeness, and to increase it if he could.

Mostly, he just wanted to be alone and experience the sensation of solitude devoid of loneliness—something quite rare for him. The experience reflects its source, he thought. You can tell the tree by its fruit. Now where had he heard that?

• • • • • •

When the boats reached the mooring place, Yarden did not stir. She remained below in her berth. In fact, she did not attend the last of the art classes that day either. And when Ianni told her that Gerdes had asked about her, she merely shrugged and said she hadn't felt like going.

"You've been withdrawn the last few days," Ianni told her. "I've noticed. Would you like to talk about it?"

"Not particularly," said Yarden. "It's something I've got to work out myself."

"You look as if you are in pain, Yarden. Perhaps I could help."

"No . . . thank you, no. I'd rather be alone."

Ianni had left her then and Yarden had stayed there, listening to the voices of the Fieri as they left the ships and began preparing for their last night on the river. Tomorrow they would begin the trek through the mountains and down to the bay—a prospect which should have filled Yarden with excitement.

But she lay on her bed in the dark, listening to the clear, happy voices, watching the circle of sky growing dim through the porthole, feeling cut off from what was happening around her. Adrift on a troubled sea.

Over and over she asked herself the same questions—the same questions she'd been driving herself crazy with for days: Should I try to contact Treet? What if I don't like what I find? What if he's dead or in trouble? What then? Oh, God, what am I supposed to do?

She rose, went up on deck, and watched the activity on shore. There was an urgency about it—the coming of night made the Fieri move a little quicker in their preparations. They were aware of the fading day and did not wish to lose the light.

I've got to decide, Yarden said to herself. I've got to decide right now. If I wait any longer, I too will lose what little light I have.

She turned and walked back along the deck to the stern, as far from the bustle on shore as she could get. She sat down cross-legged on the polished wood and drew a long deep breath. God, help me, she thought. I don't know what to do.

"The Dhogs have blasted the ductwork, Supreme Director." The Invisible commander held himself stiffly and stared straight ahead. "It will take time to reach the Old Section through the refuse pits."

"You *will* reach the Old Section," intoned Jamrog menacingly. "I want those responsible brought before me at once. Do you understand me?" The bhuj flashed back and forth in the Supreme Director's hands as he sat in the thronelike chair he had had placed in the center of the Supreme Director's kraam. His face was puffy and blistered, his scalp mottled gray and patchy where clumps of hair had been burned off. His flesh was red and painfully swollen from the scorching he'd taken on the night of the failed assassination.

"The duct is destroyed, Supreme Director," explained Osmas, realizing he was dangerously near the flashpoint of his superior's vile temper. Jamrog had been raving mad since the Trabantonna attack; it didn't do to argue with him or gainsay his whims, however unreasonable they might be. "I don't see what anyone can do."

The Saecaraz Subdirector motioned toward the door, and the Invisible backed gratefully toward it. Jamrog had killed three of them in the last two days, and Osmas wanted to save the man if he could. What with the demise of the Mors Ultima bodyguard, upper echelon Invisibles were getting scarce. "We'll find another way in," Osmas said hopefully.

"How?" roared Jamrog. "Searching is impossible, and guides are less than useless!"

It was true. For some unknown reason, guides had never been able to locate the hidden entrances and exits of the Old Section. There were many theories to explain this, but it remained a mystery why the blind wayfinders could not discover the Dhog's secret pathways—even with the help of their psi entities.

"Nevertheless, I'm told that the interrogations are proceeding successfully. We will uncover useful information soon."

At that moment Diltz, the cadaverous Nilokerus Director,

entered the kraam and crossed the floor in quick, confident strides. His sunken eyes gleamed in his skull. "I bring good news, Supreme Director," he said with a deferential nod of his long head.

"The Fieri have been located?" Jamrog half rose out of his chair.

The corners of Diltz's mouth drew down. "Ah, no, Supreme Director. But I can report that we have located what appears to be a navigational tower. I have brought a map to show you."

He produced a thin roll of yellowed plastic from the folds of his black-and-white yos, stepped close, and unrolled it for Jamrog. Osmas pushed in to see it, too. "Here," said Diltz, pointing to a newly drawn circle on a flat expanse of plain beyond the river that ran near Empyrion. "The tower is located in this area—called, I believe, a desert." He pronounced the unfamiliar word carefully.

"Desert," repeated Jamrog. "And just what is this desert?"

"Nothing—literally. The word, I am told by my readers, is an ancient mapmakers' term for *void*."

"I see," said Jamrog, looking askance at the map. "And how will examining a void help us find the enemy?"

"The tower is of Fieri design," explained Diltz, the enthusiasm draining out of his voice. "We are searching the area now. If we find another such tower, we may be able to fix a direction to the Fieri settlement."

"Or away from it," said Osmas, snapping the brittle plastic map with a fingernail. Since adopting the Supreme Director's questionable notions of finding and exterminating the Fieri using the old weapons, Diltz was enjoying a rapid ascendancy in Jamrog's favor. Osmas resented it.

The Saecaraz Subdirector thought they should concentrate solely on eradicating the Dhogs. He disliked seeing Diltz win favor through the continued support of an idea he personally considered dangerous. Moreover, he disliked the fact that the Nilokerus had been given control of the Saecaraz magicians assigned to the Archives. Diltz seemed to be making steady progress in his assignments, while he, Osmas, met with nothing but setbacks in digging out the Dhogs.

Jamrog, ignoring Osmas' remark, asked, "What of the weapons?"

"Ah, yes." Diltz smiled. "The weapons have been removed and examined." The smile turned wicked. "I am assured that there will be little problem reactivating them. Readers are working on deciphering the technical material now."

"Excellent!" cried Jamrog. He turned to Osmas and pointed a puffy, red finger at him. "You see? This is what can be done with some effort."

Diltz grinned smugly, but said nothing.

"The Fieri settlement still remains to be found," observed Osmas sourly. "Meanwhile, the Dhogs are here among us."

"And remain to be found," said Diltz.

"With more help—"

"You have all the help you need," barked Jamrog, flinging himself from the chair. "Mrukk tells me you have not been making full use of resources."

Chagrined to find himself on the defensive, the Subdirector sputtered, "Until the interrogations turn up some useful information—"

The Supreme Director thrust the bhuj in Osmas' face. "Are you questioning my directives?"

"Never! But perhaps the Mors Ultima are somewhat overzealous in carrying out their orders. Reorientation cells are crammed beyond capacity—six, eight share a space designed for one. Four of five die under the questioning. Corpses are being stacked in Hage squares—the Jamuna cannot render the bodies fast enough. The smell of death is everywhere."

"Let it be a warning to the rest!" yelled Jamrog. "I will *not* have my directives questioned!" He swung the bhuj at Osmas, missed him, and then threw it at the Subdirector. The ceremonial weapon clattered across the floor.

Osmas, already backpedaling toward the door, tripped over his own feet and landed on his backside. Jamrog, standing over him, lashed out with his foot, screaming, "Get out! Get out!" Throwing his hands up to protect his face, Osmas rolled away from the vicious kicks, gathered his feet under him, and sprinted toward the door, leaving a livid Jamrog bellowing in rage.

Diltz watched the scene with unconcealed pleasure. Here was an opportunity to consolidate his advantage: he would see to it that Osmas would no longer pose a threat to his ambitions. He approached the seething Jamrog.

"His loyalty wavers, Supreme Director. But is he dangerous?"

Jamrog turned, the veins bulging on his neck and forehead.
"Is no one to be trusted?"

"Trust me," said Diltz softly. "Allow me to deal with this
problem for you."

"It's yours." Jamrog whirled away, retreating back into his
bedchamber. "I want nothing more to do with him."

• • • • • •

The walk up through the mountain pass was more exhila-
rating than exhausting. Over the years, Fieri engineers had
carved out a generous pathway over an easy route of gentle
inclines amidst towering cliffs and plunging gorges threaded
with rushing freshets and reckless cascades crossed by graceful
cantilevered footbridges. Long tunnels bored through solid rock
laced the route—cool and damp, and echoey with the sound of
pattering feet and whispered voices.

At the summit of the pass, the travelers emerged from a
tunnel to view their descent winding down through blue-green
moss forests shimmering in silver mists. The moss flourished on
spindlelike rock spires and columns in the cool-air heights, nour-
ished by the mineral-rich spray of a hundred dashing waterfalls.

The Fieri, delighted with the beauty of the scene, ran down
through the hanging mists, laughing to feel the tingling splash on
their faces, soaking their clothing in the spray. The children ran
to gawk at each waterfall, shouting above the crash and roar as
they followed the tumbling water down and down to the plain
below.

The day was fine and bright; wonder lurked around every
corner, and glory loomed on the near horizon. Joy was conta-
gious, infecting young and old alike with a most virulent strain
that broke out in luminous smiles, songs, and laughter. Pizzle,
walking hand in hand with Starla—Anthon strolling an amiable
distance behind—felt drunk with happiness.

He chattered happily away, describing his long, lonely days
and even longer, lonelier nights to a sympathetic Starla. For her

part, his beloved appeared content merely to be in his presence. She smiled and nodded and squeezed his hand, luxuriating in his unflagging attention.

In this way they came down the mountainside, passing by tunnel through one last stone curtain to emerge blinking on the other side, dazzled by the spectacular vista of Talking Fish Bay—a great golden sweep of sand cradling a bowl of jade-colored water.

The bay was enormous—making the whole of Prindahl look like a duck pond in a park—stretching from horizon to horizon. The ragged tops of mountains formed a boundary on the right; on the left the deep blue-green of the Blue Forest smudged the distant skyline like a low, dark cloud bank. Directly ahead, jade water danced under the white sun as far as the eye could see.

The Fieri hurried down to the bay, the young ones racing ahead, abandoning themselves to headlong flight. "Magnificent!" breathed Pizzle. "I never dreamed it would be this—this wonderful." He paused, grasping for superlatives. "It's like something out of *Lord of the Rings!* I feel like Frodo coming to the Grey Havens."

"It's even more beautiful than I remember," said Starla.

Those still lingering over the view voiced similar sentiments. Anthon came to where Pizzle and Starla stood with their arms wrapped around each other. "It inspires me anew each time I see it," he sighed. "The Creator is indeed extravagant with His beauty." Then he turned and eyed the lovers. "Well, come on, we'll find our places."

"Places?" inquired Pizzle as they started off.

"For our tents—" Starla began to explain.

"And also to meditate," added Anthon. "But tonight— tonight we all come together—"

"Songs and stories," said Starla, tugging Pizzle along now. "And swimming."

They overtook Anthon, who waved them on, saying he would be along in his own good time, and hurried down to join the first ranks of Fieri now spreading out over the beach below.

• • • • • •

At the rear of the long procession making its way down to the golden beach walked Yarden, last but for those guiding the supply train—a train made up of miniature balons whose gondolas were laden with provisions and camping equipment. Bobbing and weaving through the mountain course, the long string of balons resembled a giant centipede wobbling down to the sea, flanked by attendants carrying poles and tether ropes to steer it.

Ianni walked beside Yarden, troubled for her friend, but respectful of Yarden's silence. Her attempts at conversation along the way had elicited only vague, halfhearted responses, and Ianni had given up trying to draw Yarden out and had contented herself with lending comfort by her presence. They stopped at the overlook to take in their first sight of the bay, and Yarden stirred from her reverie. "Oh, it is wonderful," she said reverently.

Ianni, glad for any response, pounced on this pronouncement. "Yes, it is. It's always been one of my favorite places. Wait until the fish arrive—that's something to see as well. The first thing I want to do is go for a swim, and then—" She broke off. "What is it, Yarden? Tell me what's wrong."

At first, Ianni thought Yarden wouldn't answer. There was a long silence in which Yarden merely stared out across the enormous bay, as if taking in the majestic sight, but Ianni saw that Yarden's dark eyes were unfocused, her gaze directed inward. The balon centipede bobbed past them. Several of the Fieri walking with it looked at the women concernedly, but Ianni gave them reassuring glances and they continued on.

"It's nothing," Yarden replied finally. She turned and smiled, and Ianni saw her force down whatever had been troubling her, and noticed that the smile was strained. "I'll be all right," insisted Yarden. "Come on, let's get down to the beach. A swim would do me good, I think."

FIFTY
THREE

Spirits improved somewhat when the missing Kopetch returned to the Old Section. He had been gone three days and was considered a casualty of the operation. But, tired and hungry, he appeared at the Chryse entrance, presented himself to the sentries there, and was brought safely in.

Now, after some food and a few hours rest, the rebel Cabal sat before a gray-faced Kopetch, listening, worry lines etched on every brow, eyes staring at a bleak, hopeless future filled with pain and death.

"I stayed as long as I could, to gather information. Invisibles were everywhere . . . I had to get out," said Kopetch, sipping from a cup of water. "I knew the raid had failed, but I could not believe the speed of the retaliation."

"He already knew what he would do," suggested Fertig. "Jamrog had it planned. Hladik helped him before he was killed."

"Likely," agreed Tvrdy. "Go on."

Kopetch gulped down some water and resumed his dire recitation. "Every Director is under Mors Ultima guard—"

"Mors Ultima *arrest!*" snorted Piipo.

"And Jamrog has disbanded the Threl," continued Kopetch. "Each Hage is under the direction of a Mors Ultima commander—except Saecaraz and Nilokerus, of course. There is talk of a quota; five thousand from each Hage must be interrogated."

"Tortured, you mean," said Cejka.

"The Invisibles have been given a free hand to question Hagemen. Work must continue, but everyone is afraid to leave the Hageblocks—although anyone discovered hiding in a kraam during work time is immediately arrested. Hagemen are pulled off the streets at random and herded into ems. Invisibles roam the walkways with lists; if one is on the list, he is taken. Or, if one is *not* on the list he is taken. It doesn't matter; the lists are meaningless—they make the arrest appear more official, that's all. If it appears official, the people don't question it; they go along quietly."

"How are the lists made?"

"During interrogation, the Mors Ultima offer a Hageman a chance to save himself further agony by giving the names of fellow traitors. If he gives them names, they might stop the torture. They get lots of names.

"Women go to special interrogation kraams where they are raped before being questioned. Often their Hagemates are forced to watch. The Invisibles get many names."

"Those who resist?" asked Tvrdy.

"Few resist," said Kopetch sadly. "Corpses are fished continually from Kyan's coves—these are said to be Hagemen who dared question their arrest or made interrogation difficult."

"What of the Hage priests?" wondered Cejka. "How can they continue to accept their rewards? Don't they see what is happening?"

"The Hagemen say the priests insist that it is a political problem and they must not take sides."

"Not take sides!" shouted Piipo. "They inform on Hagemen and say they cannot take sides. They will pay with their lives for that lie!"

Tvrdy waved him silent. "What of security?"

"It's nearly impossible to move around. If not for our Tanais on the network, and a ready escape route, I would not have made it back. The Hage borders are sealed to all—goods only may pass through. Invisibles patrol the streets. They confiscate anything a Hageman may possess, or arrest at will."

"The attitude of the Hagemen?"

"Baffling." Kopetch shook his head in dismay. "They act as if it is not happening . . . as if to admit something is wrong will turn the insanity upon them. Their Hagemen are taken from the next kraam, and they stand looking on. They say, 'He must have done something. He deserves what he gets.' " Kopetch halted, disgust choking him. "I—I wanted to kill them for their stupidity."

"Incredible," observed Cejka. "They see their Hagemen taken away to be tortured and yet think they can be safe themselves."

"The cowards!" cried Piipo.

"What reason is given for the arrests?" Tvrdy asked.

"The Supreme Director has issued a statement saying that the Fieri have infiltrated Empyrion. He says many of our people have gone over to them, that treason runs deep and must be cut out."

"He blames the Fieri?" wondered Piipo.

"There was a rumor—some time ago—of a Fieri invasion," put in Fertig. "Mors Ultima caught some people outside. No one knows what they were doing. Rohee tried to cover it up, but Hladik and Jamrog knew about it and were making plans, although the Fieri disappeared before they could get at them. They were furious over it—it's why Rohee was killed, I think."

"We know," said Tvrdy, a ghost of a smile touching his lips.

"We were the ones who removed them from under your noses," Cejka added. "And you're right—Jamrog used it as an excuse to murder Rohee."

"I should have guessed," said Fertig.

"It doesn't matter now." Tvrdy looked to Kopetch. "Anything else?"

"I heard that a Mors Ultima squad is again searching outside," the Tanais replied.

"Searching for what?" asked Piipo.

"Fierra."

"Does Jamrog actually believe the Fieri are involved in the rebellion?" Cejka shook his head slowly. "It makes no sense. He knows we are responsible. He knows . . . and yet—"

"Yet behaves otherwise," remarked Tvrdy. "He is shrewd and dangerous."

Treet, grieved and angered by Kopetch's recital, roused himself to declare, "He will not be content with ruling Empyrion unopposed. Jamrog means to destroy the Fieri, too. He's using us as an excuse to go after them."

"If he can find them," said Piipo.

"He'll find them," Fertig warned. "Saecaraz magicians are searching for maps in the Archives. Diltz has become very interested in the Fieri, and he is commanding the search himself. They will find what they are looking for."

"Jamrog means to destroy everything," Treet said. "And I'd say he's got a pretty good start."

"That is not our worry," snapped Tvrdy. "We have to save ourselves before we can save anyone else. Right now, that's all I care about."

The meeting was dismissed and, hands thrust into the folds of his yos, Treet stumped off across the empty compound toward Ernina's makeshift hospital to relieve the physician. He couldn't understand Tvrdy's reaction. The Tanais had acted as if Treet's simple observations were out of place, ill-considered, and unwanted. What was the matter with him anyway?

He was halfway across the compound when he heard a sound like a kettle drum and the ground vibrated beneath his feet. He stopped, looked around.

Earthquake?

He started forward, walked a few more steps, and the ground rumbled again. He turned and glanced back at the decrepit buildings round about. The creaky structures rattled and loose rubble fell, but they didn't sway or pitch forward.

Just then three Dhogs appeared, racing across the compound from the direction of the Isedon. Treet stopped them. "What is that? What's going on?"

The Dhogs, sweating, out of breath, gulped air and looked at one another fearfully. "Deathmen . . ." one of them managed to utter. "They be coming!"

FIFTY
FOUR

"Invisibles? Where?"

Another rumble, louder this time, shook the ground. The Dhogs looked down as if the earth might part and swallow them. They made ready to bolt once more.

Treet grabbed the nearest Dhog and spun him around. "Where are they?"

The man's eyes rolled in his head, and he pointed behind him. "Saecaraz—"

"The ruined duct." Treet held the man and forced him to listen. "Okay, we haven't got much time. You go find Bogney. Hear me?" The Dhog nodded, terror in his eyes. "Tell him to come here. Fast. Got it?" The man nodded again. "Go! Hurry!" The three raced off, rags aflutter.

Treet turned and hurried back to the briefing room, nearly colliding with Cejka and Piipo as they came flying out the door, their faces taut, anxious. "What is it? What's happening?" asked Cejka, indicating the Dhogs whose backs were just disappearing behind the wall of the command post.

"Invisibles," Treet explained. "They're blasting out the ruined duct from Saecaraz."

"Trabant take them," muttered Piipo.

Just then Tvrdy and Kopetch joined them, and Treet explained the situation. Tvrdy was silent for a moment, and Treet had the awful feeling that the Tanais was going to crack; but when he spoke, his tone was crisp and commanding. "Take some men and get down there," he told Kopetch. "We've got to know how much time we have. Keep monitor channel 3 open."

Another explosion rumbled the ground—this one louder, closer, more violent. The Invisibles were not wasting a second. Treet had bizarre visions of a whole squad of specialized subterranean Invisibles bursting up through the ground like oversized black mushrooms, thermal weapons blazing in their mole-flipper hands.

He turned and followed the others back into the building.

• • • • • •

They huddled over a crude map in the briefing room, staring at the place Tvrdy had marked—the exit shaft leading from the Isedon Zone to the refuse pits of Saecaraz. No one spoke, although the nervous shift of eyes around the table told all.

"We can't keep them from blasting through," Tvrdy was saying. "So I suggest we don't try. Let them come in—in fact, we let them come all the way through Isedon and then take them here—at Annerson Spike." He stabbed a finger at the map.

"They'll expect an ambush. They'll be ready," said Cejka.

"Yes, but I propose to offer them a first ambush before they reach the Isedon—a false ambush. We have men here and here," his finger moved over the map, "and we wait until the Invisibles get into position. We hit them, give them a fight, then break and run, leading them into New America Square and the real ambush." Tvrdy glanced up to see if everyone was following him.

"They'll still be very cautious—suspect a trap."

"Perhaps, but it won't matter. I talked this over with Kopetch, and he agrees. Once attacked, they'll have to give chase. They don't know where else to go. The secret lies in making the first ambush appear genuine. To do that, we'll have to make the attack quick and sharp. It must not appear that we're holding back our true strength."

"What happens to the men here?" asked Piipo, pointing to the other place Tvrdy had specified.

"They wait. Once the Invisibles have moved off in pursuit, they will destroy the entrance once again and then follow the enemy in, cutting off the retreat.

"Bogney," Tvrdy continued, "you will lead the first ambush and then lure the Invisibles in. You must be careful not to go too far ahead. We don't want to lose them or give them time to think. If they believe they can overtake you and finish you off, they will try it before regrouping and moving in." He paused. "Of course, move too slowly and they *will* overtake you and finish you off." Tvrdy glanced across the table. "Fertig will go with you."

"Dhogs knowing how to trick deathmen." Bogney's face

was set in a dirty scowl. Anger burned in his small, close-set eyes.

"Piipo, you will join Kopetch and his men at the entrance. You will be responsible for sealing the entrance once the Invisibles have moved off. Then follow them in, but at a fair distance. They must not see you or even suspect that you're there."

"How will I seal the entrance without alerting the Invisibles?"

"Wait until the first ambush starts. They won't hear you then."

"Cejka, you and I will take our positions here in the Isedon. We'll hit them from two sides at once. Bogney will circle back around and hit them on the blind side. The resulting crossfire should finish them. Any who try to flee back to the entrance will be met by Piipo."

There were nods and grunts of agreement all around. It was a good plan on short notice. Tvrdy glanced around the ring of faces. "Any questions?" No one said anything. "Then we go."

Treet felt as if he should say something, give a pep talk, remind them that the future of the planet was riding on this battle, but decided that no one needed that kind of pressure. Still, the thought nagged him.

"What about me?" he asked as the others hurried off to join their squads of men, already assembled and waiting in the compound field.

"You stay here," Tvrdy said curtly. "There's nothing for you to do now."

"I could help; I could fight."

"No." Tvrdy's face remained impassive. "Stay here."

Tvrdy's order struck Treet as bullheaded. Just because he and Tvrdy had had words moments before the blasting started, did that mean Treet couldn't fight by Tvrdy's side? "If you're still upset about what I said before, I'm sorry," said Treet. "But I think I should come with you now."

"You are not trained with these weapons," replied Tvrdy. Outside in the yard, the men moved off, their shouts of victory ringing hollow in the stale, unmoving air of the Old Section. "And I do not want anything to happen to you."

"You're using me as some kind of figurehead," said Treet. It suddenly dawned on him why Tvrdy was so insistent on protecting him. "You want me safe so I will look good on the platform when the time comes."

Tvrdy rolled up his map and stuck it in his yos. "I have to go."

"That's it, isn't it, Tvrdy? What for? I want to know." Treet stepped up to him. "Answer me."

"The people respect you," replied Tvrdy hastily. "You've seen how they watch you, look at you. They believe you know how to save them. We need this hope if we are to survive. Stay here, and let us handle this."

The Tanais hurried away. Treet picked up the radio monitor and went in search of Ernina, thinking they'd hold vigil together.

Upon arriving at the ruined exit, Kopetch had reported that the Invisibles were, by his best estimation, six to eight hours away. That had been an hour ago, Treet reflected. Figuring it would take another couple of hours for the squads to get into position, the main ambush might not take place for another three or more hours . . . plenty of time for Treet to get to the ambush site and find himself a place to hide.

He had no sooner thought of it than he was hanging back in the doorway, watching Tvrdy and Cejka lead their men off to their positions. As soon as they disappeared behind a ravaged wall at the far end of the field, Treet made his move, taking up the trail behind them.

• • • • • •

The comforting shadows of the Blue Forest lay two days' journey back. The man and cat walked in the bright daylight, uneasy in the open spaces, wary of the uncluttered distance around them. Since sunrise this morning, when they resumed their trek, they had been ascending a gradual incline, climbing the broad back of a rock shelf that lifted the earth in an easy tilt. Tan rock poked through the shelf's thin crust. Unable to hold the moisture, the soil was dry and dusty, the sparse ground cover withered white by the sun.

The huge black wevicat padded along, its sleek midnight coat gray with the dust that puffed up beneath its great paws.

Crocker, too, was covered in fine powder from crown to sole, except where sweat made muddy trails down the sides of his face and below his armpits. He still carried his spear, but used it now as a staff to help pull himself along.

They walked for hours watching the sun scale the eastern sky wall. By midmorning they had reached a rocky promontory that bulged up above the surrounding landscape; they climbed the mound and stopped there in the shade of a solitary fan tree to rest. The man squatted in the dust and sniffed the fitful breeze blowing from the east. "Water," he announced. The cat gazed at him with its lemon eyes and yawned, its big pink tongue curling backward behind jagged rows of clean white teeth.

There was not a sound to be heard except the breeze sliding over the rock and ruffling the wispy leaves at their feet. To skins used to the shadowed dampness of the forest, the naked sun felt hot and the air unnaturally dry. The man looked back at the bluish smudge of the forest in the distance, felt a tug: to return would be comfort, safety.

But the force that moved them onward was stronger. Ahead, just over the next rise, or the next, lay their destination. What would happen when they reached it?

It didn't matter. Reaching it was all that mattered.

When the sun stood directly overhead, the man rose and took up his spear again and began walking, his long legs swinging into the loose, ground-eating stride once more. The cat got up, shook itself all over, and stood motionless for a moment, sampling the wind-borne scents for anything of interest—warm-blooded or otherwise. There was water not far ahead, and something else.

The wevicat's nostrils worked the dry air and soon caught the human scent—very faint. The cat's tailtip jerked back and forth quickly as it put its head down and trotted ahead.

Their shadows had begun stretching out before them as they reached the edge of the cliff. The rock shelf ended in a series of bluffs overlooking a vast bowl of cool green water. The bluffs tumbled down onto the strand, and there, spread out upon the sand like colorful geometric flowers or grounded silken kites, lay a thousand tents, glowing in the afternoon light.

The sight filled Crocker with wonder . . . and fear. He looked at the strange, asymmetric tents—and at the people moving in and out of them—and his mind reeled. People! So many of them!

His first impulse was to run away, back to the hidden depths of the Blue Forest. But the voice in his head, which he had not heard for many, many days, came back instantly. *Stay!* the voice told him. *It's all right. They won't hurt you. Stay. Sit down. Rest. Watch them. You have come for this purpose.*

Crocker nodded to himself. "Stay," he told the cat and dropped to his knees at the cliff's edge, hugging his spear as he gazed out over the Fieri tent city. As they watched, cooking fires sprang up on the beach and smoke began drifting up the cliff face, pushed by the breeze.

The smoke was sweet-scented, smelling of roast meat and savory spices that brought the water to his mouth. He leaned on his spear, licking his lips and thinking of what it would be like to taste such food. The wevicat beside him lay down on its stomach, head erect, feet stretched out in front of it, tail slapping the dust into little ridges. Together they gazed down at the scene below them, drawn to it, but held back at the same time.

The stars found them still sitting there, immobile, watching the firelight sparkle on the sand, and listening to the faint tinkling sounds of music and laughter drifting up to them from the beach. Waiting.

FIFTY
FIVE

The next morning, after a long, luxurious swim, Yarden began feeling almost normal again. The day was bright, and as fresh as the breeze across the clear jade water. She ate a splendid breakfast with Ianni and some of her artist friends, then sauntered back down to the water's edge to take her place with the rest of the Fieri assembling there.

All along the strand, stretching both ways over the wide arc of the bay, Fieri settled themselves to await the coming of the talking fish. Ianni had told her that the best communication was achieved when one emptied oneself of all negative thought, all anxiety, and made oneself ready to receive the fish.

"Think only good things," Ianni instructed her. "Invite them. Ask the fish to join you, to share the joy of life with you. They respond to pure thoughts."

Yarden understood what Ianni was getting at and did not press for details. She wanted the mystery of the event to lend excitement to the wait, which Ianni warned could be several days.

Yarden dropped easily into her customary meditation pose, a modified lotus position: ankles crossed, arms resting easily on the inside of thighs, hands open, empty. She closed her eyes, emptying her mind of extraneous thought, centering herself in the moment, turning her sight inward.

The sound of waves gently lapping on the sand formed an aural background for her meditation. She pictured herself at peace, perfectly calm, a beautiful robe of glowing white, symbolizing joy, draped across her shoulders.

As she concentrated, she felt the peace she imagined flowing over her and through her, felt the calmness spreading out from the center of her being to the extremities, as if a stream of contentment ran over her, around her, through her. She drifted in its gentle waters . . . drifted . . . drifted . . .

• • • • • •

The murmur of voices roused Yarden from her meditations. She opened her eyes slowly and saw her own long shadow stretching out across the sand to the water. She realized she must have fallen asleep, for she was not aware of the passage of time. It seemed she had just closed her eyes and now opened them, feeling refreshed and at peace.

She stretched languorously and looked around. Most of the Fieri remained in attitudes of meditation, but some were on their feet staring out into the bay while others talked softly among themselves. This was the murmur she had heard. She closed her eyes again, to savor once more the sweet, drifty drowsiness, but the image of the Fieri standing, looking out over the bay intrigued her. What were they staring at?

She opened her eyes. A second later she was on her feet, too. There far out on the horizon she saw them. The fish were coming in! Yarden could see the water shimmering and breaking as the school skimmed the surface, fins slicing the sparkling water.

The westering sun glittered on their backs as they surfaced and dove, swift as torpedos, breaching and swerving, each graceful stroke multiplied by thousands. In the middle distance, Yarden could see their flashing sides dart through green-gold water. She looked down and saw that she, like all the others gathered on the shore, was striding through knee-deep surf, wading out to welcome the fish.

Yarden felt excitement ripple over her. There were shouts of joy all around her, and she added her voice to the merriment, her heart beating wildly. "Welcome!" she cried, picking up the chant from those around her. "We greet you in joy!"

The creatures slowed as they came closer, and the school separated, each fish proceeding alone to a waiting human, emitting squeaks and clicks of pure pleasure. The Fieri furthest out were met first, and the fish leaped in the water or swam circles around their human friends, who laughed and plunged after the playful animals.

Yarden laughed, too, to see the joyful play and then looked and was surprised to see one of the creatures regarding her, its head lifted out of the water, its large, clear eye watching her with bright amusement.

The animal was much larger than Yarden had anticipated, and bore a passing resemblance to the pilot whale of Earth. It had the same smooth, streamlined shape and rubbery-looking skin. But it had no dolphinian snout and sported not one, but two large dorsal fins on its powerful back. Its forebody was large, with a swelling mound atop its head over two large, disturbingly human eyes the same color as the sea.

The creature was a beautiful deep sky blue at the tips of its great dorsi and along the spine ridge of its back. The color faded gradually, however, so that its underbelly was white—it looked as if the fish had been held upside down and dipped in blue ink. The male of the species, Yarden learned later, had two brilliant parallel yellow stripes running the length of its stomach from its lower mandible to its ventral slit.

Instinctively, Yarden held out her hands, murmuring soft sounds of welcome. The fish twitched its broad, fluked tail and slid closer. Yarden lowered herself in the water and floated toward it. Her hands reached for the gleaming skin and found it warm to the touch. Warm-blooded! The animal was mammalian. She caressed the beautiful skin and said, "You're no fish; you're almost human!"

With nimble movements the creature circled her body, brushing against her, bumping her playfully, exploring her with long, jointed front flippers. Yarden dove and swam with it, holding the forward dorsal fin like she'd seen divers do in pictures. The creature swam with easy strokes of its powerful tail, propelling both of them through the water. Yarden felt the tremendous life-force of the animal engulf her, and her heart soared. She felt like a child in the great, calming presence of a wise and gentle giant.

She regained her feet in the chest-deep water and the fish swam close, nuzzling her. She put her hands on the mound of its head, and stared into the very human eye. It was a natural enough gesture, and although she knew the creatures communicated, she was unprepared for the result.

Instantly, a feeling of tremendous warmth and serenity inundated her. It was as if she had touched a live current and received a most unusual jolt. Yarden jerked back her hand, and the contact was broken.

She floated in the water and gazed at the creature wonderingly. Beneath that swelling mound of its forehead was a brain— a wonderful, intelligent, and extremely powerful brain. She reached out to the animal once more, using both hands this time and concentrating on sending a message—much as she would employ the sympathic touch—to the talking fish.

Her message was a simple greeting: *Hello, I am Yarden. I'm glad to meet you.* The words were secondary, however; the primary communication was in the emotional charge she delivered with them—welcome and acceptance.

Placing her hands on the smooth blue skin, Yarden sent her message and waited. All at once, as if rushing up through her fingertips, she felt a tingle of wonder and then excitement as the creature recognized what she had done. The excitement subsided almost as quickly as it had risen, but was replaced at once with a strange emotion, utterly alien to Yarden: a feeling of vast, boundless energy and equally expansive pleasure—an infinity of restless delight.

In a flash of understanding Yarden realized what she was sensing: the ocean! The ocean as seen through the fish's eyes. But there was more, too—a breezy, buoyant cheer combined with a sense of winsome audacity which Yarden did not understand at first.

Her puzzlement must have been communicated instantly, for the series of emotional impressions was repeated. Extraordinary! thought Yarden. It's very like the sympathic touch, only emotion-oriented rather than image-oriented.

The affect phrase was repeated yet again, and Yarden understood that the aquatic creature was giving her its name, its sense of self.

Yarden projected understanding, replaying, as far as she was able, the affect string she'd received, and was rewarded with a flourish of glee. That's what I'll call you, thought Yarden: Glee.

She concentrated for a moment, deciding how best to interpret herself for Glee, then sent an affect phrase that went: elation/hope/amity/wonder/zest and also, after a moment's hesitation, a touch of disquiet.

Glee played back understanding which was followed by a moment of fleeting uncertainty and the same disquiet—as much to say, *Why uneasy?* This was accompanied by a long, lingering, brushing stroke of a flipper against Yarden's side.

Yarden stared in disbelief. The animal was asking her about the source of the restlessness in her soul. Would it understand?

Indeed it seemed to be an extremely understanding creature. She gazed into the deep green eye closest to her and projected fear/ anxiety/depression in roughly equal proportions.

Glee was silent, and Yarden thought she'd broken the delicate contact between herself and the animal by projecting a negative emotion. But Glee replied with an outpouring of sorrow and sympathy which took Yarden's breath away. It was pure empathy, powerful, undiluted by any sense of self.

Yarden, misty-eyed at the unexpected response she had received, gave back heartfelt gratitude and, in a spontaneous gesture, threw her arms around the beast and hugged, pressing her face against the warm, wet, pliant skin. Glee presented Yarden with a sensation of peace and acceptance such as Yarden had rarely felt in life.

Then, abruptly, Glee turned and swam away. The action was so sudden Yarden opened her eyes and glanced around for her friend. With more than a twinge of regret, Yarden watched the triangular blue dorsal fins racing away from her. Apparently the meeting was over.

Yarden treaded water for a moment, looking at the spot where she had last seen the fin before it disappeared beneath the easy swell. Then, feeling sand under her feet, she turned and started back to shore.

She had not gone far, however, when she heard a squeak behind her. She turned to see Glee streaking toward her, and counted three other sets of fins speeding in her wake. Yarden waited; the fish slowed as they approached. Glee nuzzled her and clicked something to the others, who came close and stroked her with their flippers.

Yarden sank down among them and caressed each one in turn, projecting welcome and acceptance. They surrounded her then, and pressed close. Glee nudged Yarden's hand and with a mewing squeak indicated that she wished Yarden to reestablish contact. Yarden placed her hand on the bulging cranial mound and received once more the affect phrase for inquiry.

Without additional prompting, Yarden understood that Glee wanted to tell the others what she'd shared with Glee. So Yarden sent the fear/anxiety/depression string while flippers continued to stroke and caress her.

The animals went still in the water, as if stunned. Then without any of them having moved a muscle, Yarden felt herself rising up out of the water. The sensation was so strong, it took a moment for Yarden to realize it was not physical; they were buoying her up emotionally. She felt as if she were riding the crests of a rolling sea as wave after wave of consolation and kindness washed over her. The tears rose up, overflowing the barriers of her eyelashes to spill down her cheeks as Yarden allowed herself to float on the ineffable charity of the wise creatures.

The emotional tide gradually subsided, and one of the newcomers rolled over on its back, showing Yarden the two parallel yellow stripes. He repeated the action twice, leading Yarden to name him Spinner. He put his head forward, and Yarden placed her hand on his cranial mound. The fish sent welcome and acceptance, and then empathy. *I understand.*

The quality of Spinner's speech, while quite similar to Glee's, was different in some respects. There were nuances of secondary emotions interlacing the primary, making his communication feel more abstract. Before Yarden could respond to the initial string, Spinner sent a complicated string which had to be repeated twice before Yarden could make sense of it. Its main component was a feeling of vast darkness and brooding menace: danger and lurking disaster.

When Yarden responded with understanding, Spinner gave the affect phrase for inquiry, repeated the danger/disaster string and added Yarden's designation of herself. Again Yarden found herself staring at the remarkable animal. Spinner had not been anywhere near when Yarden had given her self-sense to Glee; yet Spinner knew it. Perhaps the constant interplay of flippers among the whales served to link the others to the conversation, creating a communication network.

Spinner repeated the string and waited while Yarden deciphered its meaning. He seemed to be asking whether Yarden felt the same sense of impending doom, and whether the awareness of its presence was what caused her depression.

She sent puzzlement/inquiry, and Spinner backed away; he slapped the water impatiently with his flukes. When he came up under her hand, Yarden received the sensation of threat with a virulence behind it that shocked her. The threat was powerful, all-consuming, ultimate in its expression. She pulled back her hand, and Spinner raised his head from the water to look her in the eye, as if willing her to understand.

Yarden placed her hand back on his head, and he sent the grim danger/disaster string once more, adding a soft note of hope at the end. This time, Yarden experienced a completely different reaction. The hope, however subdued, seemed to overshadow the danger/disaster motif and offer the suggestion that the menace was not certain. It was real and palpable, but not inevitable, or at least not indomitable.

Spinner gazed at Yarden with his intelligent green eyes, and slowly his meaning became clear. With a clarity that chilled her, Yarden understood what Spinner was trying to communicate to her: Dome.

Spinner's triple barrel roll in the water let her know she was right.

Dome was on the move. Treet's prophecy was coming true.

Treet lay inside a piece of old fibersteel pipe, part of a smokestack, no doubt, now nearly buried behind a collapsed bank of permastone bricks which formed a slope down to the broad plain of the Isedon below. It was a good vantage point and safe; the fibersteel formed a turret around him and the permastone a bulwark.

Safe and sturdy it might be, but comfortable it wasn't. He had spent the night in the pipe, dozing fitfully, waking at intervals to listen and look out on the night-dark plain. Now, as dawn tinted the filthy scales of the Old Section's translucent roof a sickly yellow, there was still no sign of the invaders, and Treet had begun to think that perhaps the invasion had been canceled. The blasting had stopped hours ago, and there was no indication of movement around the ruined duct.

If the ambush went according to plan, however, it would be a massacre. The Invisibles would be surrounded in the open to be picked off at will by the hidden rebels. The site was well chosen from that perspective; Tvrdy had shown his genius once again. Treet found himself feeling a little sorry for the hapless Invisibles.

The radio monitor lay at his feet; he had brought it with him so he could hear any communication between Kopetch and Tvrdy. He surveyed the battlefield. It was roughly rectangular, the burned-out shells of buildings forming the sides of the rectangle, which was open at the back end where the Invisibles would enter. At the far end, two big mounds of rock and debris formed the fourth side; the faces of these mounds were covered with straggling bushes and wispy thin trees. It was behind these and in the rubble at the foot of the mounds that Cejka and Tvrdy waited with their men. Treet could not see any trace of them, which was good. They were well hidden.

Treet yawned and rose to stretch himself; he did a few torso twists, windmills, and overhead arm pulls to loosen the kinks. He was in his fifth deep knee bend when there came a muffled rumble in the distance. He stopped to listen, and a few seconds later the monitor at his feet whispered with Kopetch's voice: "The duct is open."

Treet imagined Invisibles boiling up out of a still-smoking hole in the ground, blasters between their teeth. He waited, holding his breath, listening for the far-off sound of battle. But he was too far away. He slumped back down into his turret to wait, balancing the monitor on his knees, but the box remained silent. Most likely, Kopetch and the others were too busy to report. At any rate, it wouldn't take long. Even now the Dhogs were probably attacking the first of the Invisibles.

God help them, he thought—and then wondered if praying for an enemy's death was kosher. He amended his prayer to, God help us all.

The ambush began sooner than expected. Treet was sitting in his foxhole wondering how long it would take for the Dhogs to reach them when he heard the sound of thermal weapons echoing from across the Isedon.

He raised his head to look down upon the battlefield and saw Dhogs already running into the rectangle. They scattered as they came in, spreading out and heading for the nearest cover. At first Treet thought their actions very convincing. Too convincing. Something about the way they were running—headlong, flat-out, without looking back—let him know that something was wrong.

The first wave of Dhogs had entered the Isedon, a squad of Invisibles hot on their heels. Where were the rest? There should have been more Dhogs—at least twice as many.

Then he saw the reason for the Dhogs' severely decreased number. Clattering slowly onto the battlefield came a large, heavily armored em, spitting lightning from at least four ports as Invisibles crouched and dodged around it, laying down a blanket of deadly fire.

A tank! The infernal Invisibles have a tank!

Treet's heart sank to the pit of his stomach. We're going to lose, he thought. There's no way we can fight a tank. They've already cut down half of Bogney's squad—they'll wipe out the rest of us just as quick.

Why was there no warning? Could it be that Kopetch and Piipo had been killed before they could send the alarm?

As Treet looked on, horror-stricken, the improvised tank moved into position in the center of the battlefield and began unleashing its terrible firepower. Bolt after bolt of blue lightning streaked from its ports, screaming through the air to shatter the mountains of debris. Cejka's men are down there, he thought desperately; they're getting murdered!

The Dhogs began fighting back tentatively. But each time someone managed to get off a good shot, the tank retaliated and took the sniper out.

Where was Tvrdy? How could he stand by and watch the slaughter? Why didn't he do something?

If only I had a weapon, Treet thought. I'd . . . I don't know what I'd do, but I wouldn't sit here and wait for them to blast me to smoldering jelly. Somebody's got to do something!

His palms were wet; he glanced at his hands to see blood weltering up where his fingernails had dug into the soft flesh. Help us! Please, God! Help us now if You're ever going to!

Under the scream of the thermal weapons, Treet heard a low droning noise. Glancing at the far end of the battlefield, he saw another tank lumber into view, and behind it another and yet another. Four tanks! And each with a contingent of Invisibles hovering around it.

We're lost! he thought. They have us outmanned and outgunned. We've had it!

As the last tank came in, the others rolled forward, spreading out across the field, each taking a quadrant to scour.

In a few minutes it would be all over. There was nothing left to do now but roll over and die.

Why didn't Tvrdy act?

What could he, Treet, do? The Tanais Director was pinned down with enemy fire bursting over his head. If Treet showed himself now, it would be swift and certain death. But someone had better do something, and quickly. The Invisibles would have the whole battlefield secured in a matter of minutes. The only resistance came from the few Dhogs still foolish enough to risk popping off at one of the tanks.

But soon enough even that activity ceased. The Invisibles kept firing for a few seconds and then, seeing no further resistance, stopped. A stifling silence claimed the battlefield. The air stank of ozone and hot metal.

Treet peered from his perch. Could it be over? So soon?

The Invisibles began moving out across the field toward the mounds of debris where the Dhogs had hidden. They searched the still-smoking rubble, pulling bodies out. The corpses were lined up out in the open where, lest there be any doubt, they were scorched once more for good measure.

The stupid, sadistic scum! Treet's clenched fists pounded his thighs. Where was Tvrdy?

• • • • • •

Yarden sat cross-legged on the sand, hands resting on knees, palms upward in the classic meditation pose. She had disciplined herself to sit this way for hours at a time, without making the slightest movement, without breaking concentration. She had spent most of the flight to Empyrion in her cabin aboard the *Zephyros* in just this way: sitting immobile while her mind practiced the exercises of the sympathic art, keeping the pathways open, the process sharp.

Now, here on a different world beneath a different sun, she sat facing the dark green water as the foaming surf flung itself upon the shore before her. She had been sitting this way through the night, and now dawn broke the gloom in the east, stripping night from the horizon and peeling it back to reveal a new day.

Yarden had spent the night thinking, praying, searching for answers inside herself. There was so much to think about, to sort out, to find answers for. The familiar posture of meditation comforted her, made her feel as if she was in control once more—although, as she well knew, her life was out of control, careening for a crash.

So she sat out on the beach under the alien stars, examining the pattern of her life in the hope of finding the clues to unravel the mystery of what had gone wrong.

Before coming on this journey, she was happy, her life in Fierra full; she'd had definite plans and the sense of a future bright with promise. Somewhere along the way, however, that changed. She couldn't pinpoint the exact place or time, but she felt the effects acutely. Things had just generally fallen apart—apparently without any particular turning-point or major catastrophe. One day she was happily sketching away, developing her burgeoning artistic skills; the next day she was stumbling through ashes.

She lost sight of the bright future; her happiness leaked

away like a rare gas through the sides of a porous container. As the weeks of the journey went by, Yarden felt her grip on her life slipping, and it had slipped so far that she now no longer knew which way to turn, where to go, what to do.

That was bad enough. But worse, she could not shake the feeling that her life had become inextricably bound up with the person of Orion Treet.

It was a mystery to her how a human being could, in his absence, dominate life more completely than he ever had with his presence. Even the talking fish seemed to be talking about him—or, to be a little more accurate, talking about the same things he was talking about, which was disturbing enough in itself.

Everywhere she turned: Treet. And again: Treet.

Did she love him?

It was more than that, of course. Her anxiety and confusion were not merely the result of an inability to make up her mind whether she loved the lout or not. The roots of her dilemma went deeper. Far deeper.

As she sat there, hour upon hour, the sound of the wind-driven rollers droning in her ears, she patiently sifted the tangled thoughts and feelings that had brought her to this brink. And she began to feel as if Pizzle's remark last evening might have hit closer to the mark than she at first suspected.

She had sought out Pizzle to tell him about her experience with the fishes earlier in the day—about the warning. She found him walking along the strand at sunset, arm in arm with Starla. They walked together for a while—awkward in each other's company, Yarden feeling her intrusion with every step—until Starla excused herself and returned to camp.

After Pizzle got over being miffed at Yarden for butting in, they had a good talk. They walked along the beach, and as the lowering sun touched the water and turned it to quicksilver, Pizzle told her about his experience with the talking fish. "It was kinda weird," he said. "At first I didn't get anything from them—just a sort of lift, you know? Just being in the water with them is a blast. They're beautiful animals—a lot like those pilot whales back on Earth. Anyway, after a while I started to get something; I could tell the fish was trying to tell me something."

"Anything in particular?" asked Yarden.

Pizzle lifted his shoulders slightly. "Beats me. All I got was a warm feeling and . . . how should I say this?—a feeling of real peace and contentment. They seem to be happy creatures all right, no doubt about that."

Yarden told him what she discovered about how to talk to the fish and then, out of the blue, Pizzle asked her what was bugging her.

"What makes you say that?" she asked.

"You never want to talk to me unless something's bugging you. We're not the closest of buddies, you know. Besides, you've been chewing your lip like it's beef jerky. I figure something must be worrying you."

"I don't know what's wrong with me," she'd told him. "Honestly, I don't. I can't seem to get in sync—everything's off kilter somehow. I don't know what it is . . .

"I feel drawn and chased at the same time," she concluded.

"Then stop running," he'd said.

Stop running.

How? She wasn't even aware that she *was* running.

"The Seeker won't rest until all men know Him," Pizzle had said. "That's what Anthon tells me."

Now, as she sat watching night loosen its hold on the land, those words came back: the Seeker won't rest . . .

Fine, but didn't I *welcome* the chance to learn about You? she demanded of the Infinite. Didn't I do my best to learn, to understand? What else is there? What do You want from me? What more could You possibly want?

Stop running.

Am I running? What am I running from?

Surrender.

What an old-fashioned word: surrender. Giving up, giving in, giving yourself to another. Relinquishing control.

Yarden bristled at the notion. Ah, there was the rub. I feel drawn and chased at the same time, she thought. Drawn by a presence she did not want to give in to—so she ran. And she was pursued.

Now that same probing presence drew near once more. The Infinite . . . the Seeker. She could run, push the presence aside, and run. Or she could simply sit there, wait—whatever would happen, let it happen.

Something inside her did not want to let it happen. There was a knotty lump of defiance within her, born of equal parts fear and self-will. She'd gotten where she was in life by feeding this defiance. Would I have survived without it? Would I have gotten anywhere by giving in?

Look where it's got you, Yarden. Look at you. You're falling apart. You're sitting out on a damp, drafty beach all night mumbling to yourself. You don't know what you want or where to go. You're lost. You've lost control, because this is something that can't be controlled by you.

Your sympathic abilities are the most important thing in your life, yet they have never brought you a moment's happiness. Ever wonder why? Why? Weren't they just another way to control things around you?

Control, Yarden. That's what this is about. What do you fear most? Losing control. But tell me, who is in control now?

FIFTY SEVEN

Tell me, who is in control?

Yarden heard herself asking the question. It was her voice, the voice of her conscience, and yet it wasn't.

I am in control! she answered, and instantly felt shame wash over her in waves.

You see? Your heart knows better. Yarden, surrender.

Again, the old-fashioned word. *Surrender.*

What will I get if I surrender to You? she demanded.

Something you don't have now: peace.

Peace. Yes, that would be worth having. To shed the weight of her imperfectly borne burdens and walk away, rest, find sanctuary. But could she trust the Seeker, this Infinite so intent on winning her? Could she trust the Seeker not to crush her, not to leech away her personality and make her a drab, unthinking zombie?

Yarden, the voice chided, wake up and look around. What do you see? Are My people unthinking zombies? Are they crushed by their devotion to Me?

I am the Infinite, Yarden. I have taken infinite pains to make you who you are. Why would I now destroy what I have made? To prove a point that doesn't need proving?

You run because you fear losing yourself, losing control. Yet I tell you that you are already lost, and that the control you thought you had was just an illusion. You are just now discovering this because you have hidden the truth so well for so long. But you see the truth now, and it scares you.

Control is very important to you. But can you now see that striving after it has given you more pain than pleasure all your life? Your desire for control has thwarted you most often when you were closest to giving in to better things.

This is why you could not love Orion Treet. He had the audacity to suggest that you love him as he was. But you demanded that love should be on your terms or not at all. You gave him an ultimatum that he rejected; so you rejected him. He was a threat to you because you could not control him.

Was? Is he no longer a threat? she wondered.

We are talking about *you*, Yarden, not Treet. It is you I want now, at this moment. The choice is yours.

What choice do I have? Her inner voice was shrill, near breaking.

You can always remain as you are.

How can I? Yarden fired back. You have given me a taste of what it's like and now demand I choose. I'm not ready. I need more time.

Listen to yourself, Yarden. *A taste of what it's like* . . . First you say you fear I'll crush you, then you admit you've had a taste and want more. Yes, you tasted and found it good. Why do you hesitate? Do you think you will learn more by waiting, that the decision will become more clear? I tell you no. No. You have been given everything you need to decide. You have even been given the taste you asked for.

That I asked for? When did I ever ask for it?

Think for a moment. Who was it that pleaded to become an artist?

Artist? What's my becoming an artist have to do with this?

You yearn for truth, and burn to create beauty. Then why do you resist the source of all truth and beauty, the One who has given you your heart's desire?

There was no answer to that.

Come to Me, Yarden. Give Me the gift of yourself, and I will give you a gift far greater than you can imagine. Yarden, trust Me and believe.

All eternity vibrated in that moment. Yarden imagined that time had stopped and would remain stopped until she answered. The stars, the sea, the wind, the blood coursing through her veins—everything would wait, frozen in that instant, while she decided.

Yes, I'll trust You, she thought. *Yes!*

She expected something then. A sign of divine approval, a rush of emotion—a response of some kind. But there was only the sound of waves on sand, the breeze blowing gently, the first rays of sunlight tinting the horizon, and the sound of her own heart beating in her ears.

It is done, she thought. It's over. The running is over.

There was relief in the thought. Yarden slumped, allowing her muscles to move now; she brought her hands to her neck and rubbed gently. She rose, coming out of her trance position like a flower unfolding itself slowly.

For a moment she stood looking out across the dawn-lit water, molten green in the faint morning light—seeing it for the first time, although she'd stared at it all through the night without noticing it at all—then yawned and stretched, feeling tired and a little lumber-headed from lack of sleep. But there was something else, too—a warm place deep down inside, small but spreading outward; she was at peace within herself.

Smiling to herself, she turned and started back along the water's edge toward the Fieri camp. She had not gone more than a few steps when she saw, far off on the strand, approaching her from the direction of the line of cliffs opposite, a figure—no, two: a man and the dark, fluid shape of a wevicat walking beside him. The ghostly figures emerged out of night's quickly fading gloom.

Strange. Who would be awake at this time of the morning for a stroll? There were no wevicats in camp. Who could it be?

Yarden continued walking, and the figures drew nearer. The man appeared naked, except for a loin pouch, and carried a long staff. The cat loped easily along, stopping now and then to pounce on a wave or roll in the surf, playing in the water.

Closer now, there was something familiar about the figure. Something she recognized, but could not place. Her pulse beat faster. What? Who was it? She quickened her pace.

Closer.

No! Oh, no! It can't be.

She froze in midstride, her hands flying to her face. No! Dear God, no!

But it was.

Crocker!

• • • • • •

The Invisibles, satisfied that the Dhogs had been exterminated, now began disengaging. The tanks backed away slowly as the men on foot fell in behind, weapons at the ready, wary.

They're getting away! Black rage bubbled up like scalding pitch inside Treet as he watched the enemy retreating without so much as a single singed uniform.

Futile tears stung his eyes. It was over. The Invisibles had won. Now they would scour the Old Section, searching out all the hiding places, executing the survivors by twos, by tens, by hundreds. And nothing, nothing would stop them.

Even as these hopeless thoughts filled his mind, Treet felt the inner presence stir. Once again he felt the uncanny assurance, the strange peace that had no objective source. The despair thickening around him dissipated. The fear and frustration melted away.

He looked out on the battlefield through hanging streamers of smoke. The first of the tanks had reached the narrow entrance to the field and was turning to move into the Old Section. But as the death-dealing machine swung around, it appeared to raise slowly off the ground on a puff of gray smoke.

The levitating tank then proceeded to fly to pieces as the explosion ripped its undercarriage to slivers, scattering jagged chunks of metal in a lethal rain. The roar reached Treet a split second later as Invisibles, blown backward by the blast, tumbled loose-jointed through the fire-drenched air. Others nearby were cut to ribbons by flying shrapnel.

The two middle tanks halted at once, but the tank at the rear of the procession ground ahead, faltered, and tried to reverse. Too late. The second explosion took off its front half in a shearing sheet of red flame which billowed out of its ports. The Invisibles crouched behind the tank dropped dead to the ground, felled by the heat wave of the explosion.

Before the two center tanks could back away from the scene, however, rebels appeared from out of nowhere. A shout went up across the battlefield, and Tvrdy's squad swooped down upon the two stalled vehicles. The Invisibles, pinched between the burning wrecks of two tanks, scattered to the mound of debris behind them, where they were mowed down before they knew what had happened.

Cejka was simply not there one moment, and very much there the next—along with a squad brandishing flame-sprouting weapons.

The Invisibles wilted before the onslaught. The tanks made feeble efforts to turn the battle once again, but the attackers were too close and the clumsy vehicles were easily outmaneuvered.

The battle was over in a moment. Treet stared at the carnage, feeling numb and empty. The ferocity of the fight, the concentrated violence had deadened his senses, even as the booming shock of the explosions had stunned his eardrums.

It is over. I should feel relieved, happy, he told himself. We won.

But there was no joy in the victory. It had cost too much. Treet climbed from his bunker and began picking his way down to the battlefield to join Tvrdy and the others. He was halfway across the field when he saw men flying into the rectangle from the direction of the duct. Kopetch, Piipo, and their men reached the place where Tvrdy, Cejka, Fertig, and Bogney, who had somehow managed to come through the battle unscathed, waited amidst the wreckage. As Treet came up, he heard Kopetch saying breathlessly, ". . . too many . . . couldn't hold them . . ."

"The duct?" asked Tvrdy. He gave Treet a frown of reproach, but didn't say anything. His mind was on other matters.

"Still open," replied Piipo. "Couldn't seal it. We tried . . ."

Tvrdy cursed and began shouting orders. But before anyone could move, they heard again the menacing grumble of a heavy machine approaching from the direction of the duct.

"We can't stay here," said Tvrdy. "Too risky. We'll have to make them chase us and try to take them on the run." He shouted an order and they all started off, but not before the Dhogs finished separating a few of the dead Invisibles from their weapons.

FIFTY EIGHT

Yarden stared in disbelief at the man who had once been Crocker.

The former pilot leaned on his spear, gazing at Yarden with an odd expression, innocent and wary at the same time. The great black wevicat sat on its haunches, licking sand from a huge paw, regarding the woman with keen disinterest.

Her hands fluttered as she reached out toward him. "Crocker?"

The man did not acknowledge the name, but merely gazed back with a vacant, animal look in his eyes.

She took a step toward him. The cat's head snapped up; its lips curled back. She hesitated. "Crocker," she said, trying to control her voice, "it's me, Yarden. Remember me? Yarden . . . your friend."

He raised his hand and began scratching his stomach.

Tears misted Yarden's eyes. "Oh, Crocker . . . what's happened to you? What . . . ?" Just then the implications of what she was seeing detonated in Yarden's cerebral cortex, sending shock waves through her central nervous system. Her knees went spongy, and the horizon tilted wildly.

"Oh, no . . . Crocker—tell me what happened. Where's Treet? Where's Calin? Crocker? What happened? Can you talk?" Ignoring the cat's low growl, she stepped up to the man and put her hand to his face. Tears streaming from her eyes, she said, "Crocker, can you hear me? Can you speak? Oh, please, say something."

The man stared dumbly at her. She bowed her head, and the tears fell into the wet sand.

They stood that way for some time before Yarden drew a sleeve across her eyes, sniffed, and said, "Come on, I'm taking you back to camp. I'm going to get you some help." She put her hand on his arm. He did not resist and allowed her to lead him away. The cat watched them depart and then moved off along the strand.

• • • • • •

Jaire awoke from a disturbed sleep. She glanced around her room as if she might find the source of her disquiet in its shadowed corners. She rose and went to the curtain, then drew it aside to stand gazing out over the dark water of Prindahl.

The dream was still fresh: black, malformed shapes boiling in the seething darkness; in the center, standing in a shaft of white light, pinioned there, stood Orion Treet, his hands upraised in an attitude of prayer or supplication . . . or defeat. And then, with a terrible ripping sound, the light went out and Treet was swallowed by the roiling darkness.

That was all. But the image carried with it an emotional charge, a feeling that persisted even though the dream had ended: futility, hovering doom, despair.

Jaire shivered in the predawn light and, drawing a robe around her shoulders, hurried off to find her father.

Talus, pulled from his bed by his daughter's quiet touch and the intense, worried expression on her face, listened as she related her disturbing dream. They sat in the jungled courtyard of the great house Liamoge, drinking herbal tea as pearly daylight slowly claimed the sky.

When he had heard the dream, Talus said, "I see why you awakened me, Jaire. It is a most distressing sign." His voice rumbled in the empty courtyard like small thunder.

"You think it is a sign?"

His eyebrows went up. "Oh, yes. The Protector is trying to warn us. The dream is a warning."

"I agree," said Jaire, then looked puzzled. "But what am I to do about it?"

"That is for us to discover."

"If Orion is in trouble, we must help him."

She spoke with such conviction, her father looked at her closely. "You have a feeling for the Traveler."

Jaire smiled briefly. "I always have."

Talus nodded absently. "Well, we must consult Mathiax first thing. As acting Preceptor, he may have some suggestions. He will want to be informed in any case."

Jaire rose. "I am ready."

Talus smiled as he climbed to his feet. "We can wait until the sun is risen, I think." He hugged his daughter and planted a kiss on the crown of her head. "Don't worry. We will have the time we need."

FIFTY
NINE

Mentor Mathiax nodded gravely as Jaire told her dream. When she had finished, he said simply, "I knew something like this would happen."

"The dream?" asked Jaire.

He glanced up, held her eyes with his for a moment, smiled faintly. "The dream? Yes, I suppose—although I wasn't certain what form the warning would take."

Talus spoke up. "Then you consider it a warning, too?"

"Definitely," he agreed. "A warning. What else?"

"We have to do something," said Jaire. "We have to help him."

"Oh, yes, I agree," said Mathiax. "What to do—that is the question. Helping him may not be easy."

"Was returning to Dome easy for him?" snapped Jaire.

"No, no, child," soothed Mathiax. "I only meant that given our vow of peace, we may be limited in the kind of help we can offer."

"You are Preceptor. You could send help. Authorize—"

"Acting Preceptor, if you please." He smiled as he shook his head. "I do not have such authority. Even the Preceptor herself does not have that power. The question will have to go before the College of Mentors."

Jaire jumped from her chair. "That will take too long! We must act at once!"

"We will certainly do what we can." Mathiax looked thoughtful. "Leave the matter with me." He rose and took Jaire's hand in both of his. "I know you care for the Traveler. Can you believe that I care as much?"

· · · · · ·

Since Osmas' most timely demise, Diltz had proceeded with his plans unhindered. Jamrog began to think he'd found the perfect subordinate in the sly Nilokerus Director—smarter than the dull, officious Hladik, stronger than the weak-willed Osmas, more pliable than the inflexible Mrukk. Each had had their uses, to be sure, but the power-hungry Diltz was a tool made for Jamrog's hand.

The attribute that made him most attractive to the Supreme Director was that Diltz seemed to anticipate his moods and thoughts. Removing Osmas, for example, at the precise moment the worm had outlived his usefulness—and without the slightest hint having been dropped—what more could a leader want?

Diltz's rise to prominence had not gone unnoticed, however. Mrukk—busy putting down the rebellion, as well as overseeing Jamrog's massive reorientation campaign—still found time to keep himself apprised of the happenings in the Supreme Director's kraam. He had marked Diltz from the beginning as a quietly devious, ambitious schemer whose loyalties could be bought by the highest bidder, and was not at all surprised when Osmas' bloodless body was fished out of Kyan lacking a throat.

Mrukk entered Jamrog's kraam now and paused in the vestibule, looking out over the polished floor. Jamrog's torches—a foolish affectation from some imagined past—burned in their wall sockets, casting more shadow than light, Mrukk thought, making the kraam seem alive with insubstantial movement, as if the oversouls of dead Directors flickered among the potted greenery and hovered around the black-and-silver Bolbe wall hangings.

And there was Diltz, practically lying on the Supreme Director, leaning over him as he presented a much creased map for Jamrog's inspection, his nasal voice crooning as he described some feature there. Mrukk grimaced to see Jamrog's expression: gloating, greedy, self-satisfied, and arrogant, eyes narrowed in smug contemplation of his latest conquest.

Mrukk knew what that was: Fierra.

Mrukk had heard the reports. The devious Nilokerus had apparently discovered the fabled city of the Fieri. Out there across a near endless expanse of white nothing lay a deep lake; beside the lake was the city of their ancient enemy.

It was not proven, of course. Not yet. But Diltz had exploration teams searching outside Empyrion, while Nilokerus and Saecaraz magicians searched the Archives. This latest map had come from the Archives—from some captured Fieri artifacts. Saecaraz readers had authenticated the find. The map was genuine, if old.

Mrukk stepped from the entryway and proceeded silently across the floor to the throne. Neither of the others looked up until he was practically upon them. How easy it would be, thought Mrukk. The fools! I could have their still-beating hearts in my hand before they could open their mouths to scream.

"Mrukk!" said Jamrog, glancing up as the Mors Ultima commander came to stand before him. Diltz did not raise his head from the map. Mrukk noted the slight and filed it away for future reference. "We are to be congratulated."

"How so, Supreme Director?" Mrukk kept his tone civil, but flat.

Diltz grinned, stretching the flesh of his lips across his teeth. His head came up slowly and he said, "The Fieri, at long last, are ours."

"Are they indeed?"

"Of course," explained Jamrog. "We must dispatch an expeditionary force at once—as soon as the weapons are ready."

"You are speaking of the old weapons found in the Archives, I assume," said Mrukk.

"Yes, what about them?" Diltz's ghastly grin faded.

"I would have thought the problem obvious to a man of your intellect, Diltz."

The cadaverous Nilokerus stiffened. "I am a Director. My stent is higher than yours. You will address me as your superior."

Now it was Mrukk's turn to grin. He'd pricked the rancorous parasite where it hurt. "As you say," replied Mrukk placidly.

Jamrog chose not to notice the sparring between the two and said, "Well, mighty Mrukk, are you going to tell us? What's wrong with the old weapons?"

"They are dangerous, unstable. They will not work."

"Oh? The magicians say they will. They all agree."

"Then they are blind as well as ignorant."

"What do you know?" snapped Diltz. "You can't even subdue a handful of malcontents."

"Perhaps our leader would not dismiss them so lightly." Mrukk inclined his head toward Jamrog.

"*Dangerous* malcontents," corrected the Supreme Director,

who still felt the sting of his burns. "Still, I remain unimpressed with your success thus far, Commander. I had hoped for more immediate results."

"Which is why I have come, Supreme Director—to inform you personally that after two days of brisk fighting, we have the entrance to the Old Section secured and supply lines in place. The Dhogs have been forced to retreat."

"But they are not yet exterminated," sneered Diltz.

"Not yet," replied Mrukk. "But soon. Very soon."

"Yes, yes, of course." Jamrog yawned. "In the meantime, you will increase the interrogations. The Saecaraz and Nilokerus are to be spared no longer. I have reason to believe the treason has spread even into our own Hages. It must stop. We must eradicate all opposition." He glanced at Diltz, and Mrukk saw the look that passed between them. "If you will excuse us, Mrukk, we were in the middle of planning the attack on Fierra."

Diltz produced his grotesque smile once again and went back to his map. Mrukk offered the Mors Ultima salute, fist over heart, then backed away from the throne, turned on his heel, and walked quickly from the room.

"He resents me," murmured Diltz when Mrukk had gone. "I believe he disapproves of my success."

Jamrog sniffed. "Mrukk resents everyone and disapproves of everything—a quality I am beginning to find very annoying." He looked at the place where Mrukk had been standing. He tapped his teeth with the tip of his bhuj. "He may be taking himself too seriously of late. A very bad habit, don't you agree?"

Diltz smiled and nodded.

"Now then, where were we?" asked Jamrog.

"Fierra," replied the Nilokerus. He pointed to the map. "We were planning its destruction."

SIXTY

The breached air duct from the Saecaraz refuse pits had been secured by the Invisibles, as Kopetch reported. They had quickly fortified the position and now guarded it with a vengeance, affording themselves a small base of operations and a vital supply link with the Hage. There was nothing the rebels could do to staunch the hated flow of men, weapons, and equipment into the Old Section.

What was worse, the Invisibles did not wait to consolidate their position, but pressed forward immediately, putting the rebels on the run and forcing them to fight a moving battle. The rebels fought viciously, exacting a heavy toll in every confrontation, but still came away a little weaker each time.

The Invisibles pressed them relentlessly back and back, giving them no time to rest or regroup. At the end of the second day, the rebels were forced to abandoned the Isedon. They retreated into the Old Section's maze of ancient ruins to reorganize themselves to fight a defensive war.

Treet, ordered back to the command compound early in the struggle, watched as the exhausted fighters returned, defeat rounding their shoulders and bending their backs. He and Ernina had prepared food, and he took it to the briefing room. While the captains assembled, Treet served them and hoped the hot food would revive their spirits.

"It's bad," said Tvrdy, rousing himself after his meal. He stood and began to pace slowly in front of the others. "I won't try to tell you otherwise. In losing the duct, we've lost our best advantage. They can now strengthen themselves at will, while we can only grow weaker."

"We have already lost half our ready force. It will take weeks to get more men trained," said Kopetch. "Even then, we're grossly outmanned. Dhogs against Invisibles! We don't stand a chance."

Bogney, his hair a matted and sweaty cap plastered to his skull, frowned mightily. "Let them come. Bogney don't care. Dhogs taking care of our own."

Yes, but who takes care of the rest of Dome? wondered Treet.

The thought caused Treet to reflect on just how much of an outsider he was: the war, his war, was proceeding without him; Dome's inhabitants regarded him as either an enemy of the state, or some sort of demigod, or a propaganda tool to be applied sparingly.

He merely floated around observing events as they unfolded—which was, after all, just what he'd spent the last thirty years of his life doing. Apparently, that's what he did best: talent will out.

However, he had returned to Dome not to be a spectator, not to hover at the fringes of life with notebook in hand, not to observe dispassionately the tilt and sway of power's precarious balance. He had returned specifically to prevent Apocalypse II.

Instead, it was beginning to look suspiciously like he'd caused it.

Treet hadn't thought about it before, but his presence had somehow focused the irrational forces of Dome, thereby bringing about the current state of affairs. Now, not only were they no closer to derailing Jamrog's death machine, but it seemed as if they would soon be ground beneath its wheels.

Perhaps, he reflected, the Fieri were right—the laissez-faire approach was best. What a time for second-guessing. Now, as the tramp of enemy feet could be heard in the empty corridors of the Old Section, and enemy weapons spilled the blood of brave, foolish rebels . . .

But no. It was a trap to think that way.

The rebellion would have begun without him—did, in fact. Jamrog did not come to power through any action of Treet's. The sides were chosen long ago, and he had nothing to do with it. Ah, but whether Jamrog would have turned his cold eye toward the Fieri . . . that was another question. One that Treet could not so easily lay aside.

Treet looked at the leaders huddled together in the room, then at Tvrdy—haggard, fatigue sitting heavily on his shoulders, dark hair showing gray—and he remembered the Tanais saying to him, *Your presence here among us is a catalyst for action.*

That's me, thought Treet, the ever-faithful catalyst. Doom and destruction at your service. Treet's the name, Armageddon's the game. Have notebook; will travel.

What am I doing here? What is my purpose? Why me anyway?

"We can hold out two, perhaps three months—*if* we do not allow the Invisibles to come this far into the Old Section."

"How do we keep them out?" wondered Piipo.

"We keep them going around in circles. We make them chase us, and make certain that we stay well away from here."

"And in the meantime?" asked Cejka.

"In the meantime, we try to find a way to close the air duct. There must be a way."

"If there isn't?"

"We be fighting face to face," grumbled Bogney.

"No, we cannot afford to do that. Even when we win, we lose too much. They would eventually pare us down to nothing. They could win the war while losing every single battle."

"Without a way to close that duct," said Kopetch, "it doesn't matter what we do. They'll just keep coming at us until we can't hold them off anymore."

Fertig, the former Nilokerus Subdirector, spoke up. "Now that they know about this entrance, they'll do everything in their power to keep it open."

"He's right," added Piipo. "Even if we somehow managed to close it, they would open it again. We'd be helpless to prevent it."

Treet listened to the tension in the voices and heard the fear creeping in. It was as if an unseen hand had closed around the group and was slowly crushing out what little hope they were able to generate. He could feel the futility spreading, and looked to Tvrdy to see his reaction. Tvrdy stood before them exhausted, drained, his features blank.

He can't stop it this time, thought Treet.

The same instant he felt his face grow hot and a prickling sensation over his scalp. The presence was stirring within him again. Then he was on his feet.

"Listen to yourselves," he said quietly. The others turned, and Treet looked at their faces as if seeing them for the first time. They all looked so helpless he wanted to cry for them.

"There is fear in this room. You feel it growing," he continued, talking quietly. "You think it is fear of Jamrog, of losing against him, of death, but you're wrong."

Cejka started to object, but Treet silenced him with an

upraised palm. "What you feel comes from a different source—
It is from the source of darkness itself. It is the fear your own
ancestors felt, that crippled them and then stripped them of
their humanity. It is the ancient mindless fear that paralyzes and
consumes, that destroys first the will and then the heart."

All were silent, watching him intently.

"Listen to me!" His words, spoken earnestly, were a shout
in the room. "You think to pull down a dictator to save your
Hagemen, but the danger is greater than you suspect. We have a
world to save."

"A world," scoffed Cejka. "Right now I'd settle for saving
the Old Section."

Treet turned on him. "Do you doubt me? Jamrog does not
fear us. He believes it's only a matter of time before he catches
us. He believes that no one inside Empyrion can pose a serious
threat to his rule. At best, we are but a minor annoyance to
him."

There were mutters of agreement. "But what about outside?" Treet gestured beyond the walls to the greater world
beyond the dim crystal panels of Dome. "What about out there
across the great blight of desert? What about the Fieri?"

The others looked at Treet strangely, but said nothing.
"Don't you see it? Jamrog fears the Fieri. And what he fears, he
destroys.

"Kopetch told us, remember? Right now Jamrog has Saecaraz magicians ransacking the Archives, searching for information and weapons—the atomic weapons of old. He will find
them and rebuild them. He will send out search parties to find
Fierra, and they will find it . . . and then he will strike.

"He will plunge this world into another cycle of agony and
death that will last thousands of years."

Treet's voice had risen steadily as he spoke. He stopped so
abruptly, his words still rang in the air. The others watched him
warily, as if any moment he too might explode.

Treet continued more quietly. "We must not give in to the
fear. Our position is far from hopeless. The future of Empyrion
depends on us. We can rebuild. We can overcome; we must. We
can fight Jamrog, and we can win."

Seeing that no great upsurge of confidence met his words,
he pressed on. "Listen, the great battles of history have always
been won by shrewd generals who used their advantages, few or

many, while neutralizing their enemy's, advantages or even turning them into disadvantages. So what advantages do we possess?"

"None," murmured Kopetch.

"All right, I'll rephrase the question. What advantages do the Invisibles have? Greater numbers, superior firepower, better training, and supplies. Yes?" What else did an army need? Ooh, this was going to be tough—but not impossible. Individually, none of those advantages were insurmountable.

"Greater numbers? Under the superb leadership of Leonidas, a handful of Spartans held off the entire Persian army, the greatest fighting machine Earth had ever seen, in the Battle of Thermopylae in 480 B.C.

"Superior firepower? Fragile British Spitfires scrambled to meet the might of the terrible German Luftwaffe in the skies over England, not only once, but time and time again, until the German airforce gave up.

"Better training and supplies? A ragtag army of Afghan mountain tribesmen made do with antique rifles and pitchforks to outflank the best military minds of the vastly superior Soviets and bring the Red Giant to its knees.

"Don't you see? There is always a way." He looked around the room at the uncomprehending stares. "All we have to do is find it. We can't give up until we do."

In the hush that followed his words, Treet sat down. Tvrdy stared at him for a moment, then looked away and said, "That is all for now. We will meet tonight to begin planning our survival." At that, everyone rose and filed out silently.

Treet shuffled out, head low, shoulders slumped. Why did I shoot off my mouth? he wondered. It didn't do any good. The timing wasn't right. No one understands.

He'd walked only a few paces when Bogney approached him. Treet acknowledge the Dhog's presence with a nod and the twitch of a nostril.

"Dhogs being ready now," Bogney said cryptically; his two filthy companions gazed at Treet steadily.

"Ah—" Treet replied, "ready for what?" He studied the swarthy Dhog carefully. The greasy countenance appeared resolute, and a strange light burned in the normally lackluster eyes. "Are you talking about the raid?" asked Treet, knowing that wasn't it.

The Dhog shifted from one foot to another. "Dhogs not raiding no more. Giloon be thinking Fieri man taking us to Fierra. Dhogs ready—we living here no more."

Here was a problem. Apparently the Dhogs, having had a taste of war, wanted nothing more to do with it; they wanted to pull out, were ready to go, in fact. Treet looked around; Moscow Square was empty. It occurred to him that he hadn't seen many Dhogs since the ambush. Apparently they had been busy packing up and getting ready to leave.

But how could he explain that he couldn't lead them to the promised land? He had to stall them until he could find a way to talk them into staying. "What about your dead?"

Treet pointed to the triple row of covered bodies lined up outside Ernina's makeshift hospital, most of them Dhogs.

Bogney glanced at the bodies. "We be sending them on this night," he said firmly, turning back to Treet, his jaw set. "Then you be taking us to Fierra."

Treet decided it would be unwise to lie to Bogney. He replied simply, "I won't do that."

Giloon Bogney stared at Treet, the wheels of his mind grinding slowly, his expression one of defiance and challenge. Treet expected him to throw a punch any second, but the Dhog merely stood fingering his filthy beard, staring.

"Giloon showing you something," Bogney said finally. "You come tonight."

"All right," agreed Treet. "Tonight."

*B*y the time the mourners reached the cremation site deep
in the Old Section warrens, daylight had abandoned them.
Night came swiftly, deepening the putrid half-light of the
ancient shell. While the Dhogs set about readying the funeral
pyre, Treet gazed at his surroundings. A more depressing place
would be difficult to imagine: sun-starved trees, long dead, lifted
leafless branches to the smoke-dark dome; limp, wasted weeds
cast clinging nets of pale tendrils over reeking piles of debris;
black moss draped the stone and hung from the lifeless limbs
like tattered shrouds.

They made their way to a great heap of tumbled stone
which lay in the center of this dismal scene, and there they
stopped. Bogney surveyed the hill and said to Treet, standing
beside him, "Bogneys always burn dead. For a hundred many
years and more, Bogney men always."

Nice family business, thought Treet. Lots of trade to keep
you busy, I'll bet.

"You saying Dhogs afraid." The squat leader spat on the
ground to show what he thought of that notion. "Dhogs not
being afraid of death—it take us from *here!*" He lifted his hands.

Good point, thought Treet. "Welcome release, is that it?"

They watched while the dead, carried so carefully through
the labyrinthine byways of the Old Section, were stacked atop
the flattened crown of the man-made hill. Torches which the
women had brought with them were set in crevices around the
pyramid of dead bodies, and a huge effigy, fetched from a keep-
ing-place nearby, was trundled up the hill on the backs of some
of the men.

Treet recognized the effigy as that of the strange winged
man the Dhogs called Cynetics. Made of fibersteel crudely
patched together, the thing was erected on the summit amidst
the carefully arranged bodies. The rest of the Dhogs gathered at
the foot of the hill, murmuring in agitated voices as Giloon
Bogney ascended the hill with a lighted torch and began lighting
the ring of torches while men poured the contents of plastic
containers over the pile of bodies.

The murmurs became wails and rose in volume. The name Cynetics could be heard in the rising tumult. Then Bogney, having ignited the planted torches, stood on the hilltop holding his torch in his hand, gazing down at those below, his face shiny in the furtive light. He waved the torch in a circle and the Dhogs grew silent, joined hands, and circled the hill.

"Dhogs," he shouted, "why we be coming here?"

The Dhogs below answered in chorus, and Treet made out the words: "We coming to set free the dead."

"Where we be sending them?"

"We send them Home."

Home. It was the first time Treet had heard the word used on Empyrion. In the mouths of the Dhogs it sounded impossibly remote.

"We be sending them Home," confirmed Bogney. "We sending them Home to Cynetics."

Treet felt his flesh tingle at the realization that to the Dhogs "home" was a sort of heaven where their souls went after death, and Cynetics the welcoming deity. It made sense, but struck Treet as unutterably pathetic.

Once their ancestors had longed for a place called Home where a benevolent entity called Cynetics would receive them and care for them, grant them the pleasures so long denied in life. The Old Ones must have yearned for it, dreamed about it— those who remembered probably even told stories about what it was like, stories that grew to legend and slowly became myth— and they passed on to infant generations the dream of one day returning home.

The dream never dimmed, although it must have become painfully clear at some point that it was impossible, that they would never again make contact with Cynetics, that they could never go home. But the human spirit is a remarkably tenacious thing; it does not easily give up its dreams. So, home became *Home,* and the physically unreached became reachable in spirit: in death their souls, so desperately homesick, could travel there. Cynetics, so powerful, so remote, and so aloof, could be rejoined, if not in temporal life, then in the afterlife.

Thinking these things, Treet watched the sad spectacle unfold around him. In their profound naiveté the Dhogs still clutched at the bare threads of a tradition they could no longer understand. He felt the tears rise in his throat; he swallowed hard, and passed a hand over his eyes. The hand came away wet.

"Fire set them free!" cried Bogney, leaping with the torch.

"Fire set us all free!" rejoined the Dhogs.

"Where they going?"

"Home!" cried the Dhogs. "Home to Cynetics."

Bogney turned, took the torch to the pile of bodies, and ignited the pyre. The other Dhogs with him on the hill took up their torches and touched them to the stack of corpses. In seconds the pyre was awash in streaking red flames. In the center stood the grotesque metal effigy, its outspread wings glinting dully in the firelight, its harsh face solemn, cold, distant in the white smoke rolling up to the high arched dome.

Treet stood aghast at the cruel trick time had played upon these simple people. He felt the yearning of the blind, ignorant souls around him.

Tears fell from his eyes, and he wept.

· · · · · ·

Yarden lay in her tent in the dark, listening to the clear, happy voices of the Fieri, watching the pale slice of sky growing dim through the tent flap. In the midst of a most festive atmosphere—the arrival of the talking fish raised the ordinarily jovial Fieri into a mood of high jubilation—she felt distant, cut off from the celebration around her.

Crocker's unexpected appearance on the beach that morning had thrown her into a tailspin. She would not have been more surprised if the ghost of her greatgrandmother had taken flesh before her eyes. Seeing the lanky pilot striding up, spear in hand, wevicat beside him, had shattered the delicate peace of mind she had won as a result of her long night's vigil.

She had brought him back to camp and gathered the Mentors. One look at Crocker, and the Preceptor was summoned. The Preceptor came, and Yarden witnessed an act of touching kindness and tenderness as the Preceptor knelt down beside the naked, dirty man and took his hands in hers. The Mentors gathered round and put their hands on Crocker, and they all prayed for him quietly—with not a few of the onlooking Fieri joining in as well.

Crocker bore the experience without so much as a twitch

of acknowledgment. When they had finished praying, they painstakingly examined the man and then bathed and clothed him—all under the Preceptor's watchful eye. Crocker seemed not to mind their ministrations; indeed, he accepted the probing and poking amiably and without comment.

The examination over, the Preceptor consulted with the Mentors and, upon charging them with Crocker's care, departed once more. Yarden watched the proceedings with growing distress. The pilot was clearly not himself, and yet no one appeared concerned over this fact. Nor did they seem concerned at all with the implications of Crocker's presence.

"We can find nothing physically wrong with him," Anthon told her when the Preceptor had gone. "At least, nothing a few good meals won't put right. He's a bit sunburned, of course, but then he's been living in the forest—"

"Nothing wrong? How can you say that? Look at him. If nothing's wrong, why won't he talk? He just sits there looking at us. Why won't he tell us what's happened?"

Anthon gave her a fatherly look and patted her shoulder. "I said *physically*. He has undoubtedly sustained a severe trauma which has affected his mind."

All of which was painfully obvious to Yarden; she'd known it the second she saw him. And she saw the implications immediately, too: if Crocker was here, he couldn't very well be with Treet and Calin.

Pizzle had come by, frowning and shaking his head sadly, saying, "This is bad news. I don't like this at all. From the looks of it, I'd say the show closed on the road."

Yarden was in no mood for his analysis, so drove him away with a few barbed words and a fistful of sand.

But Pizzle was only articulating Yarden's own fears, and in doing so unleashed all sorts of grim scenarios—all of which tended to resolve into the bleak prospect that Treet, Crocker, and Calin had never reached Dome.

That's when the questions had started—the same questions that had been whirling inside her head all day: Are they all right? Should I try to contact them? What if I don't like what I find? What if they're dead or in trouble? What then?

Oh, God, what am I supposed to do?

She rose, stepped out of the tent, and stood watching the warm, convivial knots of people mingling among themselves, freely, joyously, but with a little urgency, it seemed to her, as if the fading of the daylight would steal the happiness from them.

I've got to know, Yarden said to herself. I've got to know right now.

She turned and walked slowly down to the water's edge, as far from the bustle as she could get. The setting sun had polished the bay to resemble a gleaming bronze mirror reflecting the early evening stars. She sat down cross-legged on the damp, smooth, wave-packed sand and drew a long deep breath, clearing her mind.

What she would do now was different than accepting the fleeting thought impulses she'd received before. Those were unbidden; unavoidable, actually. But the intentional, calculated drawing of another's thought into her mental awareness was something else again. Most people, especially men, resented it, considered it spying—which in a way it was; hence the reprehensible term "brain dipping."

The sympathic "touch," misunderstood though it so often was, could bring great benefit when used skillfully and responsibly. What Yarden proposed was, she hoped, responsible and not merely selfish.

Yarden exhaled slowly, drew another breath, held it, exhaled, placed her hands together, fingertips touching lightly. She cleared her mental screen—an imagined area of space right behind her closed eyelids—emptying her mind completely, concentrating her consciousness, focusing it down and down, drawing it thin as wire until she could feel it sharp and fine within her.

When she was ready, she formed the image of Calin on her mental screen. She pulled another long breath deep into her lungs, held it, and exhaled slowly. As the air flowed from her mouth, she released her rarefied consciousness, sending it out from her, a laser beam to thread the finest needle.

She waited.

Ordinarily she would begin receiving thought impressions immediately, but nothing came. She concentrated harder, probing with her consciousness, forcing it further afield, questing.

Where was she?

There was no sign, no spark, no vibration of being. Calin was not there; she had vanished. Yarden knew then that she was dead.

Fighting back the impulse to break concentration, to give in to her worst fears, she replaced Calin's image with Treet's and forced herself to continue.

Instantly a vague, flickering image floated onto her mental screen: a man with wings standing before a fire with white smoke rolling up. No, not standing before the fire . . . standing *in* the fire. Burning with it, but not consumed.

A strange image. What did it have to do with Treet?

She cleared the image from her mind and concentrated again, sending her awareness out like searching fingers.

Then she found him. Her touch vibrated with his presence; she knew it, recognized it as Treet's, but it was distant, external—as if he were covered by a thick, impenetrable shell or membrane.

He was alive, yes, or there would be no trace of him at all. Yet, something was blocking her attempt to reach him directly. Like a lead sheet shielding a body from X rays, something stood between her and Treet, something that either absorbed or deflected her probing consciousness.

Yarden forced the probe deeper, trying to pierce the membrane, all her being concentrated at the rapier-sharp tip, thrusting like a surgical needle. She felt the membrane part, slipped in through the narrow rent, and was overwhelmed by a sudden sensation of doom, of death and despair roiling fiercely, ugly and menacing. And Treet was there—somehow caught in it, enveloped by it.

And then she felt a presence, quick and incredibly strong, moving toward her through her contact with Treet. It reached out for her as if to pull her in, to envelop her, drag her down. Hate radiated from this maleficent presence like the rays of a dark star. Or a black hole which sucked all living matter into its gaping maw, vomiting lethal radiation in return.

Yarden recoiled from the contact, but tried to hold on to Treet. She felt him receding, slipping away. Then the membrane closed and she was expelled. On the outside again, she could sense Treet, but received no impressions from him. He was alive. Beyond that?

The effort at maintaining the touch was exhausting her; she felt her energy draining away.

Yarden came to herself with a shudder. She raised shaking hands to her face. Never in her sympathic experience had such a thing ever happened. And yet, as horrible as it was, it seemed familiar.

She had encountered a force of incredible strength—the merest contact had left her shaken and spent. But there was more to it than strength. There was a will, mindless and insensible, but grasping, tenacious, holding fast to all that came beneath its sway as if with countless writhing tentacles—so strong, so possessive that it could shield a human mind from her seeking touch.

It was a long time before Yarden could move again. When she finally struggled to her feet, she felt unspeakably old, weary, tired in her soul. But she remembered where she'd encountered the dark presence before: Dome . . . the Astral Service . . . Trabant Animus.

"Just what am I supposed to tell them?" asked Treet, exasperation making his voice brittle. "Why won't you talk to me?"

Tvrdy glowered and waved his hand in the air as if to dismiss the question. "Tell them you can't do it, of course. Tell them it's impossible. Tell them we need them here. Tell them anything you like." Tvrdy turned away.

"I've told them all that. They think I am a *Fieri*—remember? They believe I can lead them to the promised land, and they want to go *right now*. Haven't you wondered why it's been so quiet around here since the ambush? They think they're leaving. I've put them off as long as I can. We've got to talk to Bogney— explain to him exactly what's going on here—" Treet paused, looking at the Tanais' rigid back.

"What's wrong, Tvrdy?" he said more softly. "You've changed. What's eating you?"

Tvrdy turned on him, eyes flashing. "You ask what's wrong? You really want to know? I'll tell you: *we can't win.*"

Treet had never heard defeat from Tvrdy's lips. He stared, unable to speak.

"Do you hear?" Tvrdy's voice jumped several registers. "We can't win against Jamrog. He is too strong."

"We lose one skirmish and you're ready to toss in the towel?" Tvrdy's puzzled glance let Treet know he'd used another obscure figure of speech. "You're giving up after one battle?"

"I will never give in to Jamrog. But I know now that we cannot take him." Tvrdy paused, looked away again. "Maybe the Dhogs are right. Maybe we should leave the Old Section . . . go to Fierra."

"I can't believe it's you saying these things, Tvrdy. Look at me! Look me in the eye and tell me we're lost."

Tvrdy kept his face averted, said nothing.

"See? You can't do it. You don't believe it yourself. Besides, if we left now, it would only be a matter of time before Jamrog hunted us down. You know that."

"We could go to the Fieri—"

"I *tried* that, remember? Besides, there's the little matter of about ten thousand kilometers of nothing but nothing between here and there. Even if we were all up to a nice long stroll, where would we get the supplies? How would we carry them?"

Tvrdy's head dropped.

"Look, we'll find a way to beat him," said Treet. "Our hit and run raids aren't going so bad. We just have to hold on until something turns our way." He took a deep breath and let it out through his teeth. This was hard work, keeping all the ends from unraveling. "In the meantime, we have to figure out what to tell the Dhogs. They're waiting."

"Tell them the truth." The resignation in the Tanais leader's voice cut at Treet like a razor.

"Okay." Treet nodded. "I'll take care of it."

He went out and walked across the empty training field, trying to frame the words in his mind. The truth, yes—but what was the truth exactly? That he was not a Fieri?

That was easy enough. But if not a Fieri, what was he?

I'm a traveler. I'm from another world, another time. I'm the Ghost of Christmas Past . . .

The truth?

You think Cynetics is a god. It isn't. It's a bloated, blood-sucking corporation. (What's a corporation? Look it up in the dictionary.)

You think the Fieri are your saviors. They aren't. In fact, for all their angelic goodness and righteousness, they wouldn't give a rat's hind end to save this stinking hellhole. And I don't blame them one bit.

See, they're human beings, too. And they have long memories. They tried for peace with you bubbleheads once upon a time and paid the ultimate price for the attempt. As it happens, they aren't particularly anxious to repeat the experience. They'll leave us to die our miserable deaths without lifting a finger.

Running away across the desert won't help, either. There's a madman on the throne of this little cess pit, and he won't be happy till he's incinerated the entire planet. So even if we could run, which we can't, there's really nowhere to run to. See?

This is reality, folks. Get used to it. We're in the brown soup up to our rosy red cheeks, and it's getting hotter by the minute.

"I tried to contact Treet and Calin," Yarden said at last, her voice sounding strained. "Sympathically."

Ianni scanned her friend's features minutely. Yarden had sustained a severe shock, there was no question about that; her eyes were dull and her expression slack, drained. "You don't have to tell us—" she began, leaning toward Yarden with her hand extended. But Gerdes, with a quick shake of her head, silenced her, and Ianni withdrew the hand.

In a moment Yarden continued. "I couldn't find Calin . . . I think she's dead. There was one horrible moment when I thought Treet was dead, too. But I forced the touch, and I reached him . . ." She raised her eyes and focused on the two women for the first time.

"I'm listening, Yarden." Ianni spoke softly, her tone full of compassion and reassurance.

"Go on, daughter," Gerdes said.

"There was . . . something—I didn't know what—like a shell. It covered him, would not let me touch him. I sensed Treet's presence, but could not touch him. When I persisted, the thing turned on me, forced me out. I—" Yarden's jaw worked silently as she lost the words for a moment.

She searched Ianni's eyes for understanding, and reached out a hand to take her friend's arm. "Ianni, I have never felt such hate in my life. It was ugly. Hideous! I got the feeling that if it could have killed me through my contact with Treet it would have—instantly, without hesitation . . . and then I remembered . . ."

Ianni grasped Yarden's hand. She could sense the great struggle taking place within, a war in which Yarden fought valiantly to remain stable and rational. But there was desperation growing in her eyes; the fight was taking a toll on her strength. Soon she would buckle under the strain. She looked to Gerdes for help.

"What did you remember, Yarden?" Gerdes asked, pressing Yarden to continue. "Say the words. Release their power over you."

A spasm of fear squirmed over Yarden's face. "Trabant . . ." She whispered the name. ". . . it wanted to kill me."

"But it didn't kill you," said Gerdes. "It couldn't harm you at all. You're safe now." Gerdes spoke soothingly, but her words had the opposite effect.

"No!" shouted Yarden shrilly. "You don't understand. I'm not worried about myself. It's Treet! He's in trouble and I can't . . . I don't know what to do."

Ianni thought for a moment. "The Preceptor will help us," she said, looking to Gerdes for affirmation. Gerdes nodded her approval. "We will go to her at once."

The three were silent as they walked to the Preceptor's tent, which looked like a large, multisectioned orange, white, and blue blossom—inverted and dropped onto the sand. Ianni and Yarden waited outside while Gerdes sought audience for them within.

They were admitted and entered. Globes of pale yellow sunstone rested in sconces in the sand, bathing the interior in soft illumination. Mentors Anthon and Eino were seated on cushions on either side of the Preceptor; Preben was in attendance as well. Anthon jumped up as soon as he saw Yarden. "Come in, please. Sit down," he said, offering his place next to the Preceptor.

The Preceptor gazed at Yarden, concern and compassion mingled in her eyes. She lifted a regal hand and helped Yarden down to the cushion beside her. Yarden felt healing power in the touch as her heart calmed, and a measure of peace returned.

"Don't be afraid, Yarden," said the Preceptor. There was strength in the simple words, strength Yarden could lean on. She settled down gratefully beside the Preceptor and looked at the faces ringed around her. She could feel the kindness and sympathy flowing out to her, and relaxed a little.

At a glance from the Preceptor, Anthon leaned forward and said, "We have been discussing the appearance of your friend Crocker. We would like to hear your thoughts."

"Yes," offered Mentor Eino, a dark-bearded man with an easy smile and large hairy hands. "We are concerned, as you must be, and seek guidance in this matter. You could help us a great deal by speaking candidly."

"I'll try," said Yarden softly. Music floated into the tent from outside, along with the sound of Fieri voices, a happy evensong rippling on the evening breeze. The sound was at once comforting and remote, as if taking place in a separate and distant sphere of existence, while what was happening in this tent at this moment was all that was real.

"I am afraid," Yarden began, "afraid for my friends—I fear

that something terrible has happened." She paused, and Ianni, sitting directly opposite, urged her with her eyes. "I tried to contact Orion Treet sympathically—that is, with my extrasensory abilities. After some effort I found him, but was not able to establish contact—something prevented me, opposed me."

She explained about her attempt to reach Treet and her encounter with the evil spirit of Trabant Animus, and how just the briefest touch had left her drained and frightened. "Treet is alive," she declared, "but he is in trouble. We've got to do something to help him."

The Preceptor nodded slightly, accepting Yarden's story. "Is there anything else you would like to tell us?"

"Why, yes," said Yarden, "there is something else. The talking fish—"

"The fish?" Anthon darted a glance to Eino and leaned forward. "Tell us."

"It may have been my imagination, but I believe they were trying to warn me of danger." She then told them of the strange "conversation" she'd had with Spinner and Glee.

Her listeners were silent, their faces grave when she finished. Preben, who had followed the story carefully, spoke up. "This is precisely the matter that brought me here tonight. I have been hearing similar stories these last two days."

Mentor Eino nodded thoughtfully. "I, too, received such a warning from the talking fish, although I could not interpret it half so well." He nodded in deference to Yarden's ability.

"Exactly what I was thinking!" Anthon interjected. "A remarkable telling."

It had not occurred to Yarden that her sympathic ability might have given her a special facility for understanding the talking fish. Although she had recognized at the time that the creature's "speech" was quite similar to the sympath's touch, she did not imagine that she would prove to be a first-class interpreter.

The Preceptor, who peered over interlaced fingers at Yarden, asked, "What do you believe to be the nature of this warning?"

Yarden paused to gather her thoughts. She wanted to be as precise as possible—Treet's life might depend on her answer. Closing her eyes to aid memory, Yarden thought back—was it only a day ago?—to her time with the fishes. She could feel the remarkable presence of the wise and gentle creatures, and once more experienced their pure and uninhibited expression.

The affect string came back to her with terrible clarity, magnified by her own still fresh experience with Trabant. She felt again the swarming, pestilential darkness; the mindless hate and unreasoning malice; the all-consuming malevolence of the hideous, twisted thing; the stifling threat of creeping doom.

Yarden shivered and began to speak. "There is darkness, a seething, potent darkness, and hate—such unbelievable and total hate; it wants to destroy us, to poison us with its evil, exterminate us." She opened her eyes slowly to find the others watching her, frowning deeply, thoughtfully. "I believe the fish were warning us about Dome," she concluded.

The word seemed to freeze them all for a moment. All except Yarden.

She looked triumphantly from face to face, thinking, There! I've said it. It *cannot* hurt me. Its only power is fear, and I have conquered that here tonight. I am free of its malignant influence, and I refuse to give in to it again. I am free!

SIXTY THREE

Giloon Bogney stared at Treet with murder in his eyes. The bhuj in his hand flicked back and forth, the discolored blade glinting dully in the dirty light. "Giloon could kill you, Fieri man," he growled.

"What would that solve? You'd never get out of here then." For the last two hours Treet had been explaining all the reasons he could think of why he couldn't lead a Dhog exodus out across Daraq, the Blighted Lands. Now he was tired and wanted to sleep.

"Huh!" Bogney grunted, rubbing the bhuj against his hairy cheek. Then he pushed the weapon into Treet's face. "Maybe Giloon be killing you now, seh?"

Treet pushed it away angrily. "Look, I don't want to play games with you. I want to go to sleep. So, unless you have any further—"

"You taking Dhogs to Fieri," Bogney insisted.

"I've told you twenty different ways: n-o—no! It's impossible. We'd never make it. I can't. I won't. Kill me if it will make you feel better, but we are *not* going to Fierra. Not now. Not tomorrow. Not ever. Get used to the idea. We are not going!"

Bogney stared at him with his good eye, his zigzag scar puckering angrily. "Dhogs don't needs you, Fieri man. We be going lonely anyhow."

Treet sighed and rolled his eyes. "We've been through this, Bogney. You have no idea what a desert is, what it's like out there. In fact, you don't even have the slightest idea of what it's like to breathe fresh air! Let me tell you, words can't describe how painful it is. That's what it's like. Real air would wipe you out in a second."

Bogney listened patiently. When Treet was done, he remarked in exactly the same stubborn tone as before: "Dhogs be going lonely anyhow."

"Okay! Fine! Go! Bon voyage! Vamoose!" Treet crossed his arms over his chest and flopped down on his bed. "You're the boss, Bogney. Happy motoring. Don't forget to write. Good-bye and good luck and good riddance!"

Bogney stared at Treet for a moment longer, turned, and walked slowly out, his much-stained cloak—the one Tvrdy had given him—sweeping the floor behind him, leaving only a residual reek in the air.

What a day! thought Treet. Tvrdy's giving up, Bogney wants to leave, and everyone else is just comatose from exhaustion. If that isn't enough, the Invisibles are systematically tearing the Old Section apart brick by crumbling brick. What can happen next?

Treet knew he should not have asked that question. He didn't really want an answer. But he got one anyway—in the form of a ripping blast that raked the compound outside, spattering rocks and dirt clods against the trembling walls of the building.

Treet rocketed straight up off the bed and reached the door without touching the floor. He was outside a split-second later as people came spilling out onto the field.

"Get back! Get back, you fools!"

Treet spun around to see Tvrdy racing toward him in a crouch. He saw the flash and saw Tvrdy throw himself to the ground, but before he could do likewise, the shock wave hit him and flattened him. Brick fragments and bits of debris pelted into him, followed by a rain of hot gravel.

Wriggling on his stomach, Treet inched over to Tvrdy. "I thought they weren't supposed to be this far in," shouted Treet, his voice lost amidst the roar still echoing in his ears.

"Those were long-range seekers." Tvrdy jerked his head up, looked around. "The Invisibles will follow them in, but we still have a little time to get out."

"I know a place—the Dhog cemetery. Bogney took me there. It's safe—hey!—where're you going?"

Tvrdy was already on his feet, dashing away, shouting at the top of his lungs. "Save the supplies and weapons! Everyone carry something! Supplies and weapons! Leave the rest!"

Two more blasts shook the compound, but they landed wide of the arsenal and supply buildings. Despite the rising panic, the evacuation got under way speedily and efficiently. Treet gathered himself and ran for the ramshackle hospital.

"What's happening?" Ernina asked as he came in, her square face floating in the light from a hand-held lantern. The moans of the injured filled the darkness.

"Invisibles—they've found us. We still have some time. We're getting out."

"I can't leave the wounded." She made to turn away.

Treet caught her arm and held on. "We'll take them with us. Get all your equipment together. I'll find Bogney."

He hurried out again into the confusion. Flares burned outside the supply buildings, casting the scene into garish relief. Treet made for the far end of the compound and struck off for the Dhog leader's lair. He met Bogney and several of his underlings flying toward him along the narrow street with torches in their hands.

Treet halted. "Bogney!"

The Dhogs ignored Treet, pushing past him without a word. "Bogney! I have to talk to you." He began running after them.

"Giloon be finished talking," The Dhog leader called back over his shoulder.

"Listen to me!"

The Dhogs ran on without looking back.

"I'll lead you to Fierra!" screamed Treet. "Do you hear me? Fierra! You win. I'll take you."

Bogney stopped and turned around. Treet ran to him, and the Dhog shoved a torch into Treet's face and glared at him. "Fieri man be lying big to Giloon?"

Treet shook his head, his breath coming in gasps. "No . . . I mean it. I'll take you, but you have to help me first—help me get the wounded out of the hospital. I'll need all the men you can get; we have to carry them to safety."

"Then you take us?"

"I don't know how, but I'll take you." Another blast lit up the night. A tottering ruin several blocks over tumbled, spilling its rubble into the street behind them. "We've got to hurry. Make up your mind."

"Lie to Dhogs, Giloon killing you dead."

"If I'm lying, you can kill me all you want later. Only come on, we've got to move now!"

Bogney whirled and sent two of his companions racing off in the opposite direction. Then he and the two remaining Dhogs followed Treet back to the compound.

● ● ● ● ● ●

"It will take too long to assemble all the Mentors," protested Yarden. "We must do something now."

The Preceptor smiled, but said firmly, "We will have the time we require. The Protector will look after your friend. The Mentors must be assembled, for wisdom is multiplied when many wise come together." She rose, signaling an end to the interview.

Yarden glanced around the ring of faces and saw that pressing the matter further would gain nothing; she had done all she could for one night. She rose and said, "Thank you, Preceptor, for hearing me out. If I have spoken more frankly than I might have, it is because I believe time is short."

The Preceptor went to Yarden and put her arms around her. "Think no negative thought, Yarden. Trust in the Infinite Father to care for His own. He will provide a Deliverer."

"I will try, Preceptor. It's hard, but I will try."

The Preceptor released Yarden and stood for a moment holding her at arm's length. "I detect in you the kindled flame of belief. I sensed it earlier when you entered this evening, and it is stronger now."

Yarden bowed her head. "It's true," she admitted shyly, then raised her head, face beaming. "And it feels wonderful!"

"Feed the flame, Yarden." The Preceptor squeezed her hands. "Feed it with all that is in you."

With that, Yarden said good-night and followed the others out. Anthon was waiting for her a few paces up the beach. The campfires were mostly out, and the songs had died away. The Fieri were turning in for the night. "Walk with me a little, would you?"

"Of course," replied Yarden and they fell into step with one another. She breathed in the night air and glanced at the hard, bright stars burning in the deep heavens. Empyrion didn't have a moon, but she didn't miss it—except at rare times, like now.

When they had walked a little way, Anthon said, "It went well tonight. You were very persuasive."

"Hmmm, I am convinced that trouble is coming," replied Yarden, uncertain what Anthon was trying to say.

"I don't doubt it at all. The Preceptor is right, however, in convening the Mentors before suggesting any action—if action is to be taken, since this will likely affect all Fieri."

"Why are you telling me this?"

Anthon gave a slight shrug and made a dismissive gesture
with his hands. "I have been in contact with Mathiax and Talus,"
he said simply.

"You have? How?"

"The Mentors' crystal."

Of course, thought Yarden, I should have remembered.
Each Mentor has one. "What did they say?"

Anthon stopped walking and stood for a moment facing
the great, restless shadow that was the sea. "Jaire—Talus' daughter, you remember—"

"I remember."

"Jaire had a dream—very much like the warning you re-
ceived from the fish. In fact, in describing the warning for the
Preceptor tonight, you used almost precisely the same words
Jaire used in describing it to Mathiax. Disturbingly precise."

"So you think there may be something to the warning."

Anthon gave her a sharp look and resumed the pace. "I said
I did not doubt it, and indeed I do not. But the matter is more
complicated than that. There are those among us who have
become persuaded that perhaps the time has come to try rees-
tablishing contact with Dome. You have to understand that to
change the course we have followed happily for many centuries
is no easy thing." He looked at Yarden curiously. "In your world,
change is more quickly accomplished, yes? I gather it's considered something of a virtue in itself."

"Often it is." Yarden looked skyward and sighed. "But you
make it sound as if it will take centuries to do something to help
Treet—and to save ourselves. If the warning is genuine, and we
all agree that it is, time is running out for all of us."

"This is why I wanted to speak to you now. You can help
us change, Yarden. Perhaps it is the very reason you were sent to
us in the first place. We need your spark, your dynamic energy.
We need you to show us the way."

Show them the way? I'm just barely crawling yet myself,
she thought. I can't show anybody the way.

Anthon continued. "It's true. That's part of the reason
Mathiax and Talus allowed Orion Treet to return to Dome."

"You mean they *used* him."

"No, not at all. They sensed the Infinite was working in
him and argued for his return, hoping he would somehow show

us how we were to proceed in this matter of approaching Dome."

"We're talking about life and death here. Treet was right: Dome is out to destroy us. Surely you understand self-defense."

"We understand that self-defense is a most subtle trap. Was there ever a time when aggression was not called self-defense?" Anthon shook his head sadly. "Those who worry overmuch about defending themselves build walls instead of bridges."

"Granted," said Yarden. "But you said you hoped Treet would show you how to proceed. Has he?"

"We believe he has. And we believe you are helping, too."

"Anthon, forgive me, it's late and I'm not thinking clearly. Just what is it you want from me?"

"Only your understanding. For us, it is not so important whether Dome destroys us—believe me. We would welcome our own destruction sooner than lift a hand against our destroyer if in destroying him we become like him.

"But a few of us—Mathiax, Talus, Eino, and myself, along with a few others—have come to believe that by leaving Dome to itself, we may actually be guilty of encouraging evil."

"You're serious?"

"Very serious. You see, evil left to itself breeds only evil. By separating ourselves, we have ensured that evil would grow."

Yarden nodded slowly, finally grasping what Anthon was trying to say to her. "I understand. How will they ever find the light if there is no one to show them?"

"Yes, that's it. By withholding the light we possess, we have condemned Dome to darkness."

"But that's not your fault. They chose it for themselves."

"Did they? Take away the light, and there can only be darkness. We were the light among them and we left, taking the light with us. Only a madman blames the darkness for being dark when he has withdrawn the light."

Yarden thought about this a long time and Anthon watched her closely. They stopped walking and faced each other. "Tomorrow," said Anthon, "we will confer with the Mentors. You will have an opportunity to speak, and I wanted you to know that you are not alone."

"Thank you, Anthon." Yarden took his hand and held it. "I think I know what to say now."

A few minutes later, Yarden approached Pizzle's tent. Starla and Pizzle were sitting in front of the tent, arms wrapped around each other. As Yarden came up, she heard Pizzle saying, ". . . so after Gandalf tangled with the Balrog, and the orcs got Boromir, the Fellowship just fell apart, scattered."

"What of the Ring-bearer?" asked Starla, eyes wide with wonder.

"Oh, Frodo and Sam escaped and went on by themselves. Gollum followed them and when . . ." Pizzle glanced up. "Oh, hi, Yarden, what's up?"

"I'm sorry to disturb you," she began, glancing at Starla.

Starla rose quickly. "Please excuse me, I will leave you two to talk."

"Hey, wait a minute! You don't have to—" Pizzle protested.

Starla smiled and put a hand to his face. "It is getting late, and I must go anyway. Yarden wishes to speak privately with you. We will be together again tomorrow."

"Thank you," said Yarden. "That's a very nice young woman," she said, watching Starla walk away.

"Yeah," admitted Pizzle. "So why'd you run her off?"

"I have to talk to you."

"So talk."

"Pizzle, how much do you know about atomic bombs?"

SIXTY
FOUR

The last Dhogs carried the last wounded man from the compound ten minutes before the first Invisibles arrived. The rebels were struggling through pinched alleyways and dark corridors not two hundred meters from New America Square, each one laden with as much as he could possibly carry, when the explosions streaked the darkness behind them.

"It looks like they found Tvrdy's surprise," Treet muttered.

"That might slow them down," said Cejka, who was leading a platoon to cover their retreat. He turned to watch the torchlight procession wind through the desolate streets. "You go on, and keep them moving up ahead. I'll stay here and watch for a little while."

Treet jogged heavily on, urging those ahead of him to hurry. Ernina, bent double by the weight of the medical instruments and supplies she carried, labored alongside the line of wounded. The few that could walk tottered along weakly; the rest were slung in blanket-contrived hammocks carried by Dhogs. Treet came up beside her. "Are you going to make it? Or should I send someone back to help out?"

In the wildly flickering light her eyes glinted with determination as she glanced up at him. "I'll make it—might take all night, but I'll make it."

"If you get to lagging behind, sing out. I'll get you some relief."

Treet hitched up his own heavy packs and trundled off. Evacuation was no picnic, and the place they were headed for was no garden spot. He only hoped it would not turn out to be needlessly symbolic: making their last stand in the Dhog cemetery. At least it had two strong points to recommend it. One, it was difficult to get to if one didn't know precisely where one was going. And two, it was close to a secret exit which led to Bolbe Hage.

Still, being run out of their base was a stroke of bad luck, to put it mildly. They had counted on being able to stay there, rest, and get reorganized in their own good time. Now it appeared as if they would have to do it on the fly, if at all.

Up to the moment when the enemy began bombarding the training field, Treet had believed that a miracle would happen and that they would, by some genius masterstroke, deal Jamrog the *coup de grace;* or, if not, that they would be rescued. The chances of either thing happening grew more remote by the minute as Treet sensed time running out. If there was going to be any saving, it would have to come soon—while there was still something to save.

The evacuation was divided up into three stages or groups. Group One, under Tvrdy's direction, was in charge of weaponry and supplies necessary for survival; they had gone ahead to lead the way. Group Two was the wounded and injured, helped along by the Dhogs Bogney had provided and anyone else Treet had been able to commandeer for the task. Group Three was the Tanais and Rumon soldiery defending the rear to ensure a successful evacuation.

They reached the gloomy cremation site without incident. Piling their burdens on the ground around the massive burning mound, now studded with flagging torches instead of flaming corpses, exhausted people dropped where they stopped and sank into sweat-drenched slumber.

Treet and Ernina worked to make the casualties as comfortable as possible under the conditions, while Tvrdy moved like a ghost through the silent encampment, taking a mental inventory of what they had been able to save. Cejka, Kopetch, and Fertig, having arranged for a nominal watch between them, settled down to rest. Bogney disappeared somewhere into the Dhogs' labyrinthine fastness with a few of his assistants.

When he had done all he could for the wounded, Treet found himself a flat spot to stretch out and sank down gratefully among the stacks of gear. He was asleep as soon as his head touched the ground.

• • • • • •

Diltz examined the huge carapace with exacting care. Three Saecaraz magicians hung back uncertainly, exchanging nervous glances and fidgeting in their black-and-silver striped yoses. At a nearby workbench several Nilokerus magicians pored over an old plastic-bound text, murmuring as they vocalized the words written there.

His inspection completed, Diltz straightened and put his hands on the metallic skin. He closed his eyes and spread his thin lips in a sick smile. "I feel its power," he whispered. "Listen!" He pressed his ear to the smooth surface. "It speaks! 'Death to Fieri!' it says—'I am death to Empyrion's enemies.'"

He cocked his head to peer at the magicians. "You have done well. The Supreme Director will reward you personally." His lips twisted in a paroxysm of joy. "How soon may I inform our leader of the demise of his enemies?"

The foremost magician stepped cautiously up. "The text, Director—" He indicated the Nilokerus scanning the ancient document.

"The text, yes. What of it?"

"The text is, shall we say, vague on several points. It is . . . ah, our feeling is that . . . perhaps—"

"Speak, man! What are you trying to say? Is the weapon serviceable?"

"Oh, yes. We believe it is. The power beneath its metal shell is not, as far as we can determine, diminished by time."

"Then what is it?"

The magician hesitated and looked to his comrades for support. "We do not yet know how to . . . the word—what's the word, Geblen?"

One of the red-hooded Nilokerus raised his head. "Eh, *launch*, I believe is the word you require."

"Launch. It only remains to discover how to launch the weapon."

Diltz peered at the magician skeptically. "What is this launch?"

"The, ah—" He made a pushing motion in the air with his hands. "The sending forth of the weapon."

"The sending forth? How is it sent forth?"

"Why, through the air, Director. Or so we believe."

Diltz looked at the man as if he'd lost his mind. "Thrown through the air? By what means?"

"Engines, Director." He pointed to the rear of the weapon, the flaring exhaust ports of three huge rocket engines.

Diltz waved a hand impatiently. "Well, how long until you learn to operate these engines?"

The Saecaraz shook his head sadly. "As you see, we are reading the texts even now. Several passages look promising."

"Get more Readers. I want this weapon operational as soon as possible—two days! I'll wait two days and no more."

The magician inclined his head and went back to the others. Diltz took a last look around the Archives, and at the odd-looking death machine with its stubby, knife-thin protrusions along its narrow flanks, its snub nose and bulging engines, gray skin gleaming under a row of grid lights. He rubbed the long body with his hand and then departed, rejoining his Mors Ultima bodyguard at the door.

SIXTY
FIVE

Most of the Fieri had gone down to the sea to meet the talking fish once more. But a few, the Mentors among them and designated leaders such as Gerdes and Preben, had stayed behind to sit in council with the Preceptor.

After her talk with Anthon, and her session with Pizzle, Yarden had returned to her tent where she lay awake most of the night composing in her mind the argument she would use in helping persuade the Fieri to abandon their age-old policy of nonaggression and nonintervention and go help Treet.

They assembled in the clear morning air out beside the Preceptor's tent. The bright, white sun was warm on the sand as Yarden joined the group, taking her place in the large circle beside Gerdes and across from Anthon. Pizzle was nowhere to be seen; neither, for that matter, was Crocker.

The beauty of the day would work against her, she thought as she knelt down, digging her bare toes into the sand, feeling the cool, moist layer just below the warm, dry stuff on top. The sound of laughter and splashing water drifted across the beach. The blue backs and fins of the talking fish flashed in the jade-green water as the Fieri sported with the playful creatures. How does one take seriously a description of hell when surrounded by heaven?

Preben worked his way around the circle, distributing what appeared to be clothing tags to each person in attendance. He stopped before Yarden and handed her one of the tags. She saw that it was a flat, triangular card with a crystal affixed to the front. A thread-thin wire hung from the back of the card, and on the end of the thread was a small plug.

"You can hear with this," he explained. "It's tuned to the Preceptor's crystal."

Gerdes helped Yarden fasten the tag to her chinti and showed her how to place the plug in her ear. Anthon caught her eye across the circle. He smiled and lifted his hand in a gesture which imparted confidence. Yarden returned his smile and settled in to wait, using meditation calming techniques.

When she opened her eyes again, the Preceptor was taking her place. A large green-flecked crystal was placed on a stand in the center of the circle. Yarden put the earplug in her ear. There came a pleasant chiming sound and Mathiax's voice said, "Good morning, Preceptor. The Mentors are convened as you requested. We await your pleasure."

The Preceptor acknowledged those in the circle. "The importance of our discussion this morning is not to be underestimated because of the informality imposed by circumstance," she began, speaking slowly, solemnly.

"We understand," answered Mathiax; his voice was so distinct, so present he seemed to be standing in the center of the circle. "Your instructions have been reviewed, and we agree that a timely examination of this matter dictates such necessity."

"Then we may proceed."

"Very well, Preceptor. Mentor Talus has prepared an opening statement. As Clerk of the College of Mentors, I recognize his seniority."

"We will hear Mentor Talus' statement."

"My friends," began Talus, his voice a small aural earthquake. "I will be brief.

"It is now over eleven centuries since our fathers in their wisdom terminated all relations with Dome, leaving them to their evil. I don't need to remind you that the great riches and blessed life the Fieri have enjoyed in the intervening years are but a foretaste of the Infinite's intent for His people.

"However, less than half a solar cycle ago, Travelers were found alive in the Blighted Lands. Certain of the Mentors and myself have come to look upon the arrival of the Travelers as a signal that the time of our isolation from Dome is ending.

"We believe that the Infinite is speaking to us through the presence of the Travelers and that we must listen very carefully to learn what direction we must choose."

Talus hesitated, and it seemed to Yarden that he had been about to say something else and instead said, "Please, my friends, I urge you to open your hearts and minds to the voice of the Teacher."

There was a little silence and then the Preceptor said, "Thank you, Talus. Your words are well chosen. Since we are reminded that time is critical, I think we will be well served to hear from one of the Travelers now."

Yarden glanced around to discover every eye on her and realized the Preceptor meant her. Anthon nodded encouragingly. She took a deep breath. "Thank you, Preceptor," she said, and swallowed hard.

"I am Yarden." Her voice quavered slightly. "Although I have lived among you only a short time, I have been enriched and blessed. I have learned of the Infinite Father's love for His people, and for me.

"I have also learned something of your past, and the reason why you have chosen to allow Dome to go its own way. Rightly, you remember the grief of that terrible day—the day you call the Burning.

"Yes, you remember the grief; it is with you still. But you do not remember the horror. That too should be remembered. Let me remember for you now."

Yarden closed her eyes and began to speak in a hushed voice. No one moved or made a sound.

"The morning sun shone down on green fields around the sparkling cities on the plain. Children played, lovers awakened in one another's arms, students returned to their lessons, workers to their jobs, and the Fieri began a new day of living.

"As the sun climbed higher into the sky, you paused to eat your midday meal. Some of you took food outdoors to enjoy the beauty of your world from the shade of fine old trees. The breeze ruffled your hair and bathed your limbs. You napped and dreamed, or laughed with your families and friends around the table.

"The sunlight dimmed momentarily as a shadow passed in front of the sun. It was nothing; a cloud perhaps. But a moment later you heard the roar of engines and the whistling scream of the missiles as they fell. You looked up.

"The blue flash—brighter than ten thousand suns, yet only one hundred meters in diameter—blinded you instantly as the bomb exploded eight hundred meters above the ground. In that split second when the flash was still traveling earthward, the hypocenter reached a temperature of over three million degrees—many times hotter than the surface of your sun.

"On the ground below, stone buildings melted into pools of glowing lava, metal bridges burst into flame, as did the rivers under them, and ceramic roof tiles boiled. Your people, still looking skyward, the first intimations of terror just beginning to register in the cells of their brains, simply vaporized, the fluids of their bodies turning directly into steam and gas—leaving their shadows etched on walls and pavement.

"Due to ionization, the churning air filled with the pungent, electric smell of ozone as the blue, sunlit sky flashed to yellow and green and then red-brown as the massive fireball spread, roaring skyward on a lethal plume twenty kilometers high. The vile mushroom cloud rose so high that its intense heat condensed water vapor, and a viscid black rain began to fall— sticky wet lumps of hot radioactive mud sluiced from the skies to pelt down on the survivors.

"In the first tenth of a second, every living thing in a radius within nine kilometers of ground zero was incinerated, and every building, tree, and shrub, anything standing above the ground level, was blasted into oblivion.

"A little further out from the epicenter, the damage was more shocking. At a radius of thirty kilometers, people were charcoalized. Mothers fleeing with their babies in their arms, men running to protect their families, everyone standing in the open air when the heat flash swept by was turned into a charcoal statue.

"Winds of one thousand kilometers per hour followed the heatflash. The terrible winds lifted lighter objects right off the ground or sucked them out through doors and windows of buildings. People were picked up and hurled through the air with incredible force; they became missiles traveling at ferocious speeds to smash into walls and solid objects. Skulls, vertebrae, and long bones were pulverized on impact.

"Those safe from the winds did not escape the tremendous overpressures that accompanied them. These overpressures produced instantaneous rupture of the lungs and eardrums. Windows were extruded from their frames by the overpressure and then burst into millions of needlelike shards which sliced through the air, penetrating human flesh and producing hideous lacerations.

"At about fifty kilometers from the epicenter, the heat from the explosion spontaneously ingnited trees and vegetation. People were turned into human torches where they stood, and every building became a crematorium.

"Miraculously, however, some of you survived to wander dazed and bewildered through the glowing ashes, looking for loved ones, lost in a featureless landscape. All landmarks, all orienting points had vanished. Nothing remained but a flat, burned-over prairie.

"You felt little pain at first. The greater shock of the desolation left no room for normal human suffering. You walked around naked, your clothing having been blown off or burned away. You felt no shame or immodesty, for it was impossible to tell men from women since every sizzled body looked alike.

"Friends and family members could not recognize one another. Everyone had lost hair and eyebrows; most had their facial features burned off. A man might have the imprint of his nose 'photographed' on his cheek, or the remnant of an ear grafted to his neck. Little was left but nondescript indentations for eyes and nose, a lipless slit for a mouth.

"You reached out to help the more severely injured and drew back hands filled with skin and flesh that slid off bare bone in charred gobbets. Your wounds smoked when dipped in water, and you walked like scarecrows with your arms outstretched to prevent raw skin surfaces from rubbing and sticking together.

"The lakes and reservoirs were choked with swollen red bodies—victims who had been boiled alive when the water turned to steam. Anyone who happened to witness the flash was instantly blinded, their eyesockets burned hollow. You staggered through the wreckage as the fluid from your melted eyes ran down your cheeks.

"In the days that followed, many survivors died horribly, retching blood, skin peeling away in sheets. Within twenty-four hours, even those survivors who had escaped serious injury began dying by the thousands. Their brain cells were damaged by radiation, causing their brains to swell inside their craniums and producing severe nausea, vomiting, diarrhea, followed by drowsiness, tremors, seizures, convulsions, and finally, massive internal hemorrhages and respiratory failure.

"Fallout and radiation continued to take a toll as the weeks passed. At first you felt merely weak or tired; then you began to notice that your hair was falling out, your teeth hurt and your gums bled, you lost your appetite, vomited, and developed bloody diarrhea, you bled under your skin, painful mouth ulcers formed, infections set in, producing fever and coma. Death came slowly, a result of fluid loss and starvation.

"You died and watched your loved ones die: by the thousands, instantly, and then with agonizing slowness, one by one. Amidst the ruins of your fair homeland, you experienced the ultimate suffering that hate can devise."

When Yarden finished, she opened her eyes. The Fieri sat in stunned silence, eyes closed, each face shimmering with silent tears. The day seemed to have grown colder, the sun more distant. The wind and waves had stilled.

"This happened long ago," said Yarden simply. "But it will happen again soon. My fellow Traveler, Orion Treet, predicted it and he was right. I know that now. The evil of Dome is growing. Even now its hatred burns against us; soon it will reach out for us.

"Treet went back to Dome to try to stop his prediction from coming true. He is there now giving his life to prevent the madness from consuming us once more. But time grows short, and Treet needs help.

"The Protector has sent His messengers, the talking fish, to warn us. Crocker, who returned to Dome with Treet, has appeared in our midst a broken, pathetic husk: another warning of the malicious intent of Dome. We have been forewarned."

Yarden paused and looked around the council ring. What were they thinking? Were they with her? Only Anthon appeared supportive, gazing at her directly. It only remained for her to make the appeal.

"We have been forewarned," she repeated. "Now we must decide what we will do. As for that, I have no suggestions. I only know that somehow I must go to Dome to add my life, my light, to that of those who struggle against the growing darkness.

"That's all I have to say. Thank you for listening to me." She bowed her head in a fervent prayer that her words had done their work.

The Preceptor drew herself up. "Yarden has spoken most persuasively. Is there anyone to challenge her argument?"

The voice of Mathiax sounded over the earplug. "The Clerk acknowledges Mentor Linan."

Mentor Linan cleared his throat. "My friends, I am deeply moved by Traveler Yarden's words, as are we all. I wish to remind this assembly, however, that our response to Dome was chosen from the first. We cannot intervene and still remain Fieri.

We have chosen our path and must not abandon it at the first hint of danger. Whatever happens, our strength is not in ourselves, but in the Infinite. By Him we stand or fall."

Mentor Bohm answered him at once. "Mentor Linan speaks for many, no doubt. But I would remind him that before abandoning Dome to its evil, our 'first' response was to reach out to our brothers. We did not choose our path; it was forced upon us, for there seemed no way to be reconciled to such a hard-hearted and deadly enemy.

"The agony and horror of the Burning, so vividly rendered for us by Yarden, was fresh when we devised our plan. And while it is true that we live only by the Infinite Father's light, does it follow that we must continue on a path that has come to an end?

"We can no longer allow Dome to breed its darkness and destruction. We are responsible if we withhold the help we could give. We all know that he who commits an evil, sins against the Infinite. But he who permits an evil he could prevent is guilty of the same sin. Is this not a precept among us?

"We are guilty of that sin, my friends. Too long have we hidden our light from those who labor in darkness, thereby permitting evil to flourish. I believe the time has come to seek a new way. I acknowledge Yarden's appeal. We must go to Dome. We must find a way to arrest the evil before it destroys again."

Bohm had no sooner finished speaking than another Mentor took the floor. "Mentor Bohm is right to remind us of a most apt precept," the speaker said. "But how do we really know what Dome intends? The presence of the Travelers, remarkable though it is, does not equate with danger. For all we know, Dome is simply living out its perverse destiny. There is no cause for alarm here, surely."

And so it went: one Mentor agreeing with Yarden, and another disagreeing, the arguments seesawing back and forth, opinion swaying first one way and then the other. Yarden became weary of the talk, and disheartened. Only Anthon, Talus, and Bohm appeared to support an expedition to Dome outright. Mathiax also supported Yarden's appeal, but as Clerk of the College, he could not speak for one position or the other. The majority seemed against making any radical changes in policy regarding Dome.

As the arguments went on and on, Yarden left the circle

and went down to walk along the water's edge. She walked far up the strand, and when the Fieri encampment was small in the distance she sat down and gazed out across the shining bowl of the bay toward the chalk-colored cliffs.

Beyond those cliffs, and beyond the arid uplands lay the deep sanctuary of the Blue Forest, and beyond the forest rolled the stark and empty hill country where Dome sat brooding.

I tried, Orion, she thought. God knows I tried. I did the best I knew how. I'm sorry if it wasn't enough.

Then she put her head down and cried.

A dismal daylight awakened the rebels to the task of finding a new home among the reeking ruins of the Dhog cemetery. The prospects were not promising. The place was even more desolate and depressing than Treet remembered; besides the cremation mound, there was not another standing structure for a kilometer around. The wasted trees and rock heaps scattered over the area offered little cover and no protection.

Tvrdy and Kopetch paced off the perimeter and returned grumbling. "It's little more than hopeless," announced Kopetch. "Indefensible from any tactical point of view."

"We'll move as soon as we can find a better place," Tvrdy replied. "I will have scouts begin searching at once."

Piipo spoke up. "The Hyrgo fields are not far from here, I believe—unless I am much mistaken. Were we to go there, we would be close to our food source."

"It is not far," Cejka said, "but access is a problem. The Invisibles could reach us easily there."

"They'll find us anywhere we go," remarked Fertig. "It's only a matter of time now." He stared around the group helplessly. "It's over," he muttered softly to himself.

Treet ignored Fertig's comment. "What about the Bolbe exit?"

Tvrdy considered this for a moment. "It has possibilities."

"Isn't it a corridor?" asked Cejka.

"A tunnel," said Tvrdy. "Originally used for drainage."

"A tunnel, yes," Kopetch nodded, working it out in his head. "Even if they found us, they couldn't cut off our escape unless they somehow discovered its exit. And we'd only have one front to defend."

"An excellent idea!" Tvrdy beamed. "We'll check it out at once."

"Anywhere would have to be better than here." Treet winced as he looked around. "I've got a bad feeling about this place."

The rest of the day was spent taking stock of the supplies and arranging things for the next move. The camp was silent—depressed, thought Treet, by the dreary surroundings. By mid-morning the scouts Tvrdy had sent out returned, and also Bogney, whom no one had seen since the night before.

He came with six Dhog women dressed in frayed shreds of clothing, each one bearing a rag-wrapped burden on her back. They came into camp a few minutes after the scouts. "I wondered where they had hidden the women and children," said Kopetch as he watched the women enter warily.

Bogney and his entourage proceeded to the center of the camp where Treet, Tvrdy, and the others waited. The newcomers stared uneasily at the Tanais, Rumon, and Hyrgo gathered around. "Dhogs bringing some fine gift," Bogney explained, motioning for the women to put down their burdens.

"A gift?" wondered Tvrdy. "Why a gift?"

"Dhogs leaving soon. We be sharing goods with friends, thinking never see no more again."

Tvrdy shot a dark glance at a stricken Treet. "Oh? Where are you going, Bogney?"

"Fierra," he announced triumphantly. "Fieri man here be leading us." He grinned hugely at Treet and held out his hands. One of the women unwrapped her burden to bring forth a large plastic bladder filled with a dark liquid. "Tonight we sharing good drink. Tomorrow we gone."

"Is that so?" Tvrdy swung to face Treet directly.

Treet's mouth worked before the words came tumbling out. "Wait a minute here, Bogney. I didn't say *when* we would go. I only said I'd take you."

"No making big noises now. Giloon decides. Dhogs ready."

Tvrdy smiled suddenly. "We accept your gift," he said, picking up one of the bladders. He opened it and raised it to his nose. He coughed and shut his eyes, thrusting the bladder from him. "It is most thoughtful of you."

"We be drinking tonight. Tomorrow be going to Fierra."

Treet stared at Tvrdy as if the Tanais had parted company with his senses. As soon as the liquor had been carefully put away, Treet took Tvrdy aside. "What do you mean by encouraging this ridiculous idea?"

"What do you mean by making irrational bargains with him? You know Dhogs are like children."

"I had to do something. It was the only way I could get him to help us evacuate the wounded. We couldn't leave them for the Invisibles to find."

"Why not?" Tvrdy fixed Treet with a hard, implacable gaze. "Thanks to you, we have saved our wounded. They require food and constant attention; they are a drain on our limited resources. They will die here anyway because we cannot care for them properly. Why not let the Invisibles solve the problem quickly and easily?"

Treet listened, horrified. "You don't mean it. Do you hear what you're saying? You sound like Jamrog!"

Tvrdy made a face. "It is the voice of reason."

"Reason? It's insanity. This is exactly the kind of coldhearted expediency that loosed the monster in the first place. Tvrdy, listen to me. I know. I've read the records. When the Red Death broke out, the survivors fought back with everything they had; but when it looked like they couldn't win, they began cutting their losses. They abandoned the dying and sealed themselves into survival cells. They began systematically reducing civilization to base utilitarianism."

Tvrdy frowned. "It was life or death."

"And they chose death, Tvrdy. Don't you see? Whenever some lives become expendable, whenever some are written off for whatever reason—this one is nonviable, this one nonproductive, this one nonfunctional, this one nonconforming to the party line—when the weak or disagreeable lose their humanity—it's death, not life."

"It was necessary," replied Tvrdy sullenly. "Inevitable."

"True human beings do not make deals with death, Tvrdy. It may well be inevitable, but civilized people do not give up on life; they do not embrace death just because life becomes too hard."

"What do you know about it?"

"I told you. I read the records," said Treet. "Feodr Rumon wrote it down. I know what happened."

"You would have done the same thing. Anyone would."

"No, Tvrdy. Some would, it's true. But not everyone. They had a choice—there's always a choice. They chose wrong, Tvrdy. The ancestors of Dome chose death rather than life. It was wrong, and you've been paying for it ever since."

"It can't be undone now."

"No, it can't be undone, but we don't have to repeat the same mistake. We can choose differently. If we're ever to be free of the madness, we have to choose the right way."

Tvrdy glared at Treet in silence. It was difficult to tell what the Tanais leader was thinking. "I don't see what a few wounded have to do with this. They will die anyway."

"If you really believe that," said Treet softly, "then there's no hope for us."

With that, Treet walked off. "Think about it, Tvrdy," he said turning back. Tvrdy stood where he'd left him, staring at the ground. "You know I'm right."

· · · · · ·

Jaire walked back and forth on the curving crown of the hill. The towering obelisk, with its ring of smaller obelisks throwing long afternoon shadows down the green hill, pointed heavenward as if poised for imminent flight.

She stopped when she heard the chime, and turned toward the amphidrome. Talus emerged with Mathiax close behind him, the dismissal chime still ringing in the air. "Don't be angry, Talus," Mathiax said. "It is more than we had a right to hope for."

Jaire hurried toward them. "What is the decision?" She glanced from one to the other of them hopefully, saw their expressions, and asked, "What's wrong? Will they not allow us to go?"

"One fleet only," replied Talus tersely. "And Mathiax is to stay."

"We will be in constant communication," said Mathiax. "I will be as close as your own skin."

"It isn't the same." Talus stood woodenly, arms folded across his massive chest—like a tree taking root on the sculpted green lawn of the amphidrome.

"Accept the wisdom of the College," soothed Mathiax. "It is for the best."

"The best? The best? It is too little and too late."

Mathiax closed his eyes and shook his head gently. "It is in the Protector's good time. You are upset or you would agree."

Grim-faced Mentors began streaming from the amphi-drome and passing silently around them. Bohm approached and joined them. "I have spoken with the crew. We are clear to depart as soon as you are ready, Talus. The others will leave in the morning."

"Come," said Mathiax. "I'll go with you to the airfield."

"We're leaving at once?" Jaire glanced around expectantly.

Talus took his daughter's hands. "I am sorry, Jaire. I should have told you straight away. You are to stay here as well."

She pulled her hands away. "Is Preben going?"

"Yes. Preben, Anthon, and Yarden will be picked up at the bay."

"Who else is going?"

"Besides myself, only Bohm and his fleet crew."

Jaire smiled defiantly. "Then I will go, too. I am part of Bohm's crew." Her expression dared anyone to gainsay her.

Mathiax and Talus looked at one another. Bohm explained, "She is part of the emergency medical support group."

"The College did not say anything about medical support," said Mathiax. "It's your decision, Talus."

He gazed at his daughter. "No, Jaire. It will be difficult and dangerous. I can't allow it."

"Since it's dangerous, you may need medical support. I am going." Jaire gazed steadily at her father and saw him weaken. She laid a hand on his arm. "It was my dream, remember. I am part of this. You cannot deny me."

Mathiax watched them both. "Talus," he said stepping close, "Jaire is right. The dream was given to her. She has been called. It is in the Infinite's hands; trust in the Protector."

Talus assented. "I am overruled by a higher authority. Go say good-bye to your mother, collect your things, and meet us at the airfield. We will leave as soon as you return."

Jaire smiled slyly. "I have already anticipated your decision, Father. Mother knows, and my things are in the evee. I am ready now."

Bohm clapped his hands once and started toward the wait-ing vehicle. "Then we leave at once."

• • • • • •

It was near sunset when Anthon came to her. Yarden was sitting with her chin on knees, eyes closed. She heard the gritty squeak of his tread on the wet sand and stirred.

"Did I wake you?" he asked as he came to stand over her.

She opened her eyes slowly, and lifted a hand. Anthon took it and helped her to her feet. "I wasn't asleep," Yarden answered. "I was praying."

"Ah, yes." He paused, gazing raptly at Yarden. "You know, as I came up to you just now you looked just like my wife. From a distance, that is. She was another one who loved her solitude. I would find her like this—out alone somewhere—and I'd ask her what she was doing. 'Praying,' she'd say, exactly like you did just now. Or, 'Being alone with my thoughts.' That was another one."

They began to walk back to the encampment. "I didn't know you were married, Anthon. Were you very much in love?"

"Yes, yes. It was a good marriage. I loved her as much as any man could, and maybe more."

"What happened?"

"It was an accident. She was with our son on a boat; they were out for the day sailing on Prindahl. A storm came up, and they were too far out. I think the boat swamped, and they drowned. We never found the boat or the bodies. They just sailed off one morning and never came back."

"How tragic! I'm sorry, Anthon—I wouldn't have asked if I'd had any idea—"

"Please, it's all right. I don't mind. I have nothing but good memories. I get lonely for them sometimes, it's true, but it only serves to make our eventual reunion the more joyful. I know that we'll be together again one day. In the meantime, there is much to do. I am needed here."

"I'll say," said Yarden, taking Anthon's arm. "I have a feeling I'm going to need all the friends I can get."

"You know how the council decided?" He cocked an eyebrow quizzically.

"Well, let's just say I have a feeling my speech didn't sway the masses."

"Sadly, no. We could have hoped for a better response, there's no denying that. But we did gain something—perhaps more than you suspect."

Yarden looked up sharply. "What? Tell me," she said. "You must!"

"I thought you knew everything."

Yarden stopped. "Please, don't joke about this. It's too important."

"You're right. Forgive me; I was taken by your b—" He hesitated, turned, and looked out across the bay. "I forgot myself for a moment."

Yarden felt a warmth envelop her. "It . . . it's all right, Anthon," she said softly. "What did you come to tell me?" She let her hand slide away from his arm. They began walking again.

"The Preceptor has decided to allow a balon fleet to travel to Dome to assess the situation."

"Really? That's wonderful!"

"It is a beginning. Talus and Bohm argued most eloquently, and I did what I could, of course. But in the end the College remained unconvinced of the threat. It was all we could do to get them to agree to one fleet—six balons. They only consented because the Preceptor supported the idea—it was her suggestion, in fact. A compromise. Talus wanted six fleets; the Mentors were against sending any. The Preceptor suggested a fleet in case there were people to bring out, and the Mentors relented."

"But still, it's a victory. How soon can we leave?"

"You can believe Talus and Mathiax were already prepared. A balon is probably on the way to pick us up now."

"That'll take weeks!" exclaimed Yarden, suddenly realizing just how far away from Fierra they were. "Can't we leave for Dome now?" The notion was absurd, and Yarden admitted it as soon as the words were out. "Forget I said that. It's just that . . . well, isn't there a faster way?"

Anthon chuckled. "A balon can travel quickly. It won't take them as long as it took us. Two or three days. Anyway, you don't want them to go without you, do you?"

"You'll go, too?"

"Yes, and Preben has volunteered. Talus is going, as you know, and Bohm also, with his regular balon crews. That's all."

"Mathiax?"

"In the Preceptor's absence, he must stay in Fierra."

"Maybe I could get Pizzle to come, too. He might be useful in the clinch."

Anthon stopped and took her by the shoulders. "Yarden, this is to be an observation tour, not an invasion. We do not go in force—the Fieri have no weapons in any case."

Yarden glanced at her feet. She nodded. "I understand. I got a little carried away." She raised her eyes hopefully. "But whatever we can do to help Treet, we'll do, right?"

"Whatever we can do to help, we will do. Beyond that . . ." Anthon shrugged. "We will have to wait and see."

He stared at her for a moment without speaking. Yarden became self-conscious under his gaze and looked away, feeling that strange warmth again. "The Preceptor," he said finally, "would like to see you now. We'd better get back."

SIXTY
SEVEN

From the suddenness of the attack, Treet guessed the Invisibles had been in position and only waiting for daylight to commence the slaughter. At sunrise the rebel camp lay in sodden sleep, having dosed themselves to the point of numbness with the Dhog's rough, bitter liquor. Shared out among the men, there had not been enough to actually liberate anyone from his senses. Still, the attack caught them asleep—disaster for a soldier.

The first blasts brought the rebels to their feet. They dove for their weapons and began returning fire while the echoes still boomed from Dome's crystal shell. The rebels understood that if they did not win, this would be their last fight. They fought with dire ferocity, driving the Invisibles' assault force back by the sheer force of their fury.

When they saw their hopes for a quick victory evaporate under the rebel's blistering defense, the Invisibles withdrew to surround the cemetery mound and dig in.

Tvrdy, standing atop a stack of weapons cases, shouted orders to his men. Cejka and Kopetch dashed here and there around him, organizing the equipment for transport. "What's going on?" asked Treet as he came running up.

"We're going to try to reach the Bolbe tunnel," yelled Cejka as each blast showered smoking clods and rock dust over them.

"We'll never make it," said Treet. "It's too far. There's nothing between here and there but dead trees and broken ground."

"Treet!" shouted Tvrdy. "Help or get out of the way. We're going. We can't stay here."

"What about the wounded?" Treet demanded, hands on hips.

Tvrdy glared at him and then turned away, saying, "We take them with us—of course."

The next few hours were a nightmare of death and searing fire. The rebels—Dhogs and Hyrgo loaded like pack animals—

retreated en masse, their exit covered by Tanais and Rumon marksmen. The Invisibles sensed victory close at hand and pressed the retreat hard, hoping to divide and scatter the rebels. Casualties on both sides were heavy.

Treet, laboring alongside Ernina, assisted the wounded and helped keep up the flagging spirits of those around him as, meter by meter, they fought their way to the safety of the Bolbe tunnel. Each meter cost them dearly. When a man fell, not only did they lose a soldier—they lost the supplies he carried.

But Tvrdy, displaying superhuman leadership and tenacity, kept them all together and moving ahead, while the marksmen put down a blanket of fire behind them. This way, the Invisibles were unable to move into position ahead of them and cut off the retreat.

Firebolts streaked through the crackling air as the rebels pushed on. The Dhogs, caught in camp when the attack started, had no choice but to join the fight. They had planned to be away at daybreak, heading for Fierra with Treet leading the way.

Giloon Bogney cursed and gnashed his teeth, and worked himself into a purple rage at the Invisibles for stealing his chance to leave Dome forever. But he also put his head down and applied himself nerve-and-sinew to the task of getting himself and his people to safety.

It seemed to take an eternity to reach the Bolbe tunnel.

In actual fact, it took forty minutes to travel a distance slightly more than two kilometers. Treet was among the first to reach the tunnel. He saw the tunnel's mouth yawning from a low earthen bank covered with dry shriveled brush. He ran ahead and ducked inside. The interior was dark and cool, with a fetid, musty odor.

He took a quick look around and dashed outside again as the Invisibles, now comprehending the rebels' destination, redoubled their effort. The shriek of their weapons filled the air like a scream of rage.

The Rumon and Tanais marksmen, limping from hillock to ditch to rubble pile, dug in to face the attack while their comrades scurried to safety.

Treet helped herd the wounded inside the tunnel, and then went back to help the Hyrgo carry equipment and supplies while the Tanais and Rumon formed a semicircle around the

tunnel mouth to cover them. Tvrdy stood in the center, direct-
ing the fire and urging on the struggling carriers.

Treet saw one Tanais crumple and fall, and Kopetch appeared in the gap, snatching up the man's weapon before it
touched the ground, firing away.

The Invisibles gathered their forces together and charged
the rapidly dwindling defenses. Treet, sweating and panting
from his exertion, muscles throbbing, lightened the burdens of
others, pulling the heavier articles from their packs to carry
himself, dashing back and forth to the mouth of the tunnel.

Above the frizzling whine of thermal weapons, Treet heard
the shouts of the Invisibles as they rushed the defenders. He
turned to see a formidable wave of black-clad Mors Ultima
surging toward them, the throw-probes of their weapons white-
hot and spitting lightning.

The line of defenders buckled as the rebels shrank back.
Treet was bent over a fallen Dhog when a Rumon marksman
cried out, spun backward, and collapsed; his weapon clattered
to the ground. Treet hoisted the Dhog to his feet and rushed to
the Rumon, whose body twitched on the ground. The scorching
discharge of the weapons around him was deafening.

The Rumon had taken a glancing hit; the side of his neck
was a shriveled red welt and the flesh along the top of his
shoulder was burned away, revealing a length of fire-blackened
clavicle. Treet bent over the man, heard a sizzling crack, and
dropped flat to the ground as the air convulsed over his head.

The wash of air that hit him stank of ozone and the retch-
ingly sweet odor of burning flesh.

He saw the Rumon's weapon steaming on the ground,
rolled to it, and scooped it up. He pointed it in the direction of
the oncoming Invisibles and hit the pressure plate with his palm.

The weapon jolted in his hands as the blast discharged in a
blinding flash with a sound that pierced his skull.

Treet fired again and again, heedless of his aim—his only
intent to discourage the Invisibles in their assumption of him as
an easy target—sliding backward on his belly over the uneven
ground.

Tanais and Rumon were falling around him. The cries of
the wounded rang in the air between blasts. He choked on the
stench of hot metal and charred meat.

Somehow he reached the mouth of the tunnel once more. He felt a tug on his left hand and discovered that he still gripped the arm of the wounded Rumon and had pulled the unconscious soldier back with him.

Smoke stung his eyes, and he became aware of a tingling sensation in his right hand. He glanced down and saw his hand burning where it gripped the throw-probe of his weapon. He released the gun and stared in disbelief at his hand. There was no pain, but the palm was seared and his fingers burned bloody.

A blast ripped the dirt beside him. He felt the heatflash pass over him. The battlefield grew blurry, and his head buzzed. Treet gritted his teeth and crawled backward to the tunnel, still clutching the body of the soldier and dragging it with him.

He reached the tunnel and pulled the soldier in. People rushed by him, and he heard Tvrdy yelling for reinforcements. Then the daylight began to flicker and the tunnel to spin. Treet flung out his arms and tried to hold on.

· · · · · ·

"Please, Asquith, I wouldn't ask you if I didn't think it very important. We need you."

Pizzle scowled at Yarden in the fading twilight and said, "How come when you want something its 'Asquith, please. Asquith, we need you,' huh? The rest of the time its 'Shut up, Pizzle,' 'Get lost, Pizzle.' Just leave me out of it this time, okay? I mean, I gave at the office."

Yarden's eyes flashed. "That woe-is-little-me act won't work this time, mister! You've used it once too often with me. Now, here's the deal: we're going back to Dome to pick up Treet. I want you to come."

"You make it sound like a promenade in the Easter Parade. It isn't a Sunday fete we're going to."

"Then you'll come?"

"I didn't say that. Why do you need me anyway? You said the Fieri are sending a whole fleet."

"They're sending the balons, yes. But they're mostly just for backup and in case we can bring any people out. We're going to be a little short of manpower."

"A *lot* short it sounds to me."

"Pizzle, quit being such a baby. You're going, and that's that."

"Sure, you get to make the grand magnanimous gesture—play Florence Goodheart. All I get is orders, aggravation, and ulcers."

"Ulcers my eye! Nothing penetrates that colossal selfishness of yours. You wouldn't know a magnanimous gesture if it slithered up and spit in your eye." Yarden rolled her eyes in disgust. "This is just like you, Pizzle. I give you a chance to do the decent thing, and you throw it back in my face. I should have known better!"

She stomped off. Pizzle shouted after her, "Don't worry about hurting my feelings."

"You don't have any!" Yarden disappeared behind one of the tents.

Pizzle looked around, feeling ashamed and foolish. The whole camp probably heard the ruckus, he thought. Now they'll all think I'm a coward. He ducked into his tent and flopped down on his sleep mat.

It isn't that I'm afraid. It isn't . . . not really. It's just that now that I have Starla, I've got something to live for. I mean, I don't want to die before I really get a chance to live.

Is that so selfish?

If it is, it's just too bad. Treet made his own decision to go back to Dome. He knew what would happen, and he took his chances. I don't see why we all have to throw ourselves into fits now just because Yarden gets all excited. She didn't care all that much when he left.

But things can change. Hearts can change.

Yarden has had a change of heart, he thought. Would Starla also have a change of heart if she thought he was a coward?

The idea chilled him. Would Starla think less of him if he stayed behind? Would she think him a hero if he went?

Pizzle tossed on his mat. This is all your fault, Treet! Why can't you leave people alone?

Treet heard the sound of voices talking above him and pushed himself up on his elbows. The movement brought pain which cleared the cobwebs from his head. He was lying in the tunnel, far back. He could hear the muted roar and rumble of thermal weapons in the distance. There were bodies lying around him, some disturbingly silent and others moaning softly in the darkness.

He sat up gingerly and took a quick physical inventory. Except for his hand, which throbbed mightily but numbly, he was not hurt anywhere that he could tell. He climbed to his feet, careful not to step on anyone near him.

Someone was moving down the tunnel with a hand-held lantern. He crept toward the light.

"Does your hand hurt?" asked Ernina, holding the light to his face. She examined the pupils of his eyes, and then gave him the lantern and took up his bandaged hand.

"No, it's okay. I feel fine. Do you need help?"

"I'll manage. Some of the Dhog women have come. They're ignorant, but they do what they're told."

"Just tell me what to do. I'm here to help."

She shook her head wearily. "Tvrdy wants to see you. He told me to send you as soon as you woke up."

"What happened to me? Besides the burn, I mean. I didn't feel a thing."

"Concussion." She reached up a hand and touched his head. "Tender?"

Treet winced. "A little."

"Thermal shock wave. You were fortunate. Any closer and you would have been burned."

"How long have I been out?"

"Not long. Two hours, maybe three." She took the lantern from him and made to move off. "Tvrdy's waiting for you down there."

Treet gripped the physician's shoulder with his good hand. "Thanks, Ernina."

"I did nothing. Worse wounds than yours demanded my attention."

"And I suppose this bandage just wrapped itself around my mitt?" He gave her a hug and stepped away. "Anyway, thanks; I appreciate it. I'll come back when Tvrdy's finished with me."

He hurried off down the tunnel toward the sound of the fighting, following the curve of the large conduit with his good hand outstretched. He arrived a minute later at the improvised command post a few dozen meters inside the mouth of the tunnel.

Bright globe lights burned from the ribbed ceiling. Tvrdy stood in the center of a group, bathed in white light. He acknowledged Treet when he came up. The others shifted to allow Treet a place to stand. Treet did a quick mental roll call: there was Kopetch, and Cejka, several Tanais and Rumon commanders, Piipo, and next to him the squat Bogney, looking disgusted and angry.

In fact, now that he noticed it, everyone wore the same expression: as if they were holding something old and rotten on their tongues and didn't like it one little bit.

"Where's Fertig?" he asked.

"That's what we'd like to know. Did you see him this morning?"

"My day got off to kind of a rocky start. I don't remember much of anything."

"No one saw him," said Kopetch. "He sneaked out last night."

"Maybe he got killed in the attack," offered Treet without much conviction.

"It's possible," Tvrdy allowed, although his tone implied that he thought the possibility exceedingly remote. "No one recalls seeing him before the attack or at any time after."

"But if he died early on, that would explain it."

"It doesn't explain the Invisibles finding us so fast," replied Kopetch acidly.

The bile rising in his throat told Treet that Kopetch was right. He forced down the bitter taste. We trusted Fertig, he thought. He saved my life. Was it just so he could turn traitor?

The shock of the betrayal stung like the smack of a brick between the eyes.

"The point is," Tvrdy was saying, "we must assume he told

them where the exit of this tunnel lies. They will have begun searching for it, and they will find it."

That's it then; we're trapped like rats in a sewer pipe, thought Treet. He felt sick to his stomach at the duplicity, the treachery, and the futility of their position.

"I have sent men to the other end of the tunnel in Bolbe. They should return shortly with a status report." Tvrdy continued the briefing matter-of-factly, although to Treet it sounded as if the heart had been gouged out of the man; he spoke in a strained and hollow voice. "I doubt if the Invisibles will have had time to locate the exit in Bolbe. If it is still open, we can escape into Hage."

"And then what?" asked Piipo. "Wait for the Invisibles to pick us up? There's a Purge going on. We'll be arrested for interrogation as soon as we set foot in Bolbe."

"He's right," said another. "It would be the end of the rebellion. We'd have to split up our forces and go underground."

"Maybe that's just what we need to do," shouted Tvrdy angrily. "We have not been successful in any other way. If the rebellion is to live, we must also survive."

"How long can we hold them off at this end?" Cejka asked.

"A day. Perhaps two." Kopetch shook his head slowly. "We are well protected here, but powerless to mount an attack. We can only defend. Meanwhile, the Invisibles are strengthening their position. If we stay here, they will eventually overrun us."

Talk continued like this for some time as options were examined and discarded. When the briefing broke up, Treet started back to offer the help he'd promised Ernina. He felt a tug on his arm and turned to see Bogney glowering at him.

"Fieri man promised Giloon to be taking Dhogs to Fierra," the Dhog leader said.

"That's right. But there's not a lot I can do about it now."

"You promised!"

"What do you want me to do—walk through walls? I can't take you now. And believe me, if I had my choice right now the desert seems a better bet. But in case you hadn't noticed, we're stuck here for a while. No one is going anywhere."

Bogney spat, and his face twisted into a greasy sneer. "Dhogs going," he announced, and stomped off.

· · · · · ·

Yarden could not get over the blandness of Crocker's expression, the blankness in his empty gray eyes. She had never seen an amnesiac, but Crocker came close to fleshing out her mental picture of one, right down to the fleck of spittle gathering in the corner of his slack mouth.

"Crocker, it's me, Yarden. Do you remember me?" she asked as she came into the tent where he sat, freshly groomed and clothed in a brown shirt and trousers. The pilot appeared not to notice her at first, then, as she sat down across from him, turned his head and looked at her without interest.

"Yarden," he said. He might have been a bird mimicking a new sound.

She turned to Anthon, who had followed her in, and gripped his hand as he sat down beside her. "I don't think I can do this," she whispered.

"He's making progress," Anthon said. "You'll see. Go on."

"Crocker, I brought you something." She unfolded a cloth she carried and held out a piece of sweet herb bread. "Here, taste it. I think you'll like it."

The man took the bread and looked at it, raised it to his mouth, and took a bite. He spit the bite out at once and put the cake aside—all without the slightest reaction or expression.

"Now what do I do?"

"Just talk to him," Anthon urged. "Eino says that his periods of lucidity come and go, but mostly they come when you force him to respond to you."

"Crocker, look at me," Yarden said. "I have something important to tell you." She spoke slowly and with exaggerated care, as if speaking to a child too young to comprehend a grown-up problem. "I am going away for a little while. There is trouble, and I must go see what I can do to help. Do you understand?"

Her question brought no response. She looked helplessly at Anthon. "Make him respond," he told her.

"Do you understand what I said? Answer me if you understand."

She saw a tiny glimmer of recognition in Crocker's dead eyes. His features quickened. It was as if the man was surfacing from a deep sleep underwater and resuming consciousness. "Yarden," he said softly. "Good to see you."

"Good to see you, too, Crocker. We've been worried about you. How are you feeling?"

The man's lips drew back from his teeth, and a noise like creaking bones came from his throat. Yarden realized it was meant to be laughter. The sound sent a chill through her heart. "Feeling good. Feeling fine. Crocker's feeling all right."

Yarden shivered. Anthon slipped his arm around her shoulders and gave her a squeeze. "Go on, you're doing well."

She drew a deep breath. "Crocker, I'm going away—"

"You just got here."

"No, I mean soon—tomorrow. Treet is in trouble, and we're going to help him."

Crocker shook his head, and a vague expression of confusion passed over his features. "Treet."

"You remember Treet. He was with us, one of us. He went back to Dome, and we have to get him out."

"Dome," said Crocker. His face contorted in a ghastly smile. "Do you remember Dome?"

"I remember, Crocker. Why don't you tell me what you remember? I'd like to hear it."

He stared at her.

"What do you remember, Crocker?"

"Dome was a very big place. Very old."

"Yes, it was. But what about the people? What happened when you and Treet and Calin went back? Do you remember going back?"

"It was night. I saw them sleeping there. I should have done it then, gotten it over with." Crocker seemed to be speaking to someone else. His eyes were unfocused and hazy. "I knew there would be trouble with that girl along." He paused and then growled out, "She was trouble. I should have done it then when I had the chance."

Yarden kept her voice level. "Done what, Crocker?"

"Killed them, of course. What do you think I'm talking about? I was supposed to kill them both—would have, too. But that stupid slut of a magician interfered. She made me miss." He laughed creakily while Yarden covered her face with her hands. "I fixed her though. I shoved that thing in her throat, and that fixed her."

Yarden stifled a cry and turned away, sobbing. Anthon comforted her. "Now you know what happened. The worst is over. You're doing fine."

Presently she dried her eyes. "Crocker, listen to me very

carefully." Yarden leaned forward and put her hand on his arm, gripping it hard as if willing him to understand what she was about to say. "Anthon," she indicated the Mentor with a nod, "believes that you will get better. I believe so, too. You *can* get better, Crocker.

"You've had a bad experience, and it has upset your mind. You're safe now, and no one can hurt you anymore. You can get better if you want to. Do you want to get better?"

He nodded, watching her closely.

"Good. I want you to get better, too. It is going to take time. But mostly it's going to take a lot of work. Very hard work. No one can do it for you. If you want to get well, you'll have to work at it. Do you understand?"

"I understand."

"We will help you all we can. But it's going to be up to you. If you want to get well, *you're* going to have to do the work, Crocker."

"I'm tired," the pilot said and laid down, placing his head on his arm. He closed his eyes.

Yarden glanced at Anthon, who rose quietly and said, "It's enough for now. We'll go."

"We're going now, Crocker. But I'll come back to see you tomorrow before I leave. All right? Good night."

They crept from the tent to the sigh of Crocker's deep, rhythmic breathing. They walked a few paces away. Stars glittered in the high, wide sky and shimmered in the mirrored bay.

"He's asleep already. Out like a light"—she snapped her fingers "—just that quick. Simply talking to me exhausted him."

"The trauma was severe. It will take time to heal."

"He looks so fragile. Can he really come back?"

"Yes; it's entirely possible. Eino and the Preceptor have examined him, and they agree. But it is as you say. Recovery will take hard work, and it will be up to him to do the work. There is no other way."

Yarden thought about this. Yes, it did sometimes seem the hardest work of all to impose order on the chaos of thoughts and emotions, to think clearly, rationally. Sometimes it took all the strength of will she possessed.

Yarden shivered and rubbed her hands over her arms, feeling goose bumps. "Poor Calin. I keep thinking about her, and I can't believe it—it's like a bad dream." They walked along a while in silence and came to Yarden's tent. "Isn't there anything we can do for Cocker?"

"Oh yes," replied Anthon. "Encourage him, try to make him understand what he must do, support him. You'd be surprised how much that can help. But you must realize that ultimately he will have to make the decision to get well for himself. No one can make the decision for him."

"Thank you, Anthon." Yarden smiled wanly. "I'm glad you're here. I don't know what I'd do without you."

The balons took on color as the sun rose: royal blue, red, verdigris, saffron, violet, and bronze. They tugged at their tether lines, anxious to leave the great green field for their true home, the clean, empty skies of Empyrion. As the sun climbed above the horizon, the first airship broke free and drifted silently upward.

As if this was the signal they had been waiting for, the others rose as one, floating heavenward in slow, dignified procession, like so many puffballs rising on the wind. They ascended in silence, their bulbous shapes ghostly in the fresh light.

Fierra, the glowing sunstone of its gracious buildings fading now with the coming of day, lay peacefully below, surrounded by fields and fruit groves on three sides and the great silver bowl of Prindahl on the fourth. When each balon had gained sufficient altitude above the sleeping city, the massive engines sparked to life and with a deep, throaty purr pushed the graceful aircraft into the early morning sky.

Under power, the ships turned and headed west, their spherical shadows going before them, gliding over the hills. Only one person saw them go. Mathiax stood alone on the edge of the airfield and watched the balons rise, take power, and purr swiftly away. He watched until the huge spheres were mere colored flecks in the sky and then held up his hands, saying, "Go with all goodness and return in peace. I send you in the power of the Infinite Father, Creator of us all."

· · · · · ·

Away to the north, another balon was making its way across the ragged peaks of the Light Mountains. The sharp, red-brown spires and pyramids, flattened by the balon's altitude into a dull, featureless rumple, took on a measure of its actual shape as the shadows cast by the rising sun threw the mountainscape into knife-sharp relief.

Aboard, the crew and the passengers—Talus, Bohm, and Jaire—still slept, except for the pilot and navigator on duty. They monitored the flight and marked their hourly progress on the large projection of their destination on the flightboard.

"The wind is with us," remarked the navigator as he returned to his station beside the balon pilot. "We're making good time. I've estimated our ETA—we should reach the bay early tomorrow afternoon."

"Good," answered the pilot. "That means we can catch the others en route and arrive at Dome together."

There came a chime, and presently the relief pilot and navigator appeared to take their places. They logged in, saying, "Go get some sleep, you two. We'll take over from here." And the balon pushed on, its engines booming in the rock canyons of Taleraan far below.

• • • • • •

As the sun flamed the ocher bluffs, whose reflections shone like gold in the dark olive-tinted water of the bay, Crocker slipped from the tent. He padded silently down to the water's edge and stood for a moment gazing at the bluffs. He saw a familiar shape perched on the rim of the nearest cliff, watching, waiting.

The man's head swiveled toward the Fieri encampment. The sun's first rays were reaching across the sand as the mountain's indigo shadows receded. Soon people would be waking and stirring. They would come to the bay to swim; the air would fill with the sound of their voices. The fish would come near once more before taking their newborn young back out to the deeper waters of their ocean home.

Now, before anyone will see. Do it now.

Crocker untied the cloth belt at his waist and shrugged the brown shirt from his shoulders. He let the trousers fall and stepped out of them. He waded into the water of the bay to his waist and cupped water in his hands, drank, and splashed handfuls of water over his body. He walked back to shore and stood for a long moment, looking at the tents spread over the sand.

"Too hard," he muttered to himself. He turned his eyes

away to the west and began running toward the bluffs and the wevicat waiting for him atop the seacliff.

• • • • • •

A sharp kick in the ribs brought Fertig awake. He moaned and rolled over weakly. "On your feet. The Supreme Director wants to see you now." The guard raised his foot to kick again. "I said, on—"

"No! No! I'm getting up. See? I'm getting up."

Fertig was taken from the filth-encrusted cell and half-pushed, half-dragged through the corridor to a waiting em. Two Mors Ultima stood beside the vehicle; he was shoved in, and they drove off.

The journey went by in an anxious blur, and when Fertig roused himself from his stupor, they were stopping in Threl Square. A stupendous Jamrog stared down at him from the enormous banners ringing the square. He heard the shush of feet on the stone and saw a platoon of Invisibles marching in double time across the empty square. Then he was hauled from the em and pushed toward the immense gray columns of the Threl Chambers entrance.

They passed between the columns—and a double row of Nilokerus security men—and entered the gigantic ground-floor chamber. At the far end of the vaulted room, red streamers hung down from the ceiling over the crystal bier of Sirin Rohee. They swept past the transparent coffin, and Fertig glanced at the ashen corpse within. The shrunken, waxy remains little resembled the former Supreme Director whose life had so dominated his own.

It was just a glimpse, and they were past. They rode a lift up through the core of the building to the Supreme Director's kraam, paused outside, and waited to be announced. A moment later, the unidor snapped off and Fertig was propelled inside.

Jamrog stood on a riser in the center of a room much changed since Fertig had last seen it. In the shifting light of torches he saw sumptuous furnishings, fine Bolbe hangings, great standing jars of greenery, and tables laden with fruit and food. The Supreme Director himself was dressed in an opulent hagerobe of blood-red with designs worked in shimmering silver. It was open from neck to ankles and he stood with legs splayed, twirling a bhuj in his hands. Beside him on the riser stood the wasted Diltz, whom Fertig recognized as one of the coterie of grasping underdirectors he'd overseen as Nilokerus Subdirector and Hladik's rightful successor.

Jamrog bent his head to catch a whispered word from Diltz as Fertig was brought forward. The Supreme Director held up his hand and beckoned the guards closer. "Bring him to me; I want to see him."

The guards yanked him closer. Jamrog lowered the bhuj and pressed its point into Fertig's chest. "That's close enough." Jamrog smiled viciously. "Welcome home, Subdirector. We have missed you."

Fertig threw a dark look at Diltz. Jamrog saw it and said, "I see you remember Diltz. Yes, *Director* Diltz. What did you expect? Hladik departed life so quickly, he left a void in the Hage hierarchy. The Hage had to have a Director, and you, unfortunately, were not to be found."

Jamrog spoke so calmly, so reasonably, Fertig began to hope that he would succeed after all, that the value of the information he held would buy his life. "I am sorry, Supreme Director. I was frightened. Confused."

"Yes, and you forgot who your friends were. Didn't you, Fertig?"

"I did forget, Supreme Director. It's true."

"But now you have remembered. Is that so?"

"That's so, Supreme Director." He could feel sweat dampening the palms of his hands.

Jamrog turned to Diltz. "There, you see, Diltz? A simple misunderstanding. Nothing so sinister as you suggest. He was frightened and ran away. And now he has come to his senses and returned. Just so."

Fertig's heart leapt in his breast. This was better than he could have imagined. Jamrog must be in a supremely generous mood. Perhaps the rebels had already been subdued. The thought gave him a momentary pang. But after all, the situation was hopeless; it was every man for himself.

"Perhaps he is still frightened, Supreme Director," suggested Diltz in his sepulchral voice. "Frightened enough to withhold valuable information."

"You're not frightened anymore, are you, Fertig?" The prisoner shook his head. "There, you see, Diltz? He's not frightened anymore. And he knows what would happen to him if he withheld information that could help us crush this untidy rebellion."

Jamrog stepped down from the riser and came to stand before Fertig. "You would have to go to interrogation. Unpleasant things can happen to a man during interrogation, I'm told. The Mors Ultima are very persuasive, but tend to be somewhat overdramatic."

"They are most effective," said Diltz.

"Bah! Listen to him, Fertig. I believe he wants you taken to interrogation. You don't want to go there, do you? You'd prefer to talk to us here and now. Isn't that right?"

As Jamrog was speaking, Mrukk stepped from behind the riser and came to stand facing him a little to the left. At the sight of the Mors Ultima commander, Fertig blanched. "Answer me, Subdirector. You'd like to tell us what you know."

"Y-yes, Supreme Director, I'll talk to you now. I'll tell you everything I know . . ." He hesitated, his mouth dry, sweat starting to seep through his clothes. "Everything. But my information is worth something." He cringed as he said it. "I've already demonstrated its value—I told your commander where the rebels were hiding."

Jamrog smiled and put his face close. "Of course. A very valuable piece of information, too. And you shall be repaid. Now, tell us where the tunnel exit is."

Fertig licked his lips. "In Bolbe. It's near the material stores in deep Hage, I think."

"You'll have to be more precise than that," said Diltz, "if you expect us to believe you."

"The scouts did not say precisely."

"Are there connecting tunnels?" asked Mrukk, cold eyes glinting in the torchlight.

"No—none that I know of."

"He doesn't seem to know very much," remarked Diltz.

"I told you where you could find the rebels."

Jamrog dismissed the matter with a jerk of his hand. "We have already discussed that. Besides, we would have found them eventually. Isn't that true, Mrukk?"

"We were very close to finding them when Fertig was captured."

Fertig smiled weakly. "I—you did not capture me . . . I came to you—brought you the information."

"Is Tvrdy still in command?" asked Mrukk.

"Yes," replied Fertig warily.

"What of the Fieri?" said Jamrog.

"He is there as well. He was to lead the Dhogs to Fierra. They made a bargain."

"Does he command?" Mrukk moved closer.

"No." Fertig gave a quick shake of his head. "He tends the wounded mostly."

"Extraordinary!" exclaimed Jamrog. "Did you hear that, Diltz? The Fieri tends the wounded."

"Remarkable."

"Why does he do this?" asked Mrukk. "Do the other leaders not trust him?"

"They trust him. But he prefers to help the wounded. The others wanted to leave them behind, but he wouldn't allow it."

The three inquisitors were silent.

Fertig glanced around him. "That's all I know. I've told you everything."

"It isn't much," replied Diltz.

"Nevertheless," said Jamrog, "I agreed to pay him what he deserves." He raised the bhuj, and Fertig saw that the ornate ceremonial blade had been honed to razor sharpness.

"What are you doing?" demanded Fertig. "I—told you . . . my information . . . I gave you . . ."

Jamrog nodded, and Mrukk swiftly stepped behind the prisoner and jerked Fertig's arms back, pinning them behind his shoulders. "No! Please no!" he pleaded. "Send me away. Send me to reorientation."

The two Mors Ultima seized Fertig's yos and tore it from his shoulders, baring his chest. Jamrog placed the blade against the soft flesh over Fertig's heart.

"No! No!" he screamed. "Don't kill me!"

The bhuj bit into the skin, and blood oozed out around the blade. "I'll go back to the rebels. I'll spy for you. I'll find the tunnel exit. I'll work for you. Please, let me go."

"You're a traitor, Fertig. We could never trust a traitor."

"Don't kill me!" The bhuj sliced deeper. "No!" Fertig struggled feebly, but was held fast in Mrukk's iron grip. Blood trickled freely down Fertig's stomach. His features twisted in agony.

Jamrog laughed and forced the thick blade deeper. Fertig writhed. His head arched back, and he gasped. Jamrog saw the head go back and put his weight behind the blade, driving it in and up. The bhuj ripped upward, and Fertig went limp. Mrukk stepped away, and the body slumped to the floor.

The Supreme Director gazed merrily down at his handiwork. He put his foot on Fertig's chest and grasped the long shaft, gave it a twist, and withdrew it. "Did you hear, Mrukk? The tunnel connects with Bolbe; begin searching the material stores."

"You should have no difficulty," added Diltz. "We have done your work for you."

Mrukk inclined his head in a stiff bow, turned on his heel, and walked out. Neither Jamrog nor Diltz saw the thin, mirthless smile.

SEVENTY

The balon sat waiting on the beach where it had touched
down several hours earlier, drifting down out of the clear
azure sky as lightly as a bubble. After conferring with the
Preceptor, the passengers would begin boarding and the balon
would continue on its journey. Yarden took advantage of the
wait to have a last walk on the beach. The talking fish were
nowhere to be seen; they were birthing their young and would
not come near shore for a few days. Yarden wished that Glee
and Spinner were there now to comfort her.

She had not thought leaving would be this hard. True, she
still felt the urgency of her mission—if anything, that was more
acute—but she was beginning to have qualms about going, not
so much for herself, but for the Fieri involved.

I've talked everyone into this endeavor, she thought—what
happens now? What do we do exactly? What happens if we fail?
We have no weapons, no protection. What if someone gets
killed—what if we all get killed?

Failure had not occurred to her before. Now it seemed a
very likely outcome.

We're not prepared. We're lambs headed for slaughter, she
thought. And yet, we have to go. *I* have to go. Staying here and
doing nothing would be worse.

She saw a wad of brown cloth lying at the water's edge just
ahead; she stopped when she came to it and stooped to pick it
up. It was a shirt, and nearby lay the trousers: Crocker's shirt
and trousers.

She stood and looked off toward the seacliffs to the west.
Anthon found her standing there. "He was getting better," she
said, shaking her head sadly. "He was safe here. Why would he
leave?"

Anthon followed her gaze. "He made his decision, Yarden.
And we have made ours. Come, it's time to go."

They turned and walked back to camp. Ianni and Gerdes
were waiting for her when she returned. "I guess this is good-
bye," Yarden said as she joined them. "I'd planned it differently."

"Not good-bye," said Ianni. "We want to give you a fare-well blessing."

"Trust in the Infinite and let Him guide your steps," said Gerdes, raising her hand over Yarden's head. "Go in peace and in peace return."

"Thank you," said Yarden, reaching for their hands. She drew them both into a hug. "Thank you both very much."

"The others are boarding," said Anthon, and they turned and walked across the sand to the balon, passing among the Fieri gathered there to see them off. Yarden craned her neck as she moved through the crowd. "Looking for someone?" Anthon asked, pausing to glance over his shoulder at her.

"No, I guess not. I was only hoping . . ." She scanned the crowd, searching for Pizzle. Up to this moment she had believed Pizzle would come around. But it appeared that he, too, had made his decision. He was nowhere to be seen.

Without another word they continued on to the balon. Upon reaching the boarding ramp, Yarden turned to steal a final look back at the Fieri who had gathered to see the balon on its way. She searched the somber faces of the crowd. There would be no warm send-off, no sung farewell. They were going to Dome, and that was a matter of extreme gravity.

A chime sounded from within the balon. "They are ready to lift off as soon as we are aboard," said Anthon, moving up the ramp.

Yarden took the guide rope and started up the ramp. She reached the top, took a last backward glance, sighed, and went inside. There was a whirr of machinery as the ramp began to rise.

"Hey! Wait a second!" A high reedy voice rang out behind her. "Wait for me!"

Yarden whirled around. "Lower the ramp! We have another passenger."

As soon as the gangway touched the sand once more, Pizzle came bounding up and into the balon. "Well, what are you grinning at?" he demanded. "You're not the only one who knows how to make a magnanimous gesture."

Yarden threw her arms around his neck and planted a kiss on his cheek. "What's that for?"

"I'm proud of you, Pizzle. Thanks—"

"Whoa there, sister. You don't think I'd let you take this

luxury cruise without me? Us Earthlings stick together, right?"

"Right."

• • • • • •

The Invisibles pounded the rebels' meager earthwork defenses through the night, using three of the improvised tanks. The ditch was hastily dug and shallow, its breastwork made of dirt and rubble heaped around the mouth of the tunnel. The rebels stayed low and fired back when they could, risking as little as possible.

But the Invisibles' superior firepower made it impossible for the Tanais and Rumon marksmen to retaliate effectively, and each strike punished the rebels severely. The hours crawled by, and the rebel return fire became more random and spotty as the enemy's strength hammered the defenders down.

By morning it became clear that the Invisibles intended to grind the defense down to nothing and then rush the tunnel. Four enemy battalions were massed on the bumpy, broken plain across which the rebels had fled a day earlier.

Tvrdy appeared briefly to reconnoiter the enemy's position, gave a few brief instructions to the men, and then came back to the tunnel. Cejka met him and said, "How much time?"

"A few hours. They believe us to be trapped. They'll wait until they're reasonably certain of victory before moving in for the kill." Tvrdy rubbed his eyes with fingertips. "For now, they wait."

"We'd better begin moving into Bolbe." Cejka did not look at his friend, but gazed past him into the thin yellowish light slanting into the tunnel mouth.

Tvrdy nodded.

"I'll give the order if you prefer. You should get some rest while you can."

"No, Cejka. I'm all right. I'll give the order."

Tvrdy moved off down the tunnel. Cejka watched him go, and then went to speak with his men.

Treet came up as Tvrdy and Kopetch were talking. The occasional thunder from the tunnel entrance swamped their words as it rumbled along the ribbed walls. They turned to regard Treet as he approached, both appearing haggard and drawn. Neither had slept for over twenty-four hours. "I hear we're visiting Bolbe," Treet said.

"I've given the order."

"What happens then?"

Kopetch answered. "The tunnel will be destroyed so we cannot be followed. By the time they come searching for us, we will be hidden in deep Hage."

"Will the Bolbe agree to hide us?"

"They have no choice. They will do what we say."

Treet faced Tvrdy. "Not like that. We can't do it like that. If we just come in and start pushing people around, giving orders, and taking over, we're no better than those Mors Ultima thugs out there." He waved in the direction of the tunnel entrance.

Tvrdy nodded absently. "He's right, Kopetch. Not that way. What do you suggest?" he asked Treet.

"Well, I don't know if this means anything or not. But Bogney told me the Dhogs were leaving. I thought he meant he still wanted me to take them to Fierra when we got out of here. And then I got to thinking about something Ernina said when I woke up after my little escapade on the front line."

"Yes?"

"Well, just after I woke up, I met her in the tunnel. I asked her if she needed any help, and she said some Dhog women had come and they were helping."

"Dhog women had come? That's what she said?"

"Her exact words: 'Some of the Dhog women have come. They're ignorant, but they do what they're told.' I figured she meant the same ones that had brought the liquor the night before, so I didn't think about it again until Bogney confronted me." He peered apologetically at Tvrdy and finished by saying, "I haven't seen Bogney or any of the other Dhogs for hours."

"Another exit!" said Kopetch, his eyes alight with the discovery. "The Dhogs know about it."

"Why didn't they tell us?"

Treet shrugged. "They're unpredictable. Maybe they're trying to get even with us for refusing to take them to Fierra."

"I'll find out if anyone has seen Bogney," said Kopetch. He made to dash off.

"That can wait. First send me all the men we can spare. Get them lanterns. Hurry! We may not have much time."

• • • • • •

Mrukk stood beside a table set up in the center of a deserted plaza deep in Bolbe Hage. Squads of Mors Ultima searched among the long ranks of the material stores—the huge storage bins of highly prized Bolbe hagecloth—searching for the tunnel exit. Every few minutes an Invisible appeared, conferred with his commander, and then disappeared again. Mrukk would then move to the table and consult the map spread out there. He would make a mark on the map and return to his place to wait.

He had just finished marking off one entire section of the map when another of his lieutenants approached quickly, offered the Mors Ultima salute, and said, "Commander, perhaps you would like to come inspect what we have found."

"Where is it?" Mrukk stepped to the map and pointed. "Show me."

The Invisible placed a finger on a place already marked off. "I was returning to move the squad to a new quadrant, and I noticed a godown in the main hoarding. It is not visible from the forward approach. I went in and found a grate. Air moves through the grate. I put my ear to the opening and heard weapons discharge—indistinct, but audible. Very far away."

Mrukk slowly raised his head from the map, gray eyes narrowed. "Enjoy the fleeting moments of freedom that remain to you, Tvrdy," he murmured to himself. His hand came up and made a fist. "Soon I will have you in my grasp."

SEVENTY ONE

Treet had never felt more useless in his life. After intense, brain-numbing sessions of contemplation, he could not come up with a single idea that offered even a glimmer of hope. He ransacked his mental files, recalling every detail of every historical battle he had ever studied, dredging up every stray military fact he had ever learned.

Nothing he could come up with suggested even the remote hint of a solution to their dilemma, and he was faced with the heartbreaking conclusion that his mission had failed and that he was absolutely powerless to change the situation: the Invisibles had found the tunnel's exit and now waited to attack. It was over but for the shooting.

Curiously, he did not mind for himself. Although his failure meant death for him just as surely as for his friends, he had, upon reentering Dome—weeks? months? years . . . how long ago?—considered himself abandoned to his task, an instrument in the hand of whatever power moved him. Apparently, he had proven a poor instrument, or that power had other plans.

If anything could save them now, it was up to the Infinite. Treet had done all he could with the cards that had been dealt him, and he had no regrets—except that he would not be able to save the Fieri from the impending slaughter. The gentle, loving Fieri, so good, so pure, so vulnerable before evil's destructive power.

What did it matter if he were caught and crushed in the teeth of the doomsday machine he hoped to stop? The whole idea had been to save the Fieri from a second holocaust by interposing himself between gears. He had accepted that it might end badly for him. But he had hoped that some good might be accomplished by his presence—or if not, that some gain might be secured by his death.

Now it appeared that his death would count for nothing. This realization—growing stronger with each passing minute—filled his mouth with the taste of ashes.

And death was certain now. For while every able body

searched for the Dhogs' secret passage, the Invisibles had discovered the tunnel's exit to Bolbe. Fighting had not begun there yet, but according to Kopetch the Invisibles only awaited the arrival of additional platoons. Tvrdy had dispatched troops to secure the exit, but held little hope of holding it. When the enemy reinforcements arrived, the pinching operation would commence. The rebels would be caught in a deadly crossfire with no place to run, no way to hide. The tunnel would become a tomb.

In the meantime, every millimeter of the tunnel from the Old Section to Bolbe had been scoured in search of the Dhogs' secret passage—to no avail. There was no seam, no opening, no break that had not been minutely examined and reexamined, the search yielding nothing but frustration.

The Dhogs had vanished—Bogney, the women, the few remaining soldiers. No one recalled precisely when, but they were gone, taking the secret of the tunnel with them. And knowing that there was a way to escape from the tunnel, and not knowing how or where to find it, multiplied the agony. Nothing the Invisibles could devise by way of torture could have been worse.

The last few hours were spent feverishly inspecting the length of the tunnel yet again. Treet knew they would not find the secret, but went through the motions anyway, thinking the exercise better than sitting around waiting for the Mors Ultima to cut them down.

Tvrdy had both ends of the tunnel fortified and manned, but the narrow width mocked maneuverability and reduced movement to absurdity. A skinny tunnel was no place to fight a last battle. The rebels' only consolation was that the Invisibles would have to come in and get them one by one.

It was late when the Invisibles pulled into position. With victory now a mere matter of execution, Mrukk consulted his commanders and then left to return to Saecaraz. The Invisibles were to wait until sunrise to begin the attack. This would minimize confusion and any mishap caused by darkness, and it would also allow Mrukk time to reach the Supreme Director's kraam. He planned to be with Jamrog when the tunnel fell, and to personally announce the rebels' defeat.

• • • • • •

In the Archives, lights blazed into the night as Saecaraz and Nilokerus magicians and Readers slouched over the ancient texts. At one end of the long table, a sixth-order magician and Reader from both Hages huddled together, their heads bent over the diagrams they had deciphered.

"It is time," announced the Saecaraz magician. "We have reviewed all available lore. It is apparent that the machine responds to number impulses called 'coordinates,' which must be implanted in this device called 'systems guidance.' Are we agreed?" The others bobbed their heads and pulled on their chins in agreement.

"The coordinates for Fierra have been calculated according to the lore formula. We have adhered to the Clear Way and followed the Sacred Directives regarding the revival of machines. We must trust our lore and the psi of this place to aid us."

The others muttered approval. The ranking Nilokerus said, "My Hagemen and I are ready to proceed. Once the missile is returned to the launch cradle, the launch may progress as planned."

"I will notify Director Diltz," the Saecaraz said. He rose from the table. "Begin the procedure. The Director will wish to give the order himself."

· · · · · ·

The Dhogs, arranged by family, each of the sixteen families grouped together with their essentials and provisions, stood waiting to begin their exodus to Fierra. Since abandoning the war with the Invisibles, Giloon Bogney and the family heads had worked their hardest, scraping together every last morsel of anything edible, and filling every available container with water. When all was ready, the Dhogs put on their best articles of clothing, trussed up their livestock, and assembled by family to await the order to move out.

Bogney took his place at the head of the great procession. "Dhogs," he said, waving his bhuj to get their attention, "this here being a great day. We starting off traveling. We now going to Fieri like Giloon promising."

With that the Dhogs moved off, clattering like an army of panhandlers. They lumbered through the long-deserted avenues of the Old Section, the sounds of battle ringing off the curved sections of the skyroof above them. Like noisy ghosts, they left the familiar haunts of their ancient home, leaving for a better place they had been told lay out there, somewhere beyond the barriers of the time-fogged crystal.

SEVENTY TWO

In the clean light of the rising sun, Dome's enormous crystal shell glittered and winked like a faceted jewel mountain, its clustered peaks distinct in the early light. A multitude of giant spires protruded from its skin, each lifting an immense webwork of thick support cables, bearing up the weight of the sealed shining shell with its insane jumble of steeples, turrets, rotundas, and cupolas bulging, swelling, bellying out, one atop another as if springing from a cancerous growth. The colossal range of bulbous mounds reached skyward, hill heaped upon hill, all of them outtopped by tremendous tuberous humps and knobs and gibbous mounds.

"There it is," said Pizzle, gazing down on the sprawling mass, "somebody's idea of modern architecture run amuck."

"This isn't funny," said Yarden. It had been a long trip and a tense one for her, staring out the balon's ports at the barren hills—a deadeningly monotonous landscape, all of a uniform, unvarying soft turquoise green—watching while the interminable hours crept by, wondering, despite the many assurances that they would arrive in good time, whether there would be anything worth saving when they reached their destination. Now here it was, and she was in no mood for Pizzle's smart-aleck observations.

Talus stood like a rock, fingering his beard, staring at the glassy mountainscape of Dome. Pizzle asked him what he thought, and he replied in a strangely hushed voice, "It is arrogant and unnatural. I can feel its evil reaching out to us."

"You think it's bad now," quipped Pizzle, "wait'll you get inside."

"Will you stop!" Yarden snapped.

"He raises a pertinent question," said Bohm quietly. He, like all the other Fieri on board, was reticent and subdued as they watched the gleaming monstrosity slide silently beneath them. "How *are* we to get inside?"

"There is a landing platform on the far side," Yarden pointed out. "And large doors below it. That's where we came out."

"You know what happens to anyone who lands on that platform," said Pizzle. "I'm not about to try that again."

"But we must find a way in," said Jaire. She spoke with such intensity that all heads turned to look at her. She blushed, crimson rising to her throat and cheeks.

"I agree," said Anthon. "We must find a way in—and find it quickly."

"I will instruct our pilots to circle at the present altitude until directed otherwise." Bohm went to the command center and spoke to the pilot. He returned a moment later and said, "We will remain in this formation while we entertain ideas."

"Okay," said Pizzle, "don't everybody speak at once."

• • • • • •

With the rising sun came the Invisibles' assault on the tunnel. As expected, they attacked both ends at once, but with a vengeance that was completely unexpected. Their armored ems were moved in close, and under the cover of a fiery barrage, the first squads rushed in.

Heedless of the scorching resistance, the Invisibles were cut down in waves as the rebels, fighting for their lives, threw all they had at the reckless onslaught.

For one optimistic instant, it appeared that the rebels would stem the murderous tide. But rank on rank of Invisibles, advancing over the bodies of the fallen, began, by sheer pressure of numbers, to push their way inside. They gained the mouth of the tunnel, and then one meter of its length, and then another, driving the rebels back and back.

The fighting was vicious. The interior of the tunnel began to fill with smoke and fumes. Treet, having elected to stay with the wounded, tending them to the end, heard the shriek of the thermal weapons relentlessly drawing closer, and knew that the final battle would soon belong to the past—a brief footnote in a history that would never be recorded.

Crouched in the darkness of the tunnel, while around him the wounded began to moan and cough as the acrid fumes touched their lungs, Treet tried his hand at calming those disturbed by the wild shouts close at hand and the sound of thunder cracking ever closer. "Rest easy," he told them. "It will soon be over."

Ernina swept by him as he made his way among the wounded. "I'm going to see to what I can do up there," she told him. "Stay here and keep them quiet."

"Be careful," he called after her and wondered whether he ought to go to the front, too—not to help the wounded, but to fight. Part of him ached to be in the thick of the battle, to give some account of himself, to make the enemy feel his death. The bandage on his burned hand made that a ludicrous proposition.

Ironically, the one time he had taken up a weapon, he had incapacitated himself and had nearly lost the man he was trying to save. Yes, he reflected, it was better this way. He would wait here and do what he had determined to do since coming to the Old Section, to save life rather than waste it. There was enough killing in Dome without adding to it.

The air was thick with the stink of blood and death, the tunnel hot. The raking scream of the Invisibles' weapons echoed and reechoed, reverberating along the walls of the tunnel. The answering fire of the rebels became hesitant and less frequent. The Mors Ultima ground the resistance down, driving the rebels further and further into the tunnel.

At one point Treet heard the sound of running feet and thought the Invisibles had broken through at last. But Tvrdy appeared, leading what remained of his troops and shouting, "Now! Down! Everyone down!"

Treet obeyed. A second later the tunnel bucked under him as if it had suddenly taken life. The shock of an explosion rattled his bones in their sockets.

Tvrdy leaped up at once. "Get these supplies stacked up here!" he shouted. "Make a wall!"

Treet fell to with the rest of them and began stacking all the remaining crates and bundles in the center of the tunnel to make a wall and seal themselves in. "It won't take them long to dig through out there," Tvrdy told him. "But we'll seal this end and join Cejka and Piipo at the other end. We can hold out longer that way." He paused and looked at Treet, an expression of sorrow flitting across his smoke-blackened face. "I'm sorry it ends this way."

"It isn't over yet," said Treet.

"Come with us."

"Thanks, but someone has to stay here." Treet indicated the wounded.

Tvrdy nodded and pulled Treet to him in a brusque hug. "Good-bye, friend," he said and then was hurrying away with his men as they ran to join the fighting at the other end of the tunnel.

SEVENTY THREE

"Look, I don't know if this'll work. It's only an idea," said Pizzle. "We could try something else, you know? Yarden? C'mon, talk to me. Say something."

Yarden stood gazing at the image of Dome projected onto the map table, her fingers steepled and pressed against her lips. She did not respond.

Just then, Talus returned to where the others stood bent over the map table. He shook his head slowly. "Mathiax has consulted the Preceptor, and both agree there is no precept to cover this situation. We are to proceed according to our own judgment."

Bohm nodded and raised his head. "What do the builders say?"

Talus shrugged. "Not enough is known about the structural qualities of the materials to answer precisely. They would have to make tests. However, the principle is well known."

"We have nothing to lose," said Anthon.

"Only time," said Jaire grimly. "We could lose valuable time."

"That is a risk," Anthon assured her gently. "I only meant that if it doesn't work, we are free to try something else."

Abashed, Jaire clamped her mouth shut, glanced around at the others, and left the table.

"We need a decision," said Pizzle. "I say we go for it and see what happens."

Preben was quick to second the motion. "I agree. It is an inspired plan." He looked to his father.

Talus stared at the slowly revolving image on the table, and then nodded. "Yes," he said slowly. "We have no better plan. I say we try it. This is Mathiax's thinking as well. He points out that if it succeeds, we will all be very busy in the hours to come."

"It is settled." Bohm smacked his hand down in the center of the projected Dome. "It is time to end the madness. I'm going to give the order." He beckoned to Pizzle. "Come along. I will need you." He returned to the balon's command center.

Pizzle moved around the table to join him. Passing by Yarden, he paused and said, "Go ahead and do it."

She looked up sharply. "You know what I'm thinking?"

"I've seen that look before. Do it."

Her gaze drifted back to the gray projection. "You don't know what you're asking."

"You'll feel better. Besides, I don't see how else we're going to warn him."

Pizzle moved off, leaving Yarden transfixed before the image on the flat octagon of the table. Anthon came near and put his arm around her shoulders. She covered his hand with hers. "What should I do?" she asked. "I need guidance. Help me."

"Sometimes the itch is supplied by the Infinite, but we must scratch it ourselves," he replied.

Yarden threw him a dark look. "What is that supposed to mean?"

"We are meant to find our own way in many of life's difficult moments."

"In the doing comes the knowing—that's what Gerdes told me once. I guess it applies." She wrapped her arms around herself in a hug. "I feel so alone."

"The Comforter goes with you, Yarden. Always."

She gave Anthon a weak smile and turned to climb the stairs leading to the crew quarters. She went up and found Jaire sitting on a bench, her back against the rail of the circular balcony. She sat down on the bench and touched the young woman on the arm. Jaire stirred and looked up, her eyes wet with unshed tears.

"I know you care for him," Yarden said, and realized as she spoke the words the reason for Jaire's uncharacteristic behavior. It was obvious: Jaire had been displaying all the signs of a distraught lover. "Is there anything I can do?"

"I have been praying that he will be rescued safely. . ." Her voice trailed off.

"I know." Yarden nodded. "Sometimes it doesn't seem like it's enough. Wait here." She got up slowly. "I'm going to try to reach him, warn him."

She went to her cabin and sat down cross-legged on the floor. She took a deep breath and released it; drew another, emptying her mind of all thoughts, clearing her mental screen. She placed her hands together, fingertips touching lightly, and began focusing her consciousness into the fine, sharp probing instrument her sympathic touch required.

She gathered her awareness and sent it out from her, releasing it like an arrow from the bow.

Once again she felt the awesome oppression of the power that held Dome in its unrelenting grasp. She found herself hard against the thick membrane she had encountered before. She steadied herself and pushed through. As before, it yielded and admitted her.

There was howling darkness and the icy numbness of death. She framed Treet's image in her mind and instantly felt a shudder of rage course through the darkness. The response surprised her, but she did not retreat and did not allow herself to be unnerved or distracted. She steadied herself, pushed ahead, and a moment later Treet was there—his presence weak, distressed, shifting wildly, but alive.

• • • • • •

Treet knelt over a thrashing soldier as the sounds of battle boomed in the tunnel. The young Rumon, hysterical with fear, was intent on tearing off his bandages. Treet calmed him and was about to move on to the next casualty when, as he rose, he caught a whiff of a familiar scent. Just the barest suggestion of a fragrance—faint, but unmistakable . . .

Yarden.

He stood rock-still. The sense of her presence was irresistible. It was as if she had suddenly distilled out of the air beside him. Her nearness was almost tangible.

In the dim smoke-filled tunnel, Treet closed his eyes and opened himself to her touch, shutting out the noise and stink and pain around him. Concentrating, bending his will to the effort with every gram of strength he possessed, he gathered the frazzled shreds of his awareness and projected himself to her. He was rewarded for his effort by a violent wrenching sensation, as if a giant hand had reached into his skull and given his brain a twist between thumb and forefinger.

The sympathic touch weakened. He felt Yarden receding from him and reached out for her, strained after her, but could not hold her. Before the touch faded completely, even as it slipped away, he received a clear and distinct infusion of hope. His spirit leapt up inside him.

Help is coming, she seemed to say. Lay low and hold on.

• • • • • •

On Skywalk level of Hage Saecaraz, the Supreme Director strolled the shaded garden walkways of his pleasure grounds. Nilokerus Director Diltz walked beside him, enjoying the greenery and the sunlight shining through the huge crystal panes directly overhead, basking in the praise of his superior.

"You are to be congratulated," Jamrog was saying.

"Not at all, Supreme Director," replied Diltz. "I remind you that it was your idea. I merely oversaw its implementation."

"As you wish." Jamrog nodded solemnly. "I accept the triumph. I am, after all, the generative force of my people. I am the blood and spirit of Empyrion. I am life and beyond life." He turned to regard Diltz, his eyes glassy from flash. "Do you understand what I am telling you, Director?"

"Of course, Supreme Director, I—"

"From now on, I will be addressed as Father."

"Of course, Father." Diltz gave him a sidelong glance. "The magicians await your order. Will you give it now?"

Jamrog's eyes closed, his lips curled lazily. "My breath gives life or takes it. My word is law and death." He stopped and raised his hands to the sun, which was shining through the enormous panels of the dome above. "I am light; I am becoming one with the sun. My mind is racing far ahead. My enemies seek to trap me, but I know their plans before they are conceived. I am filled with thoughts incomprehensible to lesser beings.

"Behold me—I am advancing through spiritual realms. My incarnations fall from me and are borne away by the oversouls of my predecessors. Trabant Animus speaks to me. I will be purified in the blood of my enemies."

He stopped and lowered his hands. A fierce, wicked light shone in his eyes. "The Fieri will be destroyed. Their hateful memory will be erased forever. I give the order."

A shadow passed over them just then, and they heard a mighty booming sound that throbbed in their ears. They glanced up in time to see the curving bulk of a balon glide by overhead.

"Behold!" shouted Jamrog above the noise. "The Seraphic Spheres! Do you see, Diltz? They have come to transport me to the Astral Planes. It is a sign: I am to be made immortal!"

SEVENTY
FOUR

"The fleet is in position," said Bohm, turning from the flight board.

"Then let 'er rip!" shouted Pizzle from his place at the projection table, and the airship's engines, normally audible as a distant, burring hum, suddenly filled the cabin with a virtual avalanche of penetrating, bone-vibrating sound.

The others, clustered around the projection table, watched Dome's revolving image, their teeth clamped tight to keep them from rattling in their jaws. Talus, barely able to make himself heard over the droning thunder, shouted, "How long?"

Pizzle shrugged and shook his head, mouthing the words, "Don't know. Wait and see."

• • • • • •

The people of Dome heard the resounding boom of the Fieri airships and looked to the heavens. Far above, beyond the gigantic vault of crystal, they saw great spherical shapes gliding over the translucent roof-shell, and they stopped to stare in wonder.

Mrukk strode into the Supreme Director's pleasure garden. He found a flash-jagged Jamrog and an extremely apprehensive Diltz standing in the center of the grounds. Jamrog had his arms outspread, face upturned in the sunlight, a beatific expression on his face.

Diltz saw him and came to him. "What is it?" he demanded, glancing toward the sky as another balon passed overhead. "What's happening?"

Mrukk glared with disgust at the emaciated puppet. "Afraid, Diltz?"

Diltz drew himself up. "I am concerned for the welfare of the Supreme Director," he huffed. "As you are responsible for the Supreme Director's safety, I demand to know what is happening."

"Nothing to concern you." He moved to Jamrog, who seemed oblivious of his presence. "Supreme Director—"

"He is to be addressed as Father from now on," Diltz informed him.

Mrukk's eyes narrowed, and his lips curled in a silent snarl. "Supreme Director," he repeated, "I bring word that the attack on the rebel stronghold is effectually complete."

"Your disrespect has not gone unnoticed, Mrukk." Jamrog opened his eyes slowly and gazed at the Mors Ultima commander. "I have been made immortal. You will honor my physical manifestation with all respect."

Mrukk crossed his hands over his chest and inclined his head in a short bow. "Father, the rebels are subdued."

"That is nothing to me." Jamrog said airily.

"But—"

"Silence! You are in the presence of deity." Jamrog scowled, and then raised his hands to his head. He closed his eyes once more and intoned, "My mind sees events before they happen. All secrets are revealed to me." His eyes flew open, and he stared at Mrukk accusingly. "You imply that this disturbance means something to me. Your very presence mocks my power."

Mrukk stiffened and stared.

Jamrog continued imperiously, "This is the day of my awakening. The innermost secrets of men are laid bare before me. My words are alive, and I speak of realities beyond reality. I am radiant. Feel the power streaming from me. This is the day of my triumph." He turned to regard Diltz fondly. "Director Diltz honors this sacred day by delivering my enemies into my hands."

"The rebels are your enemies."

"The Fieri are my enemies!" screamed Jamrog. "I have given the order to destroy them."

Mrukk whirled on Diltz. "What have you done?"

Diltz fell back a step. "The weapon is ready. It has been activated—"

"You fools!"

"You have failed, Mrukk." Jamrog stepped toward him. "Your failure must be atoned. Atone to me, Mrukk. By your death you will be purified." He turned to Diltz and motioned him away. "Call my bodyguard."

There was a flash in the sun, and the knife appeared in

Mrukk's hand as if from nowhere. "Stay where you are!" hissed Mrukk. "We will see whose orders are to be obeyed."

• • • • • •

"Nothing's happening," shouted Pizzle. "Can we increase the power any more? And maybe make the circle a little tighter?"

Bohm nodded and spoke into the transceiver, then made an adjustment on the flightboard. The din of the engines, already deafening, doubled in volume. "Maximum threshold!" Bohm called back.

Through the port, Pizzle watched the airship descend toward the hills and valleys of a rumpled, crystal landscape until they flew only a few meters above the undulating contours of Dome. Pizzle gazed onto the scene, watching the shining surface slide by beneath them, staring as if entranced. All at once he whirled away from the port.

"I've got it!" he cried, racing back to the flightboard. "I've got it! It's phase!"

"What?" shouted Bohm. The others looked up from the projection table to see the two of them yelling noiselessly at one another; the boom of the unmuffled engines drowned their words.

"Phase!" screamed Pizzle. "The engines are out of phase!" He made wavy motions in the air with his hands—one hand high when the other was low. "We've got to bring them into phase—make the sound waves reinforce each other!" The wave motion came together as his hands moved in unison.

Bohm frowned and rubbed his hand over his grizzled head, squinting in concentration. He stared at the flight instruments and began adjusting the controls, listening to the timbre of the engines. After a moment, he looked up. "We'll try it," he said. He flipped a switch and began shouting instructions to the other balon pilots.

Pizzle yelled, "This is it!"

• • • • • •

The sound penetrated Dome, thrumming through the twisted mazework of its corridors; rolling through Empyrion's elaborate labyrinths of avenues, streets, and tunnels; echoing down the terraced hillsides, and into the walled valleys; pealing through the Hages like endless thunder from the hard crystal sky.

Diltz cast a frightened glance skyward as the great sphere of a balon passed by the transparent roof. The sound seeped into his skull and vibrated up through Empyrion's superstructure and into the soles of his feet. "What is happening?" He started to back away.

"Shut up!" snarled Mrukk. "Stay where you are."

Diltz froze.

The Supreme Director spread his hands magnanimously and moved toward Mrukk. "Your unbelief has blinded you, Mrukk. Turn the knife on yourself, and gain enlightenment."

As Jamrog spoke, the skydome shuddered. The immense panel above them—but one tiny scale among millions in a reptile's skin—gave forth a tremendous crack, and he looked up to see fissures streaking through the crystal.

"What's the matter, Immortal Father?" Mrukk asked sweetly. "It is just the Fieri. Even your enemies have come to pay homage to you on your most auspicious day."

"I have no enemies," Jamrog said grandly. "The fire of my being has extinquished them."

The cracking sound grew louder—as if an entire forest of trees were being snapped off at midtrunk, as if the rock cores of mountains were splintering.

"They've come to destroy us!" shouted Diltz.

Jamrog advanced, arms outstretched. "I am immortal, and all I touch is transformed. All is laid waste before me. Death is my ultimate transformation."

"Immortal? Let's see how immortal are you!"

Mrukk held his knife level while Jamrog stepped into it, the blade piercing the Supreme Director's body just below the heart. Jamrog's eyes went wide; an astonished expression appeared on his face. Mrukk threw an arm around the Supreme Director's waist, twisted the knife, and slid it up toward the sternum. Jamrog gasped and looked down in horror at the crimson rivulet streaming from his body. He clasped the knife blade as Mrukk rammed it home.

Jamrog staggered, making little mewing sounds deep in his throat as the sky panel overhead splintered and groaned.

With a terrible rending crash, the crystal ceiling high above them shattered.

The battle raged on in the Old Section. The rebels, fighting with a ferocity born of desperation, had pushed the Invisibles out of the tunnel and across the ditch and then dug in, stubbornly refusing to retreat.

The Invisibles regrouped and brought in their makeshift tanks to finish the fight. As the armored vehicles advanced, Tvrdy rallied his men to face the final assault, shouting for them to stand their ground.

The tanks bumped slowly forward over the rough terrain, Invisibles spread out behind, grinding closer and closer.

"Hold fire!" Tvrdy cried. "Make them come get us."

When they reached kill range, the tanks opened fire, laying down a blistering barrage. The air writhed with the streaking fire of their weapons.

Back in the tunnel Treet heard the awful screech of the guns—growing louder as they drew nearer. His heart sank. Whatever help Yarden could bring now would come too late. "God, help us!" he whispered to himself. "This is it!"

The guns stopped.

The silence brought Treet to his feet, and he was running toward the tunnel entrance before he knew why. He pounded along, wondering what he would find when he reached the opening. Surrender in progress? The sizzled corpses of his comrades?

Presently he saw the tunnel entrance looming ahead. After the numbing shriek of weapons, the silence roared. He reached the mouth of the tunnel and slowed, stepping hesitantly from the tunnel into a scene of suspended animation. The rebels were all standing frozen, weapons lowered and eyes skyward. Across the battlefield Invisibles stood in the same posture: still as statues, weapons at their sides, and faces raised, gazing up through the hanging smoke to the filth-dark canopy of Dome far above.

Tvrdy stood nearby. "Wha—" began Treet. Tvrdy waved him silent with a chop of his hand.

It was then that the sound Treet had been hearing for some moments registered—the sound that had stopped the battle in its final, furious throes: an awful snapping sound, awesome in its enormity—as if the very foundations of Empyrion were shifting and giving way at once.

With this sound came the howl of rushing wind. Then the sky-shell of Dome began to seesaw.

Huge rifts appeared in the enormous panels, widened, spread like stop-action lightning.

"It's coming down!" cried Treet even as the man-made heavens buckled and chunks of crystal began to fall.

Tvrdy was the first to react to Treet's warning. "Into the tunnel! Run!"

The men stood transfixed, mouths open, watching in disbelief as the only sky they had ever known collapsed upon them.

"Run!" screamed Tvrdy. Cejka and Kopetch snapped to life and began hurling men toward the tunnel entrance. "Into the tunnel! Save yourselves!" they yelled.

Treet grabbed the arm of a Hyrgo soldier and pulled him into the tunnel, returned for another, and was then pushed back by a sudden crush of bodies streaming into the narrow opening as everyone charged in at once.

They all surged forward. The floor of the tunnel shook beneath their feet as one horrendous crash after another—whole cities of glass toppling, sliding, and smashing—echoed through the conduit.

And above the tremendous din, Treet heard the raw whistle of wind rushing toward him. A second later, a blast of cool fresh air struck him, tore at his clothing, and raced on. Without considering the consequences, Treet gulped a deep breath.

A split second later he remembered only too well, remembered with every atom of his being the incendiary torture of breathing Empyrion air for the first time.

It sliced at his windpipe and spread like liquid fire into his lungs, as though his esophagus had been scoured with an industrial corrosive and the wound cauterized with a blowtorch. He reeled blindly forward.

Men around him halted in their headlong flight, gasped, clawed at their throats, and fell screaming to the tunnel floor. In seconds everyone was convulsing in agony.

Everyone except Treet. He leaned against the tunnel wall, head down, forcing himself to breathe normally, remembering a time when he, too, rolled in anguish while his lungs ignited:

The escape from Dome—Yarden, Pizzle, Crocker, Calin, and himself—traveling by skimmer over the bleak hills. Three days into the journey, Yarden had insisted that they all take off their helmets. Treet had done it, accepting and suffering the necessary pain.

And now, having once experienced sudden exposure to the rarefied air of Empyrion—with its dramatic side effects—having breathed the air and survived, Treet's pain subsided rapidly. It was nowhere near as bad as the first time. In a few moments his vision cleared, and he was able to stand upright and walk again.

The Dome dwellers were not so fortunate. Untold generations of life inside the closed and controlled atmosphere of Dome rendered them absolutely helpless in the free air. They lay unconscious in moments.

Panting just a little, Treet retraced his steps back to the tunnel's entrance, carefully threading his way over and around the still-quivering bodies of the stricken.

Upon emerging from the tunnel, he stood blinking in utter disbelief at the scene that met his astonished gape.

Clear light from the unfiltered sun streamed into the shadowlands of the Old Section, stripping away the pall of gloom. The battlefield was a glittering plain of shining crystal. It looked as if a winter ice storm had dumped frozen rain in sheets upon the land—as if Dome itself had been transported to the Arctic and set down upon the frigid silver floes.

Everywhere he looked, he saw the rainbow shimmer of broken crystal. Dome was buried in a thick layer of the stuff— like a plate-glass snowfall, making it appear eerily open and brittle. The landscape gleamed with such harsh bright light that Treet had to squint and cup his hands around his eyes as he surveyed the wreckage.

Most of the Old Section's tottering ruins were erased, flattened by the fallen remains of Dome's vast sky-shell. Broken spars jabbed up from the debris trailing snapped support cables, or lay like felled sequoias entangled in fouled fishing line.

Off to his right, he could see the ragged skyline formed by the few structures still standing in the Hages. To his left, beyond the tumbled walls, was the green rolling sea of the barren hill country, startling in its nearness.

Above, and this surprised him more than anything he'd seen so far, was the glowing blue sky of Empyrion—scintillating, radiant, so bright that Treet had to turn his eyes away. And hanging soundlessly in that infinite, empty blue sky was a multi-colored fleet of Fieri balons.

• • • • • •

Pizzle was beside himself with joy. He jumped up and down, embracing Bohm and Talus and Preben all at once. He hooted and screeched in utter ecstacy. "We did it! We did it!" he cried. "Look at that, will you?" He pointed out the observation window at the collapsed mess of Dome, which from above looked as if someone had dropped a tray of crystal bowls and stemware onto a slab of concrete.

Unlike smashing dinnerware, though, Dome's destruction took place in slow motion. First, cracks had appeared in the smooth shell of the large central dome—cracks which shifted and widened, snapping support cables and fracturing huge panes, which in turn unbalanced the gigantic supporting pillars, causing more crystal sections to break and the support poles to give way altogether.

The crazy rippling motion of the heretofore solid structure reminded Pizzle of a holofilm he'd once seen in which a circus tent had had its centerpoles yanked out from under it. The great expanse of fabric held its shape for a split second and then began to sink—not all at once—but in sections, the higher sections plummeting more rapidly, dragging the lower sections down with them, plunging from the center and working out to the edge in undulating waves.

Dome fell like that.

It was a solid shape defining an absolute space one moment, and the next a fluid mass, rippling, churning, and sinking under its own weight. One section went, pulling down another and then two more, all of them sliding, toppling, tumbling, crashing down—all of them, every cupola and mound and bubble, breaking up and falling.

Pizzle's inspired idea of using the Fieri balon engines to set up crystal-shattering sonic vibrations had succeeded. Dome was an immense fragile crystal bubble waiting for the right touch to break it. The Fieri had provided the precise touch required.

"We did it, Bohm! Did you see that? Kerplooey! Humpty

Dumpty had a great fall! Splat! Now you see it, now you don't! Fantastic!" He danced from window to projection table and back, hugging all the others in jubilation.

The Fieri shared his relief and joy, if not his enthusiasm. Talus beamed and Preben laughed out loud, while Bohm just shook his head in wonder. The women were more subdued. Jaire gazed out the window at the dreadful destruction, biting her lip. Yarden stood by her saying, "When I reached him, I had a brief image of a tunnel. He was inside it, kneeling." She looked at the awful destruction they had wrought below and said, "I think he'll be all right. I know it."

"Well, what are we waiting for?" exclaimed Pizzle. "If I'm right, our Dome friends are enjoying some fresh air, which means that we have about a half hour or so to get established before people start to come around."

"We've got to locate Orion first thing," said Jaire, turning away from the window.

"Fine," said Pizzle, "but that's not going to be easy. He could be anywhere." He turned to Yarden. "How about it, Madame Mindreader?"

Yarden closed her eyes and touched her forehead with the fingertips of her right hand. She stood motionless for a few seconds and then announced, "It's Saecaraz! I couldn't hold him; he's scared, and his awareness is shifting all over the place. But there's a huge square right in the center and this massive pyramid—all these tiers stacked atop each other—Threl High Chambers. I think he's heading for Saecaraz. I'm almost sure of it."

"That makes sense—he must be doing okay breathing-wise. Now where is Saecaraz?"

The Fieri looked at one another, and at the Travelers. "Don't look at me," said Pizzle. "I spent most of my time down there knee-deep in, ah . . . effluent. I don't know where Saecaraz is."

Yarden scrunched up her face in thought. "I went there once with the Chryse. I think I'd recognize it if I saw it again. From this vantage, the square and the pyramid should be fairly obvious."

Bohm said, "I will instruct the fleet to remain suspended in formation. We will go down for a closer look."

"We'd better find him fast," warned Pizzle. "It's going to be chaos down there once people start coming around."

SEVENTY
SIX

Treet made his way as quickly and carefully as possible through the debris and wreckage of the Old Section. He had only one hope: to reach Jamrog as swiftly as possible and take him prisoner. Then he would force the Supreme Director, on pain of death, to call off the Invisibles and stop the war. Toward that end, he had secured a large and extremely lethal-looking weapon from one of the dead Invisibles on the battlefield.

His first thought was that every one of the enemy troops had been killed by falling chunks of crystal—some of which were fifty meters or so on a side. But upon investigation, he was amazed to discover that many had survived. His next thought was to disarm the survivors so that when the rebels came around they'd have the upper hand. The only problem with that idea was that it would take far too long to find each and every Invisible survivor and collect all the weapons—what if they started waking up before he got finished? Also, it was highly unlikely that all the Invisibles were on the battlefield when Dome collapsed. There was sure to be a central command post close by with reinforcements waiting to go into battle. And what about all the other Invisibles scattered throughout the Hages?

Then Treet hit on the solution of reaching Jamrog before the effects of free-breathing Empyrion's atmosphere wore off. Bypass the chain of command and go right to the top. Jamrog, he guessed, would be found in the Supreme Director's kraam.

How to get to Saecaraz in time, though, was the problem. The devastation was almost certain to be worse in Dome's interior: whole buildings and Hageblocks demolished, galleries, commons, and arcade areas crushed beneath tons of rubble, wreckage choking the streets . . .

But he didn't have to go overland—he would go *under*: the tunnel leading to the Saecaraz refuse pits. That would take him very close to his destination, Threl High Chambers.

He scrambled as quickly as possible over the battlefield,

which was littered with jumbled slabs of crystal tossed in an infinity of angles. He kept calm, telling himself that if he broke his neck hurrying, Jamrog would have the last laugh. So he went quickly, but cautiously enough to keep from impaling himself on the jagged shards.

Once, as he was clambering over a heap of fallen brick-work, he heard the throb of a balon's engines and caught a glimpse of a Fieri airship plowing past, too far away to notice him. It disappeared among the ruins to the north, stirring up the old frustration of watching salvation drift lightly and casually by, a reminder of the bleak hopelessness he'd felt in the desert when the balons had sailed right over him and his companions without stopping.

He reached New America Square, although he had to take a good look around in order to be certain that was indeed where he was. The nearly collapsed buildings were gone, and the entire area was covered by a single flat pane of crystal over which one of the gigantic support poles had fallen. Treet grappled to the top of the pole and proceeded on. The pole was grooved, so his feet didn't slip, and he was able to run easily along the top—like jogging on a giant redwood log or tubetrain conduit.

A few minutes later, owing to the fact that he was able to travel in a straight line above the wreckage, he arrived at the entrance to the Saecaraz tunnel. Don't let it be caved in, he muttered between clenched teeth as he climbed down the side of the fibersteel pole.

It was not caved in, but the entrance was blocked by a vehicle which had been caught halfway out of the tunnel; the whole back end was smashed flat by a section of wall. Treet squeezed by the junk and was able to edge in. Once inside the tunnel, he found another vehicle—this one intact, with four unconscious Invisibles inside. He hauled them out, jumped behind the wheel, put his foot to the pedal, and sped off. The tunnel had been repaired since the rebels destroyed it so the Invisibles could bring vehicles through. Treet had very little difficulty in navigating the conduit, although it was pitch dark most of the way.

Upon reaching the Saecaraz refuse pits at the other end, however, he almost despaired of ever making it to Jamrog's kraam. He emerged from the refuse pit to look upon a scene reminiscent of the Great Tokyo Earthquake: an entire city shaken, stirred, and ground to tiny pieces fit only for landfill.

But ahead, rising from the wreckage like a building-block pyramid that had somehow escaped being toppled when all the other building blocks fell, stood Threl High Chambers, massive and gray and looking distinctly shabby in the dazzling light of day.

In fact, the whole of Dome—that is, those few structures remaining at least partially intact—had taken on a decidedly declasse appearance. While it was never a cheery place to begin with, true, unfiltered daylight revealed its flaws. Treet was struck by the incredible dullness and sameness and meanness of its architecture. Dome appeared, as never before, what it truly was: a place designed by petty, brutish men in whom the love of life, of goodness, beauty, and vitality had long since vanished.

Funny, he thought, it had always been so well hidden before. Now, however, as pure light washed over the exposed interior, the baseness of Dome was revealed in all its perverse grandeur.

Treet puzzled over this as he made his way to Jamrog's kraam. Off in the distance he could see several sections of Dome's roof that had not caved in. They arched over the ruins, ragged edges glinting in the sun, looking very fragile—as if one touch, one breath might bring them crashing down to make the destruction complete.

The Fieri balons still hovered above. What were they waiting for? he wondered.

Threl Square lay buried under a solid mass of splintered crystal, fallen with such force that it had pulverized the stone beneath. Several of the great banners bearing Jamrog's imposing image remained upright, although they were shredded beyond recognition. He hurried across the square and ducked under the columns, glancing apprehensively upward. The lower tiers of the building had caught the most damage, many of the upper terraces having been torn away to fall on the ones below.

Once inside, however, he forced down his fear of the building's collapse and made his way to the lift. He remembered the Supreme Director's kraam as being on one of the upper levels, but didn't remember which one. It took him a few minutes, and a few false tries, to find it, only to discover that it was empty.

Now what? he wondered. Time was running out. Everyone

would come to any minute. He couldn't count on being able to move around freely much longer.

Jamrog must be nearby. If not in his kraam, then where?

Treet decided to take the lift to the top and start down from there. The minute he stepped out of the capsule onto the uppermost level he knew he'd guessed right. The garden looked as if a hurricane had swept through. The miniature trees were broken, the shrubbery tattered, the grounds strewn with anomalous junk. But there, in the center lay two bodies—and one of them was Jamrog's.

He approached cautiously.

The Supreme Director was quite dead. Even without the knife handle sticking out of the chest, Treet knew at a glance. The filmy, blank stare, the slack, open mouth, the utterly vacant appearance—like that of a birdcage whose feathered inhabitant had flown—the look he'd come to know so well in the last weeks, told all. Wherever Jamrog was, he was no longer among the living.

He sighed and tossed aside his weapon. How do you threaten a corpse?

Treet was so immersed in the quandary of what to do next, he failed to notice the shadow creeping toward him over the broken ground. But he heard the rustle of clothing and the whistling sound of something flying through the air toward him, and ducked.

The meter-long splinter of crystal sliced by him and dug a furrow in the grass. Treet rolled to his knees to face his attacker, and his heart went cold with fear. Mrukk stood but three steps away, red-eyed, panting heavily, blood trickling at the corners of his mouth.

Treet took in Mrukk and his own discarded weapon in the same glance. He threw himself toward it, falling awkwardly over Jamrog's body, reaching the gun just as Mrukk scooped it up.

The Mors Ultima leveled the weapon at him, sneered wickedly, and said in a low, raspy voice, "You'll have to do better than that, Fieri, if you plan to take over Empyrion."

Treet sat up slowly. "Look around you, Mrukk. It's finished. The Fieri have already taken over." Treet wished he could have said the words with more conviction, but his heart was beating so fast, he was lucky to be able to speak at all.

Mrukk glowered at him, shook his head as if to clear it,

and spoke again with pain. "You think that matters to me? Ask Jamrog." He indicated the body beside Treet. "Now, Fieri, you will join him."

With that he pressed the gun's pressure plate. Treet saw Mrukk's palm flatten and closed his eyes. There was a faint fizzling sound, and a plume of smoke issued from the throw-probe. That was all.

Mrukk shoved the useless thing barrel-first at Treet and then dove for him. Treet pitched forward and rolled to the side, landing once more on Jamrog. Mrukk's fingers were around his throat before he could squirm away.

He grasped Mrukk's hands and tried to dislodge them from his windpipe, but Mrukk's thumbs pressed down mercilessly. Treet tried to scream and could not; his air was cut off. His vision blurred, and he felt his mind growing fuzzy. It seemed as if he was drifting away from the scene, losing touch with his body—except for the fact that something hard was digging into his back, under his left shoulderblade.

Using all his strength, Treet shifted his weight and managed to slide off the hard thing a little so that it was only digging into his side. He could feel himself slipping, consciousness fading. But the thing jabbing him in the side was uncomfortable. With his good right hand he felt for the cause of his discomfort so as to pull it away.

His hand closed on the handle of Mrukk's knife.

Treet didn't know what happened next. His vision cleared, and he saw an extremely surprised Mrukk rise up and fall backward. Air rushed into Treet's lungs in long, raking gasps. He rolled off Jamrog's body and discovered the gun, his gun. He picked it up.

Mrukk squirmed on the ground, his hands clutching at the knife which had somehow become embedded in his left shoulder.

"That's enough," wheezed Treet. "Lie still. I don't want to kill you."

Mrukk cursed and looked up, saw the faulty weapon in Treet's hand, and laughed. The fog had lifted enough by now for Treet to realize that he'd made a very silly, yet very fatal mistake: the gun was a dud.

Mrukk laughed again, a short, sharp bark that brought tears to his eyes, and then flung himself at Treet's legs. Treet staggered backward, his right ankle firmly in Mrukk's grasp. He landed on his rump and the gun in his hand discharged, sending a blazing bolt skyward.

Mrukk stopped laughing.

Treet aimed the weapon carefully at Mrukk.

"Fun time's over," rasped Treet. "We've got a lot to do, and I don't have time to mess around. You're going to cooperate, or you'll be one sorry buckaroo, *comprende?*"

He edged close and plucked the knife from Mrukk's shoulder. A spasm of pain contorted the Mors Ultima's face. "Feel better now?" Treet asked, tucking the knife into the waistband of his yos.

Just then he heard a gravelly groan and noticed that the body lying next to Jamrog was moving. Keeping his eye on Mrukk, he rolled the body over with his foot. "Director Diltz, isn't it? Why yes, I remember you. Welcome to the party."

Diltz moaned pitifully and cringed away from the gun.

"That's right," said Treet. "I'm not too good with one of these things, so you'll want to go easy. We've all had enough excitement for one day."

"What do you want?" asked Mrukk flatly.

"Stop the Invisibles," stated Treet. "That'll do for starters. Then we're going to go down to Cavern level and open some cells. We're closing down the torture shops. Like I said, it's over. Kaput. Finis."

"Kill me," rasped Mrukk. "I won't do it."

Evidently the Mors Ultima did not intimidate easily, and Mrukk had called Treet's bluff. He had no plan for stopping the assault of the Invisibles without Mrukk. They were deadlocked.

"Killing you would be too easy, too quick," said Treet. "Get on your feet. We're all going for a little stroll."

Treet felt no hope of getting back before the fighting resumed, but there was no better option but to return to the Old Section and force the Invisibles to stop the battle or forfeit their leader's life. Keeping the gun on Mrukk he shouted, "Diltz, get up. Take off your yos and tear it into strips. Hurry! We don't want to miss the opening credits."

Diltz stripped off his yos and began tearing it. When he had a few long strips, Treet said, "That's enough. Wrap one of those around his shoulder so he doesn't bleed to death before I've had my fun. Then tie his hands." He waved the weapon at

Mrukk. "Tie them good, because I'm going to check your work."

The Nilokerus did as he was told, bandaging the bleeding shoulder and binding Mrukk's hands behind him while the Mors Ultima glared death and cursed. Treet was saved from having to figure out how to tie Diltz's hands without taking the gun off Mrukk by the sound of balon engines droning nearer.

He looked up to see the huge red sphere of the Fieri craft gliding over them. He fired another blast into the air as a signal, and a moment later the airship spun on its axis and began its descent. The balon landed in the center of the garden, bouncing lightly as it kissed the earth. Before the craft has settled, before the ramp was fully down, there was Yarden, running toward him, with Pizzle a close second, and Jaire, Preben, and Talus scarcely a step behind.

Yarden took in the situation at a glance. "We saw your signal and came as quickly as possible. Are you okay?"

Treet nodded, his throat suddenly constricted by a very big lump. "I'm fine."

SEVENTY
SEVEN

"How can we help?" Yarden asked, her eyes straying to Jamrog's whitened corpse. "It looks like this situation is under control."

"I promised these boys a ride in the balon if they behaved," said Treet, handing the knife to Preben. "Watch the big one—he's got an attitude problem." He turned to Pizzle. "You'd better tie up Diltz there. He's bound to think of trying something slick."

Talus said, "Tell us what you want us to do."

"Gladly. But first things first; we've got a pressing engagement elsewhere. I'll explain on the way."

They arrived in the Old Section a few minutes later and landed on the battlefield in the midst of a handful of very distracted Invisibles. Treet pushed Mrukk down the ramp ahead of him and called to them. "We have your commander. Throw down your weapons."

The Invisibles glanced uneasily at one another. Despite the shock of seeing a Fieri holding their commander prisoner, they made no move to disarm themselves. "Tell them, Mrukk," insisted Treet. "No more killing."

Mrukk steadfastly refused to open his mouth. "Jamrog is dead," Treet continued, calling to the Invisibles. "Dome is under new management. You are ordered to throw down your weapons and surrender."

The Invisibles paid no attention to his speech, and instead began advancing slowly toward him. Treet wished he had thought of a better plan.

"Halt!" The word was raw, but forceful.

Treet swiveled his head to see Tvrdy, Cejka, and Kopetch coming around the near side of the balon. Behind them were thirty disgruntled rebels, each with a weapon trained on an enemy. The Invisibles needed no more convincing. Hardware clattered to the ground, and the rebels wasted no time gathering it up.

Tvrdy approached, his eyes full of questions, looking at Treet as if seeing him for the first time. "I don't know how this has happened," he said in a voice that sounded as if he had been gargling acid, "but I think you are responsible." He embraced Treet with the arm that wasn't holding a weapon.

"Thank you for saving our lives," said Cejka in a rough whisper.

Treet beamed at them both. "I was afraid I wouldn't get back here in time." He glanced at Mrukk—who was currently wearing the classic expression of a man who has suddenly remembered an important appointment elsewhere—and told Tvrdy, "Here, I brought you a present. Maybe you can think of a way to make him talk."

"What do you want him to say?" asked Tvrdy, squinting with pain as he spoke.

"He has a lot of people locked up. How about letting him talk about that?"

"Good," Tvrdy said. "Anything else?"

"Take Diltz here to the Archives. If I'm not mistaken, the magicians are up to some funny business there. He'll want to help you all he can, I'm sure. Pizzle, you go with him."

"Right, Chief," said Pizzle.

"I'll see to it," promised Cejka.

Treet turned and waved to the balon.

Inside the airship, Yarden saw him and said, "There's his signal. It's over!"

Bohm flipped a switch on the panel before him and said, "All balon pilots: you are free to land. Begin establishing aid stations in the designated areas."

At his word, the Fieri balons began descending into the ruins. The siege of Dome was over.

· · · · · ·

Giloon Bogney saw the balon coming toward him; he gathered up his bhuj and strode toward the alien craft purposefully. The last few hours had been extremely trying for him. Leading an exodus of eleven thousand Dhogs out of Dome wasn't as easy as he thought it would be.

In getting to the old exit, it had proven all but impossible to keep the families together. There were stragglers among the elder members, and children slowed the procession down so that it took much longer than he had planned just to reach the old airlock.

The airlock was set in the great, curving wall of the Old Section's outer rim. It was huge, and although they had known about it for hundreds of years, the Dhogs had never attempted to use it. But Bogney was determined to use it now.

He had the Dhogs gather before the outer door—the inner door of the lock had long since been dismantled and carried off for scrap—and with great ceremony lifted his bhuj into the air and waved it in a circle over his head. Two dozen of the bulkier Dhogs fell upon the opening mechanism at once. The ancient works resisted their best attempts; so the Dhogs took up long fibersteel struts and began levering the door open.

They worked themselves into a sweat with the effort, and in time heard a great sigh as the door's brittle seals cracked and gave way. The portal fell outward with a tremendous crash, its upper wheels sheared off.

What happened next could only be described as disaster. The Dhogs were treated to a rude revelation as they met Empyrion's volatile atmosphere. For Bogney it was doubly worse, for not only was it excruciatingly painful, but rolling around on the ground made him lose dignity in front of his people, not that anyone noticed.

Eventually the effects of the nasty surprise wore off. And no sooner had they regained their composure than they heard a most unsettling sound: an ominous, droning thunder which seemed to pervade all of Dome. Frightened and still groggy, the Dhogs scooped up their belongings and hustled through the portal out into the green hills of Empyrion.

They had not trooped far, however, when they were arrested by the sight of the Fieri fleet circling high above them, skimming the uppermost peaks of the crystal mountain range. That, combined with the fact that they actually had ventured outside and lived to tell about it, and the mind-boggling reality of unlimited vistas and far-distant horizons, combined to halt the exodus. They were overcome.

The Dhogs stood flabbergasted and watched the colored balons circle, their engines roaring with power, thunder booming down to them from crystal canyons.

Then it happened. Dome collapsed.

There was a horrific cracking sound and terrible rifts appeared, streaking down from the topmost peaks and mounds. The entire edifice wobbled for an instant, and then plunged inward upon itself.

The Dhogs' first reaction was to run back into Dome, which was familiar to them. But Bogney was successful in preventing this; he forbade them entrance to the crumbling bubble, turning them instead to the valleys beyond, where they watched the destruction from a safe distance. When it was over, they crept from their hiding places to look upon the shattered remains of their former home.

Bogney was at a loss to explain what had happened, but figured that the mysterious airships had to be of Fierran origin. He called the family heads together and explained to them that they no longer had any need to walk to Fierra. He pointed to the hovering spheres and declared, "Fieri be coming for Dhogs. We now be going to Fierra."

The Dhogs accepted this as reasonable, and they all went back to explain to their families, whereupon the multitude sat down and waited for the second stage of their exodus.

That was how the balon found them, sitting with their bundled belongings and livestock, ready and waiting to be taken to Fierra.

Bogney approached the craft as the ramp slid down. He stationed himself at the foot of the ramp to greet the Fieri. When the pilot appeared, Bogney held up his bhuj and said, "We being great glad to see you, Fieri man. Big thanks you coming here for us to get us. Dhogs ready. Let's go."

Tvrdy and a contingent of armed Tanais conducted Mrukk to Nilokerus Hage and proceeded to the Cavern level security cells. The groggy Nilokerus stared in disbelief at Mrukk and his captors. One word from Tvrdy, however, and they began opening the cells and setting their prisoners free.

"Now then," said Tvrdy, pushing Mrukk toward the communication console, "you're going to contact all those interrogation kraams of yours. Tell your men it's over. Any attempted reprisals will bring death."

Mrukk stood immobile. "Tell them!" yelled Tvrdy. "Tell them now, or I'll turn you over to your own prisoners."

The Mors Ultima grimaced and leaned over the console. Tvrdy flipped some switches, opening all channels. Mrukk spoke gruffly into the microphone. "All Mors Ultima squad leaders, release your prisoners. This is a special directive from Commander Mrukk. All prisoners are to be released at once." He straightened and stepped back from the console. "Satisfied?"

"No. Now we're going to begin closing down your network. We'll visit each Hage and make sure your orders are obeyed."

"My orders are always obeyed," sneered Mrukk.

Just then, the first of the prisoners began emerging from the corridors. They saw the Nilokerus standing in a clump with Tanais guns on them, and Mrukk with his hands tied behind his back and a bloody bandage on his shoulder.

One of the prisoners, a Jamuna with a battered face and eyes swollen nearly shut, fearlessly approached Mrukk and spit in the Mors Ultima leader's face. Other prisoners witnessed the act and rushed forward.

Tvrdy quickly intercepted them. "No more!" he told them. "It's over. The killing is over."

The prisoners, revenge gleaming in their dull eyes, muttered and stepped away. "Put the Nilokerus in the cells for now," Tvrdy ordered several of his men. "The rest of you come with me." He pushed Mrukk before him, and they left the cells to begin their tour of Jamrog's torture chambers.

Pizzle and Cejka, along with several Rumon soldiers, made their way to the Archives. Diltz remained silent the whole trip, staring sullenly ahead as the ems made their way through the lower-level streets and corridors.

They arrived at the Archives level and forced Diltz to open the succession of sealed doors. Upon entering the Archives, they found the stubby missile already aboard its carrier and crawling toward the Archives' huge outer doors, which were open. The magicians, wearing atmosphere helmets and oblivious to the destruction visited on the rest of Dome, were trundling the aged weapon toward the doors.

"I don't believe this!" shouted Pizzle. "They're getting ready to launch that thing!" He rushed across the floor which had been cleared to accommodate the missile, and grabbed the first magician he came to by the throat. "Stop it!" he screamed. "Turn it off!"

The magician made a movement with his hands, and Pizzle was thrown backwards through the air. The Rumon rushed forward to Pizzle's aid. The other magicians, Nilokerus and Saecaraz, turned to stare at the scene. They raised their hands, and the Rumon went down in a heap. One magician advanced to stand over them, putting out his hands to keep them pinned down.

Cejka fired his weapon at the foremost magician, who averted the blast but was slammed back into the missile by the force of the blow. Pizzle regained his feet and dashed for the missile. He reached it and tore open the hatch on its side before he was again lifted off his feet and flung back.

"Stay back!" cried Cejka and loosed another volley at the magicians, pushing two more back before the weapon was jerked from his hands by the psi force the magicians wielded.

Diltz saw his chance and hit Cejka with a body block that shoved him down the steps to the Archives floor below. "Launch the weapon!" he screamed. "Launch it at once!"

The magicians looked at one another blankly.

"No!" hollered Pizzle. "Don't do it!"

Diltz flew down the steps and scooped up Cejka's weapon. "I am Supreme Director!" he yelled. "Obey me. Launch the weapon."

The magicians, wearing their atmosphere helmets, could not understand what Diltz was raving about. They simply stared at him and exchanged puzzled glances. "Don't you understand?" he screamed. "I am Supreme Director now. I order you to launch the weapon! What's the matter with you? Do as I say."

Pizzle saw what was happening. "Ha!" he shouted. "They're deaf with those helmets on. They can't hear a word you're saying."

Diltz frowned. "Shut up!" He strode up and slapped a magician's helmet. "Take off those helmets! Take them off! I order you!"

The magicians hesitated. Diltz put down the weapon and took the helmet in his hands, gave a sharp twist, and lifted it off.

The others pulled their helmets off as well, and Pizzle watched the surprised expressions appear on their faces. Eyes starting from their heads, they clawed at their throats and sank to the floor to thrash in agony.

"Now!" yelled Pizzle. The Rumon scrambled to their feet. Pizzle ran to the missile, which was still creeping slowly toward the open doors.

"You tricked me!" screamed Diltz. He stooped to recover his weapon and, raising it, leveled it at Pizzle and pressed the pressure plate. The blast went wide as Diltz's knees buckled and he pitched forward. Momentum carried Cejka over the top of his victim. His hands found the skidding weapon, and he whipped it around.

"I should kill you, Diltz," growled Cejka.

Diltz groaned and writhed on the floor.

"How do we disarm this thing?" called Pizzle. "Hurry! I don't think we have much time."

Two Rumon hauled Diltz to his feet and dragged him forward. "You heard him," said Cejka. "Disarm it!"

Diltz stared back defiantly. "Disarm it yourself!"

Cejka slapped the Nilokerus across the mouth. "Disarm it now or I *will* kill you."

"I don't know how," Diltz spat. "*They* do." He jerked his head to indicate the unconscious magicians. "Tell *them*." He laughed, a creaking sound from the tomb.

"We've got to stop it," said Pizzle. The missile had reached the threshold and was moving out under the landing platform. "My guess is that it's set to go off once it clears the platform."

There was a grinding sound, and the missile began raising slowly up in its cradle. "It's going into firing position! We've got maybe two minutes." He raced to the missile again and peered into the hatch at the welter of blinking lights and dials. There was a row of buttons, all lit green. As Pizzle watched, one by one, they all blinked red. He heard the whir of the internal timing mechanism inside.

Cejka joined him, saying, "I know nothing of this type of weapon."

"Get one of those magicians over here," said Pizzle. "Hurry!"

Cejka signaled to the Rumon, who began trying to rouse the magicians.

"It will be a few minutes yet," said Cejka. "We can't wake them."

Diltz put back his head and laughed—an evil, hateful sound.

"I'm not going to let this thing launch," said Pizzle grimly. "I won't."

"What then?"

Pizzle drew a hand over his sweating forehead and, still gazing into the hatch, his face lit by the blinking lights, took a deep breath and said, "I'm going to start pushing buttons. I might get lucky... Then again, I might set the thing off right here."

Cejka did not flinch. "Do what you must do, Traveler."

"Here goes nothing," said Pizzle. He whispered a prayer and reached into the hatch. With a quivering finger he pushed first one button and then another. The lights continued blinking and the dials pulsing. "It's a sequence arrangement, I'm sure, but I don't know the sequence."

The missile had crawled far out beneath the platform. Pizzle could see the far edge of the upper canopy coming nearer as they approached. He began pushing the buttons and flipping switches indiscriminately, but to no avail. The missile with its atomic warhead, now in launch position, moved ever nearer the predesignated launch site.

Pizzle dashed back inside and went to a magician. He picked the insensate form off the floor and shook it. "Wake up!" The man's head lolled and his tongue bulged from his mouth. He let the body slump back to the floor. "It's no use. I can't stop it."

Diltz laughed hysterically.

Pizzle raced back to where Cejka stood watching the missile as it cleared the edge of the platform. The carrier stopped.

"It's going to launch!" yelled Cejka.

"Here, give me that thing!" shouted Pizzle, snatching the thermal weapon from Cejka. He ran to the missile, raised the weapon, and aimed at the hatch. He closed his eyes and pressed the pressure plate with his palm.

Sparks and hot metal shrapnel erupted around him. He stood his ground and kept firing into the missile. There came a rumble, and the missile shuddered.

"It's going to launch!" cried Cejka.

"No it's not!" Pizzle threw himself forward and reached into the blasted hatch. He grabbed a handful of wires and pulled. There was a sizzling noise, and the missile rocked in its cradle twice and was still.

"You did it!" yelled Cejka, running up to pound him on the back. Behind him the Rumon burst into cheers. "You stopped it!"

Pizzle staggered back as relief burst over him. He rubbed his dripping face with his hands and sighed. "Man alive!"

SEVENTY
EIGHT

The next three days were, as Mathiax had predicted, extraordinarily hectic. There was aid to be administered, order to be established, and a whole new epoch in Empyrion history to be inaugurated.

Sadly, there were a multitude of casualties, scores of which were beyond hope of recovery—although not as many as Talus and Bohm had feared. Most of Dome's inhabitants, it seemed, had been huddled in their kraams in deep Hage, hiding from Invisibles who were seeking victims for their interrogation and torture quotas. Or they were near enough to a sturdy Hage-block to run for cover when the sky-shell began to shatter and break up. Still, there was great sadness amongst the rescuers as they buried the bodies of innocent Dome dwellers who had been killed by the shattered crystal.

When the natural, vital air of the planet came roaring in, replacing the eternally recycled sterile air of Dome, the effect, while terrifying and unspeakably painful, was not actually harmful in any lasting way. The populace was instantly rendered helpless, if not altogether docile.

At first, survivors wandered dazedly through the ruins of their world, muttering incoherently, lost and forlorn, dazzled by the light of an unfiltered sun. But when they finally understood that the Fieri had come to help them, that Jamrog's nightmare reign was over, and that their lives could only get better as a result of the collapse, their spirits improved radically.

On the fourth day, reinforcements arrived from Fierra: three more balon fleets filled with Fieri volunteers led by Mathiax. The new arrivals came with supplies and heavy equipment to begin tackling the monumental cleanup operation.

For the architects of the new order, the days sped by, every minute crammed with emergencies large and small and with decisions of all kinds about nearly everything. The whole society of Dome—which wasn't really *Dome* at all anymore—had to be reorganized. There were innumerable positions of leadership to fill, and countless functionaries to appoint. Not to mention a herculean rebuilding project to orchestrate.

But by the end of the second week, the wheels of the newly formed provisional government were firmly on track, and the rescuers were able to relax somewhat. Talus announced that they would celebrate their victory with a dinner where they could all sit down together.

They assembled in Tvrdy's kraam, which had come through the apocalypse most intact, and shared a simple meal, prepared and served by the Fieri. After dinner, and a succession of souile toasts, they mingled and talked about the future.

When Talus, Tvrdy, Mathiax, and the others began discussing, as they had been all week, various options of organization for the new government and the kind of ongoing aid its leaders would require, Treet excused himself and joined Yarden, who had wandered off to sit by herself in a far corner of the room. It was the first real opportunity he'd had to talk to her alone since her arrival.

"Here's to the future," he said, raising his glass. He sank down onto a cushion beside her.

Yarden regarded him over the rim of her cup. "The future," she said a little wistfully.

"What's the matter? Having second thoughts about saving me?"

"It isn't that. I'm happier than I've ever been."

Treet laughed. "You certainly have a unique way of showing it."

She bent her head. "You're right. I'm sorry. It's just that . . . well, I've got a few hard decisions to make."

"Such as? Tell me. Maybe I can help."

Yarden took a deep breath. "A few of the balons are going back to Fierra day after tomorrow. I think I'm going back with them."

"So soon? I thought you'd stick around a while."

She shook her head gently. "I'm not needed here. What I came to do—it's finished. I'd only be in the way from now on. Besides, I've got my own life to rebuild. I've got my art, and—" She hesitated, glancing up quickly. Treet saw the light come up in her eyes and knew that it wasn't for him that it shone. "There's no way you could have known about that—so much has happened . . ."

"You're right. I've missed out on a lot."

There was a small, awkward silence then, and Yarden changed the subject. "You know we found Crocker?"

"Pizzle told me."

"And Calin—how did she die?" Treet looked away. "It might help to talk about it. She was my friend; I'd like to know."

He was silent for a few moments and then said, "We were just a couple kilometers from Dome on our way back. Crocker had started acting strange that morning, and the closer we got, the stranger he grew." Treet took a deep breath and let it out between his teeth. "He attacked us . . . he smashed Calin's throat, ripped it open with a metal bar—"

"Oh, no!" murmured Yarden.

"She never made it back. I almost didn't make it, either. Crocker was crazy, like an animal. He meant to kill us both."

"You're sure?"

"Without a doubt. He would have succeeded, too. Only Calin saved my life. She protected me somehow with her psi. She was concentrating so hard on me, she didn't see it coming."

"What happened then?"

"To Crocker? I think something snapped inside his head. He just ran off. I didn't chase him—never saw him again after that."

Yarden shook her head. "What made him do it?"

"Hladik's conditioning—that's my guess."

"The same thing they tried to do to you?"

"Probably. Only I was luckier than Crocker, that's all."

"No," she said firmly, "not luckier—stronger maybe."

Treet lifted a shoulder ambivalently. "Who knows what they did to him? I don't know if I could have lasted much longer."

"But that's just it. You stuck it out. You had the will to survive. You endured. Crocker was weak; he gave in."

"How can you say that?"

"Because I know. When Crocker came to us, we offered him the chance to recover. We gave him the opportunity to begin helping himself. All he had to do was say yes. Instead, he chose to run away again rather than endure the hard work of getting better."

Treet nodded silently. "Still," he said after a moment, "I can't blame him for what happened. It wasn't his fault. To tell you the truth, I probably wouldn't be here now, but . . . I know this is going to sound crazy, but when I was in the tank I tried to contact you and got something else instead."

Yarden's glance quickened. "What was it, Orion?"

Treet looked into his cup as if he might find the answer written there. "The Comforter," he said. "The Infinite. At least that's the only explanation I have." He bent his head and silence fell between them. When he spoke again, his eyes were focused far away. "After it was over, I carried Calin's body back to Dome and buried her outside."

"I'd like to see her grave. Would you show me?"

"Sure. She deserves a headstone or marker of some kind. I've been thinking of fixing something up when things calm down around here."

. . . . . .

The next morning Treet led Yarden to Calin's grave, and they knelt together while Yarden paid her final respects. Treet placed a simple stone marker at the head of the grave and stepped back. "That'll do until I can find something better," he said, then looked at Yarden. "You're going to be an artist; maybe you could make something. I think sunstone would be nice."

"You're right; sunstone would be perfect. I'll do it."

They turned away from the gravesite and began walking around the perimeter of Dome. The day was bright, as always, the breeze fresh, the air full of the sounds of industry as the cleanup continued full swing.

"Figured out what you're going to do, Orion?" Yarden asked after they'd walked a while.

"I've thought about it some. I guess I'd like to do what I came here to do—write Empyrion's history."

His answer brought a sharp reply. "You can't think you still have any obligation to Cynetics? Not after all that's happened. They used you, used us all."

"Easy, Yarden," Treet soothed. "No, it's not for Cynetics. It's for . . . well, for everyone really, but for the Fieri maybe most of all. The Preceptor gave me a note when I left Fierra. She reminded me that the Fieri are a people without a past, and she said, 'I ask you to remember for us who we were . . .' I guess I'd like to give them back their past." He shrugged, "Beyond that, few historians ever have the chance to view firsthand the kind of upheaval I've seen; fewer still live through it. Witnessing the birth of a new civilization is an opportunity I'd never get at home."

"Speaking of which, do you think we'll ever go home again?"

"Not much chance. Pizzle and I have talked about it. He points out that even if Cynetics sent a rescue ship—which in itself is an astronomical longshot—the chances are at least five hundred quadrillion to one that it would reach us. It could end up anywhere in Empyrion's time spectrum—like we did."

"Oh, well. I won't miss not going back. I don't think I would even if I had the chance. I'm happy here, and there's a whole world of things to learn and do. It's the adventure of a lifetime, and I plan to take a lifetime to enjoy it."

"You sound like Pizzle," Treet said. He looked at Yarden and felt her pulling away from him. Nowhere in anything she'd said so far was there a hint that she was considering a future with him. He stopped walking, and turned to her. "Last night you spoke about having to make some hard decisions. Was I one of your hard decisions?" he asked. There—now it was out in the open.

She dropped her head. "The hardest of all."

"Yarden—" He stepped toward her. "You don't have to—"

"It's no good, Treet. We don't love each other, not really. If you think about it, you'll see I'm right."

A bewildered expression worked its way across his face. "What was that we felt before? If it wasn't love, it sure fooled me."

"We'd just survived a terrible ordeal and were grateful to be alive—an absolutely normal response under the circumstances. We were in love with life, Orion, not each other."

"I love you, Yarden," he said.

"I love you, too. I hope we'll always be the very best of friends."

"It's cruel to tell a guy in love that you want to be his friend."

"I'm sorry. The last thing I wanted to do was hurt you."

Treet stared at Yarden—she was so beautiful, so alive. It

hurt to end it like this. She stepped close and put her lips to his cheek. "For friendship?" he asked.

"For friendship."

They walked some more and rounded a pile of debris to see what looked like a sizable refugee camp spread out on the hillside. "What is that?" asked Yarden. "Where'd they come from?"

"You haven't met the Dhogs? Well, you're in for a rare treat, because here comes Giloon Bogney—top Dhog himself."

Yarden stared as a grotesque little man dressed in the filthiest, most ragged clothes she had ever seen came waddling toward them. His beard was plastered to his grimy face, and a livid scar divided his forehead, warping his countenance and twisting one eye upward so that he seemed to be appraising the weather. He waved a bhuj before them and smiled broadly.

Yarden cringed at the sight. A wafting breeze carried his aroma to her, and she rocked backward.

"Steady," whispered Treet. To Bogney he said, "Greetings, Bogney. I see you managed to survive."

Irony was lost on the Dhog leader. "You no looking much dead yourself, Fieri man. Giloon be saying good-bye here now. Dhogs being gone to Fierra soon, very soon."

"You'll love it there, I know. Good luck."

Bogney leaned forward on his bhuj in a confiding way. "We no more making big stinking noises since you leaving us lonely. Giloon knowing you bring air machines to take us, so we still being big friends."

He scuttled off then, leaving Yarden agape.

"A friend for life." Treet turned to Yarden. "Well, what do you think? Will Fierra ever be the same?"

"The Fieri may have survived the atom bomb, but I'm not sure they're ready for the Dhogs."

EPILOGUE

*I*n due time Dome became Sildarin, after the nearby river, and with the steadfast help of the Fieri, sweeping changes were made. The Hages were disbanded and a new economic and social structure introduced. The Fieri opened schools and began teaching the people. The temples were closed and the priesthood defrocked. Worship of the god of Old Dome, Trabant Animus, lingered on surreptitiously for a time among the older Hagemen, but most people turned gratefully to the Infinite Father of the Fieri.

Others, however, could not accept the new era. Mrukk was found dead in his cell, a victim of suffocation, having stuffed the better part of his own yos down his throat. Most of the imprisoned Invisibles, after the example of their leader, committed suicide rather than face the justice of the new order—a pathetic and wholly unnecessary exercise since the Fieri had no thoughts of revenge. Diltz, having lost the only thing he cared about: power, lost the will to live and simply wasted away.

Tvrdy became the first Governor of Sildarin. He was installed with due ceremony by the Mentors, and immediately began working to effect the reforms he had so long envisioned for his people. Cejka took his place as Secretary-General of the new government and served with great distinction. Kopetch was appointed First Secretary and was placed in charge of redesigning and rebuilding the new city-state.

Ernina undertook the study of Fierran medicine, eventually returning to Sildarin to establish a training hospital of her own. As a result of the dramatic upswing in the Sildarinian birthrate following the collapse of Dome, *Ernina* became a favorite name for little girls whose mothers came under the care of the wise and kindly physician.

Talus established an official liaison program, a sort of Fieri embassy, for the ongoing betterment of relations between the Fieri and the Sildarins. Mathiax took on the task of overseeing the development of the new school system, which led to his becoming an extremely popular holovision personality by way of his educational programs. One of the first new projects was an airfield for the balons carrying materials and equipment from Fierra to aid the reconstruction; hence Bohm became Director of Transportation and Trade.

After the prescribed waiting period, Pizzle and Starla were married in the finest Fieri style. Pizzle grew two inches and lost most of his pudginess. Starla was credited with the remarkable accomplishment of taming his obnoxious nature, and he eventually developed into a gentle, loving, and strikingly thoughtful spouse. He also gave Empyrion its first publishing concern: a press devoted to preserving in writing all the Fieri classics of wisdom, learning, and storytelling—and also, incidentally, a few science fiction and fantasy creations of his own.

Yarden returned to Fierra as planned and applied herself to the study of art, eventually becoming a well-respected artist for her wonderfully atmospheric and intuitive paintings. She developed a unique style, which led to her taking on students of her own who wanted to learn her techniques. In Anthon, Yarden found a soulmate, and the two became inseparable friends.

The first volume of Treet's masterwork, *Darkness and the Light: The History of Empyrion,* was published by Pizzle's Empyrion Press, and was greeted with great acclaim. Work on the second volume was delayed, however, for a lengthy honeymoon cruise which Treet and Jaire undertook following an ardent, if leisurely courtship. The two divided their time between Fierra and Sildarin, and did their level best to keep Mathiax and his school system busy teaching successive editions of little Treets.

On numerous occasions Treet went to the Blue Forest to look for Crocker. He never found the pilot, but left preserved food, clothing, and simple tools and implements behind. These items were always gone when he returned the following year, and a crude present—a spear or a pair of sandals made of bark—was left in their place. In time, Treet accepted that this was how Crocker wanted it, and the yearly pilgrimage became less a manhunt than a mission of mercy for a fallen friend.

Giloon Bogney and the Dhogs found in Fierra everything they had ever imagined paradise to be. Cleaned up and fed regularly, they quickly acquired the rudiments of civilization. From the first they were fascinated by sunstone, and were delighted to learn that it came from far-off mountains. Bogney was taken to a quarry there, and upon viewing the work declared that henceforth the Dhogs would learn to work the marvelous stone and become quarriers and builders. Although they loved Fierra dearly, the Dhogs loved the Light Mountains more, and chose a place for themselves in the Star Cliffs region where with the patient expertise of the Fieri they would eventually build a shining city of their own overlooking the unlimited expanse of the jade green ocean.

THE END